PRAISE FOR

LILY OF THE NIl

"In this account of the fate of Cleopatra's daughter in the household of Augustus Caesar, Dray reveals the same events we've seen in *Rome* and *I, Claudius* from a very different perspective, that of a teenage girl. Cleopatra Selene has unusual gifts and problems, but her struggle to understand herself and her destiny is universal. The glimpses of the cult of Isis leave one wanting to know more, and the story keeps you turning the pages until the end."

—Diana L. Paxson,
author of *Marion Zimmer Bradley's Sword of Avalon*

"With clear prose, careful research, vivid detail, and a dash of magic, Stephanie Dray brings true life to one of Egypt's most intriguing women."

—Susan Fraser King,
bestselling and award-winning author of
Queen Hereafter and *Lady Macbeth*

"*Lily of the Nile* is graceful history infused with subtle magic and veiled ancient mysteries, at a time of immense flux and transition. Cleopatra Selene—regal, stoic, and indomitable daughter of the legendary pharaoh-queen Cleopatra—carries on the spirit of her mother, the goddess Isis, and the soul of Egypt itself into the lair of the conquering imperial enemy. Selene, whose skin speaks the words of queen and goddess in blood, channels the dynastic pride that is her birthright, and seals the fate of the Roman Empire. Meticulously researched, thoroughly believable, this is a different kind of book, and a true achievement."

—Vera Nazarian,
two-time Nebula Award–nominated author of
Lords of Rainbow and *Mansfield Park and Mummies*

LILY

of the

NILE

A NOVEL OF CLEOPATRA'S DAUGHTER

STEPHANIE DRAY

BERKLEY BOOKS, NEW YORK

THE BERKLEY PUBLISHING GROUP
Published by the Penguin Group
Penguin Group (USA) Inc.
375 Hudson Street, New York, New York 10014, USA
Penguin Group (Canada), 90 Eglinton Avenue East, Suite 700, Toronto, Ontario M4P 2Y3, Canada
(a division of Pearson Penguin Canada Inc.)
Penguin Books Ltd., 80 Strand, London WC2R 0RL, England
Penguin Group Ireland, 25 St. Stephen's Green, Dublin 2, Ireland (a division of Penguin Books Ltd.)
Penguin Group (Australia), 250 Camberwell Road, Camberwell, Victoria 3124, Australia
(a division of Pearson Australia Group Pty. Ltd.)
Penguin Books India Pvt. Ltd., 11 Community Centre, Panchsheel Park, New Delhi—110 017, India
Penguin Group (NZ), 67 Apollo Drive, Rosedale, North Shore 0632, New Zealand
(a division of Pearson New Zealand Ltd.)
Penguin Books (South Africa) (Pty.) Ltd., 24 Sturdee Avenue, Rosebank, Johannesburg 2196,
South Africa

Penguin Books Ltd., Registered Offices: 80 Strand, London WC2R 0RL, England

This book is an original publication of The Berkley Publishing Group.

This is a work of fiction. Names, characters, places, and incidents either are the product of the author's imagination or are used fictitiously, and any resemblance to actual persons, living or dead, business establishments, events, or locales is entirely coincidental. The publisher does not have any control over and does not assume any responsibility for author or third-party websites or their content.

PRINTING HISTORY
Berkley trade paperback edition / January 2011

Library of Congress Cataloging-in-Publication Data

Dray, Stephanie.
  Lily of the Nile / Stephanie Dray.—Berkley trade pbk. ed.
    p. cm.
  ISBN 978-0-425-23855-4
  1. Cleopatra, Queen, consort of Juba II, King of Mauretania, b. 40 B.C.—Fiction.   2. Cleopatra, Queen of Egypt, d. 30 B.C.—Family—Fiction.   3. Rome—History—Augustus, 30 B.C.–A.D. 14—Fiction.   4. Augustus, Emperor of Rome, 63 B.C.–A.D. 14—Fiction.   I. Title.
  PS3604.R39L55 2011
  813'.6—dc22

                                                                                        2010037153

PRINTED IN THE UNITED STATES OF AMERICA

10   9   8   7   6   5   4   3   2   1

To Adam,
the man who has made this
and everything else in my life possible.

Dear Reader,

In this book, I've adopted some conventions that bear explanation. To start with, I've embraced the most familiar spellings and naming conventions for historical figures. For example, I've used Mark Antony for Marcus Antonius, Octavian instead of Octavius or Octavianus, and Cleopatra instead of Kleopatra. I've also used English words for Latin concepts whenever possible. One instance is my adoption of the word *lady* when the word *domina* may have been more accurate.

Moreover, I've addressed Octavian as the *emperor* throughout the novel even though our modern understanding of the word differs greatly from the traditional Roman concept of an *imperator*. I stand by this choice because of Octavian's *nontraditional* use of imperator—a title he held lawfully in 43 B.C. and should have relinquished that same year but continued to use in front of his name until he acquired the new honorific of *Augustus*.

I've tried to respect this work as a novel more than as a biography. The historical events, such as Triumphs, battles, dedications, and weddings, actually happened, but I've altered the timeline slightly to keep my protagonist at the center of documented events. My choices and changes are explained in the Author's Note at the end of this book. Finally, this novel's portrayal of the Romans is skewed by my protagonist's biases, not my own. Whenever the historical record was in doubt, I've unabashedly adopted the slant most favorable to Egypt, Selene, her family, or to the Isiac faith in which she was raised; this is her story, after all.

ACKNOWLEDGMENTS

This book was a labor of love and there are a staggering number of people to thank, foremost amongst them: My agent, Jennifer Schober, who believed in this book and in me. Cindy Hwang, my editor at Berkley. All my friends at FiranMUX. My classmates and instructors at Clarion East, 2003. My "Writers from Hell Group" for critiquing an early draft of this manuscript. My intern, Stephanie Wolfinger. My family, for all their support. Rachel Blackman for all her help with archaeology over the years and for her horse sense. And Sabrina Darby for her insight and enthusiasm.

When it came to the academic side of this book, I enlisted the help of Dave Collier, whose keen eye for historical detail forced me to justify my choices. I also consulted with Professor Duane W. Roller. While both men were generous with their time and theories, any errors in this book are mine alone.

I'm indebted to the work of other authors who have also tried to bring Selene's world to life, including Andrea Ashton and Alice Curtis Desmond, the latter of whom also imagined Selene carrying a basket of figs to her mother. Though this novel was written before the publication of Michelle Moran's *Cleopatra's Daughter*, Michelle's wonderful book and personal encouragement helped renew my passion. However, it was Beatrice Chanler's 1934 novel, *Cleopatra's Daughter, Queen of Mauretania*, that inspired me most. My work is heavily influenced by her ideas, imagery, and lofty prose. In particular,

Ms. Chanler's book captured my imagination because of its unusual theory—that Cleopatra Selene and her twin brother were religious symbols.

In adopting and modernizing this theory by reimagining Isiac worship, I relied not just upon ancient sources and current scholarship but also upon the worship of Isis as it is currently practiced. M. Isadora Forrest's *Isis Magic* was invaluable on that count, as was Ms. Forrest herself, who kindly offered advice on rituals that Selene may have been familiar with. For other magic spells and formulations, I also consulted the classic works of E. A. Wallis Budge, with particular emphasis on his two-volume study of Egyptian mythology, *The Gods of the Egyptians*.

My idea to explore ancient sexual morality through the lens of mythic Isiac fertility rites is rooted in Merlin Stone's fascinating book, *When God Was a Woman*, itself inspired by the work of Robert Graves. While no record of Isiac mystery rites has survived, I drew upon the legend that Isis herself had served as a prostitute in Tyre. I was also mindful of Herodotus's claim that female adherents of goddess cults gave themselves to a stranger at least once in their lives—an idea echoed by Strabo. And, of course, I must express appreciation for *The Metamorphoses of Lucius Apuleius*, an Isiac work and the only Latin novel to survive in its entirety.

Additionally, I commend W. W. Tarn's scholarly paper titled "Alexander Helios and the Golden Age" as well as Duane W. Roller's *The World of Juba II and Kleopatra Selene*, Margaret George's *Memoirs of Cleopatra*, and the splashy Hollywood film *Cleopatra*, starring Elizabeth Taylor.

For an understanding of Selene's home, I relied upon Theodore Vrettos's *Alexandria: City of the Western Mind*, and to make sense of the interplay between the Isiac faith and Christianity, I consulted Elizabeth A. McCabe's *An Examination of the Isis Cult with Preliminary Exploration into New Testament Studies*.

Translations of Virgil's works were taken from the public domain, such as *Bucolics, Aeneid, and Georgics of Vergil* by J. B. Greenough and

John Dryden's translation of the *Aeneid*. I also acknowledge Henri Frankfort's scholarship in *Kingship and the Gods* as the source of Selene's ascension oath. Lastly, I'd like to thank Normandi Ellis, whose moving reinterpretation of the Egyptian Book of the Dead in *Awakening Osiris* was my model for Cleopatra's death prayer.

For additional reading, more of my sources are listed in an extensive bibliography available on my website at www.stephaniedray.com.

CAST OF CHARACTERS

Cleopatra's Court

CLEOPATRA, the Pharaoh of Egypt, Queen of Kings

    MARK ANTONY, her husband, the Roman triumvir

        Cleopatra Selene, their daughter, Princess of Egypt

        Alexander Helios, their son, Selene's twin, Prince of Egypt

        Ptolemy Philadelphus, their son, Prince of Egypt

        Antyllus, Antony's son by his deceased wife, Fulvia

    CAESARION, the queen's son by the Roman dictator, Julius Caesar

    EUPHRONIUS, the children's tutor, a court mage and priest of Isis

    PETUBASTES, the queen's cousin, a priest of Ptah

    MARDIAN, the queen's eunuch and chief adviser

    OLYMPOS, the court physician

    IRAS & CHARMIAN, the queen's handmaidens

The Court of Augustus Caesar

OCTAVIAN, or Gaius Julius Caesar Octavianus, the imperator and victor of Actium

    JULIA, his daughter by his former wife, Scribonia, and his only child

LIVIA, his wife

    Tiberius, her oldest son by her former husband

    Drusus, her youngest son by her former husband

OCTAVIA, his sister

    Marcellus, her son by her first husband

    Marcella, her daughter by her first husband

    Antonia Major, her elder daughter by Mark Antony

    Antonia Minor, also called *Minora,* her youngest daughter by Mark
      Antony

    Iullus, her ward, son of Mark Antony by his deceased wife, Fulvia

AGRIPPA, the Roman admiral and Octavian's most trusted general

MAECENAS, Octavian's secretary and a great patron of the arts

JUBA, the children's tutor, deposed Prince of Numidia

VIRGIL, the revered poet

CHRYSSA, one of the numerous slaves in the imperial household

Prologue

DECEMBER, 40 B.C.

THEY came from Memphis, Thebes, and Heliopolis to see the Savior born. Slaves and freedmen, merchants and artisans, poets and priests—they all came. Babylonian oracles came with their prophecies. Even Romans came, for their mystic poet, Virgil, had foreseen a new era and a worthier race of men. Some came on camels, some in fishing boats, some by foot. And standing wondrously tall in the harbor, the Pharos lighthouse welcomed them all.

Alexandria was the sparkling center of the world—her citizens of all races, religions, and philosophies. Where else could the Savior be born? *When* else but this auspicious night? It was the eve of the winter solstice, the Feast of the Nativity of Horus, and the crowds swarmed the squares and marble terraces. Wine flowed freely, and lute music mingled with the babble of a dozen different languages. The sweet tang of incense filled the air, heavier than any year in memory, for this was no ordinary celebration.

The people believed a divine child would be born to Queen Cleopatra and her Roman consort, and they waited anxiously, whispering, "The Savior is coming."

At dawn, the cry went up from the heralds. "New Isis has given us a sun god and a moon goddess!"

Two Saviors, not one. Twins that closed the Isis-Osiris circle, just as foretold. Two children who would change the world. And now that world awaited the Golden Age.

One

SOMETHING coiled dangerously within the basket I carried, but I'd been told not to open the lid nor to ask what lurked beneath its woven reeds. The basket smelled of comforting cedar and lush figs, but it was embroidered with emblems of Anubis— the jackal-headed Guide of the Dead.

Anubis was a kind god, so I should have taken solace, but seeing him only magnified my sense of dread. Since we'd lost the war, Alexandria was quiet and filled with ill omens.

I had once been the safest child in Egypt, but the world held terrors everywhere for me now, and the twisting motion in the basket convinced me that I held treachery in my arms. I came to an abrupt halt in the middle of the avenue, beneath a marble colonnade that cast dusk shadows over the silent street. "I don't want to carry the basket anymore," I said.

"Sometimes we have to do what we don't want to, Princess Selene," our royal tutor said, daring to nudge me forward with his divination staff. That he'd poked me offended my royal dignity, but I knew better than to chastise Euphronius, for the old wizard was unusually anxious that day. The metallic scent of dark magic clung to his white linen kilt and wafted behind him as he hurried us along. He kept glancing back at the Roman guards who accompanied us at a barely respectful distance, and even though the sun was low and the evening cool, perspiration glistened on his bald head.

Euphronius lifted my littlest brother, Philadelphus, into his arms and urged us to walk faster. "Let's hurry before Octavian changes his mind about letting you see your mother."

I tried to keep pace, but the basket was unbearably heavy and my silvered sandal caught on the hem of my pearl-beaded gown. I heard the fabric tear but managed to regain my footing, albeit with a complaint. "I could walk faster if a servant carried the basket. Why should I have to?"

After all, I wasn't just a princess of Egypt. Wasn't I also queen of all Cyrenaica and Libya? I wore a royal diadem embroidered with pearls upon my brow. Why should I carry anything for myself much less something that frightened me?

"I'll carry it for you," my twin brother offered.

But Euphronius waved Helios away. "Princess Selene, your mother wanted *you* to bring the basket as an offering to your father. Will you dishonor Lord Antony by failing to provide for what remains of his soul in this world?"

Our wizard needn't have used the blunt cudgel of guilt; the reminder that my mother had commanded me was enough to make me obey, but his mention of my dead father plunged me into a grief-stricken silence. *My poor, disgraced father.*

I first met him when I was four years old. He'd worn a sword on his belt, a tall horsehair-crested helmet, and sculpted armor beneath a bloodred cape; he'd terrified me. When his studded military sandals first thundered on the marbled floors, I'd cowered and cried. My mother had scooped me into her arms and told me not to fear, for my father had gifts for me and my twin, and a marriage proposal for her. The Romans were our friends and protected us, she had said.

But now I knew she had lied.

When the *real* Romans came—for that's what Octavian's men called themselves—they came to conquer. When the *real* Romans came, not even my father with his mighty sword could protect us, and unable to live with this failure, he plunged that mighty sword into his stalwart heart.

Now, without him, everything was crumbling. Our palace was overrun by enemy soldiers, my two oldest brothers were missing, and my mother was a captive. All I could do was stumble along behind our tutor, silenced by the enormity of our loss.

Conquered Alexandria's spacious streets were empty. Only the awnings of the marketplace stood as a colorful reminder of the usual bustle of its merchants. Even the gold-domed temples were deserted and I wondered if the gods had abandoned us too.

"Where is everyone?" little Philadelphus asked.

"They fled," Euphronius said curtly as we passed the rows of statuary inside the royal enclosure. "The people fled when they heard Octavian's legions were coming. Those who stayed have shut themselves up in their homes, doors locked and bolted."

"So only statues stand bravely before the Romans," Helios said, and I felt him bristle. My twin's dark mood made mine even blacker. With my heavy basket, I trudged up the marble stairs, unable to swish my skirts in the royal fashion I had practiced. There were no crowds to wave to me now anyway. We had come to my mother's tomb where she had hidden from Octavian, but he had found her. Now it was virtually her prison.

Euphronius approached the Roman guards. "Queen Cleopatra's children are here to see her. The honorable Octavian gave his permission."

One of the guards searched Euphronius. He actually put his unclean hands on our wizard's holy person. I watched, aghast, trying to ignore the curious motion within the basket, an echo of the fear that snaked around my heart. Then the ill-mannered Roman guard approached me and I held my basket out to him, hoping he'd reach inside. Hoping that whatever evil spirit lurked there would fly out and strike him dead!

But the guard sniffed dismissively and waved me through like a peasant. It was the first time, but not the last time, I realized how easily Romans discounted a girl. Of course, my mother had learned that lesson long ago.

WE found my mother in her tomb beside a wax statue of my father. She was setting out a meal for his *ka*, as if she were but a humble wife, and not Cleopatra, Pharaoh of Egypt.

Where my skin was fair, hers was a sun-kissed copper, befitting a ruler of a desert nation. Her hair was a curious mixture: dark strands shot through with bronze. And though her features were indelicate, her coloring was that of a golden goddess. Millions of people believed that she was just that—Isis reborn.

Candlelight glittered off the gilded walls of the tomb to surround her with an ethereal glow and for a moment, I thought she was working magic on my father's statue. The common folk said that statues imbued with *ka* could be brought to life, but Euphronius had told us the rest of my father's soul must pass through the gates into the next life, and my mother had agreed.

Now she turned to us with an expression of otherworldly serenity, which only added to my alarm, for serenity was never one of my mother's famed characteristics. She bid her servants Iras and Charmian to take the basket from me, and I surrendered it eagerly. Then she opened her arms wide. "Come."

We ran to her.

"The soldiers are everywhere!" Philadelphus wept, for he was only six years old, and frightened.

"Don't cry," Helios commanded.

"It's all right," my mother said, gently running her fingers over my little brother's tearstained cheeks. "Kings and queens cry with family. Hide your grief from subjects and strangers."

"The Romans won't tell us anything," I said, fighting back tears of my own. "Where's Caesarion? Where's Antyllus? What of our cousin, Petubastes? They're all gone from the palace!"

"Petubastes is dead." She answered simply, as if it would somehow hurt less. "And they butchered Antyllus as he begged for mercy at the foot of Caesar's statue."

We let out a sound of mingled anguish. Petubastes was a young priest of Ptah, no warrior at all. Antyllus was my father's son by a Roman wife, but he'd come to live with us years before and we'd loved him. It was unthinkable that they could both be gone.

"How could they kill Antyllus?" my twin cried. "He's one of *them*. He's Roman!"

My mother pulled us tighter into her embrace, whispering, "For all his talk of Republic, Octavian is just a despot. He respects no law nor bond of kinship. You'd do well to remember that."

"What about Caesarion?" I demanded to know of my oldest brother. "He's King of Egypt. They can't kill him too."

My heart pounded as we waited for my mother's answer. She didn't meet my eyes when she spoke. "Caesarion is gone."

Gone? What could she mean?

Sometimes it seemed that Helios inherited more Roman stoicism than even my father had possessed, for his jaw set in grim disapproval. "Do you mean he ran away?"

"Sometimes it's better to fight another day," my mother replied.

I felt my twin's burning anger. Searching for a target, he rounded on Euphronius. "Why didn't the people fight for us? Are they cowards? Do they hate us?"

The old wizard knew better than to speak without leave in the queen's presence, so he busied himself lighting the alabaster divination lamps while my mother turned Helios's chin and forced him to look at her. "Helios, I ordered the people not to fight. Once your father died, we lost all advantage. Resistance would have only made them burn the city. I know too well how the Romans love to burn things."

They had burned her harbor, storage houses filled with books meant for the Great Library, and even her husband, Julius Caesar. She seemed to be remembering it all now, as she buried her nose in my hair. "Helios and Selene. My sun and my moon. Can it already be time to say good-bye? It seems as if Isis gave you to me just yesterday and not a decade ago."

A pillar encrusted with lapis lazuli cast my twin brother's face in blue shadow as he asked, "Why are we saying good-bye?"

My mother's eyes were calm, but her voice quavered. "You children must go to Rome, but I'll be going somewhere else. Without me, Octavian will have less reason to kill you. Without me, he'll *need* you."

The dread that had coiled in my arms as I held the basket now slithered up my spine. I understood, for the first time, that my mother meant to die.

Helios must have realized it too, because his face instantly reddened. "You said that in three days' time we're all going to Rome!"

"I said that because the Romans were listening," my mother murmured.

She tried to take Helios's hands into hers. He pulled them away as if burned; I felt the panic that flittered across his face as if it was my own. It *was* my own.

"We haven't much time now," my mother said. "So listen well. When Octavian declared war upon us, he said that a woman mustn't think herself equal to a man. This was the just cause for which the Romans claimed to fight their war, so it will be hard for you in Rome. They'll try to make you forget who you are or try to make you ashamed. But you mustn't forget and you mustn't be ashamed."

"You said we were *all* going to Rome," Helios insisted, as if saying it again would make it true.

My mother pretended not to hear him. "Euphronius has taught you about the nine bodies, yes? Your father has been properly buried, so his *akh*, his spiritual body, journeys through the afterlife. Now I'm going to join him."

I looked to where my father was entombed with his armaments. He'd been a bear of a man, a warrior with a thick neck and broad shoulders who had, nonetheless, bowed to me and called me his princess. Sometimes, after his battles, he would come home and grab me up, tucking me under one arm as he walked. Other times, he would even get down on his knees, pretending to stalk me like one of the great cats of the jungle. That was the father I'd lost and now my mother meant to stay here with him, in this tomb, forever.

Her handmaidens were already laying out her royal raiment. Not the royal diadem of House Ptolemy but the ancient, long-abandoned Egyptian symbols—the white bulbous crown of Upper Egypt and the small red crown of Lower Egypt, with the crook and the flail.

I realized I was crying only when my tears splashed onto the marble floor. "I don't want you to die too."

"Selene," my mother said. "Soon I'll meet the gods of the West and pass through the gates that lead to my destiny—and yours."

I hated her distant stare. It was as if she'd already started on her journey. "Please don't die," I pleaded. "I'll do anything you say."

Philadelphus added his pleas to mine. "No, Mother, please don't leave us!"

At this, my mother's tears finally spilled over her lashes. She brought Philadelphus's hands to her lips, then kissed each chubby finger in turn. "Death, well done, is a gateway from this world into another. It needn't be the end of anything. I'm not afraid, so you children mustn't be either." Then her lips twisted into a pained expression. "I keep calling you children, but I've never let you be children. You were born kings and queens from the start and now you're as I was at your age; you see through wizened eyes. Especially you, Selene. It's your blessing and your curse."

"Your Majesty," Euphronius interrupted. "The sun is nearly set. There isn't much time."

My mother slowly nodded, blinking her tears away. "Fetch my magician's chest."

"I'll help you work the *heka*," Euphronius told her as we gathered around the oil lamp.

"No," she said. "Save your magic for the time ahead. I'll use what I have left for the children."

Then my mother stared into the flame as sweet smoke filled the tomb, the scent of light magic surrounding us. She took a more formal tone. "Tonight, I've a gift for each of you. To protect you when I'm gone."

From the chest, my mother took a Collar of Gold amulet and placed it around Philadelphus's neck. She touched her forehead to his and said, "Ptolemy Philadelphus, I give you my sight." Then she whispered the spell over the amulet to imbue it with power. *"Oh my father Osiris, my brother Horus, my mother Isis, I'm unswathed and I see."*

Philadelphus's soulful brown eyes fluttered wide, then he staggered back as if he saw something frightening. Helios and I both turned to check behind us, fearful that Romans had entered this sanctuary, but we saw only my mother's handmaidens.

Then my mother put a golden vulture amulet around Helios's neck and he bowed his head, fists balled in frustration. "Alexander Helios, I give you my power, my *sekhem*." She held his hand as she spoke the holy words. *"The sovereignty of the whole world is decreed for him. May he war mightily and maketh his deeds to be remembered. His mother, the mighty lady Isis, protecteth him, and she hath transferred her strength unto him."*

At last, my mother came to me. She fastened upon my neck a small jade frog pendant. I squinted, for my brothers' amulets seemed so much more impressive. Curious, I read the words carved on the frog's green underbelly, and I arched a curious brow.

"Read it aloud," my mother said.

My words came out bold and strong. *"I am the Resurrection."*

In that moment, a power surged through me that I had never known. Magic.

The Nile's green waves lapped at my consciousness, drawing me into the marshy reeds of a waking dream where life teemed. I saw the frog and the minnows, the life-giving silt settling onto the fields beyond, and everywhere I turned in the water, the birds flocked and water lilies blossomed. With my fingers, I traced lazy circles into the dream river bringing fish leaping to the surface. I passed dried brown foliage as I made my way to shore, and it sprouted green with life again. I gazed upon the washed-up carcass of a snake and it arose, coiled and shimmering.

It was the most beautiful thing I'd ever seen, but the intensity was too much. My knees buckled under me. My mother's guiding hands caught me to stop my fall. "Cleopatra Selene, I entrust you with my spirit, my *ba*. You are the Resurrection."

I trembled, my mouth aquiver. "I don't understand."

"Which is for the better," she said. "Because the Romans aren't above torturing children for information. Your father would tell you to live as long as you can do so honorably. I tell you to live so long as you serve Isis. Worship her and follow her dictates. You will fall short; I often did. But still, you must try. Be charitable to the poor and the sick. Help the helpless and those in need. Be kind when you can and fierce when you must. Remember that Egypt and our very faith lives in you."

Helios shook his head, not wanting to hear another word. I didn't either. I wanted to make it all stop—to make everything go back to the way it was before Octavian came with his legions. But my mother made us listen. "There are only three kinds of ink that rulers use to write their stories. Sweat, blood, or tears. So choose your ink carefully, because one day Anubis will weigh your heart upon on a scale. If your heart is black and heavy with sin, it will go to the crocodiles in the hour of judgment. But if you're faithful, Isis offers immortality."

My mother drew us into her embrace one last time, then called for our tutor. "Euphronius, take the children and these wax tablets to Octavian. They contain my final wishes. Wait until it is too late for him to revive me, because he'll surely try. His advisers will tell him to be glad that I'm dead, and he'll know it's better for him that I am. But there is something dark and twisted in that man. Octavian always wants most what he cannot have."

Euphronius bowed low. "It will be my honor to keep you from his clutches, Your Majesty. I had hoped that in this River of Time, I could finish teaching the twins . . ."

"There wasn't time, Euphronius. I understand," she said.

The old man's eyes glistened. "It shall all be done as you command."

She reached for his hand—a rare gesture by the pharaoh, to touch someone outside the family. "Your loyalty has been worth more than all the gold in the world."

Euphronius kissed her amethyst ring, then withdrew as if all words failed him.

"Now take the children away," she said.

Euphronius gathered the tablets and tugged me by the arm as I tried to stifle my sobs. I called out, "We could run away together. We could all go where the Romans would never find us."

"Selene!" my mother snapped. "I'm going now to the only place the Romans cannot follow. You're a Ptolemy, a queen, and a vessel of Isis. Remember it."

As we left, my mother pulled the basket into her lap. She slid her arm beneath the lid and I heard the asp hiss. Then she whispered the last words I ever heard her say. *"I may crumble away to dust, but my spirit remains. I journey home now, and though my lands fall fallow and my palaces turn to sand, Egypt lives a million years in me. I do not fear, for death is not the end of all things. I shall again warm myself by a fire, loved by a man, children upon my knee. In the Nile of Eternity, I shall live forever."*

Two

※

IT was hard to accept that my mother was gone. The Romans kept us locked in her chambers, surrounded by her perfumes and pearled combs. We half-expected her to burst in with passion for her latest plan; we were only now beginning to fully grasp that she'd never walk into this room again.

Roman soldiers brought our meals and kept our servants away. We asked for Euphronius, but they refused. We didn't know what they wanted with us; there was nothing to do but wait.

Philadelphus slept fitfully in my mother's bed, but Helios and I huddled together in the cushioned window seat, silent and staring out over the harbor. A breeze of salty sea air wafted the curtains around us as we looked down upon ships from faraway places like Numidia, Cappadocia, and Emesa. The ships' holds were filled with ivory, gold, fine wines, frankincense, precious dyes, and silk. Towering over this treasure, the Pharos lighthouse emerged from the glistening Mediterranean like an alert sentinel.

These sights were familiar, but the sight of Roman soldiers pillaging was something new and terrible. They seized ships and bullied sailors but it was worse on land where they dragged sacks of valuables out of buildings and tromped down our gardens. Octavian would later claim that all he took from our palace was an agate cup, but my brother and I knew better; we saw the looting Romans with our own eyes.

They showed contempt for everything they touched. They smashed my father's statues with glee. On the steps of the Temple of Isis, one of the soldiers even lifted the leather flaps of his military skirt to piss while his comrades cheered him on. If they dared all this within the royal enclosure, I shuddered to think what they might be doing in the city itself.

Helios and I watched, memorizing each outrage, taking a private accounting. But when Roman soldiers dragged an Isiac priestess out of the temple, tearing her clothes and passing her from man to man, I couldn't watch anymore.

Instead, I rifled through the papyri my mother had left behind. In all these loose sheets and pots of ink, maybe there was a note for us or a magic spell I could learn. Yet my mother had been the greatest magician in all Egypt. Now she was dead and her kingdom in the hands of her enemy, so what good was magic anyway?

I'd sorted the papers into three piles when Helios grabbed a torch from the wall. I watched him cross the room to where my mother kept the model ship he'd given her as a gift. Helios had always loved ships; he'd made this one with his own hands. I remember how he'd worked the wood, paying meticulous attention to detail, learning from our father how each part worked. Helios was very proud of that ship.

Now he set it aflame.

I rushed to him in a panic. "What are you doing?"

The toy was already on fire, its papyrus sail blackening, shriveling away to nothing. "I'd rather burn it than let the Romans take it. We should burn all of it. Everything."

When Helios started to thrust the torch toward the netting on the bed, I shrieked, grabbing his arm. "Stop it!" I started to cry again; I couldn't help it. I'd brought my mother death in a basket, yet she'd called me the Resurrection. I wept. "It's the Romans who burn everything. Not us."

Helios stared at me as smoke rose between us. Whether it was my tears or my words that reached him, I couldn't be sure, but he rubbed the ashes of his destroyed boat between his fingers before snuffing out the torch.

A few moments later, as if awakened by our argument, Philadelphus bolted upright. His eyes were wide, auburn curls plastered to his forehead with sweat as he said, "He's coming."

My twin jerked his head toward our littlest brother. "Who?"

"A man from the sea," Philadelphus said.

Helios squinted at the lighthouse-illuminated harbor as if he'd missed some special ship.

"What man from the sea?" I asked. "Philadelphus, did you have a nightmare?"

If he answered me, I didn't hear over the crash of the door being kicked open. The carved cedar edge splintered as it smashed against the wall and the bronze handle bent with the force. The bang thundered throughout my mother's chamber and through the hall beyond.

Philadelphus skittered behind me for protection while Helios held his unlit torch like a club to ward off the barrel-chested Roman who stood in the doorway wearing a carved Roman helmet with a general's crest. The stranger also wore the familiar armor of a Roman soldier, but the weathered lines of his face made him even more intimidating. When he spoke, it was in accented Greek. "So, you're the bastard whelps of Antony?"

Helios gasped. "How dare you?"

With one mighty swing of his fist, the Roman struck Helios on the side of the head, knocking him to the floor and sending his torch skimming across the marble. Rough hands had never been laid upon us, and now I was more angry than frightened. "By what right do you strike my brother?" I demanded to know.

"He's King Alexander Helios of Armenia, Media, and Parthia. Have you no respect for kings?"

"Rome has little respect for kings," the Roman answered. "And I respect them even less."

By now, Helios had scrambled to his feet. The beaded belt of his tunic was askew and his golden vulture amulet swung wildly. Where the stranger had struck him, his face, neck and ear were red, but he schooled his fair features to a royal demeanor nonetheless. "It was my father, a triumvir of Rome, who made me a king."

"He had no right," the stranger replied. "Your so-called kingdom Parthia isn't even yet conquered. We should send you there and see if you can hold it, you treacherous boy."

Helios glared. "What treachery do you speak of, Octavian?"

"*Octavian?*" The man laughed deep from his belly. "Did you think *he* would stoop to question the children of *that woman*? I'm Marcus Vipsanius Agrippa."

I knew this name. Agrippa had defeated my father at the naval battle of Actium and was Rome's most able fighter. Philadelphus must have recognized Agrippa's name too, for he tightened his grip on my skirt until I thought it would tear. Meanwhile, Agrippa folded his meaty arms, stepping closer to Helios. "Besides, when you meet your new master, you'll address him not as Octavian but as *Caesar*."

Helios said what my mother would have. "Octavian has no right to the name Caesar. My brother, the Most Divine, King Ptolemy Caesarion, is Julius Caesar's only son."

"Boy," Agrippa began. "You're in no position to talk of rights or quibble about titles. Caesar promised your mother that he'd torture and kill you if she took her own life. It'll only be Caesar's clemency that saves you now, so I suggest you call him whatever he likes."

"I'll use his title if he uses mine," Helios replied, his hubris owing as much to our upbringing as to the fact he was still a boy. He was rewarded for that hubris with a slap that brought blood to his mouth. Helios swung back at the giant but missed. Then

Agrippa grabbed Helios by his golden hair and seemed ready to beat him in earnest.

"Please don't hurt my brother!" Philadelphus cried.

I had to do something, but what? "Lord Agrippa!" I shouted. Though my hands trembled, I clutched the amulet my mother had given me and adopted my most adult voice. "You've introduced yourself. Permit me to do the same. I'm Cleopatra Selene, Queen of Cyrenaica."

"Girl, I didn't address you." The Roman clenched his fist, ready to strike Helios.

I hid my shaking hands. "Nonetheless, you're a guest in our royal palace, and I insist that you behave like one."

Agrippa peered at me from beneath the crest of his helmet, then released Helios with a shove. "How old are you?"

"Nearly eleven," I said.

"You don't speak like a child."

"I speak like a queen." Or so I hoped. "How can We help you, Lord Agrippa?"

I had used the royal *We* and the brute of a man seemed disarmed. "You can tell me how your mother managed to cheat Rome of seeing her dragged through the streets in chains. We know you were with her before she died. Who helped her?"

I did, I thought, and my knees went weak with fear.

Several Roman guards crowded near the doorway. They didn't enter but seemed to pay close attention to what was said behind their veneer of professional disinterest. But I didn't answer Agrippa's question. I *couldn't* answer.

As if to coax me, Agrippa said, "Caesar allowed your father an honorable burial and Queen Cleopatra promised not to kill herself. She broke her bargain. So who helped her? How did she do it? Was it poison?"

My heart thumped dully in my chest but I tried not to react. Philadelphus peeked at me, but I dared not meet his eyes. Helios and I stood like statues, a conspiracy of silence between us.

Agrippa removed his polished helmet, tucking it under one arm. Its gleam reflected a distorted image of my silent green eyes back at me. "We already have Euphronius in custody. It was the old warlock that brought her poison, wasn't it?"

I envisioned our frail old wizard chained in the jail, and I shuddered. Still, if they were questioning us about Euphronius's guilt, they must doubt it. So we still said nothing.

A light breeze rustled the netting over my mother's bed.

A soldier coughed in the hall.

An oil lamp flickered.

"Don't you want to prove your worth to Caesar now?" Agrippa asked. "Your mother's deception does her no honor."

But the fact she'd deceived the enemy inspired me. With my eyes, I motioned toward the cosmetics on my mother's dressing table. "My mother wouldn't need Euphronius to bring poison to her. We keep it everywhere."

Agrippa glanced over at the colorful bottles then back at us, horrified. Motioning to a soldier behind him, he said, "Get rid of that. Dump it in the Nile and let the Egyptians drink Cleopatra's venom."

The soldiers collected each harmless vial as if it contained a monster that might be unleashed with the cork. Their fear and loathing of poisons, potions, and magic was evident to me even then. If only I'd known how to use it against them. "So, your mother *did* die of poison?" Agrippa pressed.

I wasn't sure why it was important how my mother died, but the fact the Romans wanted to know meant that they shouldn't find out. I resolved to give nothing away, but Helios said, "She died by snakebite, which made her immortal. You can't hurt her now."

I wanted desperately to throttle him. Throughout our childhood, my twin's compulsive truth telling had gotten me in trouble, but now the stakes were so much higher. What would the

Romans do to me if they found out that I'd delivered the snake to her concealed in a basket of figs?

Perhaps Agrippa sensed my fear. "Girl, is this true? Did Euphronius bring Cleopatra a serpent?"

"My mother always had serpents with her," I said, and prayed my brothers wouldn't contradict me. "Three cobras adorn her headdress. My mother made them come to life whenever she wished. She said it would bring her to my father. Euphronius is only our tutor—he knows all the tongues, even the holy ones—but he's not a snake handler or a poisoner."

I said the last in Latin, because it seemed very important that the Roman understand me, and Agrippa blinked in surprise. Had he expected us to be unschooled barbarians? I was the daughter of a Roman triumvir; I spoke Greek, Latin, and many other languages.

"So, your story is that Cleopatra made a snake magically appear from her headdress and used it to end her life?"

"Yes," I said with conviction.

After all, Egypt was famed for snake magic. My mother had been a powerful magician and I'd seen her turn staves into snakes for our amusement. But when it came time to die, she'd had me bring her the serpent. If the Romans found that out, would they kill me too?

"It would have taken two cobras to kill her and her handmaidens together . . ." Agrippa's face seemed unbearably close to my own. His Roman breath was like vinegar.

"It was two, then," I said, remembering the coiling motion in the unbearably heavy basket. I doubted I could have carried two and the figs besides, but perhaps they had been small. Or magical. Or young. Perhaps there had been two. Perhaps the snakes had been lovers, or siblings, or *twins*. I dared not look at mine.

Agrippa sneered at me. "When I have the old warlock crucified and he screams a different tale, do you think I won't return to make an end to your miserable, spoiled little lives?"

I felt dizzy because I knew crucifixion was a terrible death that the Romans used to prolong suffering. "Please don't hurt Euphronius. He is just an old man!"

"He's a magician and a priest of Isis," Agrippa growled. "The Isiac priesthood is nothing but a den of witches, warlocks, and whores. Curse the day a soldier like Antony fell into their clutches." At the mention of my father, Agrippa's features twisted with sadness and regret. It took him a moment to recover, and when he did, he changed the subject entirely. "Where is Caesarion?"

At last, Helios and I exchanged glances. This question was unexpected and we both knew what it meant. If the Romans didn't know where Caesarion was, my oldest brother had escaped, after all. My heart soared with hope.

"The King of Egypt is in exile," Helios said.

"In exile where?" Agrippa asked.

"We don't know where," I replied. For that much was true. But wherever he was, Caesarion would raise an army to rescue us. Men would rally to him in the name of his dead father, Julius Caesar—the *real* Caesar.

Agrippa seemed to know it. "Is Caesarion still here in Alexandria? Will you tell me or will I have to burn down every house in the city to find him?"

The way Agrippa's face was lined with rage convinced us he was willing to do just that, so I said, "We don't know where he is. My mother wouldn't tell us." And I tried not to betray my smugness. Julius Caesar had been invincible in battle, falling only to the knives of treasonous assassins. Would not the gods shine on his son? Caesarion would save us!

Agrippa growled. "If you're lying to me, I'll see you crucified, royalty or no. Your mother's last wish was for an honorable funeral and to be interred beside your father. For reasons that escape me, my lord has granted her request. Were it up to me, I'd dump her body in the Nile for the crocodiles and you children along with her."

Just then, Agrippa's eyes drifted to the far wall where a banner hung beside my mother's bed. Upon that banner was emblazoned our Ptolemy family motto: *Win or Die.*

I had been looking in the wrong place for a note from my mother. It was not amongst her papers but here, on the wall, a message for her enemies, and for her children both. Beneath it, we stood as regal as my mother expected us to be. Knowing that Caesarion was alive, we stared at Agrippa as if he were contemptible rabble. The gods would smite him as surely as he breathed.

Helios took my hand, protectively, and I held Philadelphus in my other arm. We stood before the Roman, staring, but silent. We were Ptolemies.

"You're unnatural," Agrippa said. With that, the admiral slammed out of my mother's chambers leaving behind him wood splinters, blood, and frightened children.

Three

FOR seventy days, Octavian held us prisoner in my mother's chambers while he tightened his stranglehold over an eerily silent Alexandria. And all the while, my brothers and I waited to be liberated. When my mother's embalming was complete we were finally allowed out of our palace prison to accompany her sarcophagus in the funeral procession. We had hoped to hear the sounds of Caesarion's army marching upon Alexandria. We had hoped to hear the cheers of the crowds as they flung open their doors and windows to greet their young king. Instead, the city only came alive again to say farewell to my mother. Though it was unseasonably warm, citizens emerged from their hiding places and poured into the blistering streets. Under the pitiless sun, they jostled for shade beneath the palm trees.

As King of Egypt, it was Caesarion's duty to bury my mother, but with Caesarion missing, the duty fell to us. My brothers and I were obliged to play the trinity—Isis, Osiris, and Horus—and when the people saw us, they cried, "We love you, children of Isis!"

Though white-robed priests tried to keep them back, nobles and peasants alike wept and reached out to us. Their faces were marked with grief and fear, but the mourners offered their jewelry and furniture to replace what the Romans had stolen so that my mother wouldn't enter the afterworld as a pauper.

While citizens waved from doorways, adding their wails to the haunting music of our national sorrow, my brothers and I walked to the somber notes of panpipes. With Octavian's Roman soldiers posted on every street corner, it felt as if we mourned not only my mother but Egypt too.

Our procession passed the Soma where all my ancestors were buried beside the famous sarcophagus of Alexander the Great, but our mother wouldn't be buried there. She embraced in death, as she had in life, her native people; she asked to be buried in her own sepulcher in the tradition of all the great Pharaohs of Egypt.

Our old tutor hadn't confessed when the Romans flogged him, and he'd been released, which meant that he was on hand to see that those traditions were observed. Clad in a blue wig and panther hide, and carrying a clay vessel filled with purifying natron balls, Euphronius joined the highest-ranking priests of Egypt to lead my mother's funeral procession.

Some held my mother's organs in canopic jars and other masked priests pulled the wheel-mounted hearse carrying my mother's sarcophagus. One priest wore a false beard and the others wore masks of dogs, baboons, and falcons.

I walked behind them in a glittering goddess mask of my own, fighting tears. My neck ached from the weight of the silver moon headdress, and my black gown—which was knotted in the sacred *tiet*—seemed to soak up the heat of the bright Alexandrian sunshine. Beside me, my twin's skin sparkled with gold and he wore the sun-disk headdress that symbolized Horus; he wore it because his namesake was a sun god and because the costume was even heavier than mine. His bare arms were dewy with sweat from the effort to walk in it. Fortunately for little Philadelphus, his Osiris crown was made of dried stalks.

As we made our way down the Street of the Soma, between rows of palm trees, I saw my father's smashed statues. Chunks of marble littered the ground. Yet my mother's statues stood proud and unharmed for Euphronius knew the Romans always had a price; with the help of wealthy friends he'd helped to ransom my mother's statues with all the gold in the temple treasury.

I was glad; seeing my mother's statues, left whole, lent me strength with every step. They reminded me of my mother's passion—how she could rain curses down upon us with one breath and clutch us to her breast with the next. It could sometimes be forgotten in horseplay that my father was a ruler of men, but even my mother's kisses couldn't make us forget that she was the pharaoh; as we walked behind her sarcophagus, we couldn't forget that now.

We also couldn't forget about our enemy. I wanted to see the man who'd brought such misery to my family and who now called himself master of Alexandria. But Octavian remained a mystery; he'd allowed my mother a proper funeral, but he didn't attend. Instead, he sent other Romans, including Plancus, one of my father's generals who had betrayed us.

Plancus and the other Romans kept close watch on my brothers and me. Their armor gleamed menacingly in the sun, but their threatening glares at the citizenry were in vain. Alexandrians defiantly waved the Ptolemy Eagle in violation of Octavian's orders that all such banners be burned.

My mother had chosen as one of her epitaphs Philopatris—Lover of Her Nation—and on this day, there was no doubt her nation loved her in return.

AT last the procession reached my mother's tomb, and the bloodiest task of the funeral fell to Helios. His job was to help slaughter the sacrificial bulls and offer their meat to sustain my mother's spirit bodies.

The priests held the bull and stood ready to assist my brother if his boy's strength was not enough for the task. But Helios plunged the blade into the bull's throat with quick, merciful force. Blood sprayed crimson dots across my twin's face as the animal staggered and fell. Then it was time for the symbolic Opening of the Mouth ceremony.

This was Caesarion's task, and the crowd seemed to hold its breath waiting to see what the priests of Egypt would do in the king's absence. With a shrewd look in his eye, Euphronius lifted the iron wand to speak the holy words, and the crowd gasped at his heresy.

Only the next pharaoh could open the mouth. Not even the most holy priest in Egypt had the right. Euphronius stopped, paused dramatically, then gestured with the wand to Helios, whose blood-spattered costume glittered in the sun. "Oh, Egypt, shall Pharaoh's son open the mouth?"

At first there was silence. Then a cheer. Confused Romans looked on, the drama lost on them until the crowd began to chant. "He's Horus! Helios-Horus!"

In the Egyptian stories, Horus was the divine son of Isis, secretly nursed in the Nile marshes until he was old enough to avenge his father's murder. It was a potent Egyptian tale that the people were unable to resist. Euphronius must have known they would make the connection; he'd dressed Helios for the part.

"Helios-Horus the Avenger, open the mouth!"

As the people shouted, my brother looked to me, as if for permission. I couldn't imagine why. I was a queen of other places, but I was only a princess of Egypt, and Helios never asked my permission for anything before. Then I remembered, in this funereal play, he was Horus and I was Isis. Isis, who suckles her babe at her breast, her body seated in the shape of a throne a so that the pharaoh may rest upon her as she nourishes his people. As Isis,

I wasn't merely maiden, mother, and crone. As Isis, I was also the *throne*.

As such, it was my assent Helios needed.

Slowly, deliberately, I lowered my head, so that the moon-disk headdress dipped and signaled the blessing of Isis. Then, responding to his cue, my twin brother took the wand in his bloodied hand and the Alexandrians roared their approval.

Helios then lifted the iron to the mouth of the sarcophagus to bring my mother breath. Then Helios lifted the bloody leg of the bull in sacrifice to the mummy's mouth, to give my mother sustenance.

Euphronius shouted, *"Helios-Horus hath opened the mouth of the dead, as he in times of old opened the mouth of his father, Osiris. And just as Osiris then rose from the dead, so too shall the deceased Cleopatra walk in the great company of the gods."*

SERVANTS streamed into my mother's tomb with plates of dates and cheese, grilled flat breads, bowls of fruits, and platters of roasted meats. I noticed that it wasn't just the Greeks and the light-skinned Alexandrians who came to honor the queen. The maidens from the country came too and they had skin as brown as the beer they served.

My brothers and I had been so isolated since my mother's death that we were eager to be amongst people again. I had to actually restrain myself from throwing my arms around our prickly doctor, Olympos, when we saw him. I was even happy to see my mother's eunuch, Fat Mardian!

Mardian bowed and kissed my hand. "Princess, it's so good to see that you and your brothers are well. I have a little good news in all this sadness. I report that in your mother's final year, the Nile swelled and flooded to its greatest extent. Pharaoh's last gift to her people is a bountiful harvest."

A bountiful harvest for the Romans to gobble up, I thought.

"Where is that traitor, Plancus?" Helios asked. "If he takes even one mouthful of my mother's funeral feast, I hope he chokes on it."

"What's this about choking?" asked Olympos, his voice flat. He'd been devoted to keeping my mother alive; now his brown eyes seemed hollow. "Are the Romans feeding you children? You look thin."

"They bring us food, but never anything good," Philadelphus replied, his eyes lighting up at the treats being served.

I blinked back unexpected tears at the comfort of familiar voices and faces. Still, my mother and father's closest friends were not with us. My father's lieutenant, Canidius, had been executed. The other soldiers, scholars, and minor royalty that had once called themselves the Society of Inimitable Livers were nowhere to be found. I was afraid Euphronius would tell me that they too had been killed.

All who remained were scholars like Nicholas of Damascus, Lady Lasthenia of the Pythagorean School, and nobles like Diodromes who had sometimes teased my mother for being too Egyptian and not enough Greek. Alexandria was the epicenter of Hellenistic culture and Greek-Macedonian blood flowed in our veins too, but my mother had been an Egyptophile in every respect. She'd raised us to feel the same way, so Euphronius kept us separate from the Greek nobles. Unfortunately, we could still overhear their conversations.

"They say King Caesarion has fled to India," Lady Lasthenia said. "But I think he must be hiding here in Alexandria. He'll wait for the right moment to rally the people, then strike at Octavian."

"No," Diodromes replied. "Queen Cleopatra was all that stood between us and Rome. They'll kill the boy and crush the Isiac temples. Octavian will tolerate no rival to the name Caesar."

When he realized I was listening, the lord lowered his head and went silent beneath my gaze. He let a servant pour rich brown beer into his cup. I tasted my own and it was bitter.

I wasn't hungry either so I offered what was left on my plate to Philadelphus, who gobbled it up as if he'd never eaten before. Oil lamps kept the walls around us lit, but shadows loomed inside me. The headdress and grief weighed down on me, and I stared at my cup. The paint on my face left a smudge on it that looked like a grotesque death mask and I began to realize from the eyes of all those in attendance that they were saying farewell not just to my mother but to us too.

"They act as if this is our funeral," Helios whispered, echoing my own thoughts as he reached for a washbasin. Then he was washing his face and hands, leaving bloody water and flecks of gold in the basin. I noted that my twin resembled me, but in the fashion of a boy. His arms and legs were longer than mine, his face flatter and his thick, flaxen hair curled where mine was dark and wavy. He looked like Alexander the Great, the conqueror he was named after. I wondered how my mother had known to name him that, but I tried not to think of her, for every time I did, it reminded me that I was the one who brought her the deadly basket.

"Eat, Princess," Olympos insisted, so I nibbled at some flat bread until the temple prostitutes approached us and laid holy amulets at our feet.

One of them, with a dark braided wig, wept openly. "Holy twins, Saviors, what will we do without Isis?"

I started to make some reply, surprised as I was by her question, but Euphronius intervened, his lips drawn into sharp lines. "Don't upset the children. Be off with you."

At last, the scent of grassy funeral magic filled the air, as the priests read the words painted on my mother's tomb in ochre, carnelian, and azure. Invigorated with power from the Temple of Isis, they cast spells on the *shabti*—the small wax figures of servants and soldiers that would serve my mother in the afterworld. Then the remains of the meal were carefully gathered and placed in the burial chamber along with my mother and father's sarcophagi. The holy books were also placed inside with what treasure the citizens had gathered for her. Then, with kisses, the tomb was sealed.

Outside—where the setting sun lit the sky purple, the color of kings and queens—the Roman admiral Agrippa waited for us. "I've come to fetch the children. We sail for Rome in the morning, so make your good-byes."

Our wizard stepped in front of us protectively, planting his staff in the ground. "Lord Agrippa, winter is almost here. It's too dangerous to risk the sea."

"Have you ever commanded a ship, you old warlock?" Agrippa demanded, without waiting for an answer. "Until you do, you mind your potions and I'll mind my ships."

Philadelphus pulled the husked crown from his head and began to quake. "But we're supposed to go to Rome overland, the long way. That's what almost always happens."

Helios and I both stared at Philadelphus. Since my mother's death, our little brother didn't speak often, and when he did, he said strange things like that. Our tutor, however, didn't seem to notice. Instead, Euphronius tried to reason with Agrippa. "At least let me accompany the children to Rome. I'm sure that Lord Octavian, in his infinite mercy, will permit me to continue their schooling."

Agrippa eyed our wizard with an expression between contempt and fear. "We won't let you teach these children more Isiac witchery. We don't want you or any temple whore near them; they're now prisoners of war. Property of Rome."

Not if Caesarion came to rescue us. But for that, we needed time, and that's what Euphronius argued for now. "Surely, the noble Octavian wishes to stay a little longer in Egypt and see the riches that he has won with his great victory."

"Oh, Caesar will stay awhile," Agrippa said. "Meanwhile, I'll keep Rome for him in his absence and attend to these brats."

Euphronius winced. "Don't you wish to visit Alexander's tomb and—"

Philadelphus interrupted, staring out at the water of the harbor. "They broke Alexander."

"It was an accident," Agrippa said impatiently, eyeing Philadelphus suspiciously. "Caesar merely reached out and Alexander's nose came off in his hand."

Our wizard nearly barked with outrage. Had Octavian actually dared to touch Alexander the Great? For generations, pilgrims had come to Alexander's tomb, to see his golden body preserved in honey. Julius Caesar himself had knelt by the alabaster coffin and wept. Now Octavian had desecrated the corpse. The Romans really were barbarians!

Euphronius got hold of himself with visible effort. "If you've desecrated the tomb, you must make peace with Alexander's spirit. This is an ill omen."

Agrippa shrugged. "Or a good omen. We say Alexander's spirit recognized in Octavian his own successor and allowed Caesar to come away with some part of him. In any case, I'm taking the children to Rome."

"Lord Agrippa," Euphronius said, beseechingly. "Again I implore you to mind the seas. The Emergence has begun, when farmers sow the fertile soil left behind by the Nile flood. Stay a little longer so that you appreciate what you bring to Rome."

"Not one extra day," Agrippa said. "I've no love of this corrupting land of beast worship and black arts. Soldiers who stay in Egypt too long become like Antony."

With that, Agrippa walked away, content that his soldiers would gather us up to follow him. Philadelphus cried, clutching our tutor's leg. "Enough tears," Euphronius whispered. "Octavian worries about mutiny at home. There may be trouble in Rome, and then there are his unruly veterans. You must go and hope that your mother's visions come to fruition . . ."

Caesarion's army would come too late.

"Aren't we ever coming back home?" I asked. "Have you seen it in the Rivers of Time?"

Euphronius wouldn't lie to us, though I saw that he wanted to. "I don't know if you'll come back to Egypt, but I know that Egypt and Isis are always in you. They have desecrated her temples and rounded up her priests. With your mother gone, Isis can't live here anymore. Until her faithful sit the throne, she must go with you. We must cast you out upon the water like lilies, blossoms of Egypt still to bloom."

RIPPED from the warm embrace of Alexandria's golden shores, we were loaded onto a ship for Rome. As the enormous vessel slipped slowly through the harbor, men at several banks of oars, I saw the glittering white and gold Serapeum, where my father had crowned me queen of lands I'd never seen.

The gulls cried on the wind, the palm trees seemed to wave to us in farewell, and I clutched the frog amulet around my neck. The mysterious man who had conquered our kingdom hadn't been able to capture our mother. She had died rather than face whatever cruel fate he'd planned for her, so he had settled upon us instead. We were his captives, his war booty, and we had not even seen his face.

Euphronius said that we now carried Isis with us; if I jumped into the sea, would she save me? Even if she didn't, would it not be better to drown here instead of bringing her to Rome where we might be slaughtered? Philadelphus's eyes were red from weeping when General Plancus approached us. "Come, children. I'll bring you below to get some rest."

Philadelphus recoiled, and facing a stony glare from my twin, Plancus looked to me for help. "At least let the little one come with me, Selene. I was your father's friend once; I'll treat Philadelphus kindly."

I gripped the wooden rail of the ship, the measure of my hatred for Plancus taking me by surprise. "We don't accept kindness from traitors. Don't presume to call us by our first names again."

"Princess, don't you know how many men deserted your father in the end? We changed sides not because we didn't love Antony; we joined Octavian because your mother insisted on ruling beside him as an equal. She was the ruin of—"

"It's bad enough you're a traitor," Helios said. "Don't slander her as well."

With that, Plancus shrugged his shoulders and walked away. So it was that Philadelphus stayed with us on the deck as the sails billowed and the sparkling blue sea swallowed up more of the horizon until all we could see of Alexandria was its beacon.

Helios's features were grim and inscrutable, his cloak flapping angrily in the sea breeze. I followed his flinty gaze to the Pharos lighthouse and decided I wouldn't jump; as long as the lighthouse stood, with its beacon bright, as long as the people called for Isis, and as long as I had Helios with me, I would not jump.

Four

JUST as Euphronius had warned, the trip took much longer than it should have and I spent most of that journey huddling together with my brothers in a ship's cabin while the winds howled outside. Even after we arrived in port, we were kept onboard because Agrippa said that the alternative was to throw us into the Mamertine Prison with the rest of the captives. One might think, having spent nearly eight months on that ship, I would have vivid recollections of it, but I don't. Perhaps it's grief that stole those memories from me, or perhaps the kindness of Isis. And yet I remember our arrival in Rome with complete clarity.

The Romans dressed us in royal attire for Octavian's Triumph. I wore a Grecian gown of white and Tyrian purple with a pearled diadem upon my brow, so I tried to keep a regal bearing as Roman soldiers herded us into place. They marched my brothers and me onto the open space of the Campus Martius with the rest of the captives while slaves, soldiers, gawkers, and even caged animals witnessed our humiliation.

Foreign princes once allied with my mother were bound at the neck and hand. It did not surprise me to see those who had taken up arms against Rome now in chains, but I had not expected to see so many Isiac priests and priestesses amongst the captives, and was relieved not to see Euphronius with them. Some of the prisoners stood with grim resignation, but some of them wept with fear. They were measuring us—the children of their fallen leaders—so I knew that I couldn't cry. In older times, prisoners of war in Roman Triumphs were occasionally pardoned, but that was too much to hope for. This war had been different—and this was a new Rome. Octavian's Rome.

We could hear the anticipatory roar of the crowd from behind the city gates and knew they called for blood. Under the watchful eye of Admiral Agrippa, the soldiers grabbed Helios, to wrestle him into golden manacles. Though we had known it was coming, the reality of the situation was suddenly unbearable.

"Leave him alone!" I screamed.

Agrippa slapped me across the face; it dizzied me. Before I could gather my composure, strong Roman arms grabbed me and shook me until I went limp with fear. I wish I could say that I fought against my bonds that day, but I was too stunned by the violation. My twin, however, fought the Romans so hard, it took two of them to hold him down and snap the collar shut around his neck.

As they did, Helios delivered a kick to the groin that sent one of the soldiers down to his knees. "Spirited little bastard, isn't he?" Agrippa chuckled. "Too bad Cleopatra's army didn't have half this boy's fight in them. It might have been better sport."

The soldiers laughed and Agrippa nodded in satisfaction as my brother and I were finally restrained. Not even my Ptolemaic dignity kept me from clawing at the metal as the golden collar bit tightly against my throat. "I can't breathe!"

Speckles danced before my eyes as a Roman guard spat at me and shoved me forward. "You wouldn't be hollering if you couldn't breathe."

I stumbled three steps before the weight of the chains brought me down. I skinned my knees in the fall, but all I could think about was the tightness around my neck. I knew that the Romans strangled their prisoners and this must be what it felt like.

"She's just a little girl," another captive said. I glanced up to see that it was the Prince of Emesa, an ally who fought beside my parents in the war and now paid the price for his loyalty. "She doesn't understand what's happening."

He was wrong. I did understand, all too well.

Agrippa swaggered over. "Antony thought she was old enough to name her queen when he was giving away the Roman Empire to his bastard brats. She's old enough to march in chains."

My fingers dug under the metal, trying to loosen the unrelenting collar. It was only Helios's hand on my elbow that centered my reality. "Don't let them see you on your knees," he whispered. "Breathe slow. It's snug, but you can breathe."

Several slow breaths later, I realized he was right. I let him help me to my feet. Helios breathed with me, each of us matching our rhythm to the other until I fought the panic down. Dazed, I used my fettered hands to brush the dirt off my gown until I was yanked forward as the Romans attached our chains to a giant statue.

There she was—an enormous figure of my mother with a coiled serpent around her arm, and the images of her faithful handmaidens dead at her feet. My cheeks burned to see that they had portrayed my mother naked.

Octavian had promised the Romans that he would bring my mother before them, a conquered slave. Now I wondered if he had found a way to make good on his promise. Did the Romans know how to imbue a wax statue with my mother's *ka* and reanimate it? They said only powerful magicians like Euphronius knew how to do such things—though we had never even seen him try—but maybe the Romans had learned. Was it my mother's enemies' plan to bring her back to life only to humiliate her and kill her again?

Just then, a crimson-faced man strode past and mounted the chariot in front of us. I saw no more than the swirl of his purple toga, before guards carrying ceremonial bundled rods and axes surrounded him. A cheer went up from the soldiery and I realized it could be none other than Octavian, but once he mounted his golden chariot, my mother's statue blocked him from view. He'd not bothered to spare us even a glance, the children of his fallen enemy, who he would drag through the streets.

A man stood by in the crowd, a raven on his shoulder. It flapped its wings and called out, "Hail, Victorious Imperator Octavian!"

"A clever bird," we heard the Triumpher say. "You must be a loyalist."

"Ha!" another man cried. "He has another bird and he trained it to say *Hail, Victorious Imperator Antony!*"

The soldiers laughed until their merriment was drowned out by the deafening blare of the trumpets announcing the opening of the gates. Screaming crowds greeted the snow white sacrificial bulls that lead our procession into Rome. My mother's treasure followed: a convoy of wheeled chariots piled high, *amphorae* filled with Egyptian gold.

"You're watching the celebration of bandits," the Prince of Emesa said. "We fought for the Golden Age, but they fought for an Age of Gold."

He was angry and proud, as if daring the Roman soldiers who lined up beside us to punish him for his defiance, but his comments barely carried over the rumble of chariot wheels.

My father, Mark Antony, had told us stories of his beloved Rome. He had even once boasted that he would carry me into the city upon his shoulders. How his spirit must have wept to see us dragged through his city in chains.

"They'll kill us. We'll be strangled like common criminals," one of the other prisoners shouted. I saw that it was Lord Dio-dromes of my mother's court, but now he did look like a common criminal. The Romans let him keep only his loincloth, so that the marks of the whip could be seen plainly upon his back.

"Don't frighten the children," the Prince of Emesa said.

"They should be frightened," Diodromes replied. "Behold the legions as they form up! That is Roman might. They march before us merely to show the mob our disgrace before choking the life out of us."

Philadelphus began to sob.

"Don't listen to him," I said to Philadelphus.

I tried to think only of breathing as the legionnaires filed into the city. One by one, elements of the parade disappeared into those gates, but the crowd was waiting for us—for Octavian and his captives.

The musicians built suspense for the great moment. Horses rode past us, kicking up clouds of dust and obscuring our view as the chariot began to roll forward. As we marched into Rome, the roar of the crowd hit us almost as strongly as the stench. Perhaps it was the crush of people lined up along the narrow streets or the musk of exotic animals on display. Or perhaps it was the squat buildings, piled on top of one another so tightly as to blot out the sun.

My eyes darted left, then right. Everywhere I looked were middling structures. Some were even made of gray mud and brick. Awnings and arches attempted to beautify the parade, but having lived my entire life in the marble city of Alexandria, I could only see these efforts as a veneer to cover the squalor.

I glanced at Helios whose eyes were also wide in amazement. This could not be our father's beloved Rome, for in our eyes, this was nothing but an overcrowded encampment of barbarians! People stood on rooftops; they hung out of windows. They screamed and cheered Octavian and threw flowers in his path. "Hail, Conqueror!"

Then, as my mother's wax statue came into view, the cheers turned to jeers—the sound of adulation abruptly veering into menacing contempt. "Serpent of the Nile!" someone screamed. "Villainess! Harlot! Whore!"

Shrieks reached such a fever pitch that a horse startled and reared, nearly trampling us. The Prince of Emesa yanked the chains to pull my brothers and me out of the way.

Everywhere were screaming faces. They spat at my mother's statue, they reviled her, they threw rocks, and then their eyes came to us. I realized then why the collar around my neck was so tight and high. It was so that I couldn't look away.

This was another kind of funeral for my mother, dark and twisted. Where I'd been embraced by the love of the Alexandrian crowds, I now felt strangled by the oppressive hatred of the Roman mob. "Spawn of the Egyptian monster! My son died because of your mother," one woman shrieked at me. A stone hit my arm with a sharp sting, and I hissed at the pain.

"I want to see you die!" a man yelled at my twin. "To see you roasted! To see you flayed after you're flogged!"

Helios merely tightened his lips to show his contempt. My twin seemed so noble and brave then, unsullied and defiant, that it gave me courage.

"Is it right to condemn Cleopatra's children?" a Roman shouted above the frenzy. He was older, with a craggy face, someone who might have known my father. But he was shouted down.

Shouts, trumpets, and cymbals blurred together into a maddening mixture of hatred that Isis herself would have wept to see. From their cries, one would think my brothers and I had sprung spontaneously from my mother's womb. One might watch this spectacle and not realize that my father had played any part in the war; his partisans were nowhere to be seen. Whether Octavian had killed them all or banished them, I didn't know. Perhaps they stayed silent for fear of their lives.

Euphronius taught us that some Romans worshipped Isis and that even before my birth, the Isiac faith was spreading throughout the world. But if there were Isiacs in the crowd, they too were silent, either biding their time, or indifferent to our plight, their faith having died with my mother.

Her wax figure was on display not as a holy figure but as a naked whore. Perhaps that was to cast doubt on Caesarion's parentage. Or ours, for we too were half Roman. This fact the Romans did not want to remember, and today neither did I.

"Io Triumphe!" the warriors shouted to Octavian, but no manner of insult was too low to hurl at my mother's statue or her children. I was glad she'd died rather than face this. Glad!

Egyptians believed that pharaohs faced terrors at each gate of the afterlife, and I felt kinship with those pharaohs now. As people spit on me, swore at me, and cursed my name—wishing me dead and my brothers alongside me—I hardened my heart. I was a queen, a daughter of Isis, from the line of Alexander the Great. I was from a clean city of white marble and culture. If I would die here in Rome, I would not die a cowering child. The merciless summer sun burned my fair skin, the hours of marching leaving me thirsty and tired, but I would not cry.

A rock caught Philadelphus under the eye, and it bled. Then Philadelphus's legs gave out and the Prince of Emesa lifted him up.

"I thank you for this kindness," I said, trying to make my voice heard over the laughter of the crowd as dancers whirled past. "Thank you also for the loyalty you showed my mother and father."

Our eyes met. "My loyalty has always been to you and your brother," the prince replied.

"King Caesarion is grateful."

"Not *that* brother," he said. "You and your holy twin."

I did not know how to reply to this. I wasn't even sure that it was truly what he said. I was lost in pain and terror now. I no longer heard the obscene epithets that the crowd spat at me; they became just so much noise. A shocked exhaustion made it easier to ignore the ache in my feet.

At last the procession slowed as the chariot reached the

Capitoline Temple. The cries of *"Io Triumphe!"* began to subside. Helios held out his hand to me and I took it—a loving gesture amidst infinite enmity.

Then everything stopped.

Octavian the Conqueror stepped out of his jeweled chariot and ascended the steps in purple splendor, and the crowd hushed. Before the statue of Jupiter, the Triumpher finally humbled himself, surrendering his laurel crown and scepter. Then Octavian lifted the knife above one of the sacrificial bulls, letting it hover over the doomed beast. With a swift and efficient stroke, the Triumpher cut the bull's throat.

"So too with the captives!" the crowd cheered as the animal collapsed in death, a spray of blood showering the sacred altar, and flowing into the ready drains.

Soldiers grabbed hold of Philadelphus and yanked Helios and me up the temple stairs to face the man who held our fate in his hands. At last, Octavian deigned to look upon the children of those he destroyed.

The crowd seemed to hold its collective breath as we finally came face to face with our conqueror. I met Octavian's eyes and couldn't have been more unprepared for what I saw.

My mother had been a woman teeming with energy and boundless stamina. My father had been a broad-shouldered giant whose physicality intimidated his enemies, and whose charm won him friends. I had grown up knowing that my parents were the most powerful people in the world and had imagined Octavian must have been a colossus of a man to have conquered them.

Instead, Octavian was slight of build and pale beneath the crimson paint upon his face. His hands were fragile, his neck was thin—everything about him was small in comparison to the soldiers I had known. My lips parted in surprise, and I wondered if there had been some mistake. After all, how much more like a ruler Admiral Agrippa appeared to be.

Yet, when I looked at Octavian, I was caught by the snare of his eyes. In the narrowness of his gray stare was a wintry ruthlessness that marked him for who he was. There was a chill in everything about him—frigidity even in the way he moved—and it made me tremble.

Octavian inspected us as the crowd waited. He took my chin between his thumb and index finger, turning my face first to one side and to the next, as far as the metal collar would allow. His touch sent an icy prickle down my spine. His finger traced down my neck onto the jade frog amulet I wore and he eyed the inscription. "What does this say?" he asked, his voice soft and slightly nasal in quality.

"I am the Resurrection," I whispered, not thinking to lie.

Octavian lifted a brow. "Is that so?"

I couldn't find voice to answer. The knife was still in his hand, still dripping with the blood of his sacrifice.

"The whore's spawn is the image of her mother," he said.

"She's also the child of Lord Antony!" the Prince of Emesa dared to shout. "She's also Roman. Forget that at your peril."

I would always wonder what force of loyalty or faith drove the prince's defiance—for it cost him his life. Octavian made a single gesture, and with the efficiency for which Romans were famous, the guards plunged a ceremonial ax into the prince's chest.

Like the sacrificial bull, so too did the Prince of Emesa collapse on the temple steps. Philadelphus shrieked and my mouth fell open in a silent scream as the blood spattered my gown. The dying man's head hit the marble with a hollow sound, then his mouth frothed with bloody saliva. Hot blood poured out of him over my sandals. His wound pulsed, his chest split in gory shining halves. Then I saw the life drain from his eyes and the Prince of Emesa was no more.

The crowd cheered their approval as if they were watching a play.

In that instant everything that had been holding me together unwound. My mother had been wrong. There was nothing beautiful

in death, after all. No, the face of the dead man held gray lifeless-
ness. He was as lifeless as my mother's wax statue.

Octavian lifted the knife toward Helios and I screamed, "No,
please!"

"Don't beg," Helios hissed at me.

Win or Die was the Ptolemy motto, but I wanted desperately
to live. Where were our friends? They were all dead or left behind
in Alexandria. Where was Caesarion and the army he would raise
to smite these barbarians? For that matter where was Isis? If she
lived inside of us, what would happen to her if we died?

My mother taught us not to cry in front of strangers, but if
Octavian wanted my tears, he'd have them. I dropped to my knees
before the murderer of my kin, crying, "Mercy! The children of
the Roman triumvir Mark Antony ask for mercy."

If the plea had come from my brothers, perhaps the mob
would have reacted differently, but they saw nothing disgraceful
about this plea from a girl. It earned their sympathy, and as I knelt
in blood before Octavian, a pitying wail went up from the crowd.

The corners of Octavian's mouth twitched into a smile.

Just then, as if she'd been positioned for the occasion, a matron
draped primly in a brown gown and matching shawl stepped out
onto the temple stairs. She was an earthy-looking woman, but to
me, she was an incarnation of Isis, a goddess of salvation when she
said, "Caesar, forgive an unworthy woman for her insolence, but I
too beg that you show your great clemency to these poor helpless
children."

Octavian's voice rang theatrically in answer. "My sister, you
ask for clemency on behalf of these bastards? You must know
that they're the children of the Egyptian whore who stole noble
Antony from you and from Rome!"

When the woman spoke again, she also shouted. "Lord An-
tony would have stayed loyal to Rome were he not drugged by
Cleopatra's Eastern potions and wicked religion. As Antony's true
Roman wife, I ask mercy for these children. I'll raise them as my

own. I'll be as loyal to Antony's memory as he should have been to Rome."

I glanced up only long enough to see Octavian smile, like the master of a play he'd written and performed himself to perfection. But the blood between my fingers, soaking through the fabric of my gown was very real.

At last, Octavian said, "My sister, I will grant your wish."

"Caesar spares the children!" a herald echoed.

The mingled scent of laurel and blood filtered toward my senses. I trembled uncontrollably and my vision faded. I was only vaguely aware of the other captives being dragged away.

Rome hated me and I hated Rome, but I would live. We would live. That was all that mattered.

Five

WHISPERS tugged at my consciousness, but I tried to ignore them. I was dreaming of Caesarion and how he must, even now, be sailing across the seas with his army to rescue us. I dreamed too of the time Caesarion taught Helios and me to ride a horse. He helped us charm the animal with an apple, and every time we fell off he picked us up and made us try again. He told me that if I was ever to be his queen and Helios his fiercest warrior, we must be brave and learn to ride at his side. But we never asked what would happen if Caesarion fell . . .

The happy dream was receding, leaving me with a deep sense of longing.

"Is she awake yet?" someone whispered.

"Let her sleep," a man replied.

I was being watched, and the indignity of it made me reluctant to open my eyes. Still, if I opened my eyes, I might find myself back home in Alexandria and the memory of Octavian's Triumph just a nightmare.

I sat up to find Roman children crowding the doorway. When

they saw me awake, a hush fell. I was sticky with dried blood and dirt. Where the manacles had been, bruises ringed each of my wrists, tender and swollen; Octavian's Triumph had been no nightmare.

"Aqua," I whispered. Water. It hurt my throat to speak even that one Latin word through parched lips.

A handsome young man with desert skin came forward. "Greetings, Selene. I'm Gaius Julius Juba, a friend of Caesar's."

As if I cared who he was. All I cared about was the wooden cup that he held to my lips. I was so thirsty that I gulped until my stomach lurched. Then, afraid I would vomit, I shoved the cup away and panted. I must have seemed like an animal to them. I felt like one.

The man named Juba said, "Minora, go tell your mother that she's awake."

The smallest girl bobbed her head and ran off while more faces blurred before my eyes. "Where are my brothers?"

"They're both getting cleaned up," Juba said, and I noticed now that his features were regal, almost too perfect, like a Greek statue. He smelled of sand and cinnamon, like home, like Egypt, but his garb was Roman. "We're going to have our afternoon meal."

Was it afternoon, then? I couldn't tell how much time had passed, and there were no windows in the room. I reached again for the water and took a tentative sip while I surveyed the sparse chamber. I was on a sleeping couch with pretty ivory feet—a much simpler and more uncomfortable bed than I was used to. There was also a bronze-studded wooden chest, a carved cedar chair, and a low desk that could also serve as a dressing table. The floor wasn't marble but a patchwork of decorative tile, and instead of a brightly hewn tapestry on the wall, the plaster was painted with a mural. "Are we in the slave quarters?"

"Of course not." Juba chuckled. "Don't be such a spoiled little princess. Lady Octavia's home is modest but lovely. This is your new room."

I could scarcely believe him.

"Yes," said an older boy from the doorway. He was a youth of not more than fourteen, with a little bit of down upon his chin. "Welcome to the lamentable embassy of royal orphans."

Seeing this boy, I drew a sharp breath and dropped the cup. Water spilled in my lap but I didn't care. Perhaps I was still dreaming, but I knew my brother's face. "Antyllus! But Mother said you'd been murdered . . ."

"I'm not Antyllus." The boy smirked, and my heart broke again. "I'm *Iullus*, the son of Antony and his second wife, Fulvia."

I reeled in confusion, straightening painfully. All the adults in my life seemed to have been married many times, and I had never dwelled on the consequences of that fact before now. "Antyllus was your brother too, then?"

"Of course," Iullus replied. "Which makes me your half brother. Or perhaps of no relation to you whatsoever if the rumors about your mother's promiscuity are true."

I blinked at his taunt and the cruel surprise of seeing it fall from a mouth whose shape was so beloved to me. "But you look so much like Antyllus."

"I just told you why," he said, as if I were very stupid.

"But why don't I know you?" I asked. "Why didn't you come to live with us like Antyllus?"

Iullus's eyes darkened in a way that reminded me of our father's blackest moods. "I suppose that in all the chaos, I was somehow left behind."

Juba interrupted my stunned silence. "Selene, when your father broke with Rome, Iullus was still very young. The emperor kept Iullus here but let Antyllus go to your father. You must understand now that he was wise to do so."

Oh, I understood. Octavian had kept Iullus hostage, to use against my father during the war. Now Iullus was an orphan, just like me. I stared at him, an uncomfortable swelling in my heart. In spite of my new half brother's dark gaze, I wanted to reach out to him. Did he hate Octavian and the Romans for what they'd done? I dared not ask in front of all the others.

Juba picked up the cup. "Soon you'll be reunited with the rest of your siblings and meet the other children of the imperial family. You'll soon have lots of friends here to play with."

I didn't want to *play*, nor was I even sure I remembered how. All I wanted was to see Helios and Philadelphus, but Juba seemed to mistake my silence for encouragement. "There's Julia, Tiberius and Drusus, Marcellus, the two Antonias, Marcella and Iullus, whom you've just met."

"The two Antonias?" I asked, bewildered by all the names.

The littlest girl had returned, and I hadn't noticed. She squealed excitedly. "I'm one of the Antonias! Antonia Minor, but they call me Minora and you're my sister."

As the little girl made this announcement, a woman appeared in the crowded doorway. She wore homespun clothes that were unfit even for Egyptian merchants and kept her hair in a severe style without adornment. I recognized her from the steps of the Temple of Jupiter where she'd asked the emperor to spare our lives. "You shouldn't have let them gawk at her, Juba."

"I know you," I whispered.

She smiled warmly. "I'm Lady Octavia, dear. I'm your late father's wife."

And just like that, she crushed the gratitude out of me with her cloying familiarity. I bristled, hissing, "My father divorced you. It's my mother who rests eternally by his side. It does you no honor to claim her place."

The warmth left Lady Octavia's eyes. "Be that as it may, your parents are gone now. It's best you forget them."

I wasn't going to forget them. I would *never* forget them. "What happened to the Prince of Emesa? What was done with his *khat*?"

Lady Octavia's mouth thinned. "The dead prisoners are usually burned."

I remembered all the times my mother had wept that Julius Caesar had been burned, denied the magical funeral rites that would guarantee him entrance to the afterlife, and I now knew how she felt. It was as if they had killed the Prince of Emesa a second time.

"His body was either burned or left for the crows," Iullus added.

"Enough about that," Octavia snapped. "The bath is ready for you, Selene. After, we'll sit down to a meal with your brothers and Juba. He's your new tutor."

That wasn't possible. Juba's classically handsome features were youthful; he looked to be only nineteen or twenty years old. How could he possess the wisdom to teach anyone? "But Euphronius is my tutor," I said softly, trying to be polite.

"Not anymore," was Octavia's curt reply. "You'll have many teachers here in Rome, but Juba is a prodigy. He's already published books on archaeology. You'll like him. He's from Africa, just like you."

Juba smiled at me politely, but I looked away.

I was eager to slip into a warm bath to wash away the grime and the ache but I also wanted to get away from the rest of the children. There were too many new faces, too many new names, and too many people claiming kinship to me.

Of course, I *knew* that my father had children with previous wives, but besides Antyllus, we'd never met our half siblings. My father never even spoke of them. I'd grown up feeling *special*—his princess, one pampered girl in a household of brothers. I never imagined there could be other daughters. Especially ones like Minora, who were just a bit older than Philadelphus—conceived before I met my father for the first time.

So absorbed was I in this new and unexpected revelation, I barely noticed my surroundings. My mother had told me once—with some revulsion—that the Roman nobles sometimes bathed with the common folk at public baths. As it turned out, however, a *private* bath was readied for me. Colorful tiled steps led down into a pool and I groaned as I stepped into it.

Pain mingled with relief as the water slid over my injured skin. A slave girl named Chryssa waded in with me, a reed basket filled with oils and scrapers floating beside her. "You're Greek," I said, taking in her features with some surprise, because in Egypt, Hellenes comprised the noblest class, not the slaves.

"Yes," she said. "I'm also an *ornatrix*. It's my job to tend to your hair and make you look presentable, so let me scrub the blood off you."

Gone were the days in Alexandria when my mother and I used to soak in milk and honey before drying in the sun while servants rubbed us with oils. Thus, I endured without complaint the harsh scrape of a Roman *strigilis* even though I was sure that the slave girl took some of my skin off along with the dirt.

After I was clean, Chryssa helped me step into new garments. There were no pearl brooches or ribbons to adorn me. Just a rather plain *tunica*, the color of almonds, embroidered at the hem with white leaves. It was too big for me by far. The slaves themselves were dressed in clothing of only slightly lower quality, which only confirmed my opinion that everything in Rome was inferior. So when I saw the slave reach for my discarded silk gown, I snatched it from her hands. "Give me that."

"Your *chiton* is bloody and tattered," Chryssa chided me.

"I'm keeping it," I told her, knowing the blood on that gown was all that remained of the Prince of Emesa. It also held my memories and I wanted to remember. My mother had *told* me to remember.

The slave girl tried to yank it back. "Lady Octavia wants the dress burned."

I slapped her hands away. Such insolence from a slave! "Yes, I know Romans love to burn things."

With that I stormed out. Chryssa chased me, so I took off at a run through the corridors until I burst into the garden and was thoroughly lost. Turning abruptly, I was jarred by the sudden sensation of running into a wall. I looked up to find that the wall was actually Agrippa. The big Roman caught me by the arm. "What mischief are you up to now?"

It was strange to see Agrippa dressed as a civilian. Even so, I braced for violence. Agrippa had already slapped me once and clapped me in chains. I anticipated more brutality and was surprised when he merely stared at my arm as if he'd accidentally caught a serpent by the tail. "What did you do to yourself?"

"*You* did it. You and your chains," I said, expecting to see bruises around my wrists but when I looked, my arm was covered in tiny bloodred hieroglyphics. I lifted the other arm and my mouth fell open with a sharp intake of breath. There too pictures cut into my skin, winding around each wrist and down my arms. The cuts were needle-fine, with only the faintest trace of blood.

Agrippa's voice turned strangely gentle. "Why did you do this?"

I shook my head as fiery pain raced up my arms. "I don't know what's happening."

"Where did you get a needle to do this?" Agrippa asked.

"You think I carved them myself?"

"These symbols . . ." Agrippa was mesmerized. "What do they say?"

I tried to translate them. "It's about Isis. She saw her children shamed—" I stopped. Was this a message from my mother? Had she seen my shameful begging on the steps before Octavian and found a way to reach through to chastise me?

Agrippa's gentleness vanished. "*Isis?*" He grabbed both my arms and dragged me forward. "What vile magic is this? Caesar has brought an asp into his sister's household."

I was desperate to read my own flesh, but Agrippa dragged me when I fell behind. "Where are you taking me?"

"To Caesar!" he said, jogging up the stairs into a two-story building that apparently belonged to the emperor. We passed through a room where wax masks of Julian ancestors leered down at me from the walls. Then, together we burst into the *triclinium* where women and children readied to dine.

Agrippa threw me down to the floor where I stumbled to my knees amidst couches and low tables, dropping the bloody gown. Philadelphus cried out to see me treated thus, and Helios jumped up to come to my aid.

"Look at her arms!" the admiral roared.

Lady Octavia rose from her seat and put a restraining hand on Helios. "Agrippa, you're frightening the children."

"This is a matter for Caesar," Agrippa barked.

"And Caesar is here," Octavian said, coming in behind us.

He was the master of the world, yet he looked like an ill dressed peasant in his wool tunic. The children in the room stood to greet him and I took the opportunity to tuck my old bloody gown under my ugly new garments while Octavian turned to Agrippa. "Some civility please, Agrippa. I'd hoped for a nice family meal with all of the children. What troubles you?"

I hadn't seen Agrippa cower before; I hadn't thought the intimidating man was even capable of it. But now he shrank back from Octavian's rebuke. "My apologies, Caesar. It's just that you pardoned this girl only yesterday and already she's working magic. She's carved symbols into her arms."

They all stared at me, even my brothers.

Octavian said, "Selene, show me your arms."

Again, my mother's enemy was standing over me, and I was again kneeling before him in a trembling heap. Whatever defiance I had felt toward my captors froze within my chest. The chilling threat in his eyes was enough to contain me. I hadn't begged for my life only to anger him now, so I lifted my arms.

"Bruises from the chains?" Octavian's question betrayed his confusion. "She's a Ptolemy. No doubt she bruises easily . . ."

I looked up abruptly to see that he was right. Nothing was carved upon my arms, after all. Where tiny hieroglyphics had wrapped around each wrist moments before, there were only bruises. I was both relieved and anguished at their disappearance. What message had they carried?

"She carved symbols all over her wrists as we'd find on Egyptian temples and tombs." Agrippa stopped himself as he came closer to inspect my arms himself and flinched when he saw nothing there. Agrippa was clearly not a man who liked mysteries.

"What did you see here before?" Octavian traced his cold fingers over my wrists experimentally. I wanted to recoil from his clammy touch, but I didn't dare.

"I don't know, Caesar. I'm not feeling myself," Agrippa answered. "Were I myself, I'd never have raised my voice in your sister's presence. May I be excused?"

Octavian scrutinized me, nodded, and released my hands. Agrippa looked over his shoulder at me only once, and his eyes were as confused as I imagined my own must be.

After Agrippa had gone, the emperor mused, "We were in Egypt too long. All their talk of death and magic affects the mind."

It was clear that he wanted us to behave as if the incident never happened, but I was shaken. Careful to conceal the bloody gown, I took my seat with my brothers as slaves laid out our meal of simplest fare—porridge, coarse bread, foods you might expect at a slave's table.

Philadelphus climbed into my lap and my twin brother ate in brooding silence, while all the children introduced themselves. There were the emperor's two stepsons, Tiberius and Drusus. Then there was the emperor's daughter, Julia, his nephew Marcellus, and his nieces too. But there were too many names to remember and too many girls with the same name. Mostly, I kept glancing at my hands, wondering how Agrippa and I had both seen something that wasn't there.

As for the emperor, the women fussed over him. His sister,

Lady Octavia, scolded him for not wearing a hat outside and his wife, Lady Livia, brought him a tonic for his cold, holding the cup for him with slim, delicate fingers.

The meal could not be over fast enough for me, but the emperor seemed to be savoring it. "I love to dine with my children," he said, leaning back and stretching his arms. "You know, a soothsayer once told me that I'd have only one child—a girl child at that. But I make my own fortune. Look now how I'm surrounded by children." Then his smile turned malevolent. "Mark that you're *all* mine now."

Six

AFTER our meal, we waited in Lady Octavia's atrium. There were no breathtaking fountains here—just a well-tended pool and some stone columns. The artwork was expensive but scarce, and the paucity of furnishings would have embarrassed an Alexandrian of any standing. Later, I'd come to appreciate Octavia's simplicity, but to my royal eyes the whole of her household was inexcusably *common*.

While we waited, my wool garments itched and I fought the urge to scratch. My brothers looked equally uncomfortable in their togas bordered at the bottom with a large band of purple—an attempt to transform them into Roman schoolboys, indistinguishable from the rest. With every motion Helios showed his contempt for the garb and for me. "Stop glaring at me," I hissed at him.

Helios's green eyes flashed and his vulture amulet seemed to glow in the sunlight. "Why shouldn't I? You begged for our lives in front of thousands of Romans."

"I had to. They were going to kill you."

In the way of twins, I knew he was about to say something ugly in reply, but Philadelphus interrupted us. "Don't fight."

Everything was so strange and stark here; I could not tolerate the anger of my twin too, so I tried to reason with him. "Mother said the emperor would have less reason to hurt us once she was gone—she *wanted* us to be safe . . ."

Helios said, "And now our enemies can say they saw Antony's children beg for Octavian's mercy."

I didn't know how long we'd been waiting, but at last Lady Octavia strode into the atrium with the emperor's wife at her side. They made an oddly balanced pair. The emperor's sister had a stately bearing with arms as solid as a milkmaid's. But the emperor's wife was as thin as a reed—with a body flat and hard. Together, their matronly presence was like a wall of granite, blocking all escape.

It was Livia who spoke first. "Children, you stand here today by my husband's mercy. You've been stripped of all thrones and titles. Your dowries and fortunes are forfeit. You retain no personal possessions, slaves, nor servants—in short, you have nothing but that which we give to you. Don't think of yourselves as much above slaves."

Now it was Lady Octavia's turn. She folded her arms, making the fabric of her gown pull tightly across her fleshy breasts. "Things will be different here in Rome than you're used to. There'll be no dallying or frivolity. Caesar has laid out a rigorous plan for your studies."

Caesar. I was sure that I could never call the emperor that. That name belonged to Julius Caesar, a mentor my parents had both loved and who had loved them both in return. That name belonged to Julius Caesar's only son—my missing older brother.

Nonetheless, Lady Octavia continued. "Eventually you'll make appearances at the *ludus* with other Roman schoolchildren, but until things have settled, most of your time will be spent here at home with private tutors. You're fortunate that Juba has been chosen to oversee your studies; even at his young age, his scholarship is well respected throughout Rome."

"Will we study music and dancing?" I asked, because these disciplines had always been my favorites and I used to like to sit by the ocean and play the *kithara* harp.

But at my suggestion, Octavia glanced up with one rounded eye. "I'd beware music. Your grandfather was a flute player and no one respected him. Moreover, dancing leads to scandal and promiscuity. There'll be none of it here." With that, Lady Octavia resumed making pronouncements like a military commander. "When you're not studying, there are chores to do."

"Chores?" I asked in amazement. So then we *were* to be slaves . . .

"It's Caesar's policy that all the children in his family make themselves useful. There will be no spoiled princesses here, so don't try to cajole the slaves into doing your chores. If you can't find work to do, we'll invent some for you. We weave like our ancestors did, so Selene will be spinning and sewing in the afternoon with the rest of the girls."

My mouth opened involuntarily. Surely with all the gold he'd stolen from my mother, the emperor could afford to buy his own clothes! But I hadn't yet come to understand the importance of such ridiculous but symbolic acts in Rome.

"Meals are to be taken with the family," Lady Octavia continued. "And each night, Caesar will lecture. We have a routine that won't be disturbed. You children won't get away with indolence as you did in Alexandria. You'll learn that discipline is a virtue. Indeed, I've advised Juba not to spare the rod."

Neither of my brothers responded to this litany. A gentle breeze rustled the strange Roman trees, whose leaves were like tiny needles. The wool was itchy against my skin and it was maddening not to scratch at my arms, but it was also beneath my royal dignity, so I stole a glance at my bruised wrists to confirm for the thousandth time that the hieroglyphs were gone. "When will we worship?"

Livia gave a thin-lipped smile. "There'll be occasions for state worship."

"Do you mean the *lares* and the *penates*?" Octavia asked, pointing to an alcove with what looked to be a tiny shrine. "Our household gods are in the *lararium* right over there. We also keep some in the pantry to protect the storeroom."

"But my brothers and I worship Isis," I told them.

Octavia reacted as if the name of the goddess alone was anathema. "I won't have you speak of that Goddess of Whores!"

Livia smirked at Octavia's outburst. "Members of the emperor's household cannot worship a foreign goddess, Selene."

"But Isis isn't foreign," I argued. "She's a goddess of all places."

"Listen to the way she talks, like some zealous Vestal Virgin," Livia said, then laughed as if she'd told some grand joke. "Find a Roman goddess, Selene. Fortuna is my husband's favorite."

I stared. Did they think you chose religions as easily as clothing? How cavalierly Octavia had insulted Isis. Had these Romans no fear or piety at all?

Meanwhile, Octavia was impatient to get on with it. "I'm sending you to learn with the rest of the children. I know you've barely recuperated from your ordeal, but exhaustion is the best thing to erase pain."

Livia put a hand on her hip. "Well? Have you anything to say before you're dismissed?"

"Yes," Helios said, giving both women a resentful look before his eyes drifted across the courtyard. The walls of the house surrounded us on three sides, and the fourth side was a low fence upon which grew a green, creeping plant. There was a guarded doorway there. If Helios sought an avenue of escape, there was none. "I hope our brother King Caesarion, Pharaoh of Egypt, brings his army here to sack Rome and make you both slaves!"

Had I begged for our lives just so that my twin could throw them away at the first opportunity? As Octavia sputtered, I tried to think of something to say to lessen the blow. But before I could ask their forgiveness, Livia's eyes narrowed with unmistakable malice. "Hasn't anyone told you that Caesarion is dead?"

Her words forced the air out of my lungs. I could suddenly hear my own heartbeat crashing in my ears. My eyes studied her face, disbelieving.

"Oh yes," Livia sneered. "His own tutor betrayed him. He was strangled. A death befitting a criminal—not a son of Caesar—as if the gods themselves proved him to be a fraud."

"Liar!" Helios shouted.

"Oh, it's quite true," Livia said. "Rhodon was your brother's tutor, no? He betrayed Cleopatra's brat. No doubt, the emperor will reward him handsomely."

I felt the rush of panic and denial swelling in me. Caesarion couldn't be dead. I had loved his adventurous nature. I had loved his stories and his jests—and the fact that no Roman soldier could pass him without stopping to take a second glance, so much did he look like his famous father. He was the King of Egypt. He couldn't be dead, because so many people depended upon him. He couldn't be dead because I had loved him. And because we needed him. He was our only hope!

"Liar!" Helios shouted again as Philadelphus threw himself against me, wailing.

I hadn't thought there could be much more pain in store for us, but this news toppled me like a crumbling pillar and I was crushed beneath stone cold grief. "So, you're going to kill all of us," I said. "You're going to kill us one at a time."

"No, Selene," Lady Octavia began.

"I told you, they're lying!" Helios roared, his face red.

Philadelphus pressed his face against me, sobbing.

"Where's Caesarion's body, then?" I demanded. "If he's dead, where is his sarcophagus? I want to see it."

"There's no body," Livia said.

"Caesarion is King of Egypt," I said. "We have to give our

brother the king his funeral rites and perform the opening of the mouth. If he's dead, it's our sacred duty. Where's his body?"

"He was burned," Livia said.

It was as if the entire world went silent. I could *imagine* the words that Lady Octavia's mouth was forming, but I couldn't hear them. It wasn't that Caesarion's death crushed our last hopes for rescue; I had simply passed the threshold of loss I could bear with any composure. The emperor had given my mother and my father honorable burial, but he had burned Caesarion—the true threat. He killed Caesarion and denied him the afterlife too. The King of Egypt, the last pharaoh, was nothing but ash.

The sound in the world came back in a rush, like the crash of waves when the tides changed. My hands came up before my face and I shrieked, "You murdered him twice!"

The shrill note of my horror echoed through the atrium. As if summoned by my grief, a sudden howl of wind ripped through the open space, catching Lady Octavia's skirts up into the breeze and making the water of the pool ripple. The gust carried my words with it, exploding through the house and slamming the doors inside like a clap of thunder.

Both Octavia and Livia's eyes went wide.

I wasn't finished. "You call Julius Caesar divine, but Caesarion was his son, and you killed him. You murdering hypocrites!"

The wind strengthened. The shutters rattled. Maybe the goddess heard me and had come to leave Rome in oblivion. *Blow harder. Oh, blow harder,* I silently prayed as the wind knocked over two clay pots by the pool.

Octavia looked at the sky. "Maybe we should go inside."

"Perhaps Agrippa was right about her dabbling in magic," Livia began.

"If I could work magic I'd use it to curse you," I said.

"Oh?" Livia asked, bringing her face very near to mine. "You weren't so brave in the Triumph, were you? Do you think, before he died, Caesarion begged for mercy the way you did?"

Shame clenched in my gut, but it was Helios who flew at Livia, his fists raised to her face. Before he could come to blows with the emperor's wife, Lady Octavia grabbed him up by both arms and shook him. They struggled, my twin grasping Lady Octavia by the wrists until she said, "You're hurting me, boy."

To my astonishment, Helios let her go.

"So, Octavia saves you again," Livia told Helios. "Had you struck me, how long do you think my husband would let you live?" Then the haughty wife of the emperor straightened and drew away, leaving me weeping as the winds finally died.

"I hate you," my twin raged. "I hate all of you."

"Maybe the whip will beat some of the hate out of him," Livia sniffed, and swept past as Helios, Philadelphus, and I all clung to one another in a huddle.

Guards had come running to see what my screaming was about, and the courtyard was soon abuzz with slaves and whispers. Juba was there too, scroll cases under his arm. "Perhaps Cleopatra's children aren't ready for lessons today, Lady Octavia," he said with a polite bow of his head.

Octavia put her hand on her forehead and surveyed the sky, drawing in deep breaths. "Perhaps you're right, Juba. Perhaps you're right. Children, go to your rooms."

No matter how angry Helios was at me, he'd try to protect me. He looked ready to fight, to struggle against the emperor's guards, so I put my hand on his arm. "It's all right. We'll go."

"Our room is next to yours," Helios said, as if to comfort me. As if he knew how I would feel the moment the guards locked me alone in my chamber. It had been foolish to think Caesarion would save us. It had been just another dream, now broken like all the dreams my mother dared. The last time I saw Caesarion he'd yanked playfully on my hair, and I'd been aggravated with him. Now his lost spirit, wherever it lingered, would bother me for eternity.

When there was a knock at the door, I didn't answer it. "Selene, it's Gaius Julius Juba. May I come in?"

"No," I said firmly.

He opened the door and came in anyway, his familiar scent wafting behind him like incense. Then he sat on the straight-backed chair in the corner. In Egypt, no tutor—even such a handsome young tutor as Juba—would have dared to enter without permission and I stared, agog.

"I know what you're feeling right now," Juba said.

I snorted indelicately. "You don't know how we feel. No one does."

"I think I do," he replied, sitting beside me. "I was marched as a prisoner in a Triumph just like you."

"I don't believe you," I said, but he had my attention.

"It's true. I was a Prince of Numidia, brought back to Rome when my father was defeated in war."

"Defeated . . . ? My family is *dead*."

"So is mine," the African princeling said with a sad smile.

I stared at the smooth planes of his face, and the sensitive curve of his lips in its sad smile. Would I be able to talk about what had happened to me with the same resigned expression? "Why did you get to live?"

"Because," Juba said, "Julius Caesar saved my life. He took me into his custody from the prison where they strangle the captives. I was a child at the time and the emperor was a young man, but Octavian took an interest in me."

I found this curious. "Why would he do that?"

"Because he has foresight," Juba replied, his amber eyes warm and encouraging. "He knew I'd be useful to him someday; an African prince is helpful when converting African natives to the Roman way of life. When he came into his inheritance from the Divine Julius, Octavian housed me, clothed me, and educated me as if I were his own, and he'll do the same for you."

I chewed my lower lip. "You speak as if you admire him."

"I admire him more than any man. He's brought virtue back to Rome."

That was too much to bear. *"Virtue?"*

"Yes, Selene. You may think that he conquered Egypt by force of Rome's military might, but the emperor won because the moral fiber of his soldiers was stronger. The Roman way is the right way. It's better that this happened; you'll see that in time."

How could a man with such a beautiful face really hold the ugly belief that my family was better off dead? "I don't want to hear any more."

"I'm trying to help you, Selene. I want you to see that as difficult as things seem now, there's a future for you, just as there was for me. I have wealth, status, friends, and learning. I'm happy here, and you can be happy here too."

"I want you to go," I said.

"Not until you promise that you and your brothers will behave." Now he spoke to me like I was a little child again. "Tomorrow we'll start your lessons, and I've been instructed to be a harsh disciplinarian if there is any disruption in the classroom. I don't think Philadelphus deserves to be put through any more pain, do you?"

I felt a pang of guilt. Ought we try to bear up with more grace for Philadelphus's sake, and for our family dignity? I glanced at my wrists and wished the markings were still there. I wished I could have read them before Agrippa dragged me away. Maybe they would have helped me make some sense of everything. Then I realized that Juba's eyes were still on me, waiting for an answer.

"I'll try to behave," I said, turning over in the bed and facing the wall, pretending to be asleep until he left.

After, I heard voices in the hall. I crept barefoot across the cold floor and put my ear against the door in time to hear Lady Octavia's voice. "How is she?"

"As well as can be expected," Juba replied.

"Juba, I hope you'll help me understate what happened today when the boy tried to attack Livia. You know how the emperor meddles. He has an empire to run, but when it comes to the children of the household, no matter is too small."

"These children *are* his empire," Juba said. "They are the building blocks of what he's trying to accomplish. They are the game pieces on the board."

"I know that," she said. "But they're also children in need of guidance. Should I punish Helios?"

"No," Juba replied. "The girl will control her brothers. Our effort is best spent there."

THAT night, I resolved to hide my pain over Caesarion's death. Egyptians believed that one of the nine parts of a human soul was the *khaibit*—our shadow—where our secrets and darkest thoughts live. I put my grief for Caesarion there, where I hoped the Romans could never find it, nor use it against me as Livia had done.

But once I had put away that pain, I felt cold. Cold like Rome. No. Cold like Egypt without her pharaoh. What was to happen to Egypt? The pharaoh was the personification of the Nile—the link between Egypt and her gods. Without Pharaoh, the Nile might not rise and deposit her silt for the farmers. If the Nile did not rise, the people would starve. And if Egypt starved, the whole world would starve.

Helios and I were next in line to rule jointly, as husband and wife. This was the custom of our dynasty. The responsibility for Egypt and her inundations now rested upon us. The people were our care, but how could we help them, trapped here in Rome?

Game pieces, Juba had called us, and it lingered in my mind. Was it mercy that allowed us to live while Caesarion was burned as rubbish? Or had we been spared for more sinister purposes?

Helios and I were now the heirs to the oldest, most prestigious throne in the world. More precisely, by killing Caesarion, the emperor had *made* us the rightful King and Queen of Egypt. Now he held us both under his control. In doing so, he had taken Egypt hostage. The crook and flail of Egypt must now be placed in Helios's hands, and the bulbous crown placed upon my head, but the emperor held it all.

I tried to feel nothing as the chill embraced me and I remembered the mask room in the emperor's home. In Egypt, people wore wooden masks of baboons and leopards and goddesses. But here in Rome, people made masks of their own faces. The emperor. Livia. Juba. All of them put on faces that best suited their needs.

I took my fingers and practiced turning the corners of my mouth. Well, I could wear a mask too.

Seven

MORNING came too early. Lady Octavia unbolted my door to see that I rose and dressed. Then an impish girl came into my room. "I'm Julia," she said.

I'd seen the emperor's daughter with the other children, but it was the first time we faced one another up close. She was just about my age—maybe a little younger—with wide-set dramatic eyes and a small mouth that quivered with mischief. With her mouselike ears and upturned nose, she was undoubtedly the emperor's child. On her father, those features seemed diminutive and sickly, but on Julia, they were appealing.

"Livia sent me to teach you how to do your hair in proper Roman fashion. Sit down, and I'll comb it for you."

I hesitated, uncertain. "That's a slave's job. Why would they send you to attend me instead of the *ornatrix*?"

"Because Chryssa gets into everything. She likes to steal hair combs and jewelry when she thinks we're not looking."

It seemed like cheeky behavior from a slave, but I said nothing.

Julia tugged on my arm. "Sit down and let me do this or we'll get in trouble for dawdling."

I sat on the bed and held a polished looking glass on my lap.

"Actually," she began, working dark strands of my hair through her fingers, "I *wanted* to meet you. I saw you in my father's Triumph and you were very dramatic, like Antigone."

"No, not Antigone," I said quickly, wary of the trap. I knew Sophocles' play. In it, the heroine, Antigone, honored her vanquished family in defiance of the king, thereby assuring her own execution. I had no desire to share Antigone's fate—or Caesarion's. "I didn't defy anyone. I bowed to your father."

Julia shrugged at my answer and pulled the comb through my hair with surprising gentleness. She parted my hair in the middle then fastened it into a simple twist at the nape of my neck. The younger girls like Minora all wore their hair loose, as was the custom, and I might have preferred it to this. I frowned because even though my eyes seemed greener without adornment, somehow my skin was too fair.

"You know," Julia began. "Watching you in the Triumph was even more exciting than the theater and I love theater. Do you?"

I bristled to know she'd been entertained by our plight, and yet I was afraid to offend her. "Yes. I enjoy plays, Lady Julia."

In the mirror, I saw her doe brown eyes crinkle with laughter. "*Lady* Julia? Did Livia tell you to call me that? Just call me Julia. My father says you're not a slave, no matter what my stepmother wants."

"Livia is your *stepmother*?" I asked in surprise.

"I hope you didn't think that wretched woman is my *mother*."

"I-I'm not . . ." I stammered, trailing off in confusion, wondering if we both shared the same loss. "Did your real mother . . . did she die?"

"No," Julia said quietly. "But she may as well be dead. My

mother—Scribonia . . . she's supposed to be dead to me. I'm not allowed to see her or talk to her."

I couldn't have conceived that my heart should go out to one of these Romans, but to hear the plain suffering in Julia's voice affected me deeply. "But why can't you see your own mother?"

Julia shrugged her shoulders. "It might have been different if I were born a boy. Then my father might honor my mother, just a little. But I was born a girl, so he hates her and keeps us apart. And on the few occasions he's allowed me to see my mother, Livia throws a terrible fit. She wants no one to remember that my father was ever married to anyone but her."

"But that's cruel," I said, then bit my lower lip, fearful that I'd gone too far.

"That's *Livia*," Julia said, tugging the last of my hair into place. "We can't stand one another. Just this morning she caught me outside my father's study and sent me away. She thinks I didn't hear anything, but I did. Do you want to know what I overheard?"

I was still cautious. I couldn't decide if Julia had come to me in a spirit of malice or goodwill. "Yes, I'd like to know what you heard . . . if it's proper to share."

"King Herod's ambassador came to see my father about you."

"Herod?" I knew he was the King of Judea and that my mother hadn't liked him, but I couldn't imagine why he would send an emissary to Rome to ask after me.

"Yes, King Herod," Julia said. "He wants my father to kill you."

It was good that I was sitting down, because my knees went to jelly. Someone a world away, someone I didn't even know, was asking the emperor to kill us. "But why?"

"From what I could tell, King Herod quite hated your mother. Besides, there's a prophecy."

"What prophecy?" I asked.

Julia shrugged again. "Shouldn't you know? In any case,

King Herod thinks you and your twin might be a threat to his reign."

I'd never even been to Judea. Moreover, my mother was popular with the Jews. In her endeavors to make Alexandria a city of all nations, Jews were amongst the first to whom she granted citizenship. Yet, if Julia was to be believed, the King of the Jews wanted me and my brother dead. I tried not to panic. "What did the emperor say? Did he agree to kill us?"

"No. My father said he'd already spared you before all of Rome and that he doesn't like to be seen publicly changing his mind. The ambassador left angry." Julia snatched the mirror from my hands and made me look at her. "My father kills people, Selene. I remember the prophecy about Antigone, that if the king put her to death for her defiance, his entire family would come to ruin. Is the prophecy like that? Why did he spare you?"

"I don't know," I whispered.

Lady Octavia rapped on the door. "Girls! No dawdling."

Julia and I walked together in silence, the daughters of Octavian and Cleopatra, each wondering who might bring about the ruin of the other.

IN Alexandria, my brothers and I sometimes took our lessons in the Great Library. Here in Rome our classroom was a wood-paneled room in the emperor's home with a warren of scroll racks lining the wall from floor to ceiling. The classroom opened toward the courtyard for light. Nonetheless, the musty scent of sheepskin vellum lingered in the air and bloodstained rods rested upon Juba's desk to remind us of what might happen if we misbehaved.

In spite of the atmosphere, and the fact that Juba seemed far too young to be anyone's tutor, the dethroned African prince was actually an excellent teacher with a great deal of enthusiasm. He told engaging stories. With his breezy charm and good looks, it seemed as if every girl in the household lived to impress him.

Even so, I had trouble concentrating, tripping through the morning in a stupor. By late afternoon, I joined the rest of the women of the household, where Lady Octavia took it upon herself to teach me to spin wool.

For this, I forced myself to pay attention, for I had been raised on Ptolemy pride. If a Ptolemy was going to be forced to do the work of a slave, a Ptolemy would do it with more talent than any slave could ever muster. So I learned to tease the wool with my fingers to remove debris and then to comb it to align the fibers. I learned to use grease on my fingers to twist a little wool between them, then to fasten it onto the spindle before spinning the whorl. It was tedious, mindless work, but it helped me keep my composure in the presence of these women whom I despised so very much.

The two Antonias—my half sisters—watched everything I did. Marcella, Lady Octavia's elder daughter, ignored me as if I were beneath her. None of the girls actually spoke to me except for Julia who complained a great deal of the time.

For dinner we ate boiled fish and greens. Then it was time for the emperor's nightly lecture. We all settled into low couches, chairs, and benches while the emperor stood at a lectern. "Here under my roof," he began, then paused to cough. "I've gathered the children of my friends, my enemies, and fallen comrades. You're the sons and daughters of the old Republic and I'm the last man standing. Now, together, we'll make a new Rome."

My eyes drooped wearily, following the rows of tiny white and blue tiles across the floor to where my brothers yawned and swayed in their seats.

"I've brought the civil wars to an end," the emperor continued. "And now there are a thousand offices left vacant because of casualties or proscriptions. Rome will need moral wives and loyal public servants, and I'll make you children into able candidates for those positions."

Honestly, I can't remember the rest of what he said. By the time I climbed into bed that night, my entire body ached and I wondered if heartsickness could spread to the limbs like an illness. I held up my arms and stared at them in the flickering light. I had seen what Agrippa saw. I had not imagined it. I had seen a message carved into my skin.

Now I was waiting for another.

Eight

"THE most insidious threat to any state is the immorality of its women," the emperor was saying.

I tried not to watch him when he lectured. His cold eyes still unsettled me. Besides, I was still trying to wear my mask of royalty. Livia could say that my titles were stripped from me and that I was little better than a slave, but I knew otherwise. I was a Ptolemy princess—a queen in exile who must bide her time until she could think of some plot, some plan to return her to her throne.

"Egypt's soft religions make women licentious and independent," the emperor asserted. "Even before the war with Cleopatra, Roman women were corrupted by her example."

"He's obsessed!" Helios whispered.

I'd managed to sit beside my twin tonight, but now I regretted it. I pleaded with my eyes for Helios to be silent, for the emperor's daughter was sitting with us. Still, Helios was right. The emperor was fixated on how women should behave, and more importantly, how women should *not* behave. He'd been rambling for what seemed like hours.

In sheer boredom, I contemplated the bland red and green mural on the wall depicting a Roman matron returning at night, watched from the balconies by her neighbors—a reminder to me that my brothers and I were also being watched.

At last, the emperor's speech became more passionate. "Before Actium, women were voicing *unsought opinions*. They ignored their duty to produce children. Women were becoming stubborn and hard to live with."

The sickly ruler of the world had whipped himself into such a fury that he had to pause to blow his nose. Then he sipped at one of the tonics Livia gave him for his ailments and rearranged his notes. "It's no wonder that noblemen preferred to marry their own emancipated slaves rather than marry a true-born Roman woman."

Helios leaned over to me and whispered, "Romans fear no army on earth, but they're apparently terrified of nagging wives."

"Be quiet. You'll get us in trouble," I whispered back.

Too late. The emperor heard us, and he glowered, waiting until all attention was back on him. Our whispering had annoyed him; perhaps that's why his examples became more demeaning. "When women meddle in matters of the world, there's disaster. Fulvia, of recent infamy, meddled in politics and raised an army, shaming her husband, and bringing about the needless deaths of many."

I glanced over at our half brother, Iullus, to see his reaction to this public rebuke of his late mother, but his face was like stone, betraying no emotion at all. How long had he endured lectures like this in the emperor's home? Was he lonely here? At least I had the brothers I'd grown up with all my life. Who did Iullus have?

The emperor sniffed. "This is why women must be kept in their place. A woman needs to value purity and chastity. Monogamy keeps the voracious female appetite in check. Left to her own devices, a woman will take many men to bed and to wed, and then divorce them just as easily. Just as Cleopatra did."

Helios could not sit still, moving his hands first to his lap, then to his sides. He made a sound like a growl and my stomach tightened. My mother had married four times, it was true, but she was only widowed, never divorced. Not like all these Romans.

There was no attempt to be subtle on the emperor's part. He obviously meant to use our dead parents as examples, openly and often. "An unnatural woman like Cleopatra ruins a man. Once, the Amazon Queen of the Lydians put the great hero Hercules into bondage and forced him to dress like a woman. Mark Antony claimed descent from Hercules and just like his forbearer, he allowed corrupt Cleopatra to emasculate him and make him weak."

At that, Helios was on his feet. "Endless lies!" I stiffened in my chair as Helios continued, "My mother wasn't corrupt and my father wasn't weak. His soldiers told a thousand tales of his valor."

Part of me was angry at Helios for risking the emperor's wrath. Another part felt proud of him. Unfortunately, it made me feel like a coward for silently enduring insults against our family honor. The emperor lifted his cold eyes from his notes and stared at Helios dispassionately. "If your father wasn't weak, he wouldn't have lost the war."

I could see Helios wrestling with his anger, his hand twitching. "What would you know about it? You let Agrippa do all your fighting for you. At Philippi, it was *my father* who avenged Julius Caesar's murder while *you* hid in a swamp."

The emperor's daughter gasped beside me and a nervous rustle went through the room at what Helios had said. The master of the world tilted his head as if evaluating my brother anew. I expected the emperor to shout a denial, but he was often quieter when angry. "So he taught you about Philippi?"

"My father taught us about all his battles," Helios replied, and it was true. He would pull out maps and tell us about the people in each country, and show us where he'd marched.

The emperor said, "Then he must have taught you that

Philippi was a very unpleasant place. I don't breathe easily in such climates."

"You breathed well enough to make a father and son draw lots to see which would be spared," Helios argued. "My father's soldiers told us how the conquered at Philippi were so disgusted with your ruthlessness that they cursed you even as they saluted my father as the merciful victor."

I closed my eyes, fearing to breathe. It couldn't be wise to remind the emperor of all the people he'd so cruelly put to death. We could still be next!

When I opened my eyes again, the emperor was staring hard at my brother, his gray eyes sharp and flinty, but he made no move to deny any of it. "Antony may have been a valorous warrior at one time," he said. "But then he was enchanted by your mother and her orgies of wine and excess. She forced him to abandon Rome and every shred of honor he ever possessed."

I felt warm with embarrassment at the picture of my parents he painted. They had entertained the finest artists and scholars in the world, yet Octavian made the joy of our court sound perverse.

"Your parents clearly didn't make the time to school you in your manners," the emperor said. "It's time you were properly educated. Helios, you'll be whipped three times for speaking out of turn."

My twin's jaw set in the same way it had when he burned his model ship. "Is it three strokes per interruption? I have at least six strokes' worth more to say."

A ripple of fear went through the room; I could feel it and the emperor seethed. "You can have fifteen."

Livia rose from her seat to fetch one of the disciplinary rods Juba kept in his classroom. Meanwhile, the emperor crooked a finger at my brother, summoning him to the front of the room.

"Remove his tunic," Octavian instructed a male slave. The slave rose, but my brother pulled off his tunic and threw it on the floor before anyone could undress him. Then Livia returned with the beating sticks and handed them to Juba, who regarded my twin with some disappointment before pulling out a bench for Helios to lean over.

Juba readied the switch while I observed the faces of the children and slaves in the room. They were a study in marble. The children might giggle and bicker outside, but before the emperor, they showed nothing. Even Lady Octavia was subdued, her hands neatly folded in her lap. I couldn't read her expression—whether it was stern approval or distaste—but she told Marcella to put Philadelphus and Minora to bed, for which I was grateful. I didn't want Philadelphus to see Helios beaten, and I tried not to feel grateful to Octavia for sparing him.

As soon as the younger children had gone, Helios lay face-down, his smooth royal back exposed. His hands gripped the wooden legs of the bench as Juba lifted the switch and brought it down. The whip whistled through the air, then cracked against my brother's back.

I yelped, but Helios didn't make a sound.

"Where was I?" the emperor asked. "Oh yes. The immorality of women is dangerous to the state. One day, I'll pass new laws that will bring us back to the older, more correct, Roman values."

The second strike of the rod was just as vicious. The third welted Helios's skin. My twin twitched, then lowered his face so that we couldn't see his expression.

The emperor continued his lecture throughout it all. "The new laws will require a man to immediately divorce an adulterous wife and report her if he knows her to be unfaithful, or else be convicted for pimping."

The sixth stroke broke Helios's skin and my twin brother's knuckles whitened around the legs of the bench. I tried to look away but couldn't. He was my other half and I felt the echoes of his pain upon my own skin. It seemed to me almost as if the legs of the bench were straining under my brother's grip. Still, he made no sound.

As I writhed in my seat in empathetic agony, comfort came from a most unexpected source. Julia touched my fingertips. She was the emperor's own daughter, but I squeezed her fingers in return.

The tenth stroke sent a slow trickle of red blood over Helios's ribs. He let out a smothered groan. The eleventh stroke brought more blood with it and my eyes flooded with tears. It was the fourteenth stroke that finally broke Helios. He cried out.

But Juba would never reach fifteen.

Like a crack of lightning, the legs of the bench snapped under my brother's iron grip. Wood splintered, the bench crashed to the floor, and Helios tumbled forward, stupefied as he held broken wood in each hand.

The marble facade of all the faces in the room finally shattered— Julia squealed and one of Livia's sons laughed nervously. Disgusted, the emperor stormed out of the room.

Once the emperor was gone, I ran to Helios's side, helping him up from where he lay amongst splinters. How could a bench break in such a way? It seemed impossible that it should've fractured to pieces.

"Selene," Juba began, reaching for me as if to apologize.

"Barbarian," I said, jerking away.

The crisscross pattern of welts and blood on my twin's back was truly horrible to behold, and Juba had done that. Was this the happiness that he told me we'd eventually find here? Had Juba endured *his* family being insulted day after day? He'd whipped my twin and I wasn't sure I could forgive him no matter how sorry he was.

I wrapped my arms around Helios even though his blood smeared on my hands. It was warm like the Prince of Emesa's blood had been when they chopped his chest with an ax. And that memory sickened me and made me sway on my feet.

As for Helios, he was angry and embarrassed. That much I could tell. He wiped his teary eyes with the back of his hands.

Then he turned on the women and children in the room. "Only three of Cleopatra's children were here to defend her," Helios said. "But if everything we're told is true, six of Mark Antony's children sat here. Lady Octavia even claims she was his true wife. Yet I'm the only one who defended him."

Our half brother, Iullus, flashed his eyes at Helios with barely disguised fury. "Why should I defend him? How can one defend the indefensible?"

Helios all but spat at Iullus. "He was your *father*."

"A regrettable fact of my life," Iullus replied.

Iullus was three years older than Helios, bigger and with a longer reach. Even so, the two of them looked ready to come to blows.

"That's enough, boys," Lady Octavia said. There was an edge to her voice and she looked away. "It's time for bed . . . We're all very tired."

"SELENE!" The whisper cut through the darkness and startled me awake. I rolled over on the thin mattress, squinting in the dim light.

"Helios? Where are you?"

"Look for me under your dressing table," he said.

I climbed out of bed and crept across the floor. Ducking under the table, I found a hole in the wall and saw my twin's face on the other side, illuminated by his oil lamp.

"The slave girl told me that there was a loose brick between our rooms," he whispered through the hole. "I waited for Philadelphus to fall asleep and pulled it out."

"Which slave girl?"

"Chryssa. The Greek."

I scowled into the darkness. "You can't trust her. I fought with her after my bath when she tried to take my dress from me." That bloody garment, trophy of Octavian's Triumph, was now hidden under my mattress, which was the only safe place I could find for it. "She's just trying to get us in trouble."

"No," Helios said. "I don't think Chryssa means us harm. She said she wanted to help us."

He reminded me very much of my father then, with that firm and misguided belief in the honor of others. "Why would she want to help us?"

Helios wet his lower lip as if he were afraid to tell me. "She saw what Agrippa saw. She saw hieroglyphics on your arms, but she was afraid to say anything. Now she's in awe of you."

So the slave girl had seen it too. Still, I was guarded. "We just can't trust anyone here. Not even Iullus."

Helios nodded. "Should I put the brick back, then?"

"No." Since we'd come to Rome, we'd had only a few moments alone and I missed him terribly. I put my fingers through the opening and touched Helios's on the other side. "Does your back hurt from the whipping?"

He looked as if he might deny it, then nodded instead. "It was worth it, though. I didn't think I could break the bench just by gripping it like that." Then he stared down at the spread of his hands with troubled eyes. "In the courtyard, when they told us they killed Caesarion, Octavia shook me, and I grabbed her arms, hard. I hurt her. I didn't mean to grip that tight, but then tonight . . ."

"You were angry," I said, tracing the jagged plaster where the missing brick had once fit into the wall. "But Helios, you mustn't provoke them even if it's the least they deserve."

Shadows passed over Helios's expression. "How can you ask me not to provoke them?"

I felt weak, and childish. "Because I'm scared," I admitted, though it wasn't queenly to do so. "I hate the Romans. I swear it. I hate them as much as you do. But I'm scared to do anything that might make them change their minds about letting us live."

Helios sighed. "Your fingers are shaking, Selene. You should go back to bed."

The cool of the floor was now cutting through my sleeping

gown, but I shook my head. "I don't want to. I'll only dream of Caesarion."

"Me too," he said, for we often shared the same dreams, in every particular, down to the detail.

"He's gone. He's really gone. And he's not coming to rescue us. No one is."

"Then maybe we have to rescue ourselves," Helios said. It seemed to me quite suddenly that my brother was much older than I was, even though we were twins. In a day's time he'd changed in a way that I wasn't able to quantify. "Selene, when Euphronius had me perform the Opening of the Mouth ceremony, do you think he knew that Caesarion was dead?"

Growing up, it had always seemed to us that our old wizard knew everything, but the idea that he'd known Caesarion was dead and let us believe otherwise was too horrible to contemplate. "No, he can't have."

Helios's voice was strained. "But don't you remember how the crowd kept calling to me? They called me Horus the Avenger."

I could feel how badly my twin wished to avenge our father, but we shared more important burdens now. I leaned close and whispered, "What I remember is that with Caesarion gone, you're now King of Egypt."

"And you're Egypt's queen," Helios said.

We were also two children huddled in a corner, reaching through a crack in the wall to comfort one another. That was the legacy of Octavian's Triumph.

Nine

❧

ISIS came to me.

I woke in terrible pain. Stinging fire ran up and down my arms and I wondered if I were still dreaming. As I sat up, the glow of the oil lamp fell across me and I saw bloody handprints on the coarse linens. I lifted my hands before my face and they cast wavering shadows on the walls. Blood dripped down my arms.

I screamed.

Hundreds, maybe thousands of tiny cuts etched symbols into the palms of my hands and down my arms with precision. The pain was like the sting of many insects. Tiny birds, waves, and symbols danced in my blood. Trembling, I used the bed linen to wipe off my right hand so that I could read the hieroglyphics. I had trouble translating. The more commonly used demotic Egyptian was easy, but hieroglyphs used only pictorial clues for context.

I heard footsteps down the hall. My scream had awakened the household, so I tried to read quickly. As I translated, I could almost hear words spoken in a beautiful voice—an echo of my mother's.

"The Athenians call me Athena. The Cyprians and Romans know me as Venus. The Candians say I am Diana. The Sicilians call me Proserpine. The Eleusians know me as Demeter. Some call me Juno, others Bellona, and still others Hecate. But the Egyptians, who are excellent in ancient doctrine, and by their ceremonies accustomed to worship me, do properly call me Isis. I am one goddess. I am all goddesses."

"Praise Isis," I whispered in wonderment as Philadelphus and Helios burst into my room.

"She's hurt!" Philadelphus cried, coming to my side, his eyes wide with panic.

I could hear other members of the household stirring, awakened by my scream. The guards would be here any moment; their boots were already pounding down the walk toward my door. "There's a message on my arms. Block the door and I'll try to read it!"

Helios glimpsed my blood and his face went ashen. He looked at the doorway uncertainly, then back at me. Then he closed the door behind him and braced himself against it.

I read aloud, my voice shaking.

"I am the natural mother of all things, and I know suffering. The dark god murdered my love and I was forced to wander the world collecting his dismembered limbs. Grieving, I gathered mangled flesh, spilled blood, and broken dreams, then knit them together in love one last time so that I might conceive a child. Alone, and frightened, as you are, I secreted away my joyous miracle until he was powerful enough to again make me mistress of the elements and Queen of Heaven. Behold, children of Isis, I know thy fortune and tribulation."

Someone tried to open my door, but Helios put his shoulder into it to keep it closed. I knew a boy would be no match for the guards, but when they crashed against it, Helios's feet only slid back slightly.

"Read faster. The symbols are fading," Philadelphus urged.

I tried to remember the sounds and words. There were so many of them, and the pain blurred my senses. Then I realized that they were changing. I'd read the first part of the message and now there was a second part too, symbols healing and cutting anew. Thrones, disks, feathers, snakes, and cow horns swam before my eyes, and I wiped more blood on my sleeping gown.

"Open up by order of the emperor!" Another bash followed the command. The door started to splinter, but Helios held it closed.

Finally, the last of the symbols became clear to me.

"Children of Isis, leave off thy weeping and lamentation. Put away thy sorrow and behold the beautiful day, which is ordained by my providence. Like babes hidden in the reeds, attend to my commandment. Live, love, and learn."

Then there was no more.

"That's everything?" Helios asked, incredulous.

I couldn't disguise my disappointment. Isis had reached through me to deliver a message, and yet it told us little. It urged acceptance of our fate and I was crushed.

I stared down at my hands as my skin began to heal. The soldiers outside continued to batter against the door. It finally cracked and Helios took a step back, letting one guard fall into the room with a clatter.

In the doorway with the soldiers was Lady Octavia in her bedclothes, her face puffy with sleep. "What's happening?"

Octavia rushed to me, pulling back the bedcovers. She stared at my arms, but the message left only blood in its wake. For a moment, genuine concern washed over Octavia's face. She took my arms, searching for a wound. "Send for a healer!"

I noticed her wrists, encircled with bruises where my twin had grabbed her days before. Helios *had* hurt Lady Octavia, after all, and she'd kept it to herself. She could've told the emperor, but she hadn't. I wasn't sure what to think about that.

"Maybe the girl has come of age," a guard suggested.

Lady Octavia gave him a withering glare. "Where are you hurt, Selene?"

Perhaps Isis meant to give me forgiveness. She'd commanded us to live, love, and learn—so perhaps begging the emperor for our lives hadn't been the shame my brother thought it was. Perhaps this message was to ease my guilt. "But now it's gone," I whispered miserably.

Octavia's concern became suspicion. "What's gone?"

I just shook my head. Something about Lady Octavia always brought out rebellion in me when I least expected it. It was *my* message and I wasn't going to tell *her*. It was meant for my brothers and me, from Isis herself.

At my refusal to answer, Lady Octavia's eyes flashed. "Have you been working magic in my house?"

These barbarians knew nothing about *heka*. "How could I work magic? You won't even let us worship properly. The markings on my hands were the work of Isis and she'll judge your actions."

"I won't be judged by some whore," Octavia said, pulling me out of bed by the arm.

"Isis is the natural mother of all things," I replied.

"Stop it." Octavia shook me. "They'll call you a witch as surely as they did your mother. They'll kill you. Is that what you want?"

"Let us worship," I said, dazed. "If not at the temple, then here, with candles and sage. Isis is our mother now."

Octavia's handsome face crumpled as she dug her fingers into my arms. "Why are you doing this to me? Why? Even though your every gesture reminds me of your mother, I've taken you in with my own children. My husband abandoned me, yet I honor his memory by raising his bastards. This is the thanks I get?"

"My father never loved you," I said, remembering all the bits and pieces I'd heard from my parents over the years. "The emperor threatened war if he didn't marry you. Then you both betrayed my father anyway—and you expect us to thank you for it?"

Lady Octavia was stricken. The corners of her mouth tightened as if she were in great pain. There was something frightening about seeing a formidable person crumble. She seemed frail and I regretted my words. I tried to utter an apology, but Octavia had already withdrawn.

Her voice was shaky. "Take her to the emperor."

THE guards led me to the emperor's house and up the stairs to his private study, a room he called the Syracuse. This is not where he received guests, but where he worked alone and where he permitted only intimates like Agrippa and his advisor, Maecenas, to enter.

Still, he admitted me.

The emperor glanced up from his work as I appeared before him in bloody nightclothes. The guards pushed me to my knees, and I stayed there, beneath his chill gaze. He let me kneel there in silence, finishing whatever he was writing.

And while he made me wait, I dared to glance at my surroundings. Here, hidden behind the plain doors, the ruler of the world's riches finally shone. His desk was ornate and gold; beautiful art adorned the walls. Silk bunting draped from the ceiling in red, like the interior of a tent. The gold dolphins that had once adorned my mother's bath now hung in one corner of his study. He liked to say that he had taken nothing from Egypt but an agate cup, but all of Egypt was now his personal property and I saw that even the rug beneath my knees had been stolen from my mother's palace.

"Selene," the emperor finally said, "would you like to see what I'm working on?"

I was too frightened to do anything but nod.

He tilted a group of sketches so that I could see them. They

were architectural in nature—plans for some kind of building—
and he was making notes in the margins. "This will be my mau-
soleum," he said. "They say the Egyptians have a fascination with
death, so I thought it might interest you."

What I saw momentarily startled me enough to stop the trembling in my limbs. The design was a bastardization of Etruscan,
Greek, and Egyptian architecture. It was a circular building with
a vaulted ceiling. It also rose up on an earthen mound, like the
tomb of Alexander the Great, but he'd ornamented it with obelisks like the ones my mother used to adorn her sepulcher. Yes, if
I squinted, it was reminiscent of her tomb . . . and the implicit
threat in his showing it to me made my blood run cold.

"Don't you like it?" the emperor asked. When I didn't answer—
because I couldn't answer—he asked, "Selene, didn't you beg me
for your life at my Triumph?"

I dared not look up at him. "Yes," I whispered.

"Did I spare you gladly at my sister's request?"

"Yes," I whispered.

"Then why are you and your brother so determined to die?"

I shivered. "I swear to you, I was working no magic."

"Why is this blood all over you?" the emperor asked, rising
from his desk to approach me. "Did you sneak out of your room
somehow? Did you kill an animal? Tell the truth and don't hesitate, for while my patience is legendary, it's not unlimited."

I'd been so defiant with Lady Octavia, but before the emperor
I cowered. "I woke up and my hands were cut everywhere with
tiny symbols—a message from the goddess Isis."

"You don't dare lie to me," the emperor whispered, crouching
in front of me as if to get a better look at my face.

Desperately afraid, I jumped as if he'd shouted. "I'm not lying.
I did nothing to bring it about. I swear it. It was the same as when
Admiral Agrippa saw the symbols. They appear and disappear."

The emperor's jaw worked, then he motioned to the guards.
"Summon Agrippa and shut the door."

Now alone with him in this sumptuous apartment, I felt a terrible sense of foreboding. In the center of one wall, given the highest position of glory, was a statue of Fortuna, who stared down at me with a mocking wink. If Isis embodied all goddesses, was she watching me now through Fortuna's fickle smile? "You have to believe me."

The emperor scrutinized my face. I could feel his breath on my cheeks. "Your mother lied prettily too."

I wasn't brave like Helios. I couldn't bring myself to argue in her defense. "I'm not lying."

The emperor narrowed his eyes. "What did this message say?"

I didn't want to tell him, but I was too frightened to refuse. "The message told us to live and love and learn." I fumbled through my memories for more. "And the message said that we are the children of Isis."

He leaned back on his heels. "Your mother's propaganda."

I stayed silent as the emperor rose and stormed back to his desk. "It's also the propaganda of the Isiac temples. You and Helios have been brought up on this rubbish. Don't deny it. Night and day since Cleopatra's death I've heard this prattle. Isiac priests coming to plead for your lives. Even Herod, that old suspicious fool, is panicked by whispers of the word *messiah*."

"Why should King Herod fear us?" I asked.

"He probably hates you more than he fears you," the emperor said simply. "Your mother created in Herod a bitter enmity that survives her death. He was a powerful client king, you see, but Antony put your mother above him and called her the Queen of Kings. Besides, Herod's people are always waiting for a savior of one type or another. Herod doesn't want the Jews getting unpatriotic ideas. For that matter, neither do I. So let me assure you, in case you have doubts, you and your brothers are *quite* mortal. Don't make me prove that to you. They called your mother an incarnation of Isis and your father an incarnation of Bacchus, and they're both dead now."

It wasn't just Bacchus that people called my father. Bacchus was also Dionysius, who was Osiris, who represented the mystery of rebirth and was the divine consort of Isis. As my mother's husband, he could be no less, but I dared not explain that to the emperor as he perched himself on the edge of his desk and stared down at me. "Selene, we all choose our propaganda and the peasants believe. I'm just the son of a middle-class household. Not a drop of royal blood in my body, but now, for the first time in my life, I'm without rival. I've conquered where every other Roman has failed. So I'll pick some god to be. Which one shall I choose?"

I bit my lip at his heresy.

"Isn't Julius Caesar a god?" he asked me, sipping his tonic before a cough wracked his frame. "Since he adopted me as his son, it stands to reason that I must also be a god, but which one? My family descends from Venus, but she hardly strikes fear into the hearts of my enemies." I just stared at him until he said, "Apollo might suffice."

Apollo. Cool, reasoned, Apollo the Purifier. That's how Octavian saw himself—anointed to rid Rome of foreign influences and new ideas. Apollo was also known as the Pythian, for having slain the Python of Parnassus. At the emperor's Triumph, they had called my mother the Serpent of the Nile, and I saw now that Octavian meant to build his legend upon her death. Not my father's death—never that—for Mark Antony was Roman. No, Octavian wanted to be remembered for having rid Rome of Cleopatra.

At last, Agrippa burst into the doorway, pounding one fist against his breastplate. "Hail, Caesar."

My father had once told me that war garb beyond the *pomerium*—the old city wall that protected the heart of the city— was forbidden. But I knew the emperor's guards secreted daggers and weaponry beneath their togas. Agrippa also wore armor where he pleased. Despite the emperor's constant praise of tradition, the old Roman rules that my father had cherished and my mother had derided were set aside at the convenience of those who ruled; it was a lesson not lost on me.

The emperor motioned Agrippa inside. "The girl claims that all of this blood came from symbols cut in her hands. But they're gone now, Agrippa. What do you say to that?"

The brawny admiral looked at my blood-smeared appearance, eyes flickering with alarm. "It's what I saw before."

The emperor crossed his arms over himself. "The guards can't find any sharp instruments in her room, and I don't see any wounds. The blood seems to be real, but I'm not sure where she would get it if it weren't her own. She's watched all the time."

"Magic," Agrippa said. The emperor waved a dismissive hand. Agrippa seemed abashed and it made me uncomfortable to watch the way the emperor made the stronger man squirm. "Then illusion, perhaps."

"What's the difference?" the emperor asked.

"Illusion is when you see things that you don't see. When you think . . . I'm not sure."

"Bah," the emperor said.

"It's like the omens and augurs," Agrippa explained.

At that, the emperor's mouth tightened. From the beginning of her founding, Rome practiced ritual divination and paid careful attention to good and bad omens. I could see, on the emperor's face, a mixture of superstition and skepticism. "If I were to believe that this is magic or illusion, where did it come from?"

"It's the work of the Isiacs." Agrippa's weathered face was filled with conviction. "Cleopatra and Antony are not without partisans, even now. They just hide in this city like rats, waiting."

The emperor had said that he was completely without rival, but Agrippa's words told a different story. No matter how much Octavian tried to make the war about my mother, the truth was that it had been a civil war. Romans had fought Romans in a bitter struggle. Octavian was the victor, but I'd just learned his power wasn't secure. Some still opposed him, and thanks to

Agrippa, I now knew that some of Octavian's enemies were right here in Rome. They might even be willing to fight in our cause.

The emperor lifted up his hands in a helpless gesture that seemed feigned. "If you're right, where do we strike?"

"Are you not Master of Rome?" Agrippa asked. "We know the Isiacs have a dangerous faith. They encourage wives to stand equal to their husbands; they tempt slaves to rebellion; they threaten the social order. Their priesthood operates in the shadows. Who are they to stand in your way? Leave nowhere for them to hide. Destroy all the temples in Rome devoted to Isis."

This aroused a visceral reaction from me. "You can't!"

Agrippa glared at my outburst, but the emperor's voice was cautious, as if he were standing on the edge of a blade. "The girl is right. You know the cult makes adherents of nobles and slaves alike. Tearing down temples in Rome would seem *impious*."

"Yet, there's precedent for it, Caesar. In days past the Senate ordered the temples of this Egyptian cult destroyed in Rome."

The emperor's cool expression betrayed that he already knew this. He'd drawn it out of Agrippa, making it seem as if he was reluctant to attack. But for whose benefit was this show of reluctance? Mine or his?

"When we destroyed Isiac temples in Rome," the emperor said, "the people rebelled. No, we need to slowly undermine their faith before we make such a bold move."

As I would later come to understand, it was a classic strategy. Octavian never risked open battle until he'd weakened his opponent through treachery; that's what he'd done to my father too. Agrippa, apparently content to play his role in the emperor's theatrical construction, asked the question he was supposed to: "How will we undermine the cult?"

"We'll first demonstrate that the twins are merely children. They'll be seen often as members of the imperial family, doing normal things children do. They'll be seen to be happy and content."

Then he looked my way and I realized he'd reserved a special part in his play, just for me. "If Selene suffers more of these *illusions* upon her body, she's to come to me immediately. We'll accuse the Isiac temple of using magic to attack her because I've taken her in. They attack her, a mere child, because she no longer advances their anti-Roman agenda."

Shocked, my tongue worked slowly. "But it's not true."

"It *is* true. You've been attacked, Selene. Did you not claim this makes you bleed and causes you pain?"

"Yes, but—"

The emperor hovered above me with an aura of threat. "You'll tell us if it happens again. Won't you?"

He'd made me betray my family dignity before all Rome, and now he asked me to betray my religion as well. But the goddess had commanded me to live, love and learn. I'd be able to do none of that if I openly defied the emperor.

Masking my hatred like a pharaoh dons her headdress and face paint, I nodded my assent.

Ten

I waited for days for Isis to come to me again—half fearful, half
eager—but she did not. There was nothing to do but fall into the
rhythm of my new life. My world now was the collection of brick
houses on the Palatine Hill, an imperial compound connected by
gardens and surrounded by low walls. There were no gold-capped
columns or marble walkways like in Alexandria, but what the
Romans lacked in splendor they made up for in thievery.

From the emperor's household on the Palatine Hill, I could
see the Forum Romanum, where plentiful Egyptian gold sparked
a buying frenzy. What's more, the hillsides were dotted with
columns, obelisks, and statues—the plundered spoils of Egypt.
They looked like mismatched ruins—captured and displaced,
just like me.

On clear autumn days I could make out the aqueducts that
linked the Alban Hills and the Sabine Mountains to form the
walls of my prison and I was acutely aware that I was not the only
prisoner. Here in Rome, slavery was an overwhelming presence in
my life for the first time.

There had been slaves in Alexandria too, of course, and I told myself that I had no cause to be disturbed by their presence in Rome. But in Egypt, treating a slave well was a moral duty because the status of a slave was temporal—he was a valued member of the household and could eventually buy his freedom. This was supposed to be true also in Rome, which boasted that the sons of slaves could even become citizens. But in practice, this was a dream realized by too few. Whereas labor was scarce and valuable in Egypt, slaves here in Rome were plentiful and cheap. Livia herself owned more than two thousand slaves and this was quite beside the number owned by the emperor, or by the state. Many slaves lived in abominable conditions and I even heard talk that some Romans fed their slaves to pet lampreys for entertainment. I didn't doubt it because the suffering that etched itself on the faces of these subjugated peoples was haunting.

It made me realize how much worse off my brothers and I could have been. How much worse off we could *still be* if we couldn't find a way to turn our situation to our advantage.

Still, in everything we did, we were watched. It wore Helios down like wheat on a grinding stone, but as the Romans watched me, I studied them too. I knew that both Livia and Octavia loved the emperor and fretted over his health all while putting on a public face that he was tireless and immortal. In return, the emperor doted on each woman. If he praised his wife he'd find something nice to say about his sister too. If he gave one a gift, he would give a gift to the other as well. I searched for some crack in the unity of the adults, some fissure to exploit. But I found none.

I was the emperor's bitterly resentful captive but grateful that he let us live. Grateful too that he'd reunited us with all the remaining members of my family. He'd gathered here all my surviving half siblings and in spite of myself, I wanted to know them.

Unfortunately, they didn't want to know me.

My half brother, Iullus, seemed to think we were tainted— that being seen in our company would remind people that he was also Antony's son. My little half sister Minora sometimes stared at me curiously, but she took her cues from her older sisters, who shunned me without regret.

In light of this, I clung to Helios and Philadelphus. Before bed each night, Helios and I would remove the brick from the wall between our rooms, and say our good nights. Sometimes I woke with nightmares of carrying that basket to my mother's tomb. Then, in bed, I'd trace my hands, trying to memorize the symbols that had cut themselves into my flesh, and I couldn't decide if I should wish them away or pray for them to return.

Each morning we woke at dawn to do our chores. My task was to fill all the oil lamps, and I relished this time because it allowed me to whisper my morning prayer to Isis as I had in Alexandria. After chores, while the emperor received his many clients, we children were ushered through the crowds of favor seekers and loyal partisans, to the classroom.

There Juba rewarded correct answers with figs. Helios refused to answer and went hungry, but I usually answered correctly and gave away all my figs when Juba's back was turned. Since my mother's death, I had a loathing for them.

Occasionally, the emperor himself stopped by our classroom and though his visits always disturbed Juba's lesson plans, the emperor enjoyed moralizing above all. "For the good of the empire, I expect you children to work just as hard as I do," he'd say.

And in that, at least, Octavian was no hypocrite. My mother had said that rulers write their stories in blood, sweat, or tears. It seemed to me that the emperor used all three. He read scrolls, signed papers, and discussed politics with his intimates from dawn to dusk. He had to work so hard, he said, because the civil wars had cost Rome her best leaders and he couldn't wait for our generation to grow up and take the burden from his shoulders.

The emperor's nephew Marcellus barely had hair on his chin but already carried responsibilities, and he wasn't alone. The emperor had no sons, so it was understood that even Livia's boys from her first marriage, Drusus and Tiberius, must do everything possible to prepare for public office. The girls were to be educated and useful wives—political bargaining chips in marital alliances. This was drummed into us every day.

In the afternoons we broke for sport and baths. The boys learned hunting, riding, gymnastics, and wrestling. And whereas Helios was always so quiet during class, he could not suppress his physical talents. He was a powerful wrestler and could beat even the older boys. Once, he pinned Iullus while Agrippa happened to be passing and the admiral said, "Aye, get it all out, boy. Get it all out."

I had no such outlet. I had danced in Alexandria but dancing, Octavia insisted, was what men did when drunk and women did in brothels. Instead, she insisted that we sew. So every day, after our afternoon meal, I'd retreat with the other girls to spin thread and weave fabric for the family clothing and linens. Meanwhile, in the courtyard beyond, the boys trained in the art of war.

For the emperor's wards, nothing less than Agrippa's expertise would suffice. On a semiregular basis, the celebrated soldier was actually obliged to interrupt his business to attend to the sword craft of boys not even old enough to join a legion. Afterward, Agrippa would join us for our evening meal, which we took together with the emperor. Almost always present was the emperor's wealthy advisor, Maecenas—a shrewd little man who kept the emperor's papers and schedule. He was officious and extremely influential; he looked at my brothers and me the same way he looked at the trade goods he purchased for Rome.

I didn't like him, or his pretty wife, Terentilla, but they both had exquisite taste in clothing, and I was given leave to believe that most of the attractive artwork in the household had been acquired by the two of them.

In my mother's court, royal children had always been welcome to join in the discussion. Here, the emperor expected us to impress his dinner guests with our quiet solicitude. There were rarely lavish feasts; the emperor preferred simple fare. In fact, Julia sometimes mocked her father's habit of picking at his meals, jesting that nervous guests probably left hungry.

Then, before bed, the emperor lectured. Oh, how he *loved* to lecture, spouting priggish platitudes about chastity, virtue, and austerity. Helios wasn't exaggerating when he'd said the emperor was obsessed, and these speeches always seemed to be for my special benefit. Helios would roll his eyes, but he didn't interrupt a lecture again.

Meanwhile, I began to envy the affection the emperor bestowed on my half siblings. He doted on the Antonias and seemed fond of Iullus. It made me feel like a caged animal, pulling on my chains while the domesticated pets roamed free.

I wondered what my mother would have done in my place. She won Julius Caesar and Mark Antony to her cause with charm, wit, and faith. She could discuss in many languages the subtleties of Plato or jest with bawdy soldiers. She could hunt all day and throw dice all night or play the lyre to soothe tempers.

Perhaps I too could make the Romans love me, change the way they saw things, open their eyes to the beauty of the Isiac faith. My mother had done it. She hadn't just preached partnership and trust as a political creed; she'd lived it. Two Roman generals had taken her as a wife. In so doing, they proved by personal and political example that women and men could work together as rulers and equals, just as East and West could come together in peaceful partnership.

If my mother could do all that, I resolved to try to do the same. If we were to ever return to a land where Isis was loved and magic was revered, I would need to win allies to our cause.

"IT'S market day," Julia whispered to me one morning as I tried to help her with her Greek. "We're going shopping."

"Where?" I asked, trying to keep the excitement out of my voice; anything that interrupted the routine of the emperor's household was a welcome change.

Julia tucked a strand of errant brown hair behind her ear, and copied some poetry into the wax tablet with her stylus. "We'll probably visit the Forum and browse shops along the Via Sacra."

I remembered being dragged through the streets of Rome in chains and suddenly this trip didn't sound as enticing.

"What are you whispering about, girls?" Juba asked.

"Greek."

The way Juba smiled, he must have known I was lying, but he left a fig on my desk anyway, prompting Julia to tease, "You're his star pupil. He's inordinately fond of you."

I thought often about all he'd said to me the night we learned of Caesarion's death and remembered how he had said I would control my brothers. However, I'd seen the way flirtatious slave girls looked at him and I wasn't immune to his charms either, which made me desperate to talk about something else before Julia saw the blush upon my cheeks. "Never mind Juba, what will we shop for?"

Julia's lower lip jutted out. "Probably nothing interesting. My father just likes the citizenry to see us doing ordinary things. But maybe I'll be able to show you the Temple of Venus Genetrix."

The Temple of Venus Genetrix is where Caesar had famously installed a statue of my mother. Now both of them were dead, but the building remained, a stone ghost of my family's past.

"Don't be so glum, Selene," Julia said, as if reading my thoughts. "Iullus always buys me a sweet cake when we go shopping and I'll share it with you."

Was the daughter of the emperor really so deprived that such a simple thing could make her happy? Then again, I realized that my mouth watered for cakes too.

After class, Octavia lined us up for inspection while Agrippa insisted that we take a larger retinue of soldiers with us. Octavia laughed warmly at his concern. "There's no need for a retinue. The emperor wants us to mingle in the crowds like the humbler citizens."

"With this city infested with gangsters and thugs?" Agrippa growled low in his throat and shook his head. "Order isn't yet fully restored. Murders take place in broad daylight, even in the temples. There should be no mingling."

Lady Octavia ran her fingers through Philadelphus's unruly auburn hair as if to make it straight. "Is it still that bad, Agrippa?"

Agrippa's hand worked at his side. "I'll go with you."

It was nonsense that a man of Agrippa's importance should accompany us like some lack-wit bodyguard, but Octavia took him up on the invitation at once, lowering her eyes submissively to say, "As you wish."

A flush worked its way onto the big man's features. There was a dynamic between the two that I was proud of myself for noticing because something, however small, might be used to win them over. In fact, I'd have liked to watch more of the exchange, but Livia interrupted.

"Children, I'll give you each some coins," the emperor's wife said, jingling a pouch of gold. "But spend them only at the windows of respectable merchants and friends of the family. And keep close to the walls so as to avoid the sewage the *plebs* dump from their upstairs windows."

Julia and Iullus giggled, though whether it was at the idea of dumped sewage or at some secret joke shared between them, I couldn't tell. In any case, their merriment annoyed Livia. "Julia! Keep your eyes down and don't attract the attention of men passing by. That goes double for you, Selene."

Why she'd singled us out, I didn't know, but I just bobbed my head. I was too eager to escape our prison, even for just a few hours. My last trip through the streets of Rome, I'd been a captive. Now I traveled with the *Julii*; I wondered if anyone would spit on me this time. We descended from the Palatine Hill on

foot, following the winding road past green hillocks and twisting trees. It had none of the beauty of Alexandria, but there were
lovely villas and serene landscapes along the way. Only once we
entered the narrow streets of the city proper did I sense a restless-
ness that made me strangely glad Agrippa was nearby.

The population of Rome seemed to be twice, maybe even
three times, that of Alexandria. And it was overcrowded. They
said Alexandria was home of the mob, but Rome showed that to
be a lie. Some streets still had toppled debris and litter from old
riots. Graffiti was everywhere, and some of it was lewd enough to
make me blush. Crowds gathered quickly and menacingly. The
traces of anarchy remained.

Perhaps they thought Octavian was just one more dictator who would soon be challenged by the next. I could see why
he worried about the public reaction to destroying temples. He
may have conquered Egypt, but he had not yet fully conquered
the hearts and minds of Rome—and that was a battle Agrippa
couldn't fight for him.

Though the people had hailed Octavian in his Triumph, the
Romans seemed to hold no awe of his family now. We were jostled like the rest of the citizenry as we made our way with the
never-ending traffic. I furled my nose, for in spite of its sewage
system, Rome was still dirtier and smellier than Alexandria on
its worst day. Meanwhile, Helios and I held hands as I gazed up
at the tall crooked *insulae* that lined the road and shadowed the
narrow streets.

"Some of these buildings are going to blow down in a strong
wind," I said.

"Or burn up in a puff of smoke," Helios replied.

Whatever I was going to reply went unsaid because two young
men shoved past us, stealing a basket of bread from a merchant
before running off. Seeing this, my foolish twin actually let go
of my hand and bolted forward to pursue the thieves. Luckily,
Helios didn't get far.

Agrippa caught him by the back of the tunic and let out a belly laugh. "You're full of fire, boy."

"But they're thieves," Helios said. "They stole right in front of me."

"These days everyone is a thief. Let the *tresviri capitales* handle it," Agrippa said, letting Helios go, and diverting our party down another street.

Crowds pushed from behind, and Helios and I, unaccustomed to moving with the flow of pedestrian traffic, soon found ourselves surrounded by strangers. We'd been separated from the others and now gaunt faces blocked our path. Hands reached out at us from every direction.

"Bread or coin, please!" begged one woman. She had a filthy face and two little boys at her knees.

There were throngs of citizens in rags, demoralized and desperate. There were rich and poor in every society, even in Egypt, but we'd never seen poor such as this. Crowds would never dare approach me in Alexandria in this way, nor be so demanding. After all, I was the daughter of Pharaoh then. Now I was merely a well-fed child with money.

My brother took the coins that Livia had given us and gave one to the woman with the children at her feet. "Thank you, my lord!" she said. "Thank you. Whose name should I praise?"

"Isis," Helios said to the woman. "Praise Isis who understands suffering."

Then he gave the rest of his coins to the others and still they pressed him for his name. I wondered what he would say, for I wasn't sure it was wise to admit we were Cleopatra's children. Helios seemed to worry too, because he lowered his green eyes, as if summoning all his courage. "I'm King Alexander Helios," he said.

I turned to gape at him. The crowd seemed just as astonished and pulled back. Such was the power of the word *rex* to the Romans.

Someone tittered nervously. "But he's just a boy."

Another man in rags spit at the ground in front of Helios. "You aren't King of the Parths anymore. You never were."

Helios stared at the man, as if memorizing his face. "Perhaps not. But I'm the rightful King of Egypt now . . . and my sister is its queen."

Cyrenaica, Libya, Parthia . . . all those lands we'd ruled only in name. They meant little to us beyond Ptolemy avarice. Egypt, however, was in our blood, and it was a calling beyond mortal aspiration. Egypt was a mantle that had fallen, and I could see now that Helios was determined to take it up, whether we were prisoners or not.

In the end, the beggars did not care about thrones or boys claiming to be kings. It was all a blur as people kept pushing and crowding. "Selene, give them your money," Helios said.

I frowned at him and my fingers curled around the edges of the coins possessively. The money in my hand was all I owned in the world except for a frog amulet and a hidden bloody dress. "After these people spit at us and threw rocks at us?"

"You don't know that any of these people did that," Helios said. "And even if they did, Isis teaches us forgiveness. Please?"

Why this small, futile gesture was important to my brother I didn't know, but Helios so seldom pleaded that I could do nothing but surrender the coins to his hand. Something in me lightened as I did so. I watched Helios give away every single coin, then hold his hands up to show they were empty.

"Praise you, my young lord!" an old woman said to Helios.

"Praise you, Holy Twins of Isis, for her followers are always with you and watching you," another man said in a voice I thought I knew. My eyes snapped up at the familiar sound. I thought I'd imagined it, but there he was!

Cloaked beneath a white cowl was the face of our wizard, Euphronius. At my look of shock, the old man brought a finger to his weathered lips to silence me. A range of emotions passed over me in an instant, from fear to joy. I'd last seen Euphronius in Egypt and thought I'd never see him again.

I turned to Helios for his reaction, but my brother was facing in the direction of Agrippa who was barreling toward us, muscling through the crowd. Octavia followed with Minora on one hip and Philadelphus on the other. "There you children are!"

I turned to warn Euphronius, but his white garments had already vanished into the sea of peasant gray and brown.

"What are you two doing?" Livia snarled at us once she caught up. "I told you to spend your coins at respectable shops. There's no telling what pestilence you may have picked up from beggars. Helios, if you can't follow simple instructions, I'll have you beaten until you can."

"I gave away my coins too," I said, unwilling to let Helios take all the blame.

"Helios is a *boy*," Livia snapped. "He's responsible for what you do."

I sputtered with indignation as Agrippa marshaled us back into line with the rest of the children. "Next time, do something worth the beating," Julia said to Helios, then offered me a sticky pastry. "Here. I promised you half."

I took the sweet, but my eyes were in the crowd. What was Euphronius doing in Rome? Had he been sending the bloody messages to me? If so, how could I warn him to stop?

Eleven

WINTER arrived without our seeing Euphronius again and I began to wonder if—wishful and homesick—I'd only imagined him in the crowd. Helios, however, had faith that the old wizard was in Rome. "He has a plan, Selene. He's come to take us home where we can reclaim the throne."

I wasn't so sure. And though we exhausted ourselves thinking of ways to contact Euphronius, we were isolated and watched, with no avenue of escape. The Greek slave girl had offered to help us, but she'd been caught trying on Livia's jewelry, whipped for her insolence, and sent to work at a country estate.

I was sure we'd get no more help from her, but seeing Euphronius again had given both my twin and me a renewed sense of purpose, and we were more conspiratorial than usual. Lady Octavia seemed to notice, and kept us separated at every turn. She and the emperor's wife kept a constant and suspicious eye on me, which I felt most keenly during the long afternoons after we'd retired from the schoolroom to work the looms.

In Egypt, weavers often did their work from the floor, but

my loom was vertical and warp-weighted, which meant I had to walk back and forth to add the weft thread. Unfortunately, I also needed Julia's help, and she wasn't very attentive. "This will have to all be unraveled," Livia scolded. "Don't you pay any attention, Julia? Notice how neatly Selene always does her work!"

When Livia turned her back, Julia made a face at me while mimicking in mock whisper, *"Notice how neatly Selene always does her work!"*

Livia turned around just in time to see Julia's antics. "You're a wicked girl, Julia, and I hope to prove it to your father one day. In the meantime, I have errands to attend in preparation of the Saturnalia. When I get back I expect this to be fixed."

After Livia left, Julia rolled her eyes and whispered, "I'm not so wicked a girl that she doesn't want me to marry her son Tiberius, of course."

"What are you girls whispering about over there?" Lady Octavia asked, her strong hands working the wool. "Just because Livia has other business doesn't give you an excuse to dawdle."

"Someday," Julia whispered, "when I'm grown with my own house, I am going to dawdle all day. Dawdle, dawdle, dawdle."

"What's that?" Octavia asked.

Julia gave her best innocent look. "Oh, I was just telling Selene that it's important to be a modest lady in Rome if you want men to admire you."

Octavia's lips thinned as she looked at me. "Both of you are too young to be worrying about how to earn a man's admiration."

"I'm not worrying about it," I said, defensively, giving Julia a dark look for having created mischief. "Besides, in Egypt, a woman cares not so much whether a man admires *her*. She worries, instead, about what a man has that *she* might admire."

Lady Octavia looked scandalized. "That's a presumptuous attitude."

"Perhaps men prefer presumptuous women," I said, though I was of an age when I had more questions about men than I could answer. "Why shouldn't a man find a woman's strength comple-mentary to his own?"

Octavia stared at me for a moment, as if I'd said something seditious. "The emperor has spoken on this subject at length. Men need women for heirs, not for partnership."

I don't know what got into me. Perhaps it was the stifling room with its false frescoes. Perhaps it was merely that I couldn't wear a mask every moment of every day. "My father wanted a partner," I argued. "He was the first Roman to put women on his coins and he *preferred* strong-minded and independent women like Fulvia of Rome and Cleopatra of Egypt."

Even before I'd finished, I knew that I'd gone too far. I could have added that my father had put Octavia's likeness on coins too, but it wouldn't have helped matters. I'd reminded Octavia of my father's love for my mother and her face went ashen. "I endeav-ored to be the perfect wife to your father. Did Antony never have a kind word for me?"

I couldn't answer truthfully, especially not with my two half sisters, the Antonias, listening to every word, so I spoke care-fully. "My father said that you were modest and righteous, Lady Octavia."

Self-righteous, in truth, but it wasn't necessary for her to know that.

"That was kind of him," Octavia replied.

I thought the matter was settled, but then she asked, "Did he say anything else about me and my daughters?"

Oh, how I wished she hadn't asked. My parents had mocked Octavia as her brother's creature. My father had even jested that being married to her made him feel a kinship to Roman matrons who lay back with a shudder to do their duty for Rome.

I could have hurt Octavia with that knowledge. A part of me *wanted* to hurt her. But the Antonias were finally looking at me with rapt attention, eager to learn anything they could about the father they'd never known, so I pieced together truth and fiction as convincingly as I could. "My father said a man couldn't have a more dutiful wife than you and that he regretted the circumstances that prevented him from gathering his children under one roof."

I'd lied as artfully as I could for her sake, but Octavia's silence settled over the room like a suffocating blanket as she worked. She only looked up when Agrippa passed by the archway.

"Will you marry again, Lady Octavia?" I asked, desperate to lighten her spirits.

In answer, Octavia's thick fingers twisted in the wool. "Not unless my brother commands it. I love my children too much. If I married, my daughters would all have to be left behind."

"But why?" I asked.

"A Roman man shouldn't be asked to take girl children from another marriage into his household."

This shouldn't have astonished me. Nonetheless, my mouth fell open. Octavia looked up to catch me gawping and asked, "Besides, who would I marry?"

"Agrippa favors you," I suggested.

Octavia's hands stopped moving and her voice went lifeless. "I'm too old to give Agrippa heirs. He's marrying my eldest daughter, Marcella."

From the look on her face, Marcella already knew. Shyly, she showed us her betrothal ring. It was a twisted signet of gold and iron, and she wore it on the fourth finger of her left hand, where the nerve of love was said to run straight to the heart. Upon seeing her ring, the other girls squealed. Minora clapped and Antonia wrapped her arms around Marcella in a rare show of affection.

Julia was alone amongst the girls in seeing this as a bad pairing. "But Agrippa is so *old!* He's dirt common to boot."

Lady Octavia scowled. "Julia, he's the emperor's most trusted friend. Agrippa is a fine match for Marcella."

"And he's old enough to be her father." Julia yanked at some stitchery. "How can Marcella ever love Agrippa?"

"She doesn't have to *love* him," Octavia replied. "She just has to marry him. Love causes pain, but good marriages benefit the state. It's your central purpose and duty, girls. Remember that because you'll all be married off soon enough."

THE cold weather sent the emperor's household into frenzied preparations for the Saturnalia. Slaves adorned the buildings with wreaths of evergreen. Feasts were prepared throughout the city, and the spirit of gaiety so often found on the streets of Alexandria only now made its way to Rome. Where laughter was usually discouraged as an affront to Roman gravitas, smiles and merriment now appeared even in the emperor's household.

Helios and I had the sense that something important would happen soon. Something would *have* to happen soon. We just had to be prepared for it when the opportunity came.

A few days before the Saturnalia, Octavia saw me and Helios with our heads together, so she sent me to the emperor's house to work with Julia making gift baskets. Trudging into Livia's salon, Julia and I piled heaps of baskets and evergreen in one corner, piles of red fruit in another, and placed rows of white candles in the middle.

"At least Marcella will get a pretty wedding gown," Julia said, clearly wanting to gossip more than she wanted to work. "Poor consolation for marrying Agrippa, though. Can you imagine marrying a man who moons over your own mother?"

I glanced at her, surprised that she too had noticed the affection between her aunt Octavia and the admiral. "Do you think Marcella knows?"

"How can she not? Octavia is heartsick, but she and Agrippa just do whatever my father wants them to do."

"What choice do they have?" I asked, tying a bow on a basket of candles and fruit.

Julia made a face. "I suppose not much. My father kills people who don't do what he tells them to."

I swallowed. "Surely he wouldn't kill his own sister."

"I think he might," Julia said quietly. "Or at least . . . he would send her away like he sent my mother away and we'd never see her again." I didn't know what to reply, and the moment stretched on until Julia said, "So tell me about Africa."

The cool air nipped at my cheeks and I was grudgingly grateful for my ugly wool clothing. "It's warmer than this place, I can tell you that much."

Not far from where Julia and I toiled, the emperor conducted business in the uncovered atrium. The emperor's doctors had advised that cool winds might help his numerous ailments. So there he was, bundled against the chill. He seemed annoyed with the merchants who were pestering him and I did my best to ignore them until a breeze blew through the courtyard carrying the sweet scent of light magic to me. That's when I realized that the merchant was Syrian and spoke through an interpreter. I was startled to hear him talking about Helios and me.

I stopped working, straining to hear more.

"No here, do it like this." Julia grabbed my basket from me and placed the fruit in an aesthetically pleasing way. "Is that all you're going to tell me about Africa? It's warm?"

"We also celebrate the solstice and yearly rebirth," I said distractedly, trying to listen to the exchange in the courtyard as the Syrian made feverish appeals, holding up a polished mirror and other pretty trinkets for the emperor, whose patience was finally at an end.

"Maecenas granted you an audience for this?" the emperor snapped. "Livia buys for the household. I don't want these baubles."

The Roman interpreter said, "We're just trying to make an honest living."

The emperor threw the man a pouch of money. "You're lucky

it's the season of Saturnalia and that I'm in a generous mood. Here, take these coins and be gone."

Leaving Julia and the baskets behind, I walked toward the courtyard. I knew better than to interrupt the emperor's business, but the injustice drove me to action. "The Syrian isn't a merchant," I said.

The three men glanced my way as Julia loomed in the doorway behind me.

Exasperation made the lines of the emperor's pale brow furrow. "Child, be silent."

"Would Caesar have me let a man lie to him?" I asked.

Caesar. This was the first time I gave him the honor of that name; it left a taste in my mouth like ash. Still, it was the only way to convince the emperor to listen to me.

The emperor motioned me forward. "What lies is this man telling?"

A twist of anxiety crossed the interpreter's face, confirming my suspicions. "He's mistranslating everything. The Syrian isn't trying to sell you baubles."

The emperor's gray eyes tightened nearly imperceptibly as he peered at the interpreter. "Is this true?"

"Emperor," the interpreter answered, "the Syrian offered me a cut of his business if I would help sell you his goods from the East. What does this little girl know?"

I lifted my chin with an imperious air. "I know Syrian."

The courtyard went silent. The interpreter's hand trembled, and I wasn't the only one to see it.

The emperor finally asked, "If he isn't a merchant, then who is he?"

"He's a wizard," I said. "A magi bearing gifts, and he's giving them because of me."

"You, Selene?" The emperor's eyes widened. "Why?"

At the mention of my name, the Syrian dropped to his knees before me, pressing his forehead to the floor in abasement.

Startled, I took a step back. I'd seen people worship my mother as pharaoh but this was different in quality and intensity.

"What's this nonsense? Make him get up!" the emperor demanded.

I touched the magi's shoulder and whispered in Syrian, "Please rise or you'll make the emperor angry. Who are you? Why are you bringing gifts?"

The magi smiled into my eyes with joy that made me tingle. He got to his feet, his stance unsteady as his head bowed before me. He actually began to weep. "I come from the East to honor Isis. Octavian of Rome has spared the holy twins who are saviors. I bring offerings for his family and gifts for you as the holy day of your birth approaches."

Warmth spread through my chest at the realization that people in faraway lands still cared about us. My brothers and I had felt alone in the world, yet people we had never met gathered their wealth and sent it to us as a gift. I'd all but forgotten my own birthday, as I'd spent the last one in the belly of a warship awaiting my arrival in Rome. Yet other people still remembered it a world away.

"What did he say?" the emperor asked.

I knew I'd have to surrender the truth, but I waited a few moments more to savor the loving words before Rome stole them from me and turned them ugly.

When I translated, the emperor struggled to hide his surprise. He loathed the unpredictable, so I was relieved when his dangerous gaze rested upon the interpreter instead of me. "Why would he lie and tell me that this man is a merchant?"

"Maybe he doesn't speak Syrian well," I suggested, but I suspected darker motives.

So did the emperor. "Perhaps he meant to make me pay for goods that were being given as gifts? Perhaps he meant to *steal* from me without my ever knowing it."

The interpreter blanched as if struck, perspiration gathering on his brow. "Surely not, Caesar! Perhaps I misunderstood a few words, but my Syrian is more expert than the girl's and maybe *she* misunderstands."

"Send for Juba," the emperor said to Julia.

I'd nearly forgotten she was behind me. Now she dashed off at her father's command. We stood waiting as caged birds in Livia's atrium sang to fill the silence.

As if prompted by the uncomfortable wait, the Syrian addressed me, "Holy One, to honor you and your brother as the children of Isis, my ship is filled with gifts. Perfumes and silks. Gold and myrrh."

I translated quickly to allay the emperor's suspicion, then added, "Perhaps the truth can be found in the ship's papers."

The emperor lifted one finger. "Just as I was going to suggest, Selene."

The interpreter interjected, "Caesar, this Eastern barbarian didn't show me any papers!"

It was too late. The emperor wasn't even listening to the interpreter anymore, only to me. "If this man is guilty of trying to steal from me, Selene, what should I do?"

Even at my age, I understood I was being asked to condemn him to death. I examined the interpreter's face, noticing the hollowed cheeks. There was a desperate, hungry look about him. "His soul is for Isis to judge. I pray that Caesar is merciful."

The interpreter snarled. "You'd believe the daughter of an Egyptian whore instead of a citizen of Rome?"

I'd suggested clemency, and yet when he called my mother a whore, I found myself adding, "But I wonder . . . would he have laughed afterward at how great a fool he'd made of you?"

From the slight darkening in the emperor's eyes, I could see my arrow had not missed.

Just then, Juba arrived, sweaty and winded. He was only wearing a tunic and toga, but saluted as if he were in military garb. "Juba, do you speak Syrian?" the emperor asked.

"Some," Juba replied.

Then he smiled at me winsomely, not yet sensing the tension between those gathered. Julia eavesdropped from the doorway behind him and the emperor tipped the brim of his hat toward the sky. "Juba, ask the Syrian who he is."

I didn't flinch, but the interpreter quaked as Juba did as the emperor asked. "Caesar, he says he's a priest who brings offerings."

"Offerings? Gifts? Not merchandise?" the emperor asked.

"Perhaps gifts," Juba said, abashed.

The desperate interpreter pointed an accusing finger at the Syrian. "He's only saying that now, hoping to avoid the offense of having annoyed Caesar with his baubles!"

The emperor plucked a red berry from one of the bushes in the courtyard and flicked it away. "What merchant offers his entire cargo for free when he could have left with the bag of coins I offered? Guards, arrest this man."

The interpreter maintained his composure even while understanding he was doomed. He didn't struggle as the emperor's soldiers seized him. That was the Roman way and I could almost admire it. The Syrian, for his part, left my presence with tears in his eyes as if in holy rapture.

Snow began to fall.

I'd never seen snow before and I held out my hands to catch the crystalline flakes while the emperor tucked his hands under his armpits for warmth. "Your reasons were self-serving, Selene, but you did well. What other languages do you know?"

I startled as the snowflakes melted to water on my fingertips. This was like a new kind of magic altogether, and it took me a moment to remember that the emperor had asked me a question. "Our tutors in Alexandria saw to it that we learned the languages my mother knew. Ethiopian, Arabic, Syrian, Latin, Greek, Egyptian, Parthian, Hebrew, and a smattering of some other Eastern languages and African dialects."

Juba's gaze took on an intensity too admiring by far and his chest seemed to puff up with pride. "Selene's work in my classroom demonstrates a strong grasp of history too. She's very accomplished, Caesar."

"And quick-witted," the emperor said. "Agrippa says she's unnatural."

Juba draped his arm over my shoulder, ostensibly to warm me. "Were it not for her sex, I'd recommend her as a scholar."

The emperor brought his fingers to his temples. "Must I now doubt all my translators? I'm of half a mind to have the girl report their accuracy to me. Interpreters wouldn't dare dissemble when Maecenas is near, but they won't worry about the presence of a girl."

My consent wasn't needed or sought and suddenly, the emperor's mood was buoyant. "How shall I reward your good service today, Selene? What do you want?"

I wanted to go home to Egypt, but I knew better than to ask. "Will you let me speak with the Syrian?"

"No."

"Can we send a letter to our friends and loved ones in Egypt? Fat Mardian and Olympos and the servants don't know what's become of us here . . ."

"No."

"Will you let us worship at the Temple of Isis?"

"No. Ask for something practical, Selene."

I clenched my fists. "I want the gifts that the Syrian brought my brother and me."

"Ah, a girl's avarice," Juba said, trying to be helpful. "One can't accuse her of being impractical there."

The emperor chuckled. "True, but I can't encourage Isiac fantasies. You saw the Syrian's ecstasy. He thinks Selene is a savior of some kind."

Juba tilted his head and asked, "If it appeases the Isiacs to think of you as the benevolent father of their holy twins, is that so bad a thing?"

It was painful to even consider. Octavian was *not* my father and would never be. Wasn't it enough that he drove my parents to their deaths? Must the emperor also try to steal their places? It seemed so, because the emperor's thin lips stretched into a smile and he handed me the polished mirror the Syrian had left behind. "Why not, then? The Saturnalia approaches and I'm feeling generous. I'll have my sister weed out any inappropriate gifts and give the rest to you. Run along, Selene."

Reluctantly, I returned to the baskets and fruits where labor alongside Julia awaited me, but I could still hear the emperor as he rose from his chair. "Come, Juba, it's time for a warm fire and maybe just a sip of wine. Fortuna has a sense of humor. A thousand important positions to fill and my most talented child is a Ptolemy princess!"

They both laughed.

JULIA had overheard everything and within hours the rest of the children knew. Overnight, I transformed from a shunned interloper into an exotic princess of the East—a tragic demigoddess still worshipped across the seas. Whereas only Julia had shown me any warmth before, now all the girls of the household wanted to share my tasks. When adults were near, they babbled about their plans for the Saturnalia—wondering what gifts they should give, what gifts they might receive, and who might come to entertain. But when we were alone, they plied me with questions.

"But why do they worship you?" Minora asked. "Is it because you can work magic?"

"I can't," I said hurriedly, both because it was true and because I knew how dangerous such talk was.

"There's no such thing as magic anyway," Antonia sniffed.

I shouldn't have challenged her, but something compelled me to say, "Yes, there is. Magic comes through Isis. Ordinary people bring power to her temples every day, and she lets her priests draw upon it to work *heka* in her name. I've seen them do it, so I know it's real."

Marcella scowled. "Next you'll tell us that crocodiles and hippos and baboons were meant to rule over us and be worshipped. We ought not even be speaking about such matters."

Marcella was the oldest girl in the house; they all deferred to her and I was eager to change the subject anyway, so I enchanted them with tales of Egyptian gods and described Alexander the Great's gold and alabaster sarcophagus. They asked about Egyptian customs, about our slaves, our palace, and my wardrobe. Even Marcella wanted to know about my inglorious reign as Queen of Cyrenaica.

As we worked, the smells of the kitchen were spicy and there was natural warmth to our shared endeavor—making treats for street children. Meats roasted in the fire, skin sizzling and crisping with spices in the heat, and slaves kept checking on them; everything needed to be prepared to Octavia and Livia's exacting standards. In Egypt, we'd never have performed such lowly tasks alongside the slaves, but the emperor liked for his family to keep up at least a pretense of industry. Besides, in Rome, any excuse to be near the stoves was a good one and I found myself enjoying the moment in spite of myself.

"What was your kingdom like?" Marcella asked. "Did you have your own palace?"

"I never visited Cyrenaica," I confessed. "But they say the soil is fertile and dotted with many oases."

Minora used too many fingers to tie a sloppy ribbon and Antonia ripped it out of her hands to fix. "What's oases?"

I tied my bow carefully lest Antonia snatch it away from me too. "An oasis is where the tears of Isis fell onto the desert sand and brought life out of death."

"Your country was filled with tears?" Minora asked.

It seemed to me that every place that had anything to do with me was filled with tears. "Picture nothing but sand and desert.

Then where you least expect it, trees and fruit and water spring up, like a hidden treasure trove. Like magic!"

I'd said the forbidden word again, and Julia put a finger over her lips to quiet me. The steam from the pot Julia stirred made her brown hair curl into a frizzy halo around her head and to cover my mistake she asked, "What do they eat in Cyrenaica?"

I finished tying a ribbon and started on a new one. "Rosemary, almonds, and a special bitter honey. They sent the honey to me as a gift and I had a chance to taste that."

"And who was your king?" Julia stole a wine-soaked plum from the pot when the slaves weren't watching, then tried to wipe the telltale purple off her fingertips.

"I was sole ruler, and a coin was even issued in my name, but my mother was regent for me until I came of age."

"Sole ruler?" Julia asked. "Not even your mother ruled alone!"

"Well, she did. In practice," I said. "Besides, many women ruled Egypt—mostly from my family."

"I don't believe you," Marcella said, her face a stern imitation of her mother's.

"No?" I countered. "Egyptian women are the freest in the world."

Marcella wasn't having it. "Well, you *say* you're Egyptian, but we all know you're really Greek and the Greeks treat their women worse than sheep."

The Antonias giggled and I felt my cheeks grow hot. "Not *all* the Greeks. The Athenians said that Spartan women were equal to their men. And in any case, my blood is *Macedonian* and some of my ancestors were Illyrian warrior princesses."

Marcella snorted. "Warrior princesses, indeed. Women don't make war."

"My *mother* did," I reminded her.

It was an imprudent thing to say and several of the girls stared pointedly. I was rescued only by Julia's quick intercession. "You should learn from what Selene's trying to tell us, Marcella. I've heard Egyptian women have rights in the law courts. They can be scribes or physicians or scholars."

Marcella scoffed. "They *cannot*, Julia. Whoever told you such tales? Egyptian women even need perfumed eunuchs to guard their chastity."

The things they'd been taught! It was true that my mother had eunuchs like Fat Mardian, but I never had any watching over me. My tutor was Euphronius, a priest, a magician, and a whole man. Reminded of him, I now missed him terribly. How could he have shown his face to us on the very streets of Rome only to disappear again?

Taking a deep breath, I continued, "I'm just saying that there's nothing unnatural about women ruling a country."

Julia offered me a plum. "Would the people allow it?"

I took a bite—it was rich with wine and spices, and the best thing I'd tasted since leaving Egypt. I savored the flavor, indelicately licking my fingers clean. "Sometimes the people *demand* it. Since the son of Ptolemy took his sister to wed, women in my family have ruled with men in partnership or even on their own."

They all startled, and I wasn't sure which part of what I'd said alarmed them. From the way a half-eaten plum dangled from Julia's lips, I gathered that maybe it was everything and my stomach knotted.

Antonia hissed, winding the ribbon around her bough too tightly, crushing the treat beneath. "You speak as though there were no shame in a sister wed to a brother!"

She was my half sister, but there were no traces of our father in her. The set of her jaw was all Octavia and I felt thoroughly chastised. "Why should there be shame in it?" I asked slowly. I had to remember that these people were nothing like my own. "It's a long tradition in Egypt. Sometimes a son can't even become pharaoh without wedding Pharaoh's daughter—his sister."

"That doesn't make it right," Antonia returned.

I felt their gazes upon me. They were trying to make me

ashamed, just like my mother warned they would. I tried to explain it the way my mother had explained it to me. "Brother and sister marriages prevent rival families and civil wars. It keeps foreign princes from coming to Egypt to court Pharaoh's daughter and steal our treasure. Besides, the royal family of Egypt descends from the gods. Isis and Osiris were siblings, and no one would question their pairing."

"Jupiter and Juno are siblings as well, or so the stories say," Julia added, giving me a reassuring smile, but the rest of them still looked at me sourly.

"Are you going to marry Helios, then?" Minora asked.

The question caught me entirely off guard. I used to believe I would wed Caesarion. He was king and I was Pharaoh's daughter. But those had been the old ways, and my mother hadn't always adhered to them. Now that Caesarion was dead, what would that mean for the royal line of Ptolemy? As Pharaoh's only daughter, I must wed the ruler of Egypt, or the Nile might not rise. But who now was the ruler of Egypt? Wasn't Helios the rightful king?

"Helios is betrothed to Princess Iotape of Media," I murmured, and then realized that I didn't even know what had happened to her. Perhaps she'd also been dragged through the streets in Octavian's Triumph and I hadn't even seen her.

Just then Livia swept through the kitchen, berating slaves and checking over our progress. "You girls are dawdling! If you don't finish your boughs, I won't let you attend the poetry reading."

"A poet?" I tried to seem less interested than I was. "Is he talented?"

Livia scowled into the pot of plums, as if she'd counted each one and knew some were missing. "Of course. It's Virgil, you stupid girl."

Twelve

THE emperor kept his promise to give me the gifts offered by the Syrian magi. The most wonderful gift of all was a spotted cat for my brothers and me. Cats were sacred in Egypt and there were strict laws against harming them, or even taking them to other countries. This sleek gray huntress had obviously been smuggled from Egypt, but as she bounded around my room chasing after a ribbon that Philadelphus wiggled for her, we couldn't disapprove.

"Let's call her Bast!" Philadelphus said.

It was hardly original to name her after the cat-faced Egyptian goddess, but if Bast too was an aspect of Isis, this was one way in which we could honor our goddess even on the Palatine Hill. "Yes, Bast," Helios insisted. "Selene, you should let her sleep here in your room."

Then the little wild cat leapt into his lap and made him laugh. I couldn't remember the last time I'd seen Helios laugh so I said, "No, you and Philadelphus keep her. She fancies you."

Besides, with Bast's dappled fur coat and her bright eyes, I was already growing to love her, and I was terribly afraid to love anything new. Things that you loved could be taken from you, or used against you, after all.

Fortunately, the cat wasn't the only gift the Syrians gave us in honor of our birthdays. There had been a bed netting with silver stars that reminded me of the drapes that swept over my mother's bed in Alexandria, but Lady Octavia called it licentious and wouldn't let me keep it. A shimmering silk gown, a box of cosmetics, and vials of perfume were also deemed inappropriate and sent away. Octavia did, however, allow me to have an incense burner shaped like a cornucopia. My room was also now adorned with a colorful new woven rug and a chest full of silken gowns that Octavia deemed modest enough for me to wear. A carved *kithara* harp rested against the far wall, and in spite of Octavia's warning about music, I'd been allowed to play it. In fact, the emperor said I might even have some talent for music.

Finally, Octavia allowed me to keep a blue linen *tunica* cinched with a silvered girdle to wear during the Saturnalia—a Roman festival that I was about to experience for the first time.

FOR the Saturnalia, the emperor's household was strewn with ribbons to mask its architecture in seasonal charm. Dried spices and gilded pinecones—an unusual extravagance—were set in decorative bowls as centerpieces in every room. Everything seemed touched by green sprigs or red berries.

The Saturnalia was to be our first official public appearance since the Triumph, so care was taken that Helios, Philadelphus, and I looked every bit the part of happy Roman children. I was even allowed to style my hair more fashionably, held in place with pearl-tipped hairpins that I borrowed from Julia.

As the guests filed in for the emperor's banquet, they shouted to one another in greeting: *"Io Saturnalia!"* The men wore colorful muslin tunics with loose-fitting bottoms. The women wore gowns that would normally be too immodest for public. And everyone wore a red *pileus*—a loose peaked hat that was the sign of freedom.

The emperor's guests included nobles, merchants, freedmen, and even valued slaves. In fact, during the Saturnalia, the masters served the slaves, so Livia sent the children of the household mingling with trays of treats. But when Minora and Philadelphus were caught eating more pastries than they gave out, Lady Octavia sent them to play in the courtyard.

I refilled goblets with spiced wine and Julia handed out the boughs of sweets that we'd fashioned, gossiping about the guests all the while. Lady Octavia had impressed upon us the importance of our manners and modesty, so I feared the smallest misstep. I needn't have been so worried. When I sloshed some wine out of the side of one senator's cup, he merely winked at me and shouted, *"Io Saturnalia!"*

I overheard snippets of conversation, some of which I understood and some of which left me confused. I'd occasionally hear the emperor complain that seven days of Saturnalia was too long a time for courts to be idle; he felt that the celebration should be shortened to three days, but no one seemed to agree with him. Livia bragged about the talents of her sons and everyone was in high spirits—even Helios, whose natural earnestness gave way to sportsmanship when the other boys invited him to wrestle outside.

I learned that night that even Agrippa had a sense of fun; I saw him demonstrating a thrust of the sword to some soldiers and they all burst into laughter at whatever jest he told. Then Octavia offered him some fruit from a platter and allowed her fingers to brush his. They stood there for several moments, just smiling at one another until Agrippa's fingers closed around her hand as if he held a precious jewel. This made Octavia scurry away, crimson-cheeked.

The other guests were less inhibited. Flirtation abounded. The emperor scolded Julia for "flashing her eyes" at male visitors, but when Tiberius and Iullus flirted with pretty girls their own age, no one counted it amiss.

The food was plentiful for a change and singing was encouraged. Some of the guests even danced. How envious I was! In Egypt, this was also a time of celebration; this was the time to honor Isis and Osiris for the yearly cycle of life. They brought forth the bright sun rays of Horus, the divine child, so that another year of planting would commence. The Romans viewed it differently, and Juba delighted in telling the tale as children gathered around him.

In truth, it made me smile to watch Juba with the children. He liked to tell stories almost as much as he enjoyed hearing them. When I refreshed his goblet of wine, he took in my silvered girdle and smiled. "You're lovely tonight, Selene. The blue of your gown brings out your green eyes."

"Thank you," I said, altogether flattered that such a handsome man should compliment me. In truth, I liked Juba more than I would have admitted.

"It's good to see you smile," he added. "I hear that a little gray cat might have something to do with that. You know, I'd like to buy a cat and then maybe Bast can have kittens."

I grinned. "And I hear that with your writing, you're a wealthy young man. But Egyptians don't sell their cats. There are some things money can't buy."

He laughed. "Quite so, my pretty princess."

I blushed again, nervous that Julia's too-big ears could eavesdrop at long distances when she smirked at me from across the room. She took special gratification in sending me knowing looks whenever Juba and I spoke.

"Tell more stories!" Philadelphus interrupted.

Juba laughed in surrender. "Very well, Philadelphus. When the end came to Saturn's earthly reign, this time he wisely chose to set aside his crown." I'd heard darker tales about Saturn, but I kept quiet as Juba continued his story. "He sailed away beyond the Northern Wind where he now sleeps upon a hidden island at the top of the world. Thus in the coldest season, we send our prayers to Saturn's snowy realm to wake from sleep the ancient and kindly king. One day, his divinity will be reborn into this season and we will enjoy the blessings of a Golden Age."

A Golden Age. This was what the Prince of Emesa said before the emperor ordered him killed, before his blood spattered me and the life went out of his eyes. The amphora of wine seemed heavy in my hands. I was unsteady on my feet. "Selene, are you all right?" Juba put a hand at my elbow.

The crush of people around me was suddenly overwhelming. "I need a breath of air."

I left him with the wine and searched for Helios, but couldn't find him in the crowd, so I slipped away into the gardens. Even there children shrieked and played in the snow, so I receded into the *cubicula* where the family normally slept.

The Saturnalia was a celebration of life, but so many members of my family were dead. Julius Caesar, Mark Antony, Antyllus, Caesarion—all gone. My mother was dead too, and I had killed her. Why hadn't I dropped that basket and let the snake slither away? Because of me, she was dead, and here we were in Rome, being taught lies about our family and expected to smile.

I fought again to make a mask of my face. If I let myself feel everything in me, I'd scream like I did the day they told me Caesarion was dead. I'd scream and never stop. And that wouldn't help me find my way back to Egypt.

As I fought these thoughts, my fingernails digging into my palms, I realized that I wasn't alone. Outside the emperor's bedroom, Livia and the pretty daughter of one of the senators stood talking. The girl was rosy and slightly disheveled.

"You'll do what he tells you to," Livia told the girl, softly caressing her pink cheek.

I knew, even then, that I'd stumbled upon something illicit, but I didn't understand what. I stayed where I was, in the shadows, paralyzed with curiosity. The girl glanced toward the emperor's bedroom and trembled all over. "But I wasn't encouraging him, Lady Livia . . ."

Livia's sweetness gave way to anger as her hand moved from the girl's cheek into her hair and grabbed a fistful. "Don't *Lady Livia* me. I know your kind—what you really want from the emperor, despite what you say. Don't deny it."

The girl tried to look away, and when she did, she saw me. Then Livia did too and turned on me in fury. "Didn't I tell you to serve the wine, Selene? How dare you spy on me?"

"I-I," I stammered in surprise at her anger, but before I could finish, I was rescued by shouting throughout the house.

"It's time to choose the Lord of Misrule!" the cry went up, and the guests cheered.

Taking advantage of the merriment, I gathered my skirts and fled from Livia's presence. I reached the festivities in time to draw a pastry to see who would be nominal ruler of the emperor's household for the rest of the Saturnalia.

I worried when I saw my littlest brother push his chubby fist into the bowl and draw out the pastry with the hidden bean. This pastry marked him as the winner of the dubious honor. The crowd tittered awaiting the emperor's response. Philadelphus was the son of Antony, as anyone could tell by looking. But he was also the child of Cleopatra, and they hadn't forgotten.

A Ptolemy child to be the ruler of the emperor's household? Even in the jest of the Saturnalia, would that be too much for the emperor's honor to endure? All eyes were on the emperor as my little brother crushed the pastry between his fat fingers. I could see he was confused by what was happening, but the emperor hovered over him like a doting nursemaid. "Ah, Philadelphus, my child. You're the Lord of Misrule! What's your desire? How may I serve?"

I prayed that my little brother wouldn't command something insulting. Thankfully, Philadelphus smiled up at the emperor and asked, "May I have another pastry?"

The emperor laughed and gave Philadelphus a pastry for each hand. "The Lord of Misrule has commanded sweets for all, and we must obey."

A cheer went up from the crowd as the emperor took Philadelphus into his arms. It made me cringe to see him holding my baby brother and smiling a smile I recognized. A sly smile like the one I'd seen the day of the Triumph.

How gracious and noble the emperor was, the guests all seemed to agree. How forgiving and merciful was this ruler of the world, just like his uncle, the Divine Julius. How lucky it was for the children of Cleopatra to be taken so lovingly into Octavian's family. I knew they'd spread this story on the streets long after the Saturnalia had ended and so did the emperor. To complete the picture, he called me to his side as he told his guests the story of the lying interpreter. "Then she says to me, 'But Caesar, I know Syrian!' Isn't that right, Selene?"

I bobbed my head and he patted my shoulder with his chilly fingers. His face could affect warmth, but his fingers always revealed his underlying cool. He was generous with his praise of me, telling the story in a way that put us both in the most flattering light and so the Romans could take that story home with them too—how the emperor had so easily won over the loyalty of Cleopatra's daughter.

AT last it was time for the poetry reading. So many guests crowded into the salon that they had to line the walls. When Juba saw me, he scooted over to make space on the bench next to him. "Sit by me, Selene. I can't wait to hear what you think of our Roman poet."

I squeezed beside him, our arms tangling briefly. He smelled good, the scents of the Saturnalia mixing with the desert smell that always lingered on Juba's clothes. I followed his pointed finger to the poet who stood at the front of the room.

Though Juba had called him the Roman poet, Virgil had the

heavily browed features of a Gaul. His mysterious eyes were deep-set and his forehead was creased with intensity. The poet swept a lock of black hair across his forehead when Maecenas asked what tale Virgil would spin and Virgil's answer came easily in verse:

> *"What makes the cornfield smile; beneath what star*
> *Maecenas, it is meet to turn the sod*
> *Or marry elm with vine; how tend the steer;*
> *What pains for cattle-keeping, or what proof*
> *Of patient trial serves for thrifty bees;*
> *Such are my themes."*

That Virgil could answer with poetry delighted the guests. An awed hush fell over the room as he recited the rest. Virgil's poem spoke of the land and harvest. He spoke of the farmer's life with such poignancy that even a Ptolemy princess like me wished to dirty her hands with a plow. He finished to applause, and women held their hands over heaving chests, as if they couldn't contain their emotion.

Juba's eyes twinkled. "Selene, when you hear tales of her fertile soil, doesn't it make you love Rome just a little?"

"Egypt is *more* fertile," I said quietly, wondering whether the Nile had risen this year. It was the season of Emergence again, and if the Nile hadn't flooded, there'd be famine. "It's Egypt I love."

Juba's eyes were sympathetic. "Egypt feeds Rome; that's why Rome can't afford to lose her ever again. The emperor has taken Egypt as his own private domain; he's even forbidden anyone above the rank of an *equite* to visit there without his permission. You must forget Egypt, Selene."

I stared at my hands. "As you've forgotten your kingdom of Numidia?"

Juba smiled sadly. "I haven't forgotten Numidia."

By now, Virgil had finished his reading. Juba stood to

congratulate the poet on his work, sweeping me along with him. "Publius Virgilius Maro, I'd like you to meet Cleopatra Selene of Egypt."

I lowered my eyes in the way Lady Octavia did when she met new people, waiting for the man to address me before speaking. Virgil smiled. His cheeks were ruddy and he had an unexpected shyness to his demeanor. "Why, my dear, you are the incarnation of your lovely mother."

For the first time, someone in Rome had mentioned my mother in a kindly fashion, and I felt myself smile without guile. "You knew my mother?"

"We did. She once stayed in Rome at Julius Caesar's estate and was a great patron of the arts. I was painfully young, but had the good fortune to be introduced to her by a mutual friend, Crinagoras of Mytilene, the great epigramist. I look forward to seeing you again, Cleopatra Selene. I'll make time to visit you again before the end of the Saturnalia."

I'd been dismissed so I let my lips form the expected words. *"Io Saturnalia!"*

Then I turned to see Helios. The urgency of his expression seemed at odds with the jovial red cap he wore upon his head. He grabbed me by the arm and pulled me into a quiet corner.

"Chryssa has returned from the country," he whispered. "And she's seen Euphronius."

Thirteen

IN my room, I lit the oil lamp beside my bed while Helios ushered Chryssa inside and quietly shut the door behind us. Bast looped affectionately around his feet, rubbing her whiskers and muzzle against his legs. All at once, the slave girl fell to her knees. "Forgive me, lady!"

For a moment, I wondered if we'd been betrayed, but Helios shook his head as if she did this often.

"What is there to forgive?" I asked her.

"I was petulant with you the day after the Triumph. Then I saw the marks of Isis upon your hands and I knew you were holy to my goddess!"

I remembered how she'd fought with me over the bloody dress, but she'd revealed something far more important now. "You're an Isiac?"

"Of course," she said. "Isis is the only goddess who truly cares about the lives of slaves. Her temple admits everyone to worship. Lady Livia would feed me to the lampreys if she knew, but I love Isis more than I fear Livia."

"You *should* fear Livia," I said, worried. "She holds the power of life and death over you."

"Only *this* life," Chryssa said, and kissed the hem of my gown. "Euphronius teaches that death is not the end of all things and that you will help us find salvation."

She looked at me then as if I were capable of ending the suffering in her world, but I couldn't even end the suffering in my own. "How do you know Euphronius?" I asked, wondering what else our old wizard had taught this slave girl.

"Before I tell you, won't you bless me?"

Helios motioned for me to go ahead, but I felt every bit the pretender. Chryssa was asking me to convey the blessing of Isis but I wasn't pharaoh. I was no priestess and this was no temple. How could I?

"I've lain with no man and dedicated my virginity to Isis. I've tried to treat others with kindness and compassion. Your brother found me worthy and gave me his blessing. Won't you give me yours as well?"

I tried to remember what my mother did. I put one hand upon my frog amulet. With the other, I brushed honeyed wisps of hair out of Chryssa's eyes. She looked to be fifteen or sixteen; she was older than me, but kneeling before me like a child at her mother's knee.

"You're blessed," I told her, and felt warmth flow through me like a strong wine—likely the heat of my embarrassment and the flash of fear that Isis would be angered by my fraud. But if Chryssa sensed artifice within my blessing, she didn't let on.

Instead, her pupils dilated and she trembled when I withdrew my touch. Helios helped her to rise. "Please, Chryssa. Selene has done as you asked. Now we must know of Euphronius."

She nodded quickly. "I met Euphronius at the Temple of Isis on the Campus Martius."

"*Io Saturnalia!*" someone shouted outside, and the three of us were silent until they passed by.

Only when I heard the laughter of the guests echo in the distance did I speak again. "But why is Euphronius in Rome? Agrippa had him flogged in Egypt. It can't be safe for Euphronius here."

"There are many foreigners in this city, my lady. They aren't looking for him here. He says he's come to help prepare for your glorious reign."

Could sweeter words have ever been spoken? But where would Euphronius take us? Even if he spirited us away, where in the entire world could we hide from Romans or have a prosperous reign? All of my worldly possessions filled this room. My brother and I were without country or army. We reigned over nothing. It felt vain to hope, and yet, I had to ask, "In Rome, the Isiac temples have no sway. The emperor opposes them. What power could Euphronius have here?"

"The faith is powerful, my lady," Chryssa said. "There are thousands of Isiacs within the city alone who are ready to help you. I'm not even the only Isiac within *this* household."

"Who else?" Helios prompted, his eye on my repaired door.

"Many slaves and one even more important than that. Gaius Julius Juba frequents the temple and has been trying to study minor magics there. Euphronius wants me to ask you if Juba can be trusted to be a messenger."

"Juba?" I suddenly understood the scent of the Romanized African prince who was our tutor. It had been magic I had smelled all along.

Helios removed his red cap and scrunched it in one hand. "Juba has been fair with us. Would you trust him, Selene?"

I fumbled for my reply. I liked Juba. Sometimes when he looked at me, I felt something flutter inside. I *wanted* to trust our handsome young tutor, but I still remembered how he once spoke of us as game pieces. I remembered too how he'd beaten Helios until he bled.

"Juba has been kind to us when he could," I admitted. "But

he performs for the emperor like a well-trained pet. You must tell Euphronius not to reveal himself until we can learn more about Juba's true loyalties."

Helios thumped his hands against my desk in frustration. "That's all Euphronius wants to know? If he can trust Juba? He appeared to us once, why not again? Tell our wizard we want to see him with our own eyes. Tell him that we *command* it."

"Helios . . ." I cautioned, though when I looked at his face now, I saw no recalcitrant twin brother, but the face of my king. "You could get him killed."

Helios looked away in frustration and my mind whirled around the memory of the emperor's promise to undermine the Isiacs and accuse them of attacking me with magic. "Chryssa, did Euphronius send me messages upon my skin? If he did, tell him to stop or he'll give the emperor an excuse to destroy our temples."

"Won't Isis protect her temples?" Chryssa asked.

I loved Isis, I believed in Isis, and I'd been her conduit in the mortal world, but Octavian had smashed Egypt. He could smash the temples of Isis too. "Just tell Euphronius that I can't have these messages. They anger the Romans."

WHEN Chryssa was gone, Helios turned on me. "How could you say that? Isis spoke through you, and you wish her words away because they might anger the Romans?"

He made me feel small and unworthy, but *he* wasn't the one whose hands bled and burned with pain. "Helios, I don't want to argue. Not tonight. Euphronius will come for us. That's good news, isn't it?"

Helios shook his head. "I don't think we should wait for him to free us. I think we should find him ourselves."

My heartbeat fluttered beneath my breastbone. "What if we're caught? To risk such a thing now, just when we've achieved some semblance of—"

"Some semblance of what?" Helios demanded.

"Safety."

The word *happiness* would not pass my lips, but things had changed a great deal for us since we'd come to Rome as prisoners. Though I never forgot that we were at the emperor's mercy always, he was starting to show some fondness for me. There might be some way that we could get him to put us back on the throne of Egypt.

"Safety?" Helios's lips turned with disgust. "It's only the safety of a bird in a cage—like the ones Livia keeps."

"All I know is that Philadelphus has stopped crying all the time," I said, worrying at the ribbon of my gown with my fingers. "Octavia treats him well. To see him smile again makes me glad."

"And you think I'd rather see him sad and afraid? We can't just sit here and wait for Euphronius to come to us again."

"Why can't we? He's a wise man. He knows things we don't. He asked us to find out if Juba could be trusted as a messenger, so why can't we be content to do as he asks?"

"Because every day we're here, we're in danger. The emperor could change his mind and kill us at his whim. We're in his power. And what if we learn that Juba *can't* be trusted? What if Chryssa can't get to the temple and carry messages for us anymore? Then it will be as before, and we'll be alone. Egypt will be alone. We should find Euphronius ourselves—it's worth taking a risk."

"I know you're desperate to do something, *anything*. But maybe the emperor is right when he says to *make haste slowly*."

I winced at my own words even before they had escaped my lips. Of all the means I had at my disposal to convince him, I'd chosen to quote one of the emperor's favorite sayings. Infuriated, Helios got up, walked out, and slammed the door behind him. I tried to catch it before it slammed, but was too late, so I wrenched it back open and gave chase. Nearly tripping over my *tunica*, I caught up with Helios and grabbed him by the arm. "Helios, please. I'm just scared!" It shamed me to say, and I couldn't remember the last time that fear had not informed my every action. I thought he'd yell at me. He had that thunder in his eyes that made me quake. "Aren't you scared too?"

"Kings aren't allowed to be scared," Helios said. "Besides, sometimes I think that everything I'm afraid of has already happened."

"Just wait a little longer to go looking for Euphronius," I pleaded. "Just until the snows melt and its springtime. Until we know more. After all, how do we know Chryssa isn't the emperor's spy?"

"She's not," Helios said, scowling, but I could see he didn't want to be at odds with me. "Perhaps you're right. You've always been the clever one. So, we'll wait until springtime. Let's hope we have that long."

THE last day of the Saturnalia was a time to exchange gifts with the imperial family. Helios found the idea particularly galling, but I convinced him that if we didn't give something to each member of the family, we'd cause offense and make our situation worse.

We gave away the Syrian incense and I gave each girl in the household one of the silver stars I'd plucked off of the netting before Octavia had gotten rid of it. I also gave Julia an ivory comb, and she embarrassed me with a basket full of hairpins, ribbons, and rings.

"I'm touched by your gifts," I reassured her.

Livia snorted and stretched out upon her plush couch. "Don't be too grateful, Selene. Julia is particularly free with her possessions in a way that only someone can be when they tire of things quickly."

Julia's cheeks reddened and she looked away, and I wondered why the emperor never defended his daughter from Livia's barbs. He ignored the exchange, tossing us each a pouch of Egyptian gold coins.

Then he gave my mother's jewelry to the women of the

household. "Here, Selene. Your mother was famed for her pearls. You should have a strand of them."

They should have been mine anyway, but I was obliged to thank him while he fastened my mother's gold and lapis lazuli bracelet around Livia's wrist. The emperor was in a good mood, which meant that the rest of the household could be in a good mood as well.

Over and over he told the story of how I'd helped him catch the lying interpreter, though in his version of the story, I'd merely confirmed what he already knew. Then the emperor glanced down at the wax tablet he often kept with him for notes and reminders. "Ah yes, I almost forgot. Tomorrow, Selene and Helios will have a birthday and I've heard that Helios has taken a fondness to the slave girl Chryssa."

I held my breath. Did he know about the conversation we'd had with Chryssa in my room about Euphronius? I braced for the worst. The emperor, however, smiled. "I bought her away from Livia and now I'm giving Chryssa to Helios as a birthday gift. A young man of his stature should have an attendant."

I tried not to gasp with relief. A slave was a generous gift and everyone praised the emperor's largesse. Helios could only stammer his thanks, but if the emperor was put off by my twin's ingratitude, he didn't show it.

"I've not forgotten Selene's birthday either. I'm gifting her with the works of the greatest poet of all, a Roman at that."

The emperor opened a trunk before me and I ran my fingers over the smooth skin of the vellum scrolls within. They were copies of Virgil's poetry. A complete collection. It was a generous gift indeed. "Thank you."

"Good," the emperor declared, satisfied with himself. "You'll even have a chance to speak with the poet himself. I've always thought he doted overmuch on my nephew Marcellus, but now he's quite taken with you, Selene. He says he's going to pay you a visit before the end of Saturnalia."

Fourteen

WITH the gift exchange over, I went with the girls to the kitchen to clean up dishes from the feast. Helios had also been sent to work with the girls as punishment for a smart remark he'd made to Agrippa.

Philadelphus and Minora swept the hearths while the rest of us tackled the mountain of filthy platters. Meanwhile, Bast made herself useful by gobbling up the scraps of food we spilled, her spiny cat's tongue scratching against the floor.

Julia whistled while she scrubbed. "I wonder if Virgil has grown fond of you in a certain way, Selene."

The way she said it made Helios bristle, so I quickly interceded. "Julia, you think *everyone* is fond of me in a certain way."

"And why not?" she asked. "You're of marriageable age now. Once Marcella marries Agrippa, you'll be the oldest girl in the emperor's household and everyone will be interested in you. After all, you *do* come with a great legacy."

"Of death?" I asked, brooding.

But Julia only laughed and rolled her eyes at my dramatics.

"Why else would Virgil wish to see you if he didn't want to marry you?"

Helios turned so quickly I thought he might strike Julia. "Marry her!" He slammed the platter in his hands down so hard it cracked. "Virgil can't marry Selene. He's just a rich poet. He's not even noble and completely unfit to marry the daughter of Pharaoh."

"This much is true," Julia allowed. "Now that Selene is a member of my father's household, she'll have to marry someone of a certain stature. A distinguished old senator or maybe a soldier like Plancus."

I shuddered more that I should be married off to a traitor than that I should have to wed some wrinkly old man, but either way, I must have lost all color in my complexion, because Julia put a hand on my arm and said, "No matter who my father marries you to, your wedding should be glamorous, Selene."

"Glamorous?" Helios slammed down another platter, as everything Julia said seemed to make him angrier. "A Roman wife is subject to the complete authority of her husband. That's hardly glamorous, Julia."

He was right, and if the emperor married me off, I'd be separated from my brothers.

"Don't be angry with *me*," Julia said to Helios. "It's not as if I wrote the Roman laws on marriage. In any case, I'm sure my father will find someone of proper age and stature to marry Selene."

My twin and I said nothing. We were both all too aware that there was only one person left in the entire world of proper age and stature to marry a Ptolemy princess, and that was Helios.

"I hope you don't mind the brisk weather, Selene," Virgil said, offering his arm to me. Mindful that the emperor might marry me to him or to any other man that he chose, I was afraid to take it.

"Come, Selene," Virgil coaxed me. "Rome isn't normally so cold in the winter, but I thought a walk might do you good. Pretend we're on a country stroll."

I pulled my cloak tighter and wrapped my fingers around the poet's arm. "I don't mind the weather, but I thought you'd be reading me poetry today."

"I'll *show* you poetry," Virgil said, sweeping one arm across the landscape. Trees were silver spires, and Rome finally looked clean under a blanket of white snow. I could hear laughter and the tunes of minstrels in the distance as everyone made the most of the last day of the Saturnalia.

"It's good of you to meet with me," I said. "The emperor gave me all of your works but one. The Fourth Eclogue is missing."

"No, you have the whole set," he said, and I saw that Virgil too could make a mask of his face, for he forced a smile as he guided me toward the construction site where lightning had years ago struck and burned down part of the emperor's home. "In any case, Selene, I have a different gift for you, something I've wanted to give you for quite some time."

Julia's words came back to haunt me, and I tried to show indifference. If the emperor wished to marry me to a poet, I'd have no say in the matter, but no matter how kindly Virgil's face was, I couldn't imagine being married to him. "I'm afraid I have nothing to give you in return."

"Your company is gift enough," the poet said, steering me round a snowcapped tree where a group of slaves passed around jugs of wine while meat roasted on an open fire.

"*Io Saturnalia!*" the slaves shouted to us in greeting and our presence chilled their celebration not a whit. I was desperately glad for their interruption.

Impervious to the cold that made their cheeks and noses red, they danced amidst the construction. The open congress between men and women was enough to make even an Alexandrian blush. Modestly looking away, my eyes settled upon the ivory doors of the unfinished building and wondered if the emperor was finally going to construct something beautiful for us to live in. "Is this the emperor's new home?"

"No, my dear. But it's quite lovely, isn't it?"

That's when I noticed the stolen pillars and war booty. Was it a shrine to the nations that Octavian had conquered? Then I stared in wonder at the bas-relief myth of Niobe who had offended the gods with her arrogance and had watched each of her children struck down by Apollo's arrows.

A slave offered me a cup of warm spiced wine. Though the cold would have made it welcome, the dread inside me prevented me from even holding a cup. "Wh-what is this place?" I asked with foreboding.

"This will be a temple to Apollo," the poet replied. "The emperor has chosen Apollo as his patron. Here the most precious artwork in the world will be housed alongside libraries of Greek and Latin."

Had not the emperor boasted to me that he would claim to be the incarnation of Apollo? Had he sent me here with Virgil to witness these doors as a warning? Did he mean to kill all my mother's children as Apollo had killed Niobe's?

Virgil mistook my hesitation for chill; he took my hands and rubbed them between his to warm them. "Before you freeze, I must give you your gift. It comes with a rather strange story."

"What kind of story?"

"A personal story," he began. "You see, as I mentioned before, I knew your mother. When Julius Caesar brought her to Rome, every young artist sought out her company. I was no exception. The Queen of Egypt was a dazzling visionary."

When Virgil spoke about my mother, his eyes lit up with such affection and admiration it gave me pause. I had to wonder at all the stories the emperor told of my mother's promiscuity and an impertinent question rolled from my lips before I could stop it. "Were you her lover?"

"Oh no." He looked down shyly. "Your mother was too infatu-ated with Caesar to notice me and I prefer men."

Embarrassed, I fumbled for a reply. "I see."

He noticed my discomfort. "I hope I haven't disturbed you. Your mother was never offended by my preference."

"Nor am I offended," I said quickly. Men who preferred other men were common enough in Greek society. My mother's court had viewed it with indifference. In fact, because of Julia's taunting about how Virgil might like to marry me, I found myself quite relieved.

Virgil's hands were warm on mine as we slowly walked away from the slaves. "Your mother was here at Julius Caesar's invita-tion, but those were dangerous times—before the Ides of March that year everyone in the city was seeing omens and having dark dreams. The very night Julius Caesar was assassinated, I went to reassure her she was still welcome in Rome."

"But she'd already resolved to leave?" I knew my mother had fled Rome for fear of her life. Still, I couldn't help but be entranced by the telling of it from someone who was there.

"Yes. I found Queen Cleopatra in a state of disarray, over-come with grief. The air was thick with burned incense and her eyes were wide as if she'd taken a draft of magical potion. She clutched my arm, gave me this bracelet, and said, 'Give this to my daughter.'"

From a pouch at his belt, Virgil now took a golden coil—an armlet shaped like a hooded snake with emeralds inset for eyes. He pressed it into my hand.

I narrowed my eyes at him skeptically and stared at the snake bracelet as if it were a live serpent about to strike. Virgil *had* to be lying and it angered me. "I wasn't even born when Caesar died."

Virgil nodded as if he expected my objection. "I reminded her that she had no daughter, but she couldn't be reasoned with. With her hair wild and magic talismans of Isis clutched at her breast, she said, 'Give this to my daughter and tell her that it wasn't her fault.'"

The words washed over me as if I'd somehow plunged through the ice into a frigid pond. The guilt of my mother's death was still with me, and I hurt to remember. "You're lying."

"No," the poet said. "I always wondered if we'd laugh about it later, but I never saw her again. When news came that she'd given birth to a daughter, I considered sending this bracelet, but by then everything had changed. Partisans of Antony and Octavian were already choosing sides in the civil war, and it seemed unwise of me to continue any association with Cleopatra."

How could he know about the serpent I brought my mother to kill her? Even the emperor didn't know I carried the snake in that basket of figs. No one knew that but Euphronius and my brothers. "Stop lying!"

"I'm telling the truth," Virgil said, sadly. "Looking back now, I think she foresaw the tragedy. She was an Isiac oracle, so maybe she could see beyond the veils that separate this world from the others. Her request left an impression on me that I never forgot."

I squeezed the bracelet until my knuckles whitened, rage at Virgil and my mother burning just beneath my skin. "Why are you saying this to me?"

Virgil's eyes softened with sympathy. "I didn't mean to upset you, my dear, but when I saw you marching in Octavian's Triumph with such royal bearing, I became eager to fulfill the only request Cleopatra ever made of me. Now I feel relieved to discharge the duty. It's been weighing on me these years."

If my mother had known the future, why would she have done everything she did? Had my mother known the futility of her fight against Rome and fought anyhow? Could she have absolved me of her death even before it happened? Before I was born? My throat tightened with my efforts to remain composed. I couldn't cry in front of Virgil and all I wanted was to be alone.

"Selene, are you well?" the poet asked gently.

I was *not* well. I shook my head and bolted for Octavia's house, running away from the poet without so much as a reply. He called after me, but I didn't turn back.

Seeking out my room, and the simple pallet that was my bed, I curled up miserably beneath the blankets. Why would my mother have devoted herself to a losing battle? How could she have foreseen her own death and played out the farce of the war so fearlessly anyhow? I remembered the banner in her room that she placed there for the emperor to find—our family motto—*Win or Die.* Was it just to make a point that the Ptolemy dynasty, the last of the Pharaohs, would rather die than lay down their arms? Had she risked the lives of her people and her children for the sake of that gesture? Did she want me to do the same, or was this latest message meant to release me from her fate?

HUDDLED with Bast in my bed, I squeezed my eyes shut and buried my face in her fur. I tried to deny the truth in what Virgil had said, but something inside me knew it was true.

Terribly, horrifically, true.

My mother had seen everything and let it happen anyway. I remembered the way she'd said good-bye to us, and now the words of Isis, as they had carved themselves into my hands, also seemed like a farewell. In spite of the pain, in spite of the danger, I had gloried in being a vessel of the goddess. It had marked me as special and reaffirmed my faith, but as I stared at my hands now, I didn't even feel the tingle of *heka* inside the lines of my palms. Whatever magic lay inside me had gone dormant, and I had best forget it ever happened lest I wind up like my mother.

When anyone asked for me, I told them I was ill, for I was sick at heart. Livia sent Chryssa the slave girl to bring me one of her elixirs, but I wouldn't open the door. I didn't even answer Helios when he removed the brick from the wall and called for me. "Did Virgil hurt you, Selene? Why won't you talk to me?"

I was too lost in anger to soothe him. "Just leave me alone. I don't want to bleed anymore or learn magic or see Euphronius. I don't even know that I want to be Queen of Egypt anymore."

"That's not something you can choose." He sounded incredulous. "Selene, what's wrong with you?"

How could I tell him that some of the terrible things the Romans said about our mother might be true? That she'd been so ambitious that she'd fought the Romans from spite and left us helpless against their power. She left us. She left us!

Angrily, I got out of bed and ducked under the dressing table so that I could see my twin through the hole in the wall. I slid the bracelet down to my forearm. "A gift from Cleopatra, the Queen of Egypt. Virgil gave it to me."

Shock registered behind my twin's green eyes as he took in the shape of the golden serpent—for my brother too had been there on the day my mother died. "How would Virgil have anything that belonged to our mother?"

I was relieved of the need to answer by the knock at my door. Without my having to tell him, Helios put the brick back as I slipped the bracelet beneath my mattress, then straightened my clothes. "Who is it?"

"It's Juba. I've come to check on you."

"Please come back later."

"Octavia says you're ill," Juba replied. "Let me check you for fever, Selene. Open the door."

I crossed the room, opening the door a crack—enough to see that Juba's eyes were suspicious. "Who were you talking to?"

I spun a quick lie. "I was just singing a tune from the Saturnalia."

He sniffed the air, then pushed his way in. "It sounded more like a spell than a song."

I stepped back. "*You* would know, I suppose."

Juba lifted an eyebrow at me in the way he did in his classroom when we misbehaved. "Selene, you know how Lady Octavia feels about spells. Are you working magic?"

Now was the time to test him. Euphronius wanted to know if Juba could be trusted. It was time to find out. "Are *you* working magic?"

Juba's cheeks puffed with surprise. There was a moment's hesitation before he said, "*Someone* has been telling tales."

I covered my mouth with both hands, then whispered, "Juba, you're an Isiac, aren't you?"

His face went carefully blank, and then Juba closed the door behind him. He risked Lady Octavia's wrath by being alone with me behind bedroom doors now that I was of marriageable age, so I knew he took my question quite seriously. He sat at my dressing table, staring down at his smoothly elegant hands. "I visit the Temple of Isis from time to time."

My heart surged with joy. "Sweet Isis!"

I wanted to throw my arms around him. Though he was a man grown, Juba was still an African prince in the same situation as my brothers and me. He might be able to help us protect the temples. After all the turmoil of the last few days, there was good news at last. Perhaps Euphronius was right when he said that the followers of Isis would be watching us and watching over us. First Chryssa and now Juba.

"This isn't something to spread," Juba cautioned.

I clasped my hands before me. "Juba, you have to believe me. I would never tell the emperor your secret!"

Juba frowned. "It's no secret, Selene. The emperor knows of my interest in various cults, especially in light of the book that I'm writing. He asked only that I be discreet and not shame his house."

His words came crashing down around me like a house in collapse. Reeling, I sat down hard on the edge of my bed. "But the emperor hates Isiacs!"

"No, he hates anything that threatens the peace. I mean nothing to the Isiacs so there's no harm in my curiosity. You, on the other hand, are a symbol of their faith . . ."

Curiosity? Did he think our worship could be studied like all the scrolls in his library? "But—"

"But nothing," Juba interrupted. "Say what you will, but the emperor has very simple and admirable goals. He wants to preserve his own legacy, preserve the peace, and bring the advances of Roman culture to the rest of the world."

"What about Greek and Egyptian culture?" I asked.

Juba brushed this aside and spoke with the conviction of a disciple. "For the first time in decades we don't have one bully fighting another using Africans as pawns. We don't have pirates plaguing our seas and starving the citizenry. An entire generation has grown up knowing nothing but civil war, and the emperor has put an end to it. He wants to build things instead of tear them down, if they only accept the Roman way."

I fingered my arm where the bracelet had been. "But the Roman way is built upon oppression."

"Oppression?" Juba sighed. "Sometimes it's easy to forget that you're only a girl. Then you say something like that."

It made me stiffen. I was not *only a girl*. I was a Ptolemy. I was the rightful Queen of Egypt. I'd even been, at least for a short time, an embodiment of Isis. When I spoke, I didn't hide my indignation. "So, you're going to defend the Romans and their way? Juba, someday Rome will run out of new countries to conquer and steal from, and then what?"

"We'll both be long dead by the time that happens. Besides, Rome doesn't *choose* war. She fights *just* wars. She's pushed into war."

That's what Romans told themselves, but the generals, like my father, knew better. And so did I. "Juba, don't you realize that Rome looks for excuses to wage war?"

Juba met my eyes. "Is it really so different than anything Alexander the Great did?"

"Yes, it's different," I said, remembering what my mother had taught me. "Alexander wanted to bring people together as citizens of one world. He had a design behind his conquests that went beyond booty. Does Rome?"

"Of course," Juba said.

My chest rose and fell and my face was hot. Juba was confusing me. How could I explain that even Alexander's Egypt had been different than Rome? Where Egypt fed the world, Rome tamed it. Where Egypt fostered, Rome disciplined. Egypt was seductive as a temptress, nurturing as a mother, and wise as a crone. To me, Rome's spirit was all male.

"Selene, you and your brothers are the last of a distinguished line. You're the last of the Ptolemies. Don't you want to honor that legacy? Serve the emperor loyally and perhaps some place in Africa can be found for you—"

"The emperor wants us all dead!"

Juba reached out his hands as if he wanted to shake me. "Stop thinking like a *child*. The emperor has done everything possible to keep you alive. Africa isn't fully subdued. She chafes under Roman rule. Why would he kill you and ignite the spark that might rekindle the flames of war?"

"In other words, he might lose Egypt if he killed us."

"You're his investment in the future," Juba explained. "Remember how masterfully he set the scene the day of his Triumph so he could offer you clemency. Even if you hadn't begged for your life, Lady Octavia would have."

My mouth went dry with humiliation. I hadn't *had* to beg for our lives.

Juba leaned forward and made me look at him. "If you and your brothers threaten the peace, he'd have no choice but to destroy you, but what threat can you be to him as a loyal member of his own family? Your glory reflects upon him. I happen to know he wants to let you go home to Africa."

"My home is Egypt."

"Then convince him you can hold Egypt without betrayal. In Egypt, Octavian is letting them call him the father of the country.

There's symbolism in that. So give the emperor your loyalty as a good daughter might."

I hated myself for letting the hope swell in my breast. Still, I was skeptical. "And where has your loyalty gotten you, Juba? Are you King of Numidia or just the teacher of ungrateful royal orphans?"

I expected some show that he harbored resentment. Instead he gave me his most patronizing smile. "Patience is the hallmark of the emperor's regime. If you learn nothing else about him, learn that. He moves slowly and surely. I've had to prove myself to him, but one day he'll send me back to Numidia."

I all but snorted at him. "The Romans have turned Numidia into a province. Do you think the emperor can snap his fingers and turn it back into a kingdom for you to inherit? Is he so powerful now that he can anger the senators in Rome, each of whom vies to be the thieving governor of a province like Africa Nova?"

"I think he *is* that powerful," Juba said. "And if he isn't, I'll help him *become* that powerful. And you should do the same."

"Why should I?"

"Because he's the only man who can make you queen of anything. And because he spared you, Selene. You owe him your life."

My stomach dropped at the memory. "He only spared us to keep as hostages."

"Just the same, Selene, would you be a Brutus or a Cassius?"

How dare he make such a comparison? Offense heated my cheeks. "I'm no Brutus or Cassius."

Those were men that Julius Caesar had pardoned—men to whom he'd shown mercy—and they murdered him. But neither was I like Plancus, who'd sworn his life to my father and been turned with bribes and lies.

"Selene, aren't you even a little bit grateful to the emperor?"

In truth, it was hard for me to tell the difference between what I felt and what I made myself feel. Tears of frustration started to rise. "I am . . ."

Juba used a fingertip to brush them away. "You're not the only one who has lived through Roman conquest. I know what you're going through because I suffered it too. I saw my father die . . ."

And I had watched my mother put her hand into a basket with an angry cobra. This common history made me look into Juba's princely face. I sensed no guile in his warm honey-colored eyes. "How did your father die?"

It was as if he'd only been waiting for me to ask. "The night my father realized that Caesar's legions had defeated him, he and a loyal Roman general got themselves drunk. Then they made a toast to death before taking up arms against one another."

I sat perfectly still, transfixed.

Juba continued, "The general swore that his last duty of friendship would be to give my father an honorable death. I was younger than Philadelphus, but I remember watching as my father and the man rounded one another, locked in bloody tearful combat. Their swords clashed and they grappled, until a sudden lunge erupted in blood. It was my father's sword that struck true. The other man lay dead by my feet, but my father had been fatally wounded. I cried as a slave slit my father's throat."

I felt a shiver at the base of my spine. "I'm sorry," I whispered, though I knew there were no words that could ever make appropriate reply to such a story. I wanted very much to comfort him then, so I reached out to grasp his fingers in simple empathy the way Julia had done with me.

"It took time, but I'm past it," Juba said, bringing my fingers to his lips and planting a gentle kiss there. "You'll get past the death of your parents too."

At the feel of his lips against my fingers, I flushed warm. He'd *kissed* me—my fingertips at least—and my stomach was all aflutter. I felt the pull between us. He drew closer, leaning toward me, his eyes on my lips. Then—abruptly—Juba rose and walked to the doorway.

"Juba . . ." I started, but I had no idea what to say.

He cleared his throat, and looked back at me. "Now, you must think about everything I've said, Selene, and decide. Will you and your brothers be the last sad chapter in the history of the dying Egyptian dynasty? Or will you make a new glorious beginning under the Roman banner?"

Fifteen

"THEN Juba can't be trusted," Helios whispered from his side of the wall. "And he can't be our messenger. If Juba even knew that Euphronius was in Rome, he'd tell the emperor and they'd arrest our wizard before we could do a thing to help him."

I was irritated that after having conveyed the entire conversation to my twin, *this* was the only thing Helios had taken from it, but I couldn't disagree. "You should send Chryssa back to the Temple of Isis to warn Euphronius away, then."

"I can't send Chryssa again. She's my slave now, which means they'll follow her and trace all her doings to me."

"You think that the emperor gave Chryssa to you because he means to trap you?"

"Could there be any other reason?" Helios asked. "Fortunately, I'm not the slow-witted boy the emperor thinks I am."

No, he wasn't. From a sense of pride, I'd tried to impress upon the Romans that we were royalty, that we were smarter and better than they were. But Helios had smothered his talents in the schoolroom. He'd shown them nothing, and maybe there was an advantage in that too.

"Then what are we going to do? Euphronius can't come to us. The Romans had him flogged in Alexandria; surely, he knows they'd do worse if they caught him here."

"We'll have to find a way to meet with him secretly," Helios insisted, raw determination in his eyes. "Egypt needs Pharaoh. Egypt needs Isis. We need a throne to carry her back to. We'll find Euphronius, and he'll help us to escape before the emperor marries you off to some horrible old man."

He didn't seriously think we could simply run away, did he? I was aghast, wondering if Helios was like my mother, fighting even when he knew he'd lose. I tried to hide my rising panic. "Helios, remember that you promised we'd do nothing until springtime." He scowled and began to protest, but he was never one to break his promises and I reminded him of that now. "A king doesn't break his word. Especially not to his sister."

Helios growled. "We'll wait until the *Navigium Isidis*, then, when the city is filled with revelers and it'll be easier for us to get lost in a crowd."

The *Navigium Isidis* was an Isiac festival that celebrated the opening of the sailing season in early March. That my brother had chosen it was a testament to how serious he was about his plan. There was no more likely day in which we could find Euphronius in Rome, or at least find someone who had seen him. "We lose nothing by trying," Helios said.

He was wrong—there was much we had to lose by trying, but before I could tell him so, Lady Octavia was pounding on my door. "Wake up, Selene! The morning lamps need to be lit, and after that you can help Marcella gather up her childhood things."

THE slaves were already scurrying in and out of Marcella's room when I got there, and I found her standing in the midst of the bustle, wan and drawn. Since Chryssa now belonged to Helios, who gave her precious little to do, the imperial family relied upon another *ornatrix* named Phoebe—who was now explaining to Marcella how her hair must be divided with a spear tip into six braids for her upcoming wedding. "It's to drive curses and evil spirits out of your hair," she explained, and Marcella just kept nodding her head, her eyes somewhere off in the distance.

I was loathe to interrupt, but I said, "Your mother said I should help you gather your childhood things. Are you going somewhere?"

This made Marcella frown. "I'm marrying Agrippa tomorrow. I'm going to live in his villa."

Now I frowned too. "You're marrying *tomorrow*?"

When Lady Octavia had told us that her eldest daughter would marry Agrippa, I certainly never thought it would happen so quickly, and I also thought it would be attended with some pomp and circumstance. Marcella was, after all, the emperor's niece. "Isn't there to be . . . a celebration?"

"What is there to celebrate?" Marcella asked, biting her lower lip and turning to stare at the saffron veil draped over her bed as if it were her burial shroud. "Livia says that on account of Agrippa's low birth, we shouldn't mark the occasion lavishly. The patrician families won't approve."

"Not even a banquet?" I asked.

"Oh yes. A small one. Then a wedding breakfast the next morning at Agrippa's villa. But nothing so grand as the Saturnalia."

Like her mother, Marcella often wore a carefully guarded expression, but I could see she was miserable. I tried to offer what comfort I could. "I'll help you pack."

"You don't need to," Marcella said. "Most of my things have already been sent ahead. All that remains now is to burn the rest."

"To burn?" I thought I'd misheard.

"Tomorrow I'll be a bride," she explained, tracing the charm she wore at her neck. "Tonight I have to offer up this *bulla* and the rest of my belongings from girlhood."

That night, we all gathered round as Marcella removed the *bulla* from her neck and burned what remained of her childhood in offering to the household gods. Agrippa and Octavia were both on hand to watch her feed these things to the flame, but neither of them spared one another a glance.

The next day, the slaves slaughtered a ewe and erected an altar before which Marcella and Agrippa were to be wed at dusk. Octavia was in a temper all day, and I made sure to stay out of her way, busying myself by helping the slaves light the candles and lanterns to welcome the few guests and witnesses required to make the marriage legal. Then I sat together with my brothers and Julia who viewed the entire proceedings with distaste. "When I get married, my veil is going to be embroidered with gold thread," she insisted. "And there will be an enormous party to celebrate."

The musicians took up their instruments and Marcella finally appeared, emerging from the house.

"She looks like a bejeweled mummy," Helios whispered to me, and that wasn't far from the truth. Marcella wore a long white tunic, the bright orange veil drawn over her face like a hood, showing only the coiffure of her hair. With her fair complexion and the wreath of flowers that adorned her, the emperor's niece looked like a Vestal Virgin, a veritable symbol of innocence and purity.

Her groom, however, was unquestionably drunk. Looking awkward with his burly warrior's frame draped in a toga, Agrippa gulped down the last of the wine in his goblet before lumbering to his place beside his young bride.

Was I the only one to catch Agrippa and Octavia share a meaningful look? They stared at one another as if there were years of unspoken longing between them. For a moment, I even wondered if they might rebel and call an end to this wedding. But in the end, in their way, I think each of them loved the emperor more than they loved each other, or even themselves.

"Who is the little girl?" Philadelphus asked, noticing the child in Agrippa's wake, about his own age.

"That's Vipsania," Julia explained. "Agrippa's daughter."

Octavia had said that a Roman husband shouldn't have to take in the girl children of other men, but Marcella would clearly be expected to mother Agrippa's daughter, who eyed the whole exchange with wide-eyed wonderment.

I was only four years old when my own parents married, but I actually remembered the wedding and the riotous celebration that attended it. I still had flashes of memory: my mother's golden gown and my father's glittering eyes. The wine, the dancing, and merriment had tired me out long before Iras and Charmian had fetched me for bed. So it was uncomfortable to see the stoicism with which Agrippa and Marcella now approached the altar. Marcella held her lips tight. Sewn up. Fastened down. I wondered whether she had ever breathed a day in her life or whether she'd always been that girl arguing with me while we decorated boughs for the Saturnalia.

In short order, while the guests looked on, the bride and groom exchanged bites of spelt cake, then said the simple Roman vows. "When and where thou art Gaius, I shall be Gaia," Marcella murmured.

"When and where thou art Gaia, I shall be Gaius."

Then it was done, as simply as that. They were married, and all the guests cried out their congratulations. All except for Julia, that is. "Poor Marcella," she said, but as I glanced around at the faces of the rheumy old senators in attendance, I decided that things could have been worse.

The banquet that night wasn't lavish, but the menu had been chosen by Octavia and included some truly tasty dishes. My brothers, both of whom missed living by the sea, gorged themselves on shrimp and oysters, but I couldn't find my appetite. I kept thinking of my mother and how she must have banqueted here in Rome. No doubt, wearing the serpent bracelet that she'd asked Virgil to give to me.

When the candles had burned low, it was time for Agrippa to take his bride home. Marcella was supposed to cling to her mother and Agrippa was supposed to rip his bride from her mother's arms. But only too well did Marcella play her part, weeping openly. Too little did Agrippa play his, standing there stammering and wine-soaked. Even in the face of jubilant taunts, he could barely bring himself to touch his new bride.

At last, at the emperor's impatient glare, Agrippa took Marcella by the shoulders and yanked her backward, hoisting her up into his arms. *"Talasio!"* our guests cried, an ancient Roman encouragement.

Agrippa looked like a bear with a child in his arms as he let the torchbearers lead them away. I rose from my seat, all too well imagining myself in Marcella's place and wanting nothing but to flee.

Julia stopped me. "Where are you going, Selene? You'll miss the procession!"

"You're all too young for the procession," Octavia said, overhearing us. "I don't want your innocence spoiled by the bawdy jests that the guests will make as they lead the bride and groom away. Off to bed with you, and take poor Philadelphus with you. He can barely keep his eyes open!"

"I won't let that happen to you," Helios said after we tucked Philadelphus into bed.

"You won't let *what* happen to me?" I asked as the two of us sat on my bed.

"I won't let him marry you off like you're chattel. You're the Queen of Egypt, even if you don't want to be."

I watched the lantern burn. "When I said I didn't want to be queen, I didn't mean it." And in any case, it wasn't a choice. It was in my blood. I was the last queen of the Ptolemies. The very last. I could no easier cut off my arm than turn my back on that legacy.

"I know you didn't mean it," Helios said. "And I promise, one day I'm going to bring you back to Egypt."

It was a reckless promise, but he sounded so very sure that it made me smile in spite of myself. "On the prow of your warship . . ."

"Yes. And when we see the lighthouse, we'll know that we're home. At the docks, the people will throw flower petals in the harbor."

"To greet you as their king," I said, wanting to lose myself in this fantasy, for just a moment.

"I'll take you straightaway to the Iseum, to be anointed before all the people and have the royal diadem placed upon your brow . . ."

"But that won't be enough," I protested. "Egypt needs a pharaoh. She needs the blessings of the old gods, and the magic that makes the Nile rise. We'll have to go down the Nile."

"All the way to Aswan," he agreed. "On a luxurious river barge. And when we've ensured a bountiful harvest and nourished the people, we'll go to see the pyramids and we will restore Thebes. We'll reform the laws too—"

"It sounds like a great deal of work being queen," I teased, easing my head down onto the bed and closing my tired eyes.

"It won't all be work," he said, resting beside me. "We'll invite all the finest minds to our court, all the dazzling, brilliant people. And if the harvest is good, we'll actually feed them and serve expensive wine. We'll have music and we'll dance, you and I. So that any Roman who happens to see will faint in horror."

I liked this idea. "I'll wear silk and put netting over my bed and wear perfumes," I murmured, getting sleepier all the while.

"And I'll give you jewels," Helios said. "I'll give you emeralds to match your eyes and black wigs with beaded braids to wear in the Egyptian style and no one could chastise you for it, because you'll be my queen . . ."

THE next morning we woke before dawn, but not of our own accord. We heard shouting and slammed doors—such a commotion that I wondered if Octavia's house were not being overrun by barbarians. I'd barely had time to slip on my sandals when Julia came bursting into my room. She must have run all the way from Livia's house, because her cheeks were rosy and it took her a moment to catch her breath. "What are you both doing in here?"

I glanced over to Helios, who was still wiping the sleep out of his eyes. "What are *you* doing here, Julia?"

"Marcella's come back!" she crowed.

"So?" I hadn't even seen the bride leave the night before, so I wasn't sure why Julia's eyes were gleaming with gossip.

"How could you have slept through the wailing and crying?" Julia asked. "Marcella's run away from Agrippa and locked herself in her old bedroom and won't come out."

Poor Marcella, I thought. "Oh no . . ."

But Julia burst into a peal of laughter. "Agrippa's going to fetch his wife back for the wedding breakfast, but first he needs to sleep off his enormous hangover! I almost feel sorry for the great big lout, having to chase after his bride like some cuckolded merchant—"

"Keep your voice down," I hissed. "What will Lady Octavia think if she hears you rejoicing in Marcella's misfortune?"

"Oh, I'm not rejoicing," Julia replied, dutifully lowering her voice to a whisper. "I feel rather sorry for Marcella. Can you even imagine what Agrippa must have done to her to make her run away?"

Actually, I couldn't, and in spite of myself, I was very curious. I glanced at Helios once, and he said, "Go."

So I followed Julia out into the hallway. Lady Octavia was standing near Marcella's old room, shouting, "You open this door at once, you wicked girl!" When she saw Julia and me standing there, Octavia put her face in her hands and let out a long breath. "You girls tell my daughter that if she's not come out within the hour, I'm going to get the guards to break down the door and march her right back to her husband's household."

As it turned out, Marcella responded neither to our knocks nor our shouts for her, until Julia wondered aloud, "Perhaps she's died. Perhaps she drank one of Livia's toxic tonics and now she's lying in there rotting—I hope she left me something in her Last Will. I quite like the embroidered shawl Marcella wore to the Saturnalia and I think it would look very nice on me."

Marcella unbolted the door and opened it just wide enough so that she could direct one black but bloodshot eye at Julia. "I'm not dead," Marcella finally said. "And if I were, I wouldn't leave *you* anything, Julia."

"I don't see what you should have against *me*," Julia huffed. "It wasn't *my* idea to marry you to Agrippa. I was the only one who was against it!"

With the door already unbolted, Marcella opened it a little farther. Julia and I both went into Marcella's room and sat together at the dressing table, which was empty because her belongings had been packed up and sent to Agrippa's house the day before.

"Are you unwell?" I asked, for Marcella was still in her bed clothing and she hadn't bothered to fasten her hair, which fell in a messy tangle of dark waves over her shoulders.

"You have no idea how awful it was," Marcella said, clasping her hands together. "Agrippa was so big and heavy, and he stank of wine!" Her nostrils flared as if she were recalling a pungent scent. "He was *frightfully* drunk. Then he was on top of me, and he was sweating. Actually sweating. Dripping onto my face as he moved above me."

The emperor's daughter and I were both aghast. Julia's eyes

riveted on Marcella's tearful face. Meanwhile, I leaned so far on the edge of my seat that I nearly lost my balance.

"And it *hurt*," Marcella continued, her lower lip trembling. "I tried to lie still, to be stoic, to do my duty for my family and for Rome. But every which way I turned my hips, it seemed to hurt worse!"

Octavia would have liked to think I was too young to know anything about the way men and women came together in intimacy, but I'd worked beside the slaves in her household long enough to have overheard a thing or two. Even so, a heated blush came to my cheeks. "But it can't have lasted long, can it have?"

"You would think not," Marcella snapped at me. "After all, he promised it wouldn't last long. His face got red, his arms bulged with effort, the bed creaked like mad, and he cursed like he was leading a battle charge. But even that I could have endured, at least until . . ."

Here, Marcella broke off in a gale of sobs as she buried her face in her hands. I watched her cry, at a complete loss as to how to comfort her. It was Julia who quite naturally went to Marcella's side and wrapped her into a hug.

"He said *her* name," Marcella whispered. "Agrippa said *her* name, and then he found his pleasure. Grunting and calling her name as he . . ."

And then I knew. He'd said Lady Octavia's name. Something beneath my stomach fell away at the awfulness of it. No wonder Marcella couldn't bring herself to tell her mother what was wrong.

"That's perfectly terrible," Julia said.

"It's perfectly *humiliating*," Marcella cried. "How can I tell anyone? How can I go back to Agrippa's house?"

"You know," Julia said, her eyes lighting up with sudden mischief. "You can hold this over Agrippa's head. He was likely too drunk to even remember what he said last night. You could embellish the incident to make him ashamed. Why, you could even claim it was my father's name that he called out in bed. Octavia becomes Octavian. It's only one letter off."

"Julia!" Marcella and I cried in unison.

But the emperor's daughter wasn't the least bit chastened. "Agrippa won't want *that* story repeated, and to keep your silence he'll likely give you anything you want."

"Julia!" we both cried again.

She only shrugged. "If I were Marcella I'd make a list of all the things I wanted, knowing full well that Agrippa won't say no."

I thought this was a spectacularly bad idea, but it made Marcella laugh through her tears, so I helped find a wax tablet for her to start writing.

"No more sewing and weaving for Marcella!" Julia declared, putting a request for a seamstress at the top of the list, and the three of us laughed. It was hard not to like Julia when she was like this, openheartedly instigating rebellion that she could only enjoy vicariously. For a moment, she'd made me laugh—earnestly laugh—and I hadn't thought that possible ever again.

Sixteen

LATER that morning, we were guests at the wedding breakfast at Agrippa's villa on the Palatine. In the hours since Marcella had run away, she'd managed to wash her face, fix her hair, and return to her husband's home. Married women wore shawls called *pallas* over their shoulders, for modesty, and Marcella seemed to use hers to remind herself that she was now a woman grown. Squaring her shoulders, she directed the slaves and did a fair impression of her mother as hostess. It was actually Agrippa, with bags under his eyes and bloated cheeks, who looked green and ready to bolt for the door.

Agrippa's villa devoted an entire wall to engraved gemstones, and I stood to admire the sparkling stones while the other guests arrived. "You have an eye for expensive things," the emperor said, coming up behind me. "Do you like them?"

I nodded my head, remembering that my parents had collected these carved stones too. "Were these my mother's?"

"No," he said. "I have hers in my study, in the Syracuse. I like to keep her things near."

There was something about the way he said it that made me look up at him. Something about the way he always spoke of my mother, as if contempt and fascination had coiled together for him like twin snakes of a *ureaus*. As if her death had made her that much stronger an influence over him. "Sometimes I cannot fathom how much you remind me of her," he said. "Your face isn't the same. Nor your hair. Nor your skin. But somehow . . . my sister is right. Cleopatra is in your every gesture . . ."

I couldn't tell if this was meant to frighten me, but it did. The moment Maecenas arrived with his wife, Terentilla, she began fawning over the emperor and I used the opportunity to slip away to my seat.

"Did you enjoy the wedding, Selene?" Juba asked, sitting together with Helios and me. "Don't tell Marcella, but I think you'll make an even more beautiful bride."

This made me flush and I took a bite of leftover wedding cake to hide my flattered expression. Then Helios whispered to me, "This was our father's house."

The cake went sour in my mouth. "Here?"

"Marcellus told me," Helios explained. "This used to be our father's house, but after Actium, the emperor gave it to Agrippa as a gift."

I let my eyes follow the intricate design to the balcony that overlooked the Palatine. I noticed the gilded handles on the doors and the engraved gemstone collection on the far wall. I could almost imagine my father here in this room. His laughter would have boomed off the walls and I imagined its faint echo. And yet, instead of making me smile, it filled me with melancholy. My mother may have known what was going to happen to her and risked our lives anyway—her accursed bracelet was testament to that—but I felt certain that my father always thought he'd return. Perhaps to this very banquet room. Maybe some part of him *was* here. I felt the sudden urge to touch the mosaic floors, the bronze-banded doors and the painted walls, as if I might somehow reach through time to my father and his comforting arms.

"It's wrong that Agrippa should live here," Helios said, keeping his voice low.

It *was* wrong, but there was nothing we could do about it. Meanwhile, as the guests cloistered together around the banquet tables, the emperor looked as if he'd set things to order according to some master plan. Raising his wine goblet in toast to the couple, the emperor announced, "*Feliciter!* This is a good day for the happy couple, and for me. I've purged the Senate of undesirables, and those senators who remain have voted me new honors. Amongst them, a new title, suggested by General Plancus."

At his name, Plancus stood and announced, "To our first amongst equals . . . to our first citizen . . . to the new *Augustus*."

Augustus. It was a strange title, carrying with it neither lawful authority or regal connotation. In fact, it was more religious in nature, as if he'd somehow become a sacred person. Octavian, a holy man? My father would have laughed in mockery if he were here, but my father was dead and the men who had betrayed him were making toasts here in his old banquet hall.

"To Augustus!" Agrippa said and all the guests repeated it.

And Augustus seemed pleased. "Not only do I add a new title to my honors, but I will now have Agrippa as my nephew-in-law in Rome to watch over things while I'm gone."

"Gone?" Livia asked, her cheeks pink.

"To fight the Cantabri in Spain," he replied. "The mountain tribes are in rebellion, and it's time that I made a conquest of my own."

I bit my lip. It couldn't have been Helios's barb alone that worked its way under the emperor's skin, but I remembered well how my brother had taunted the emperor about letting Agrippa do all his fighting for him.

"I'll be taking Juba with me as he's almost as skilled a soldier as he is a scholar," the emperor continued, and Juba nodded his head in gracious acknowledgment of the compliment. I looked at him as if for the first time. How had I never known that there was a warrior in him?

"You've fought in the legions?" I asked.

"Not exactly," Juba replied. "But I'm a cavalryman."

The Numidians were famed for their horsemanship and I had seen Juba ride before, so I should have put this together, but before I learned more the emperor announced, "Also, the older boys of the family need military experience, so I'll be taking Iullus, Marcellus, and Tiberius with me to serve in the legions."

Iullus puffed with pride as the other two boys looked up with surprise. Marcellus had been sitting close to Virgil, and now the poet reached out an affectionate hand to reassure him, even as his mother paled.

Livia kept silent, her lips thinning as she considered tall, broody Tiberius. But Octavia couldn't be still. "The tribesmen in Spain are brutal savages! At least Iullus is fifteen, but Marcellus and Tiberius are only fourteen years old. They haven't even donned the *toga virilis* of manhood yet."

"We'll remedy that shortly," the emperor said. "Besides, the boys are nearly the age I was when my father, the Divine Julius, called me to serve with him in Spain—"

"You were too young at that," Octavia broke in. "You never did serve because you were a frail boy who nearly died en route, and my son—"

The emperor silenced his sister with a dark look of warning. "And your son may one day marry Julia and rule the Roman Empire in my place . . . or don't you want that?"

Octavia flinched. I saw maternal worry clash with all her hopes and dreams for her son. Had my mother looked that way when she risked all by claiming Caesarion's rights as Julius Caesar's heir? My mother had raised three sons, but Octavia had only one. Marcellus was everything to her, so she said, "Of course I do. He should rule this Republic."

"Then Marcellus needs to experience war," the emperor said.

"I think it's a marvelous idea," Livia finally added. "You'll find Tiberius to be a quick study in the field, and if Marcellus is too frail to serve you, *my* son is hale and hearty."

Octavia slammed down her goblet. "Marcellus isn't frail. He's sensitive but not frail."

Livia seemed to enjoy having tweaked Octavia in this way. "Once things are settled I'd like to join you in Spain, husband. I know you suffer so when you're away from home and no one could tend to your needs the way I can."

"It's settled, then," the emperor said, looking tremendously smug. He wasn't the only one. Helios was sitting beside me, an expression on his face that I could read plain as day. If the emperor, Livia, Marcellus, Juba, Iullus, and Tiberius would all be away in Spain, it'd be that much easier for us to escape.

WINTER thawed into spring and the next weeks were filled with my brother's schemes. "A week from now, the *Navigium Isidis* will be celebrated," Helios told me as we peered down at the city from the height of the Palatine Hill. "There'll be a great procession through the streets. The priestesses will be carrying flowers and the initiates will make offerings to the ship that they plan to let loose for the goddess."

Huddling against the cold in my wool cloak, I pressed against the gate, trying to imagine the parade. "And you think the new *Augustus* will just let us take part in an Isiac festival? You're mad."

"He won't let us, no," Helios said. "But the slaves will go. I've heard them talking about it. There are tunnels they use to come and go, and with all the construction we might not be noticed if we went with Chryssa. Then all we need to do is make our way into the crowd and let ourselves be swept along. Soon after that we can exchange clothing with initiates and when the priestesses are pouring out milk libations and filling the ship with spices, we can ask the worshippers about Euphronius."

"And what if he's not here?" I asked. "What if Euphronius has gone back to Egypt?"

"Then we'll board the ship that they dedicate to Isis. They'll cut her free of the moorings and let her loose down the Tiber. I can sail a ship. I know I can."

"By yourself?" I asked, blinking at his desperation. Finding Euphronius was risky, but it had a certain amount of sense to it. Sneaking aboard a sacrificial ship and using it to sail away was foolhardy. And I told him so.

My twin's hands tightened on the iron bars that separated the imperial compound from the rest of the world. "Do you want to stay here? Do you want to become some Roman girl and be married off like Marcella? It's Juba's influence on you," Helios accused. "Ever since your talk with him, you've been different."

But he was wrong. It wasn't Juba who had changed me—not *just* Juba anyway. It was our mother's bracelet. It was that coiled serpent that slept beneath my bed, reminding me every night how I had killed my mother, and how she had known that I would. It was my burning resentment for her and my determination that we shouldn't share her fate that made me hesitate. And what if Juba was right anyway? What if we could return to Egypt and rule it for Rome, just as my mother had ruled Egypt for Julius Caesar? "I'm going inside," I announced and didn't see Helios again until the next morning.

We were sitting together eating porridge when Lady Octavia glanced at us, and seemed to know us at once for the guilty conspirators we were. I couldn't guess if some spy had reported back our whisperings or if she simply had a preternatural sense for intrigue, but I'd barely finished eating when she informed us that we'd be leaving Rome at once.

"Leaving?" Helios asked, the color draining from his face. "But why?"

"Marcella needs time to adjust to being a married woman," Octavia said. "I can't have her running back to cling to me whenever Agrippa says a cross word. Besides, Augustus needs time to plan his new glorious conquest. While the men concentrate on military matters, they don't need women and children about. We'll spend some time at Livia's country estate. It will be good for you children to be in fresher air."

I hadn't liked Rome, and not only because I was being held there against my will. The dark alleyways, the teetering buildings, and the sour scent of the Tiber River hadn't endeared the city to me. Moreover, I didn't like to remember that my mother had been here, seen her fate, and carried on. But this new journey filled me with foreboding. In the country, we might be isolated. Easier to murder in our beds and make up a convenient excuse to tell anyone who might still care about what happened to the children of Antony.

I fought back my fear long enough to ask, "But what about our studies?"

"We'll hire new tutors," Octavia chirped, warming to the subject. "Think of the brilliant scholars who will all want to teach the emperor's family. We'll bring Julia too, and the younger boys. Now get to your rooms and help the slaves pack your things. I want to leave at once."

The color in Helios's face now came rushing back again. We both knew that we couldn't escape during the *Navigium Isidis* if we weren't even in the city, and Octavia's sudden announcement had given us no opportunity to formulate an alternate plan. I feared that Helios might sweep everything off the tables in a rage. Somehow, he steadied himself long enough to stand and storm away, and I chased after him down the corridor to our rooms.

"It only means that we must wait a little longer to find Euphronius," I told him.

Helios didn't even answer me. He brushed past Philadelphus and threw open the door to his room where Chryssa was already at work, collecting his things and putting them into a traveling chest.

"Where is Livia's villa?" Helios asked her. "How far is it?"

"Six miles from Rome," the slave girl answered. "No more than that."

It might as well have been across the sea.

"Are there any temples near Livia's villa?" Helios asked. "Any altars? Anywhere we could meet with Euphronius in safety?"

"Euphronius?" Philadelphus asked, his eyes wide. "He's here in Rome?"

"Hush," I told him, not wanting to explain, and not wanting to involve him in my twin's scheme.

"There's nowhere to meet him there," Chryssa said. "Nowhere to worship Isis either. Livia's estate is well guarded and isolated."

At hearing this, Helios bunched his golden hair in his fist. I wanted to say something to him. I wanted to find the words to comfort him, but his mood was as dark as mine had been the day Virgil gave us our mother's bracelet. There was nothing we could do, and even Helios knew it. Once we'd been packed off in the carriage with the rest of the children, his anger smoldered dark as soot. He couldn't even be comforted by Bast, who kneaded gently upon his lap as we rolled along the Via Flaminia, away from Rome.

LIVIA'S country estate overlooked the Tiber valley and had a magnificent view of the sloping Italian hills. She called it *Ad Gallinas Albas*, after the white hens that populated the place. She told us that on the day of her marriage to the emperor, an eagle dropped a white hen into her lap with a sprig of laurel. As a young wife, she then planted the laurel and used branches of its leaves for the emperor's wreath during his Triumph.

Even if I'd believed her story, I couldn't hate the magnificent laurel groves that encircled the villa and lent it a sweet bay perfume. I was unexpectedly charmed by the place. I'd been a city dweller, first in Alexandria and then in Rome. Here we seemed entirely apart from the rest of the world. The gardens featured fruit trees, every hedge thrived with herbs. Even though imperious columns hovered over the pool like hulking guards and everything was designed with the exacting lines the Romans preferred, Livia's villa still felt less like a prison than did the houses on the Palatine, and my fears about it being an out-of-the-way place in which to murder us began to subside—especially when I learned I was to share a room with Julia.

Our beds were inlaid with shells, and Julia and I each had our own elaborate dressing tables. Gilded braziers heated the room, each of them shaped like a sheaf of wheat. The mosaic floor was covered in a thick woven carpet of crimson and gold, and it was more luxurious than anything I'd seen in Rome. "If you like this, you will love the palace in Capri," Julia said. "It's only in Rome that everyone watches and wants us to be humble."

Before we unpacked, Julia and I explored every nook and cranny of our new apartment, including the ivory-trimmed wardrobe filled with old-fashioned garments handed down by *Julii* women, which we took turns trying on. I was grateful that the emperor's daughter was so absorbed with her image in the mirror that she didn't notice me slip my mother's serpent bracelet— wrapped carefully in my old bloody dress—under the mattress. I buried it, like I buried my own discontent. I'd been angry since my mother's death, but I'd blamed all my troubles on the Romans. Now I blamed my mother too.

I wondered which of the things the emperor said about my parents might be true. Sometimes, in the darkness, I even wondered how Isis could have loved us and let all this come to pass.

When the weather warmed, our days were spent chasing after Bast to keep her from hunting the white hens. Since Livia wouldn't

join the emperor in Spain until much later, she made sure we were
also given chores to do. It didn't matter that our childish efforts
were often more of a hindrance to the slaves than a help—Octavia's
girls were put to work in the gardens tending the fruit trees, the
boys collected eggs and tended the barn animals, and perversely, it
was Julia's task to milk the goats. Meanwhile, I was to spend most
of the day in the house helping the kitchen slaves.

Since the night of the Saturnalia, when I discovered Livia
caressing the cheek of the senator's daughter, she seemed to single
me out for unpleasant tasks. But if Livia thought to exile me to a
life of kitchen drudgery, she misunderstood my nature. For me,
the scents of the kitchen were like magic—a safe kind of magic,
which I could enjoy without reproach. Over the smoke of the
hearth, as the slaves brewed up porridge, I cherished the earthy
scent. In the mornings, I loved to make rose-honey, squeezing
petals in a press and extracting the sweet perfume. At dinnertime,
I loved to grind tart sumac for the stew. Try as I might to forget
Egypt, my fingers always formed our olive oil cakes into the shape
of pyramids. Sometimes I packed these cakes into leather satchels
so that we could take our lunch in the hills.

While the emperor planned his campaign and the rest of us
lived in exile, the mirror showed changes. Green eyes still dominated my face, but my lips were fuller and more distinct. I wished
that I was as adorable as Julia with her dimples and upturned
nose, but my face had the grave look of a temple statue, long and
regal. I worried too that Julia's form was still boyish, while my
hips were curving and my breasts growing round.

It was at Livia's country villa that I first began to bleed—not
in carved messages from Isis, but with the blood of womanhood.
I knew it meant that I would now be able to bear children. What
frightened me was the thought that the emperor would marry me
off to make babies for some dour old senator. So I told no one of
my monthly flow and buried the bloody rags behind the house

before my morning chores. I also bound my breasts so that the Romans might not yet know me for a woman.

Here in the country, I wasn't the only one to get lost in the chores of daily life. Philadelphus enjoyed feeding the birds in the poultry yard—especially the peacocks with the iridescent feathers that reminded me so much of home. With his auburn hair and apple cheeks, Philadelphus fit in with the imperial family more easily than Helios or I did, for he had an easygoing nature. When I watched him playing with the Antonias, I wondered if my littlest brother would forget that we were once Egyptian royalty. I envied him and wondered if I too could forget.

But Helios didn't forget. He busied himself sketching ships—his mind always on the sea that separated us from Egypt.

WHEN at last the emperor and his entourage left for Spain, I began to wonder if my brothers and I were being kept in the countryside precisely because he suspected we might run. Helios must have realized it too, because I often found him pacing in front of the marbled balustrade of the terrace like a caged animal paces behind bars. His eyes were often in the direction of Rome, where he imagined Euphronius might be, waiting to liberate us.

For my part, I wasn't so sure.

"Why don't you come inside," Octavia said to us one afternoon. "It smells like rain. Besides, Virgil is visiting. He's grown quite fond of Marcellus and knows how much I worry for my boy, so he's come to entertain us. Isn't that kind of him? You know the story of Rome's founding, don't you?"

"Romulus and Remus," I said as we followed her inside. "Two wolf-nursed brothers who fought to the death to see which would rule Rome."

"That's right!" she said proudly, and I could do nothing but shake my head at her. Egypt too had her story of fratricide, when

Set murdered Osiris—but in Egypt, Set was loathed as the dark god of chaos. In Rome, the murderer was revered.

With the older boys gone, the good-natured, clownish behavior of Livia's youngest son, Drusus, came to the fore. He was throwing dice with Philadelphus when we came into the library. "Ah, the *children* are here," he said in the exact tone the emperor always used, mimicking his stepfather. Helios rolled his eyes, and I stifled a laugh just as Octavia sailed into the room with our poet in tow.

A slave started a fire in the brazier, for it had, indeed, begun to storm outside, and Virgil began to speak.

Virgil called his new work the *Aeneid*. It was not about Romulus and Remus, after all, and it began:

> *"Arms, and the man I sing, who, forced by fate,*
> *And haughty Juno's unrelenting hate,*
> *Expelled and exiled, left the Trojan shore.*
> *Long labors, both by sea and land, he bore,*
> *And in the doubtful war, before he won*
> *The Latian realm, and built the destined town*
> *From whence the race of Alban fathers come,*
> *And the long glories of majestic Rome."*

Perhaps no one in the room was more enthralled than Philadelphus, who sat forward on his couch, straining for every word. But as the poet read, I didn't like what I heard. Virgil's Aeneas was an upright warrior who was tempted from his true Roman destiny by a seductive queen; I couldn't help but think Virgil was commenting upon my parents. Worse—much worse by far—was the denigration of our beliefs, all the passages mocking Anubis and setting the gods of Egypt against the gods of Rome. Then his poem went on to glorify the emperor, implying that Octavian would bring about a Golden Age!

I tried not to show my open displeasure, but on the couch next to me, Helios folded his arms and stared into the crackling fire. I heard my twin grumble, close to my ear, and the flames seemed to rise and fall with his breath, flashing brighter the angrier my twin became.

Afterward, when all the others had gone to supper, I lingered, helping Virgil roll up his scrolls. "Ah, Selene, you didn't like my poem?"

"I prefer your other works—at least, the ones the emperor gave me. I'd like to read your missing Fourth Eclogue, though."

"You have quite a memory," Virgil said, his thick fingers pushing through his dark hair. "Won't you let this matter go? The Fourth Eclogue has been banned by orders of Augustus."

I was astonished, for Virgil was the emperor's favorite. "Why would he ban your poetry?"

Virgil watched me carefully, as if to test me for what I knew. "The Fourth Eclogue is just a flight of fancy I once had, brought on by too much wine. Those were strange days, when prophecies ran rampant. Even before your mother's influence was at its zenith, the world was on the cusp of transformation."

"What kind of transformation?"

"Slave revolts. Land ownership reforms. The start of giving citizenship to people outside Rome. Ptolemy women vying for power and wielding it without reserve. Roman women led by Hortensia protested in the Forum, agitating for justice. Your father put Fulvia's face on coins and though she was just a woman, she led a military revolt without him. And then came your mother . . . The Sibylline Books warned against a woman like her. Do you know of Rome's most ancient books of prophecy?"

"I only know that they warned if an Egyptian king came to Rome in need, you should turn him away, but when my grandfather came begging for help, he received it. No one seemed too scared of the prophecies then."

"People have a way of interpreting the prophecies the way they want," Virgil allowed. "The Sibylline Books said that a woman would rule and there would be fiery destruction in Rome, but then there'd be a time of reconciliation and *harmony*. A Golden Age."

I drew my feet up under me on the couch since Octavia wasn't here to scold me for it. "And that's what you wrote about in your poems? You foresaw the same?"

"I saw an eclipse that heralded a new age. I foresaw that Antony's progeny would bring about a Golden Age. That's not something the emperor wants known, so the poetry has been banned."

I was mesmerized. "There was an eclipse near my birth . . ."

"Yes, but you weren't the child of Antony I was thinking of. I thought it'd be Lady Octavia's son—that child combining the blood of Antony and Octavian, ending our civil wars at last."

I frowned. "But my father had no sons with Lady Octavia."

"Alas," Virgil said quietly, "had she given Antony a son, he might not have gone back to your mother and there'd have been no war."

This I refused to believe, for my father was a different kind of Roman. "He didn't *need* more sons. He had two Roman sons already—Antyllus and Iullus. And he had Helios! Your prophecy was wrong."

"I've told you it was wrong," Virgil said gently. "You see?"

I narrowed my eyes. "But if your prophecy was so wrong, then why should the emperor want to ban it?"

"He's banned everything that might encourage the people to latch on to you or Helios as a savior. Not just my poem. He intends to seize the Sibylline Books themselves and safeguard them in his new Temple of Apollo."

How curious I suddenly was to know what else the Sibylline Books said. "Then what's all this talk about a golden child in the *Aeneid*? Are you talking about the emperor? Are you predicting Marcellus will be his heir?"

"Selene, I'm the closest thing that the Romans have to a mystic, and prophecy is tricky business. It is like scrying the—"

"Rivers of Time?" I asked, remembering it the way Euphronius taught us.

"Yes, exactly like that. You can see streams of all possible futures, but it's hard to predict which one this world will follow. When your mother asked me to give you that bracelet, I think she was seeing one of *all* her possible futures. She was better at it than I, and when I tried, I upset the emperor. That's also why you and your brother must put it out of your minds."

"What about the poem you're writing now? In this *Aeneid*, you make it seem as if you're seeing into the future and that the emperor is a savior and Rome's way is the only way. Were my parents really the bad people you portray? Is the emperor right?"

"My dear," Virgil said ruefully. "A poet has to eat."

SUMMER swept over the peninsula fetid and hot. Even the laurel trees around the villa wilted beneath the sun. To escape the heat, we normally studied in an underground room which boasted bright garden frescoes on the wall, but since Juba was away on campaign with the emperor and the older boys, we spent the day at play.

Drusus and Philadelphus threw a ball on the marbled terrace while Julia and I splashed them with the crystalline waters of the pool. "Do it again and I'll drown you," my little brother threatened. He was teasing, of course. Even so, it was a challenge we couldn't resist. We continued to douse him, flinging white ribbons of water through the air until he came running toward us, arms outstretched, knocking us both into the pool with him.

Julia and I came up out of the water shrieking, our careful hairstyles utterly ruined; our sopping clothes clung to us like fur on wet hounds. Then all the children were in the pool as Helios tried to dunk us. Minora squealed with delight, climbing on Philadelphus's back and all of us—even Helios and dour Antonia— swam and splashed and laughed until our sides hurt.

It was during this rare moment of levity that Livia came sweeping in, her eyes red, her hair wild, and her *palla* trailing the ground behind her like a funeral shroud. "Gods of Olympus, what is there to laugh about on a day like this? You little ingrates!"

"Mother, are you all right?" Drusus asked, instantly sobered.

He climbed out of the pool to go toward her, but she slapped him away. "Don't drip on me. You and your brother are of no use to me now."

None of us knew what had caused Livia's sudden outburst and she disappeared into the house before we could ask. Behind her, slaves and messengers filed in, nervous as cats. Then one of them whispered the news, eyes low, "Augustus is dying."

WAS the emperor wounded? Had he been hurt in the campaign in Spain? Or was it a fever, as the slaves suggested? We had a thousand questions, but no one to answer them. As Livia fled to her chambers, Lady Octavia took command of the household and ordered us to our rooms. I'd just started into the house when we heard one of the hens make a ghastly sound in the poultry yard.

Octavia snapped, "Selene, go fetch that wretched cat of yours. It's not bad enough the lot of you are sopping wet. If Bast kills one of Livia's hens, she'll flay you." Given Octavia's mood, I didn't stop to argue, but instead obediently started down the lane toward the coop. I tried to keep my wet clothes from dragging in the dirt as I rounded the barn and saw Bast, crouched in hunting position.

"Bad kitty!" I cried, clapping my hands together. Chastened, Bast slunk under the fence and began to lick her spotted fur as if this had been her plan all along. I stooped to take her into my arms, but she slipped away from me, running a few steps toward the road, her tail twitching violently. Frustrated, I called to Bast again. I knew she heard me because one ear rotated in my direction, but infuriatingly, she trotted away from the villa.

"You'll never catch her," one of the guards said, all but dozing in

the heat of his lazy country post. If he was alarmed at the news of
the emperor's ill health, he didn't show it and simply waved me after
the cat. Gathering my wet skirts in my hand, I chased Bast down
the hillside. There wasn't usually much traffic in these parts, but
owing to the news about the emperor, there were messengers and
wagons aplenty, and our cat ran right between the wagon wheels.

My heart jumped to my throat. "Bast!"

But when she leapt to safety in the tall grasses, my worry was
replaced with irritation. It would be hard to find her and the
adults in the house were already upset; if I tarried too long, Octavia would be wroth. With the sun beating down on me, I pushed
through weeds and brambles, some of them snagging my clothes.
Then I saw Bast stop, her whiskers stiff, her mouth open to the air,
scenting the breeze. Unthinking, I did the same, and caught the
unmistakable metallic notes of dark magic in the air.

That's when both of us saw the vagabond hidden beneath the
canopy of an acacia tree, asleep in the summer sun. I was wary
of the stranger, whose face was obscured beneath the folds of a
surprisingly white cowl, but Bast approached him with increasing
confidence and nuzzled his hand. The stranger came awake at
Bast's affection, and invited her into his lap. "Could you hold her
for me, please?" I said, catching up. "I've come to fetch her home."

"As I've come to fetch you," the man said to me in Egyptian,
turning to face me with a smile. "Child of Isis."

I had to stifle my cry when I recognized him. "Euphronius!"

I didn't wait for him to rise but went to my knees in a most
undignified fashion and threw my arms around him. He smelled
of sand and magic, of salt and the sea, of swords and the forge. He
smelled of home. "We've missed you," I said, my eyes brimming
with tears. "We've missed you so much."

"And I you," Euphronius said. "It's been difficult to get word
to you."

"Have you been sending the bloody messages to me, the ones
on my arms?"

He shook his head. "That's the doing of Isis. It's a miraculous thing, and not your only power."

"It isn't a *power*. It comes to me unbidden. I can't work *heka* and the Romans would forbid it even if I could."

"Oh, you *can* work *heka*, you just haven't learned how," the wizard said, turning my arms over to inspect the pale undersides.

"There aren't any scars," I explained. "The hieroglyphics vanish. The marks are gone."

"Except for this one," he said, tracing a birthmark just below the inside of my elbow. "You were born with this. Don't you recognize the symbol?"

I didn't. It looked like a darkened patch of skin, a cluster of freckles perhaps, but as he continued to trace lines between them, I saw his meaning. "The hieroglyphic of a sail? The sign for wind?"

Before Euphronius could explain, we both heard rustling in the grasses and I trembled at the thought of Roman guards finding us. Then I realized it was just the breeze. "They'll be looking for me soon. What should we do?"

I felt like a little girl again at my lessons.

Euphronius whispered, "Before dawn, you and your brothers must escape the house and find your way back to this tree."

My mouth ran dry in contemplation. I'd come to this tree by happenstance and had already been gone long enough to tempt Octavia to beat me. I couldn't imagine how we might sneak out of the villa, past the guards, and somehow find this tree again in the dark. I just wanted Euphronius to wave his divination staff and use his magic to make everything better. "Can't you just use your magic to bring my brothers here now?"

Euphronius smiled softly. "I'm not as great a magician as that, and even if I were, I used most of my *heka* to make your guards sleepy and to lure you to me. I can perhaps guide you with a bright moon this night, but you must find the courage to escape."

"Then what?" I asked, tucking tendrils of damp hair behind my ears.

"We'll run," Euphronius said. "It's only six miles to Rome, and with the emperor dying, the city will be in chaos. From Rome, we'll make our way to Ostia. If Marcellus is Octavian's heir, the boy will have more to contend with than a search for missing Ptolemies."

My stomach churned. "What if the emperor doesn't die?"

Given the furrow of Euphronius's brow, it was perhaps a question he wasn't expecting. "If we're in a River of Time where the emperor does *not* die in Spain . . . things will be more dangerous."

"Where would we go? Back to Egypt?" I asked.

"If we can raise an army in Egypt to fight for you," Euphronius said. "Otherwise we must make our way East and beg the help of your mother's old allies."

I could hear my own breath slow. "Like Caesarion was to do?"

The old wizard narrowed his eyes, seeing that I'd learned much since we'd parted, then nodded his head sadly. "I'm so sorry about your brother, Selene. Caesarion was to seek refuge in India—he didn't make it there."

He didn't make it to India because the emperor had him hunted down and killed. Even if Caesarion *had* made it, he would have been a wealthy king in exile, but Helios and I were penniless and had not even been crowned. We'd be fugitives, tempting prizes for an Eastern ruler like King Herod to offer to Rome in exchange for favor. Euphronius sensed my discontent. "You must be brave, Selene, and trust in Isis."

I wet my lips nervously. "Does Isis protect us?"

"Of course," he said. "You're sacred to her."

"Wasn't my mother also sacred to her?" Euphronius sputtered at my question, his hands knotting at his side, so I told him, "Virgil gave me her snake bracelet. I know my mother saw her own end . . ."

He didn't seem surprised. "Still, your mother tried to steer our River of Time to its best course, as you must do."

"Euphronius," I said, very seriously. "When you look into your

Rivers of Time, does Isis save my brothers and me from every harm?"

"No, child." Our old wizard stroked my wet hair with a liberty he would never have taken in Egypt, and I saw the lines of his face had grown deeper since my mother's death. "But many times, you save Isis."

What could he mean? Bast's ears perked up and this time I knew it was not just the wind. Someone was coming. "I have to go," I whispered.

"I'll be here," Euphronius said, "Waiting for you until dawn. You and your brothers must come to me, Selene. There won't be another chance such as this one."

I kissed him—my pink lips against the weathered skin of his cheek. Then I scooped up Bast and rushed back toward the road where a sullen guard was cutting a path through the grasses with his sword. "Damned cat," the guard said when he saw me. "And look at you, all full of nettles."

Not daring to look over my shoulder at our wizard hidden in the grass, I followed the man back to the villa, clutching Bast against my chest. She gave her nervous purr and her heart beat only a little faster than my own.

It was a testament to Octavia's upset over the news of her brother that she didn't have me beaten when I appeared before her, bedraggled and clutching the cat. Instead, the emperor's sister sniffled into her kerchief, and it was clear she'd been crying. "I should never have let you keep that creature for a pet. Go to your room without supper and I don't want to see you until morning."

IT was just as well that I'd been forbidden supper, because I was too nervous to eat. Once I changed into dry clothes, I paced beside the window of the room I shared with Julia, staring out at the sun as it lowered in the horizon. Each dip brought me closer to the predawn escape that I must somehow engineer.

"Will you sit still?" Julia asked. "And what's wrong with your arm? Why do you keep worrying at it?"

Without realizing it, I'd been touching the birthmark on my inner arm, the one Euphronius had traced. "It's just stinging nettle or something," I said, wishing fervently that the emperor's daughter would absent herself so I could plot and plan. Had we been in Rome, I'd have been alone in my room. I could've removed the loose brick from the wall and told my brothers everything in whispers. But with Julia as a roommate, how could I tell them Euphronius's scheme?

"I don't see why *you're* so nervous," Julia said, flopping dramatically upon my bed. "It's *my* father they say is dying."

"Perhaps you should visit the household shrine," I said, but regretted it instantly. I could see from her expression that Julia was genuinely grieved by the possibility of losing her father. I felt selfish and small for trying only to be rid of her.

Julia sighed. "What good would that do? I don't think gods listen to girls . . . but I have heard the slaves. They think Isis listens even to them. Is that true? If your father were ill, what would you do?"

"I'd pray to Isis," I said, remembering how my mother had asked us to do just that when my father contemplated his suicide.

"In her temple?" Julia asked, trying to draw me to sit beside her. "What kind of ritual offering would you have her priests make for you?"

"You can pray to Isis anywhere and she doesn't require offerings." This wasn't the Roman way, I knew. More often, they treated gods like faraway rulers, sending ambassadors and gifts. Worship, for them, was a matter of proper ritual and behavior. It had nothing to do with personal faith—a concept that sounded to them more like philosophy than religion. So it surprised me when Julia looked at me very earnestly and asked, "Will you pray with me for my father's life?"

Oh, Isis, how you tested me that day! I sat down on the bed

near Julia, drawing my bare feet up under the linen and trying desperately not to meet her eyes. Isis taught us to show mercy and have goodwill in our hearts, but how could I pray for the emperor when his death was the only possible thing that could free me? I could neither ignore nor rejoice in the pain I saw in Julia's eyes. I'd lost both a mother and a father—I knew how lonely it was, and I couldn't find it within myself to wish such pain upon the only girl who had ever been my friend.

"I want to learn about your faith in Isis," Julia said, her fingers twined with mine. "Teach me to pray."

Outside the sun dropped below the horizon, and I felt the blackness of night enter my soul. A lump rose in my throat. What would Isis have me do? Why didn't I know? If Isis dwelt in me, if I carried her words, why was I denied communion with my goddess? "I-I can't," I stammered.

Julia sucked her rosebud lips inward, then let out a little cry. "Because you hate my father! You *want* him to die."

I'd read the words of Isis upon my own skin, and they'd only told me to live, love, and learn. They hadn't commanded me to hate or even to wish for the emperor's death. They hadn't commanded me to run away in the night with our wizard. Moreover, they hadn't commanded me to raise an army to fight the Romans.

"No," I said, despair forcing the breath out of me. "I can't pray with you because Isis can't help your father!"

The bitter pain of it burst like a boil in my heart. Isis hadn't protected my parents. She hadn't protected my brothers Caesarion and Antyllus. She hadn't even been able to protect Egypt. Her priest Euphronius was hidden beyond this villa in the grasses, waiting for me, and he'd said that Isis couldn't protect us from all harm. Perhaps Isis could save no one at all. No different from those little stone statues of household gods who never really listened to little girls, or anyone else.

"Then no one can help me," Julia finally said. "If my father dies, what will become of me?"

I had no answer for her.

"I shouldn't care," she said. "My father wouldn't care, if *I* were the one dying."

"That's not true. He does care for you," I said, though I'd never seen any warmth between the two.

"No, he doesn't. He divorced my mother the day I was born. He waited just long enough to snatch me away from her. Then he rushed off to marry Livia and all her noble Claudian connections. I'm only a tool for him."

"Your father is just a distant man," I told her.

"But if he dies . . ." Then she put both hands over her face. "What if there's been some battle and the boys are hurt too?" Tiberius was her stepbrother and Marcellus was her good-tempered cousin, so it seemed natural to me that she'd be afraid for them. But it surprised me when she said, "Iullus. What if Iullus is dying too?"

My Roman half brother was still a stranger to me, a brooding teenager with a sardonic wit. I'd noticed how he'd pampered and flattered Julia and always assumed it was just one of the many things he did to please the emperor. But Julia's fondness for him wasn't feigned. "I'm sure the messengers would've said something." That's all the comfort I could offer.

When darkness finally fell, I lay on my bed listening to Julia's breathing. As the crickets chirped outside the window and the moon rose in the sky, I thought that Euphronius might as well have asked me to simply swim my way back to Egypt—and I wondered if such an ocean crossing wouldn't have been less dangerous.

Tossing and turning in my bed, I wondered if I was made of the stuff of the Ptolemies. My own mother had smuggled herself to Caesar through enemy lines wrapped in bed linens, or a carpet, some said. She'd gambled with her life. It was foolhardy, it was reckless, and it was marvelous. That was my legacy, but I couldn't live up to it. I could scheme and manipulate, but I couldn't seem to throw the dice and let them fly high.

My mother had relied on magic and defiance, even knowing how it would end. I refused to share her fate. I wanted to live a long life with what remained of my family. I thought about Juba's words to me and how, through the emperor, perhaps I could regain some of what had been lost to us. Thriving under a Roman banner seemed a surer path back to Egypt than the one Euphronius promised. Helios would consider such thoughts treason and perhaps he was right. Perhaps I was already becoming one of them, becoming Roman. Lost to Egypt. Lost to Isis.

I didn't care.

I wouldn't go to Euphronius. I couldn't save Isis; I could only save myself. And if that was true, then I wasn't the Resurrection, after all.

Realizing it was the death of some part of my soul—though I couldn't name which one—I took the frog amulet from my neck and rolled the delicate jade carving between my fingers. In the dark, I let the inscription scratch along my fingertips one last time, then slipped it under the mattress with my mother's coiled bracelet and the soiled dress, all these things that must now be in my past.

Seventeen

IN my River of Time, Augustus did not die in Spain. While his armies fought in the cold mountains without him, he retreated to the fortified city of Tarraco. Livia took the first opportunity to join him there and cared for him during his convalescence. Meanwhile, the boys returned, riding up the road toward the villa with Juba at the head of their procession. The Numidian princeling rode as if he'd been born on horseback, and seeing him in Roman armor was a startling sight. I knew it would be hard to envision him as only a tutor or even a scholar from now on. I understood as I hadn't before that Juba was as much a trusted lieutenant as Agrippa.

The servants clamored to make ready and we all came rushing out, eager for news. Marcellus, Tiberius, and Iullus were young men now, tempered from war, and prideful in their armor as they dismounted their horses. In an instant, Julia pulled up her skirts and ran toward them, flying past Marcellus and Tiberius to throw herself into Iullus's arms. I watched Iullus as he hugged Julia; he'd grown as tall and handsome as Juba now, but he had a thick neck like our father's and had the makings of a warrior. He wasn't yet broad-shouldered, but he made Tiberius and Marcellus seem like gangly youths beside him.

"Oh, Marcellus, I've been so worried," Octavia gushed at her son. "Were you wounded?"

"Just a scrape," Marcellus said with a sunny grin. "The Cantabri are savages who jump out at you from the forest!"

Octavia looked as if she might faint just imagining it. "I'm so glad you're home. You're my life. You're all my hopes. You're *everything* to me, don't you know that?"

"Don't embarrass him," Tiberius said glumly, though I wondered if it was because Drusus seemed to be the only one glad to see him.

I couldn't contain myself. "Is Augustus . . ."

"He's on his way home, with my mother," Tiberius replied, and he wasn't wrong. When the emperor finally returned to Rome—which had been transformed into a more modern city thanks to Agrippa's building projects and Numidian marble—he claimed to have dealt the Cantabri a decisive defeat. But he never did celebrate a Triumph. Perhaps his illness had made him too weak to drag conquered peoples behind his chariot in chains, or perhaps he knew that more than a few people in Rome had celebrated his death. Restoring himself to power swiftly, he paid large amounts of money to appease the citizens and ensure their loyalty. To ensure stability of the city, he replaced the *tresviri capitales* with an urban cohort and guarded himself and the imperial family with a praetorian guard that was loyal to him and him alone.

It was a testament to the effectiveness of the praetorians that Helios stopped talking about escape. In truth, as the chaos of the emperor's return swirled around us, Helios stopped talking almost entirely. It was as if my sense of malaise and helplessness had infected him too, both of us paralyzed as Augustus efficiently and ruthlessly killed or exiled enemies who had revealed themselves during his health crisis and persecuted Isiacs and friends of my father.

And when Helios wondered aloud if Euphronius was dead, part of the purges, our last hope lost, my tongue swelled with silent deceit inside my mouth. I told myself that I'd made the prudent choice in not running away with Euphronius, but I couldn't tell my brothers that I'd seen him because they would never forgive me. I couldn't tell *anyone*; it was a dark secret held between me and Bast, and I knew I'd lost a great deal in keeping that secret.

In the year that followed, I returned to Rome with the rest of the family and became someone I barely recognized. I didn't pray. I smothered my thoughts of magic. I became accustomed to the noise of Rome. My naturally gregarious nature gave way to introspection and melancholy. I lost my taste for food and cried easily—not only because I was thirteen. It was because my *khaibit*, the shadow soul that held my darkness, now felt bigger than the rest of me.

ONE morning Helios removed the brick. "Selene—"

Since my first menses, I'd been binding my breasts, trying to look the part of a little girl. Helios had startled me, caught me in the middle of dressing, so I spun to shield myself from his eyes. I wasn't sure he'd seen, but embarrassment pricked at my skin. When I finished, I crept beneath my desk to face him and saw that his cheeks were flushed too.

"What were you doing?" Helios asked.

Perhaps if I'd been in Egypt, I would've been straightforward about my body's changes. But we were in Rome and the constant stream of shame had begun to soak into me. "I wasn't doing anything."

An awkward silence passed between us. My hastily fastened gown had come open and Helios was gawking. "Is it a bandage?"

"No," I said quickly. Mortified to see the visible bumps of my nipples beneath the fabric, I wrapped my arms around myself and my stomach tingled with an unfamiliar, sickly sweet sensation. It was pleasant but somehow made me want to run away. Redness crept from Helios's cheeks to the tips of his ears. He opened his mouth as if to say something, but no words came. "What did you want to tell me?" I finally forced myself to ask.

Helios stared as if he wasn't sure what language I was speaking. "I . . . I'm going to the port at Ostia. Agrippa has business there and has offered to take me with him." I was instantly wary of intrigue. What purpose would Agrippa have for taking my brother anywhere, if not to dispose of him? But Helios was enthusiastic. "Agrippa said he'd take me to inspect the ships in the harbor—bigger ones than can come up the Tiber."

"Why would Agrippa take you?" I asked suspiciously.

"He's taking Marcellus, Drusus, and Tiberius too, but he said that Iullus and I could join him, so I'm going."

We might have friends in Rome, old partisans of my father who would make life difficult if the emperor harmed us, but what friends did we have in Ostia? Who would call foul if a boy slipped and fell into the harbor? "I don't want you to go."

"I *have* to go," Helios said. "Ships from Egypt come into Ostia every day. I might hear news from Alexandria or be able to send messages to our people, to let them know that we haven't abandoned them. I may be able to find out what happened to Euphronius."

I wondered what happened to the wizard too. That summer in the country, when morning dawned outside Livia's villa and we hadn't come, had he been angry with me? Had he understood? Or had he given up on us the way I'd given up on Isis?

I stood at the gate, watching the road long after Agrippa and the boys had disappeared from sight until Julia tried to draw me away. "How can you be so glum, Selene? We'll have a whole week without boys to boss us around!"

The anxiety of being separated from Helios was too great for me to laugh. Being apart from Helios, even for a few days, seemed unnatural. You must understand that I'd loved all my brothers. Caesarion, Antyllus, and Philadelphus too. So I knew the deep and sometimes exasperating way a sister loves a brother.

But my connection to Helios was something different. Helios was my twin in this life, but I'd always felt certain he'd been with me before. We came into this world together and had never been separated. We sometimes even shared the same dreams. Perhaps once, in Egypt, when we were little children, we'd only been siblings. But when Caesarion died, Helios and I became something else entirely. He wasn't my brother anymore. Not truly. He was my king. He was my other half. Being without him made me feel as if I'd been cleaved in two, and I told Julia so.

She just sighed at me. "I don't know if I can stand a week of both you and Chryssa brooding just because Helios is gone. I think she's half in love with him. Your brother spoils that slave girl."

She was right, of course. Though Chryssa had been raised to do domestic work for Livia, Helios wasn't the most exacting master and almost never treated her like a slave. Instead, he let Chryssa study with the rest of us. Juba objected, naturally, but the emperor surprised us all by approving of my brother's choice, saying, "Helios is wise to want an educated servant. What other use is there for a Greek slave?"

In truth, Chryssa was a quick wit. She was better with numbers than any of us. But I resented her. Perhaps it was the way she was always at my brother's elbow, her eyes wide with devotion. Even Iullus sometimes remarked on her eager attention to her master and Marcellus would laugh.

I was brought back from these thoughts by Julia yanking on my arm, trying to get me to let go of the gate. "You should feel sorry for the boys gone on a trip while we get to stay here and glory in the sameness of it all. We'll make a game of it. We can try to live yesterday over again today, exactly the same, to avoid bad luck, just like some people did when they fixed the calendar." She started walking backward, laughing all the while.

I wanted to laugh with her; her laugh was lively, vibrant, and warm. Unfortunately she could also be self-absorbed and impatient, so when she saw I couldn't be comforted, she skipped away, leaving me alone.

At long last, I pried myself away from the gate and went looking for Juba. A part of me believed the answers to all that vexed me could be found within a scroll, if only I looked hard enough. Accordingly, I'd been studying every school of philosophical thought from Roman Stoicism to Greek Epicureanism. I studied mathematics and astronomy too. Now I needed something new to distract me.

Juba was in the courtyard; it was early spring, and the sun made his skin glow tawny and tan. "Come join me, Selene! I was thinking of writing a poem for you."

"For me?" I asked, blushing furiously. Marcellus and Tiberius had come home with scars from Spain, but Juba returned much the same as he'd left. Perhaps the muscles on his arms were harder, and when I looked at him, I sometimes thought of the nude Greek statues where the carved stomach gave way to a phallus beneath, but such thoughts were scandalous and I pushed them away. I'd once hoped that Juba was an Isiac, that he could help my brother and me escape. I now knew better, but I still considered him a friend. Or perhaps it was just that sometimes, when he looked at me, my skin tingled. I liked the slope of his shoulders and his elegant hands. So smooth and tan. And I remembered the way he'd once kissed my fingertips. I'd relived that moment more than once and thought I might swoon if he did it again, but then I thought of Helios and the danger he might be in, and it sobered me. "I didn't know you were a poet, Juba."

Juba smiled. "Everyone thinks themselves an artist this year. Virgil has taken a special interest in Marcellus, and Iullus has been studying with Horace. He's written a few love poems. Even the emperor has begun writing the story of Ajax in Greek. He's been working on it all morning."

That Iullus would be writing about love surprised me, but that the emperor was writing surprised me even more. After all, the emperor didn't consider himself a great intellect—relying more on his animal cunning. He'd been raised from humble beginnings and had never mastered Greek. As if we'd conjured him up by speaking of him, the emperor strolled through the courtyard just then wearing his ridiculous broad-brimmed hat. He breathed in and seemed terribly satisfied. "I'm feeling much better these days. Can you smell that, Juba? It's going to rain!"

The emperor was never in so good a mood as when it rained, for rain was a grand excuse to avoid the sun. No one avoided the sun more than the emperor because his physician had assured him that it aggravated the blotches on his skin. He held his hat with one hand while tapping a tablet against his leg with the other.

"How goes it with your Ajax epic?" Juba asked, cheerfully.

"A tragedy, Juba," the emperor said, screwing his face into a mask of mock grief. "It seems Ajax fell on his sponge."

He flipped the tablet open so we could see it sponged clean. Juba laughed at his jest. The emperor was not, after all, a man incapable of wit or charm. He could be generous, and there were even days that I could see hints of greatness. He genuinely believed his own propaganda—that he was the benevolent father figure to the orphans he'd gathered together. So when I didn't laugh at his joke, he adopted the tone of a kindly *paterfamilias*. "Selene, why the long face?"

I looked up at the darkening sky. "If it rains, Helios's trip to Ostia might take even longer."

"No worries there. Agrippa consulted the augurs this morning and the omens looked good."

I forced myself to smile, but I knew the emperor was skeptical about mystical divinations. He sometimes mocked the idea that anyone could read omens. Even so, he was careful to observe all public religious ceremonies. It wasn't because he was a pious man—he simply didn't like taking unnecessary chances. In that, perhaps we weren't so very different. "Come, Selene, play your *kithara* for me today," the emperor said. "It will cheer you up, and I know you want to please me."

That much was true. The night I'd forsaken Euphronius, I made pleasing the emperor my only choice.

SEVERAL days later, Helios returned from his trip, and I was so relieved I actually whooped with joy. I threw my arms around him, and he spun me so that my sandals brushed the carefully manicured grasses by the walkway. Helios had gifts for us. A basket of pomegranates for Philadelphus and a new gown for me, made of blue and green diaphanous silk. He even brought back ribbons for Bast to play with.

All the young men of the family had enjoyed their trip to Ostia with Agrippa, but Helios didn't share any of his stories until we were alone. "I've bad news from Egypt," he whispered from his side of the wall between our rooms. "Isis has abandoned Africa. Since our mother's funeral, the Nile hasn't risen above the cubits of death. Without a pharaoh, it won't rise."

My mother had stored grain in case of just such an emergency, but it wouldn't last. There'd be famine, and because Egypt fed the world, her famine would cause suffering everywhere. "What will the Roman governor do?"

"The Romans know nothing about Egypt!" Helios raged.

Philadelphus hushed him. "Be quieter or they'll hear you outside."

Helios lowered his voice but was no less passionate. "The Romans think they can manage Alexandria, but what of the Upper Kingdom? Did you know that when the emperor was in

Egypt, he refused to visit the Apis Bull at Memphis? He said he was accustomed to worshipping gods—not cattle."

I gaped at the emperor's irreverence. "He said that?"

"The Romans have contempt for all the old religions." Helios tapped the loose brick against his stone floor with agitation. "I wrote a message on papyrus for them to take back to Alexandria, but Agrippa caught me and threw it in the harbor without even reading it."

My heart leapt to my throat. "You're lucky he didn't read it!"

Helios snorted. "As if Agrippa knows how to read."

"Agrippa may seem simple," I protested, "but there's a genius about him and not just with his military tactics. Have you seen his projects? The roads, the aqueducts, and the buildings! He can most certainly read. What if he'd showed your note to the emperor?"

"Then Augustus would be shocked to find out how much I hate him." My twin's uncharacteristic sarcasm gave away the true depths of his upset. "Selene, Egypt is dying. The Isiacs aren't even allowed to celebrate the *Navigium Isidis* anymore here in Rome. Our faith is in danger and you and I haven't even learned to master the powers that we have."

"I don't want to bleed in hieroglyphics. It's not a power, and if you're talking about *heka*, well, I don't want to learn it." I'd put all of that behind me the night I took off my amulet.

"Then I'll learn for the both of us, but either way, we can't just sit here and let Octavian use us."

"What else can we do?" I asked.

"I've told you countless times," Helios said. "Let's escape. Let's find out what happened to Euphronius."

I shook my head vehemently to cover my guilty secret. I wanted to say, *I've seen Euphronius and I couldn't run. He came for us once and it was the end of my faith.* But instead I said, "How can you even think that after all these years Euphronius is still in the city? It's done, Helios. It's over. I'm not going to help you look for him, and don't go dragging Philadelphus into it either. Do you remember all those pretty stories you told me about how you'd bring me back to Egypt? Those were just stories. The only way to help Egypt is to make friends and allies in Rome, which is exactly what I plan to do."

Eighteen

FOR my brothers and me, seasons passed quickly without the familiar cycle of the Nile to mark time for us. Another birthday came and went. I didn't see Euphronius again and no more bloody messages carved themselves into my hands; I felt cut off from all that we'd known and forced myself to believe I must be Roman now. It's what Juba had done as an exiled princeling and he believed his efforts would see him back home one day. I wanted to believe the same held for my brothers and me.

By the time I was fourteen, I understood the actors and the stage that was set for me to play my part. I had only to choose the right moment for my entrance. That moment came on a warm spring day during an afternoon meal. It was the emperor's habit to quiz the boys with questions about military matters, but today his question was of a more peaceful nature. "Marcellus, the harbor in Alexandria is too crowded. There's no room for expansion, and our goods are getting bottled up in Egypt. What would you recommend?"

Marcellus had been caught chewing and was, therefore,

unable to answer. "Anyone?" the emperor asked. "Iullus, can you say what you'd recommend regarding the overcrowding of the harbor in Alexandria?"

Our half brother gladly jumped into the fray. "I'd burn down the old unusable facilities to make room for expansion."

I cast a dark look at Iullus. "Burning things isn't always the answer!"

All eyes turned to me. I was supposed to be silent, but they were discussing the fate of Egypt. My hands felt shaky as I said, "I'd build a new port in another region of Africa entirely."

None of the other girls of the household would have been so bold. Julia coughed. Livia scowled, cutting a sliver of cheese for her bread, and Octavia said, "It's impolite to speak out of turn, Selene. No one asked you."

Still, Juba cast me an encouraging glance and the emperor leaned forward in his seat, his brow arched curiously. "Where would you build the new port, Selene?"

"In Mauretania," I said. "In West Africa."

"That's too far," Julia piped up, suddenly emboldened.

I didn't wish to contradict her, but I had to. "Mauretania is far from Alexandria, but only a week's travel from Rome—perhaps less than that with a fast ship and good weather. A Mauretanian port would receive goods from Spain. It'd also bring prosperity to the downtrodden peoples of that region."

The emperor's mouth tightened. "I believe you mean *rebellious* peoples of that region, Selene. Since old King Bocchus died without an heir, the area has been utterly ungoverned."

Rome had overextended herself and that had contributed to the rebelliousness, but I was sure I was right. "In Africa, many people worship Isis. The right person could bring them together under a common faith."

By the right person, I meant a Ptolemy. My ancestors excelled at taking patches of deserted sand and turning them into places the world held in awe. Everything in my blood cried out to leap at any chance to build and create. The emperor tapped his plate. "Helios, do you agree with your sister?"

My twin tried to school his features into neutrality, but he'd never been gifted with artifice. He cared deeply about the issue, yet he said only, "I haven't given it much thought."

"Well, give it some thought," the emperor snapped.

I glared at my twin; he glared right back. Helios, who loved all things nautical, knew better than I did where a port should be. He'd most certainly given it thought, but he refused to share those thoughts with the emperor.

It was Agrippa who broke the tension. Shoving himself up from the couch, he plucked some purple grapes from a platter and popped them into his mouth. One always got the impression that Agrippa would rather eat standing anyway. "Maybe a little knockabout will get the blood flowing to his mind," he said, not bothering to stop to chew. "Iullus, Marcellus, and Tiberius should make time to show the younger boys what they learned fighting in Spain. It's time for practice, Helios. You want to be ready to ride in the Trojan Games."

The emperor flicked his wrist with a sour expression of dismissal. He'd finally finished building the Temple of Apollo and it was nearly time for the dedication. In celebration, he planned to hold athletic contests that showcased the flower of Roman youth. The emperor wanted the boys of his house to set an example, so he let them go with Agrippa without further complaint.

Meanwhile, we girls fled to the sewing room to escape his foul temper. But as I made my way there, I noticed a certain lift in my step. As Juba had encouraged me to do, I'd inserted myself into the emperor's plans for Africa, and it might even make a difference.

I had no sooner begun to weave at my loom when we heard shouting in the courtyard. Julia, curious as a monkey, was up in a flash for the doorway to see what was going on. She didn't have to wait long before Chryssa came running in.

"Master Helios is fighting with Iullus," the slave girl panted. "And there's blood drawn!"

I dropped my sewing and raced toward the atrium. By Isis, what had Helios done now? We found Helios and Iullus grappling, dirt kicking up underneath them. Terra-cotta pots holding the blooms of spring overturned, petals crushed beneath trampling feet. Iullus was three years older than Helios—a hardened youth with the training of a soldier, but he was the one who was most bloody and battered. My twin's face was red and furious, his hair wild as a lion's mane and as Marcellus and Tiberius tried to pull Helios back, the hairs on the back of my neck stood up too; a part of me always responded to my twin's strongest moods as if they were my own.

"Stop it!" I shouted, but my voice was drowned out by the shouts of the other boys as Helios broke free. He and Iullus again came to blows—both my father's sons, trying to kill one another. "You never even knew our father!" Helios screamed at Iullus.

"Whose fault is that?" Iullus shouted in return. "Your Egyptian whore of a mother lured him away!"

Helios roared, his fists flying wildly. "I'll kill you."

Tiberius grabbed Iullus by the right arm, yanking him back, and my twin's stray punch caught the wrong boy. Cursing, Tiberius stumbled to the ground with one hand out to the side to catch his fall. He landed on some shattered pieces of pottery, cutting his hand. Meanwhile, Iullus kept taunting Helios. "Shouldn't I call your mother a whore? Isn't it the family profession? Augustus already favors Selene. Next, she'll wrap her legs around Juba!"

I gasped with indignation, but Helios seemed as though he might go mad. He tackled Iullus and this time I was glad. The two combatants only narrowly missed dashing their heads against the stonework of the pool as Helios pummeled Iullus into the ground. My twin's lip was split, there was a cut under his eye, and his knee was skinned, but Iullus was getting the worst of it by far and I thought his nose might be broken.

At last, Lady Octavia caught up. "Boys! Stop this at once!"

They ignored her and little Minora began to cry, big round teardrops flowing down her cheeks. "Make them stop."

At Minora's plea, both Drusus and Philadelphus moved to enter the fray, but I held the younger boys back. "Enough!" someone bellowed. I looked behind me to see Agrippa barging into the courtyard.

Livia came running behind him holding her skirts up in each hand. Her eyes came to rest on Tiberius's bleeding hand. "What's happening? Who hurt my son?"

"It's nothing," Tiberius said, though blood dripped down his fingers onto the ground. "Helios struck me accidentally."

The fires that raged in Livia's eyes let me know that this wasn't an offense she'd forgive. Having once tried to strike her, Helios had made an enemy. Now that he'd injured Tiberius, he'd sealed his fate in her eyes. Agrippa waded into the melee and neither of Antony's warring sons was a match for the seasoned warrior. Agrippa swept one foot under Helios to knock him off balance with a lightning-quick maneuver that stunned us all. With his knee in my brother's back, Agrippa held my twin's face in the dirt, and Helios flailed. "You're strong as an ox, son, but you lack discipline," Agrippa said. "It's no wonder your father wanted to make you King of the Parths. You're as savage as they are."

"He's rabid!" Iullus cried, holding a dirty hand over his bleeding nose.

"Shut your mouth, Iullus!" Agrippa barked. "I doubt you're innocent either. What did you do to antagonize the boy?"

My twin's nostrils flared as his breath came out in desperate little puffs. "He called my sister a whore!"

Helios thrashed until Agrippa twisted an arm behind his back and I cringed to see my twin so helpless. "Iullus, is that true?"

"Yes, it's true." Iullus replied. His hair was matted with sweat, marring his patrician air. "Cleopatra *was* a whore; the emperor says so. And Selene would be one too, if allowed."

I'd known from the first day I met Iullus that he was a covered cistern of hatred but I hadn't realized that the hatred he harbored was for *us*. Iullus and the Antonias were my father's Roman children, but they'd never been true siblings to me. I glowered at Iullus as the burly Admiral shook his head and stood up, bringing my brother to his feet.

"Helios hurt my son," Livia hissed. "I want him tied down like a slave and beaten."

"I'd imagine they've both been beaten enough," Agrippa said. "They got each other pretty good. Besides, there's enough to worry about with the dedication and the games tomorrow."

Livia wasn't so easily appeased and pointed at Helios. "That boy is an animal. I want you to beat him, Agrippa."

Agrippa stood with his feet stubbornly apart. "I won't beat him for defending his family. Not even *that* family."

"I told you to beat him," Livia insisted.

"Do you give me orders now?" Agrippa asked, letting go of my brother's arm. "If you want him beaten, get one of your slaves to do it. That is, if you can find one strong enough to hold him."

With that, the admiral stormed off.

"Livia," Octavia scolded. "You ought to know better. Agrippa isn't yours to command."

"Nor is Agrippa *yours*, Octavia, however much you'd wish it so."

With those words, a look passed between the emperor's wife and his sister that resounded like an earthquake. A schism between the two women opened so wide that even we children could recognize it. I'd always considered the two women to be inseparable thirds of the emperor's household. Now I knew that I'd missed something crucial. Livia and Octavia may have shared in common their love for the emperor, or perhaps their dependence upon him, but their unity only ran so deep. They were not friends or companions by choice, but bitter rivals.

BRUISED and bleeding, Helios sat on the edge of his bed, his fist closed around his sparkling vulture amulet. I found a washing basin, then knelt on the carpet, rinsing the cloth and moving it toward his face. He gently pushed my hands away. "Leave it be."

"You're hurt," I said.

"Iullus is hurt worse," Helios gloated. I could see another part of myself in his green eyes—the raging part that I buried every day. "Besides, you had to be a little bit pleased that I defended you. You can't hate me for it, Selene."

"I could never hate you," I whispered, in a sudden rush of honesty. "You're the dearest thing to me in this world. But you didn't have to defend me."

Helios made me look at him. "I'll always defend you. You're Egypt and I'm Egypt's king. I will always, *always*, defend you."

I was both moved and frightened by his conviction. It was as if by fighting Iullus, he'd been emboldened by the realization that he *could* still fight. "But Helios, if you always defend me, then Iullus knows how best to goad you."

"He wasn't goading. That's what Romans think of us. They pretend to welcome us, but that's what they really think."

"It's what Iullus thinks," I said. "And even he doesn't believe it. He's just bitter that he doesn't have a mother, or father either. He's alone here. At least we have each other."

Helios, whose heart was always more tender than mine, lowered his eyes, suddenly less proud. "You're getting blood on your hands. Stop fussing, Selene; you're not my slave."

No, I wasn't his slave, but I wouldn't let him call for Chryssa. I dabbed at the blood with a wet cloth, then rinsed the blood into the washbasin. "If you can always defend me, then I can always fuss over you. Remember the little song our mother used to sing to us? '*The sun lets the moon rest and the moon shines when the sun is tired.*'"

"I'm not tired," he said, but he let me clean the blood off his face. "I'm frustrated. Why do you listen to Juba? Has he such a hold on your affections? Why are you always trying to impress the Romans?"

"Why are *you* trying to make them hate us? What did our grandfather do when he was struggling for our kingdom? Did he make enemies with the Romans?"

"He went to the Romans for help, and look at the price. Once they got a foothold in our country, they never let go."

"That's not the point."

Helios grasped my wrist gently. "That's exactly the point, Selene."

"You and what army will defeat the Roman Empire, Helios?" It was a cruel question but one that had to be asked. The night I let Euphronius wait for us in vain, I'd determined to use Rome even as Rome used me. It was time I convinced Helios to do the same.

"I don't know," Helios replied, tortured. "But maybe Euphronius does. Our first Saturnalia he sent word with Chryssa but we've heard nothing from him since. If he could have come to us, he would have. We have to find a way to go to him."

Guilt burned a hole inside me, the horrible truth of what I'd done searing my tongue. "Helios—"

"Selene, we aren't helpless. We have gifts, if only we learn to use them. I'm strong. Too strong, sometimes. I think . . . I think I could have killed Iullus today."

"He's our father's son," I said, because I couldn't bring myself to call Iullus our brother. "How would killing him have helped us?"

"I'm not saying that I *should* have killed him; I'm saying that I *could* have. I have the strength of Isis. Philadelphus has her sight. You've carried her words! The Romans can't hold us here forever if we master our powers and learn to work *heka*."

"Isis doesn't speak through me anymore."

"Have you tried to call for her?" Helios asked.

I reached to touch my frog amulet, and—not finding it there—I remembered the night I'd taken it off and left Isis behind. I shook my head. "I don't feel magic here in Rome. I don't. We haven't been to a Temple of Isis in so long I can barely remember what one looks like, and she sends me no more messages. She's forgotten us."

"She hasn't forgotten us," Helios said sternly, his faith so black and white in my world of gray. "But if we don't try, people might forget *her*."

Looking into my twin's emerald eyes, I saw the green waters of the Nile and the beckoning light of the Pharos lighthouse. I remembered the camels and the merchants, the palm trees, the spices, and the pyramids—Wonders of the World built thousands of years before I was even born. I remembered the night calls of the frogs and the silky feel of the desert sand slipping through my fingers. But I was still in Rome and there was no getting around that fact. Flinging myself down onto the scarlet coverlet on Helios's bed, I threw my hands over my face. "Euphronius is the wizard, not me. If he's here in Rome, then Chryssa must find him. Not you."

Helios lay beside me and I made room for him. "Selene, Chryssa's already risked too much for us."

The protective note in Helios's voice made me angry. I'd heard the jokes the older boys made. I knew what Tiberius and Iullus did with the slave girls. I imagined that even though my brother was younger, he must have the same desires. I could barely ask him, but I forced the words out over a scalding tongue. "Do you . . . take Chryssa to bed?"

Helios didn't blush. "No."

I turned to look at him. "Why not? She's pretty."

"Because she's devoted her virginity to Isis."

He stared at his wall where an artist had painted faux garlands to brighten the room. I stared at it too, wondering if Helios's chivalry toward Chryssa wasn't actually worse than the alternative. It did nothing to alleviate the burning emotion inside me that I could only identify as jealousy. I couldn't let this awkwardness go on between us forever, so I leaned on his arm like a pillow and let my fingers trace along the inside of his elbow, noticing that he too had a birthmark there, though in a different constellation than my own. His looked almost like the shape of a cobra, the *uraeus*, the spitter of fire.

He wrapped his arm around me as our breathing fell into the same pattern and I remembered that Helios was another part of myself. Euphronius had taught us that we each had nine bodies of the soul, but I thought our old wizard was wrong; surely, Helios and I shared at least one between us. We'd come into the world together, and in the afterworld, I felt certain we wouldn't walk separately, but in one *akh*.

Still, my twin brother smelled like dust and sweat and crushed grass, but neither of us smelled like magic. I'd given up *heka* and broken from my faith. I wanted him to understand, so I repeated the arguments I'd made to myself the night I left Euphronius standing in the dark beneath that acacia tree. "Even if we escaped, Helios, we have no army, and we can't use magic to fight another war. What would we do if we ran away?"

"I don't know. But as long as the emperor holds us hostage, our people suffer."

"If Egypt starves, so will Rome. The emperor knows this."

"What he knows is the Egyptians will starve *first*," Helios said. "Rome will steal Egyptian grain, then conquer someone else for more. Why do you think he wants another seaport in Africa?"

I hadn't thought of that when I suggested another port in Mauretania. "But you see how the emperor longs to be loved. How he performs for everyone. He wants to be admired. We must convince him that partnership with Egypt makes the whole world prosper. Alexander, Julius Caesar, our father—they all changed once they truly saw Egypt. The emperor can change too."

"Octavian is *not* our father," Helios said. "He's not Julius Caesar, and not Alexander. Octavian won't change; he'll change us. He's already changing us."

He was changing *me*. That's what Helios meant. Helios had always been the beacon of our faith when I had wavered, but now I tried to beat down his spirit like I buried my own. "Warriors shape the world, not wizards, Helios. We don't have soldiers. We don't have generals. But we have the emperor's ear. I want to protect Egypt and if I have to win the emperor's trust to do it, I will."

Nineteen

THE next morning, the imperial household lined up before the emperor, entirely chastened. As the gardeners worked on prettying up the courtyard, he evaluated us as if we were slaves on the block. Livia, Octavia, and Agrippa stood behind him, still as stone. Neither Helios nor Iullus said a thing. Drusus drew near to his older brother, Tiberius, who fidgeted with his bandage, while Marcellus stared at the ground.

"So," the emperor finally said. The word hung in the air with dramatic effect until the tension nearly crackled. My parents had been fiery, temperamental people. My father had smashed things. My mother had shouted. Even Agrippa was prone to bellowing. But not Augustus. How I wished he'd shout, or strike, or throw something. Instead, we had to strain to hear him when he was angry. "You all know how important tomorrow's games are to me and how much effort and expense went into them. It was to be our reintroduction to all of Rome as a family. Yet now we have Tiberius, Iullus, and Helios all bruised and battered, tangible proof for my enemies that there's strife in my home."

The older boys had tried to stop the fight, but the emperor's anger leveled itself at all of us, as if there'd been some grand conspiracy to upset him. Julia's shoulders rounded defensively. Her voice was a whisper. "But father—"

The emperor gave his daughter a withering look. "Julia, if you wanted the right to argue with me, then you should have been born the son and heir that I need. Now be silent."

Just then, Philadelphus yanked on my sleeve, whispering to me, "Both you and Helios are going to save lives at the games tomorrow. I've seen it."

"Shhh!" I hissed at my littlest brother.

The emperor's eyes fell upon me. "Do you have something to say, Selene?"

I swallowed. A light breeze stirred the laurel trees and the fragrant bay scent wafted toward us. Falling white blossoms from the almond trees seemed to swirl with my upset. They smelled heady and sweet, calling the scent of light magic to my mind. "Just . . . are a few bruises and cuts really so bad? Would anyone notice? And if anyone did, wouldn't it just make them seem more manly? More . . . Roman?"

"Don't you understand that we're being watched at all times?" the emperor snapped, and I realized that defeating my parents, celebrating his triumphs—none of it had yet made him secure. Even something so small as a scuffle between Antony's sons could shake him.

It was Agrippa, again, who stepped into the breech. "Caesar, what Roman would think ill of boys roughhousing for sport?"

"True," the emperor admitted. "But no more fighting. Iullus, Helios, you'll get along. And when we mingle with the people, you'll smile and show no traces of this feud between you. You *will* be a part of this family. You *will* wave to the crowd. You *will* be charming. And Helios, since you seem to like beatings so much, I won't bother. Whatever displeasure you bring to me from now on, I'll take out on your slave girl. You may consider your every frown to be a lashing on her pretty back. Do you understand?"

The emperor's generosity regarding Chryssa became clear now. She had never been a spy. She was more like a Trojan horse who had infiltrated my brother's affections, and now the emperor would use her against him. Helios knew it too. His jaw worked slightly, grinding his teeth. Then he nodded his head.

Agrippa growled at Helios. "Don't nod, boy. Augustus asked you a question. Do you understand?"

"I understand the emperor perfectly," my twin replied.

THE Temple of Apollo stood complete, pure white marble gleaming in the sun. Rome might be made of mud and brick, but this building and its surroundings were truly magnificent. On the top of the central arch was a carved masterpiece—a chariot drawn by four horses—and it was marvelous even to my jaded Ptolemy eyes. The emperor puffed with pride as he announced, "As of tomorrow, I'll become chief priest of Apollo. I've moved the great books of literature from around the city to this temple. Next, I'll move the Sibylline Books from the Temple of Jupiter to the sacred vault beneath Apollo's statue. What's more, one day, I'll convene the Senate, when it needs convening, in this temple. This temple, my home, my gift to Rome."

While the emperor made his pompous pronouncements and the crowd cheered, Helios squinted up at the sunlit chariot, but I was more awestruck by what I saw at eye level. I'd thought the horrid temple doors depicting Apollo slaying the children of Niobe was dark enough warning, but I now took in the red and amber statues between each column. Fifty dagger-wielding women, each looming beside an ill-fated husband. The statues were breathtaking, beautiful, and macabre. For these were the Danaids, daughters of Danaus, a prince of Egypt—who, to make peace with his brother Aegyptus, betrothed his fifty daughters to his brother's fifty sons. According to the myth, on the night of the wedding, the unwilling princess brides all murdered their husbands with a poisoned dagger; now the scene was reproduced here in marble for all Rome to see.

"Do you know this story?" I asked Helios.

He nodded. "But what does he mean by it? Is he celebrating the murders? Is he saying Egyptian princesses are kin murderers and Egyptian princes are weaklings?"

"He's accusing our mother," I whispered. "He's accusing her of murdering Julius Caesar and Mark Antony just as the Danaids murdered their husbands."

In truth, I feared it wasn't just an accusation against my mother but an accusation against all women. These statues mocked the notion that men and women, or neighboring nations, could live together in partnership. The message was: Ally with a foreign power and she'll betray you. Love an Egyptian princess and she'll put a blade through your heart. "I hate this temple," I muttered, and it was true. I hated the sound of the boy's choir as they sung their dedication. I hated the way Apollo's statue was slim like the emperor. I hated Apollo the Pythian, Apollo the Torturer. If Apollo existed, I only hoped he wouldn't see into my heart and strike me dead. "And I hate how it seems like the guests are all staring at us."

"Of course they are," Helios replied, leaning toward me to touch his forehead to mine. "Aegyptus and Danaus were twins, like us. The Romans just want to see which of us has the dagger."

FOR the occasion of these games, I wore a green *tunica* bloused and cinched at the waist with two blue bands of ribbon embroidered with acanthus leaves. Though Octavia preferred me to wear white, I'd made this dress myself and she agreed it was modest enough. My hair was parted in the middle, with my braids knotted at the nape of my neck, and I kept my eyes low so that Roman wives might compliment Octavia on my behavior.

As we made our way into the arena, I couldn't help but notice the giant obelisk at the center, a treasure of Egypt that the emperor had stolen from Heliopolis. I gritted my teeth and joined Julia and the rest of the women of the family in the imperial box.

From my seat, I had an excellent view of the emperor when he entered the arena arrayed like a Triumpher, leading the procession of athletes and entertainers in a chariot of gold. I remembered the last time I'd seen him that way, when I'd been dragged behind his chariot in chains. This time, I wasn't to be displayed as a hated captive but as a member of the imperial family, so I watched the emperor drive his chariot in tight circles and made a halfhearted effort at cheering along with the rest of the crowd. In seeing that Apollo's shield was emblazoned upon the emperor's armor, I wondered if today he would finally abandon the disguise of a simple Roman citizen and declare himself a god.

But if that had been his intent, he soon thought better of it. The Romans cheered, but there was impatience too. People pushed for better seats in the arena, and I worried that the wooden risers would collapse under their weight; the people had come for games, not to glorify Augustus, and he seemed to know it. When he finally stepped out of his chariot, he didn't make the speech he'd prepared, but instead, started for the imperial box. His *lictors*—the ax-and-rod-wielding guards that always accompanied him—had carefully arranged which citizens might be in his path and eager hands reached out for his attention and generosity. I watched him, astonished at how poorly he handled this, in spite of the orchestration.

When my mother appeared in public, she was the New Isis, swathed in black silk and silver stars; the people stood back in awe. My father, by contrast, was a glad-hander, comfortable with beggars and kings alike. He loved to mingle with the commoners and charmed them with his good-natured buffoonery.

The emperor was like neither of my parents. When he spoke with the *plebs*, his manner was stiff. He cringed when a particularly dirty child touched his toga. He scowled at a flirtatious woman. It sometimes still bewildered me how he'd become the ruler of the world, but then the heralds announced the spectacle he was about to give and it became clear once again.

As the attendants quickly prepared the arena with a maze of obstacles and thatched blinds, the emperor brushed past me and made his way to his seat on the dais where he signaled that the Trojan Games should begin. In previous years, Tiberius, Marcellus, and Iullus had participated too, but now that they had each nominally served in the legions in Spain, they thought themselves too grown up. It didn't stop them from cheering when the trumpets blared and the boys of Roman aristocracy came riding out in even ranks.

The whole crowd rose to its feet. On prize steeds, the sons of senators and important families were arrayed in every finery, and Helios was amongst them, his hair held back tight. Like the others, he looked like a young warrior, for he carried a glittering quiver on his shoulder and a wooden lance in each hand. But mounted upon a tawny Iberian horse, even in the midst of this proud boys' army, Helios's regal bearing set him apart from the rest.

With his knees tightly pressed into the sides of the sleek but sturdy animal, Helios deftly wove in and out of the columned formation with the troops. He performed even the most intricate maneuvers with studied grace, and it was hard to look away. Helios led one squadron of boys, Drusus led another, and the third was led by some Ahenobarbus boy. According to the emperor, this was a Roman tradition that spanned back to the days of Aeneas, but his intent was clear to me. He wanted the flower of the next generation to be accustomed to following the men of his household.

"Helios is quite good!" Juba said, handing me a loaf of bread he'd purchased from a vendor and it was still warm when I bit into it. I tried not to appear too grateful; I'd secretly hoped that Juba and I might sit together, but my pride still smarted from

Iullus's taunts. Was it wrong for me to hope my handsome tutor would notice my new dress today? Did it make me a wanton to hope he might compliment me?

At last, a whip cracked overhead and the squadrons split apart, parading into the maze until the boys were two matched forces readying for a mock skirmish. I knew it was meant only to be a terrifying display, only the mimicry of war, and that their lances were blunted. But the fierce look upon their faces as they galloped over barriers, their weapons lowered for the charge, made me slide forward to the edge of my seat.

It might be only sport to those of us watching, but to the boys in the arena, it became war in earnest. Helios bellowed out his commands as the two sides clashed. Beside me, Minora squealed and Tiberius gave a mighty shout of encouragement to his little brother just as Drusus's lance caught another boy by the shoulder and threw him from his horse.

I hadn't seen this kind of display before, so I didn't know whether or not it was *supposed* to dissolve into melee, but when it did Helios was grace in motion. Twisting at the torso to avoid the lances that reached for him, Helios was untouchable. What's more, there were none who could stand against him, and as the thunder of hooves beat the ground and sent clods of dirt into the air, the mood in the arena changed.

All eyes were riveted upon my brother's skill. Even the emperor leaned forward in his seat for a better view. Agrippa motioned for some dark beer and said, "Look at Helios riding like a Numidian. The boy is a natural-born soldier. If he can harness that talent, he may conquer Parthia yet!"

Livia greeted Agrippa's statement with serene indifference, as if every bit of praise for Helios came at the expense of her sons. "And have you no admiration for Roman boys?"

Agrippa was never one with a quick reply, so I broke in with, "Oh yes, how very smart Drusus looks upon his horse!"

It was Octavia whose mouth pinched tight as her fingers

worried over one another in her lap. She thought these games were too dangerous, I knew. And given the intricacies of these cavalry maneuvers atop frothing war horses who seemed eager for a fight, I couldn't blame her.

That's when it happened.

Drusus's horse reared up under him and Livia shrieked with surprise as her son toppled backward to the ground. I too cried out, because Drusus all but disappeared under the stomping hooves. It was a maze the boys battled in, and some of his own troops didn't see him in the clash; it looked as if he'd be trampled to death.

"Stop them!" Tiberius cried, his adolescent voice cracking.

But before the emperor could even rise from his seat, I heard Helios bark out orders. I'd sought out a stage for my strengths, perhaps now my twin saw his own part to play because Helios *literally* leapt into the fray. He flew off his horse, dodging lances and deadly hooves as he ran. His formerly pristine white tunic was instantly grimy with dirt. It looked as if he cut himself leaping over a barrier, but his composure never wavered.

To see him risk his life like this made me weak all over. Losing him would be to lose myself, and I couldn't bear it. But down in the arena, Helios reached Drusus easily and attempted to pull him up from the ground. As he lifted Drusus, Helios's golden hair broke free of its tie, flowing behind him like a lion's mane. His face was red and sweaty with effort as he called out to his horse. The Iberian shook its mane and thrashed its golden tail, but even in the chaos of battle, came at my brother's command.

With lances aimed for him, somehow my brother still managed to heft a stunned but seemingly unharmed Drusus onto his horse. Then Helios mounted behind him, and rode away from the lashing combat, delivering Livia's son to safety.

As he galloped off, the mob cheered for Helios as if he'd been their most loyal son. Women clutched at their breasts and men shouted praise for his daring. My brother may have been the son of Cleopatra, but they now remembered he was the son of Antony too. They stomped their feet until the timbers of the arena shook, and I feared the whole thing would come down. And when at last the Games of Troy were called to a close, the mob demanded a wreath be awarded to my brother.

I watched the reluctant emperor stand to make a personal presentation, but I couldn't read his expression. He can't have predicted my brother's acts of valor, but neither did he seem displeased. From the imperial box, he shouted and the heralds spread his word. "I hereby award a wreath for excellence in the games upon my ward, Marcus Julius Alexander!"

For a moment, the arena quieted. Who was Marcus Julius Alexander? Someone laughed. A baby wailed. Murmuring buzzed the crowd like a lazy bee. Then realization dawned. The emperor had just renamed my brother before all of Rome.

"A new family name," Juba said excitedly. "Not just another Gaius or Lucius. Unconventional choice, but good."

It was not only unconventional but *outrageous*. The name recalled three men: my father, Julius Caesar, and Alexander the Great. It did all this without making any overt reference to my mother, the hated Queen of the Nile. What kind of game was this? It can't have been legal for the emperor to make such a declaration, but he didn't seem the least bit troubled.

Helios, on the other hand, was more than troubled. Even from the stands, we could see my twin's anger at being publicly renamed . . . and his astonishment at the way the crowd roared its approval. How fickle these Romans were. Had they not been baying for our blood only years before? But now, because he'd been the best at a boy's military game, the Romans wanted to claim Helios as their own!

Marcus Julius Alexander, indeed. With this name, the emperor had declared my brother both a Roman and a child of his house. It was as if the emperor actually believed he could finally heal the wounds of the civil war by claiming Antony's son as his own.

Meanwhile, another son of Antony, the one who had fought beside the emperor in Spain, glowered. My Roman half brother looked as if he saw himself being supplanted by the very boy who was to blame for his bruised face, and I saw Julia reach out her hand to comfort him in silence.

But if Iullus was angered, it was nothing next to the rage of Helios himself. Beneath the wreath being fastened on him, I saw Helios struggle with his anger. Perhaps mindful of the emperor's earlier threats, he kept his peace, and when my twin finally rode his fine Iberian horse out of the arena without making a scene, I was grateful.

"This turned out better than I'd hoped," the emperor said, taking a loaf of bread from a passing slave. "Let the Isiacs see this and take note! Come, Selene and Juba. Sit closer to me. Tell me the names of the animals now being led into the arena."

Were we to watch the rest of the games as if nothing had changed? I wasn't the one who'd been renamed but some part of me could feel what Helios was feeling. My hands nearly shook with it as Juba and I rose to join the emperor.

Livia made room for us with a nearly imperceptible sniff of resentment as hordes of African animals were led into the arena. There were wild beasts of all varieties: some in cages, others in yokes. "Ah, Selene, this is a glorious day," the emperor said. "Don't you feel the change? I've accomplished everything—everything is changing."

"Yes." I did feel it, but it wasn't a good feeling. The emperor was remaking the world in his image and things might never be the same.

Just then, Drusus came bounding up the stairs, sweating but invigorated. It wasn't his mother, Livia, but his older brother, Tiberius, who reached him first. "Are you hurt?" Tiberius asked. "Drusus, are you hurt?"

"He's fine," Livia said. "No doubt, he's as humiliated by his fall as his mother is, but maybe this will teach him a lesson to practice more."

"Don't embarrass the boy," Augustus said as Helios made his way up the stairs to shouts of gratitude. Marcellus and Tiberius both clapped him on the back as if they didn't notice my twin's dark expression.

I threw my arms about his neck, hoping my embrace could convey all that I couldn't speak. I'd been afraid for Helios and I'd been proud of him. Now I was angry for him too and he seemed to feel it, his hands clasping my waist.

"Well done," Agrippa said.

Even the emperor nodded graciously. "Yes, well done, young man. I'm very pleased."

That's when Helios disentangled himself from me long enough to rip the wreath from his head and crush its leaves in his hands. "My name is *not* Marcus Julius Alexander."

"Why shouldn't it be?" The emperor spread his arms in a gesture of benevolence. "You did me honor today and I honor you in return. I've bestowed upon you your rightful place as a Roman. It shall be the start of a new relationship between us."

The strangest thing was I believe he meant it, but his apparent sincerity did not touch Helios. "I'm Alexander Helios of House Ptolemy."

And with that, the fragile peace was destroyed.

"You are who I say you are," the emperor hissed. "The House of Ptolemy is no more, so sit down or I'll feed your slave girl to the lampreys."

My brother's nostrils flared, but he took his seat. Meanwhile, the emperor turned back to the arena and unclasped his breastplate; he wasn't accustomed to wearing even the decorative kind. "What's that animal there, Selene?"

At this moment, I didn't dare look back at Helios. For once, I feared him more than I feared the emperor. "That's a rhinoceros."

"It looks fierce," the emperor replied. "And that animal there?"

"A hippopotamus," I whispered, staring at my hands. "It looks less fierce, but it kills as many each year as crocodiles do."

"Really?" the emperor asked, astonished. "I admit to being fascinated by creatures that are more than they seem to be."

The emperor too was more than he seemed to be. That's how he'd risen so high. My father had mistaken him for a malleable boy. Now the emperor seemed to be making the same mistake when it came to Helios. I felt the heat of my twin's glare upon my back and I knew better than to spare him a glance.

In the arena, hunters entered with nets and spears. These animals had been captured for a slaughter—like everything else from Egypt—and my throat constricted. The hippopotamus fought best in water. Here in the arena, though, the hippo stood stunned. An ostrich ran past. Then a stately giraffe. I could smell the fear, the musk of terror. The animals, cornered and panicked, fought wildly. Some of them tore into one another. Animals died as the crowd chanted.

Blood splattered and the crowd roared. Hyenas feasted on the gore and let out hideous laughter. The crowd laughed in return. A rhino charged a wood barrier and sent several people climbing over one another to get away while spearmen plunged their blades through its thick hide. The rhino fell to his knees.

It was something uniquely Roman to kill with such waste. In Egypt, the spirits of animals were revered and holy—part of the great family of the divine. We killed them only for food or holy ceremony, mummifying some for eternal life.

"This isn't fair," Philadelphus objected as a graceful gazelle met with an angry lion and the hunters tried to prod the lion into attacking it.

"Life isn't fair, though, is it?" the emperor asked as the lion attacked one of the hunters instead, leaving a gash in the man's thigh, spurting blood. The Romans cheered for this too, the torture of man and beast equally entertaining.

Half my blood was Roman, and I'd tried for the past two years to become like them. I read their poets, I learned their traditions, and I'd even come to love the Saturnalia. I looked like them, I dressed like them, and I sat with them. But as I watched this Roman spectacle of gory death, absolute conviction dawned upon me that I would *never* be one of them.

The emperor waved toward me with his cup. "The hunt grows stale. Juba, why don't you share with Selene the good news?"

Juba smiled. "We're going to scout for a site to build a port in Mauretania. Your idea was a good one."

"Selene, what do you think of this news?" As the emperor smiled, I felt guilty for having made the suggestion.

Aware of Helios's eyes on me, I copied Octavia and folded my hands in my lap. Helios's words about how the emperor would starve Egypt and steal grain elsewhere weighed upon me, and so I settled upon, "If it pleases Augustus, then it pleases me."

The trumpets started again and the emperor leaned forward in his seat. The volume of the crowd's cheers grew impossibly louder. I'd not heard such a wall of sound since Octavian's Triumph. My heart beat faster as the noise brought back to me all the fear of that day. "Have you seen gladiator games before?" the emperor asked.

When I shook my head, he looked surprised. "I'd have thought your father held them in Alexandria."

He must have been feeling very confident indeed to bring up my father. "My mother didn't care for them."

In truth, my mother had said that the most arrogant pharaoh in Egypt wouldn't dare ask her people to fight one another to the death for the sake of amusement. Besides, such games were strictly against the teachings of Isis.

"I think you'll enjoy them, Selene," the emperor said as helmeted gladiators trooped their way into the arena and saluted. I watched their grim faces and their grimy armor with apprehension. As two novice gladiators took to the ring, the crowd began placing bets.

One gladiator was a Gaul armed with a sword and buckler. The other was a native Egyptian who fought with a trident and a net. I noticed the scars of the whip on his dark skin and wondered what had brought him here. Had he served in my mother's forces and been dragged here to die? Did he have family that he would never see again? He looked frightened, and I became frightened for him.

As the two gladiators rounded one another, they didn't want to fight, but the officials lashed them with the whip and promised a slower death than they'd find in the ring.

"Don't watch," I whispered to Philadelphus, and tried to cover his eyes.

"I can still see it," he said, so I closed my fingers tighter.

At last the two men clashed, wounds opening, each man dancing back. The crowd jeered their self-preservation. Then the men went at one another again. The trident missed its mark, but the swordsman dashed the net out of the Egyptian's hand and sent him scrambling for it. A sudden cheer went up as the Egyptian, who seemed to be getting the worst of the battle, tangled his opponent within his retrieved net. But soon the Gaul was thrusting his way free and tackled the Egyptian to the ground where he lay helpless and pinned.

This was over too quickly for the mob and they booed. The legs of the prone Egyptian were soaked with sweat or urine, I couldn't tell. I thought the death blow would come, but it did not. Instead, the victorious gladiator looked to the emperor for his approval, and all eyes turned to the imperial box. It was for the emperor to decide the gladiator's fate.

"Spare him!" Helios shouted.

Instead, the emperor's eyes fastened upon me. "Shall I spare him, Selene?"

With a slow dread, I turned to look at the wan face of the Egyptian on the ground as he contemplated death. His lips were moving, and I saw her name upon his lips. *Isis.* The doomed man called for my goddess and I saw his eyes soften. Was he already looking from this world into the next? Did he hear the beautiful voice of Isis calling to him? Did it sound the same as it had in my own ears when her messages had cut themselves into my skin?

I tell you truly, that even with a weapon at his throat, her name brought a smile to the gladiator's lips and his faith nearly broke me. Trembling, my first bitter thought was that Isis could not help him now . . . or could she?

Before my mother died, she told us to adhere to the dictates of Isis, to care for the less fortunate, and I remembered the lightness I felt the day Helios and I had given all our coins to the beggars. Perhaps I had been a naive child expecting the magic of Isis to work always in a flash of *heka*. I had given up my faith without truly understanding it.

My faith had been tested, and I had failed, but did Isis still dwell in me? Could she still work through me if I gave myself to her again?

Iullus had accused me of being the emperor's favorite. Surely that must have its advantages. "Please, spare him," I said to the emperor, my lower lip aquiver.

Isis. The gladiator mouthed the word again and it echoed in my head as if he'd shouted it. I had been without Isis. I had lost my way. In difficult times, I had given up my amulet and my goddess. But this man, when faced with his end, still called to Isis and I was humbled.

The emperor, a consummate showman, seemed to enjoy keeping the crowd in suspense. "Selene, would you ask for mercy if the Gaul were defeated instead of the Egyptian?"

"Yes," I said quickly. "Mercy is universal."

"Yet, you had little mercy for the cheating interpreter."

A lump rose in my throat at the reminder of that far-off day before my first Saturnalia. I remembered the hungry look of that interpreter and how I'd helped condemn him. How long had the emperor waited to put this mantle of guilt upon my shoulders? But perhaps it was no less than I deserved. I cringed to think how many times I had failed my goddess.

Isis, forgive me. Please return to me.

"The interpreter was a thief," I said. "But what crime has the gladiator committed?"

The emperor's thin lips twitched into the hints of a smile. He was enjoying playing my emotions, I knew.

My fingernails dug into my palms. "If you spare him, he might live to fight and entertain you another day when he's better trained."

"Selene?" the emperor asked me. "What is your brother's name?"

All of the other times the emperor had pressed me to betray my family or my faith, I had struggled with my choice. Not this time. The fate of that interpreter had been the emperor's to decide; he was Roman. But if any part of Helios and me were still Egypt, then this gladiator belonged to us. All I had to do was give the emperor what he wanted. Simple words in exchange for life. Cooperate and my people live. Fight and they die.

With clear enunciation, I said, "My twin's name is Marcus Julius Alexander."

Helios lurched forward in his seat, but I didn't cower before my twin's wrath. There were prices for pride that I would never pay. I felt my surrender was unquestionably justified when the emperor made a gesture with his thumb, and the Egyptian gladiator was spared.

It all began to meld together—the dirt, the arena, the sea of peasants. The stink of death mingled with the scent of sausages and beer. Above it all, I caught magic on the breeze, like sandalwood and jasmine, poignant and sad. My fingernails dug so deeply into my palms I feared that they'd bleed. In fact, I could almost feel the wetness of the blood and the sting of the cuts. No, I *did* feel it.

I turned my hands over and slowly uncurled my fingers as blood began to drip down my arms.

Twenty

❁

I'D never before seen the emperor shocked. Not truly. The petulant lines of his mouth fell lax as he watched hieroglyphics scroll
across my palms and down my wrists in blood. He wasn't the only
one to see it, for Julia let out a scream that sent Agrippa to his feet.

I'd invited Isis to return to me, but now I was seized with
fear. I called out for Helios as speckles danced before my eyes. He
rushed to help me, but Juba was in his way.

They would kill me for this—they would accuse me of witch-
craft again. I remembered how Octavia reacted the last time this
happened, and that hadn't been in public. The crowd's attention
shifted to the uproar in the imperial box and the emperor was
conscious of their stares.

"Up!" the emperor shouted, and the family rose, obstructing
the crowd's view. Then praetorians encircled us, as if there'd been
an attempt on the emperor's life.

"Is she hurt? Is she ill?" Octavia asked, trying to quiet the little
ones. Agrippa didn't answer her but snatched a *palla* off Marcella's
shoulders and bound my hands with it.

It was then that Juba lifted me into his arms and shouted, "Make way!"

Held aloft by Juba, I saw Helios and called his name again, but this time he looked away, down at his hands, spreading them as if they were helpless and foreign to him. His gaze finally fell to the crushed wreath at his sandaled feet, an unreadable expression on his face.

"Helios!" I cried again, but he made no move to reply and it was as if my whole world went dark. Like the blotting out of the sun. Helios had said he'd always defend me, but perhaps I'd finally gone too far when I helped the emperor strip him of his name. I'd thought the bond Helios and I shared was unbreakable. But then, I'd been mistaken about many things.

Juba cradled me against his chest as he carried me through the path that guards cleared in front of us. The heralds reassured the mob that the emperor was unharmed and that one of the girls had simply swooned from the excitement as women were wont to do. Curious Romans strained their necks as Juba carried me out of the arena, but most of them were eager to return to the games.

A sob tore itself from my throat and Juba said, "Shhh, Selene, don't cry."

I didn't want to cry. Queens didn't cry, but I wasn't a queen anymore. Even my name didn't belong to me if the emperor could take it away. Then visions swam before my eyes and I realized I was fainting after all.

"SELENE, wake up," Juba said softly, getting me to stir. I was on a couch in the emperor's study with a wet cloth upon my brow. I had no sense of how much time had passed. Juba lifted a cup to my lips as he'd done on the very first day we'd met. "Here, drink this. It's a restorative."

"Is it one of Livia's tonics?" I turned my head away.

"No, Octavia sent it. You should drink it."

I took a sip and it tasted like grass and beer. Then I lifted my hands and found each one tightly bound with bandages. "I need to read my hands."

Juba smoothed my hair onto the pillow behind my head. "I don't know if the emperor would want that. Besides, you've lost much blood."

If the blood smeared on his clothes belonged to me—and it must have—then he was right, but I didn't care. "Isis is with me!" Frantically, I tried to pull my hands free. "Help me read her words."

Juba surrendered, his long fingers gently unwinding the ruined *palla* from my arms. Then we both stared in amazement at the figures still carved into my skin. "You can read that?"

I nodded, slowly translating the figures I knew and puzzling at those that were more difficult. Serpents, wings, and scales wriggled into my skin. All of it bled so that I had to wipe my hands to see the red lines in my rent flesh. I'd only read as far as the wrist of my right hand when the emperor arrived. His skin was paler than usual and the unhealthy circles under his eyes accentuated his furious expression. The last time I'd been in this study, he'd reminded me there were still kings like Herod demanding my death, and now I'd given him an excuse to oblige them. "I didn't work magic," I said quickly, though I wasn't entirely sure that was true.

The emperor didn't answer right away but pulled up a chair beside me, waving Juba away. The ruler of the world looked so thoroughly unnerved that it frightened me and he stared at my face as if he would never stop staring. "Calm yourself, dear child," he finally said.

It wasn't his habit to use terms of endearment, so that terrified me even more. He'd seen the blood on my sleeping garment before, but he'd never truly believed that symbols carved themselves into my hands. Not until now. Even so, he didn't show the joy of religious revelation—he displayed the grim determination of a man who'd seen the enemy. "This is the work of the Isiacs," he said.

"Please believe it's Isis herself." I let my passion show, hoping it would convince him, that he would allow himself to understand the beauty and mystery of the goddess I would no longer deny.

"That's what they want us to believe," the emperor said, touching my shoulder in a gesture that might have passed for compassion. He was an actor with a thousand roles, but he seemed to believe each one. "Selene, when Agrippa first suggested it years ago, I didn't believe him, but now I understand. They've attacked you with their magic and they won't get away with it." His fingertips were cool to the touch and I wanted to recoil, but I found myself unable to move. A mask of possessiveness fell over his face as he asked, "Are you in much pain?"

I nodded because my hands burned like fire. This was the longest the inscriptions had stayed on my hands, and as much as it hurt I hoped it wouldn't go away before I could read it. The emperor put his elbows on his knees and clasped his hands together under his chin, contemplatively. "Since coming into my household, you've been a good girl and done what I've asked of you. I'll protect you in return. I've drawn up a formal accusation against the Isiacs for working magic against you, and when you're better I want you to sign it."

"They didn't do anything." My eyes sought out Juba's support, but he didn't meet my gaze.

"How do you know?" Octavian asked.

"I just know," I said, feeling the power of a presence inside me. "Why do you need my signature or seal anyway? Since when do the Romans give merit to the testimony of a girl?"

"Romans don't, but Isiacs may," the emperor said as I bled. "I'd like you to translate the words on your hands. Juba will write it down."

Where I had hurried to read the inscriptions before, now I

hesitated. "I want Helios. I want my brothers. Where are my brothers?"

"They're downstairs waiting for you," the emperor said in a coaxing tone. "I'm going to let you see them shortly. You did well today, and a man even owes you his life. You're a very good girl. I just need this one thing from you."

My hands trembled, but I translated the tiny precise cuts, spirals and feathers, vultures and flags, all scrolling as I tilted my head to the side at the change in tone from the last message.

"Do you feel secure, Master of the World?"

The emperor leaned forward in his chair and Juba's reed pen paused over his writing as if he doubted me. I started reading from the beginning.

"Do you feel secure, Master of the World? Will your star shine brighter if you harness my moon and my sun? You have my throne, but will you sit on it? Will you nourish my people as Pharaoh must? You think the war is well and truly won, but perhaps in this River of Time, it's just begun."

The emperor's eyes flickered with something akin to panic. His pasty face shined with sweat and he lifted an unsteady hand to wipe it. "Are you lying, child?"

"I swear it by Isis. That's what it says," I told him.

Then each tiny carving healed, each wound closing perfectly until only bloody bandages remained as evidence of my wounds.

"It's just the propaganda of zealous Isiacs," Juba said. "They do work magic. I've seen it in their temples."

"You've seen this before?" the emperor asked.

"No," Juba admitted. "These bleeding messages . . . no."

The emperor strode to the window that overlooked Rome,

where we could see the colossi that he'd stolen from Egypt. The folds of his purple-bordered toga swayed as he stared out the window. "It's not the Isiacs," the emperor said.

"It's Isis," I replied.

"No," the emperor said with his back to us. "It's *Cleopatra*."

Twenty-one

❦

"ALWAYS Cleopatra!" he shouted. "I thought I had shaken her, but here she is again. Always in my way. She took my uncle from me and when he died, she claimed my rights for her brat Caesarion. Even before I could ally with Antony, she was already in *his* heart, blocking my path."

I stared at the emperor, entranced. Afraid to interrupt. "But I saw her *dead*," he continued. "She had no pulse or breath. She lay as cold as marble. I should've gone to that funeral and watched them seal her up in that tomb."

Juba tried to soothe him, "Queen Cleopatra *is* dead. The Egyptians are skilled with magic, Caesar. They're using their powers to give you doubts."

The emperor's eyes were shadowed as he turned back to me. "What causes these outbreaks of blood upon your hands, Selene? Do they happen at the same time of day? Do you eat or drink anything unusual?"

"I don't know," I answered quickly and honestly. "Twice it happened in the early morning, this time in the late afternoon."

Now that he'd abandoned the charade of protective warmth, his gray eyes sent that familiar chill through me. "Where is your mother?"

"She's in the afterworld," I whispered.

"*Where* is Cleopatra?" the emperor demanded again. "She's speaking to me, through you, so I know she's alive. Was there a double? How did she escape, and where is she now?"

"I told you. She's in the afterworld."

"No," the emperor said. "Death is the end of all things."

"Then she's dead," I said bitterly. "She's *dead*."

The stark brutality of my tone seemed to take Juba aback. He set his tablet down and lowered his head. It also seemed to snap the emperor out of whatever madness had possessed him. He took a seat behind his desk and ran his fingers over the golden dolphins that had once adorned my mother's bath. Then he took a blank scroll and tossed it to Juba. "Write."

Juba took the emperor's dictation. "'I, Cleopatra Selene of House Ptolemy, ward of Gaius Julius Caesar Octavianus Divi Filius, did on this day fall prey to a magical spell that made my hands bleed and forced me to be carried from the games. Magic is an integral part of the Isiac cult and was used against me in retribution for my loyalty to Rome. I ask that the perpetrators be punished for this treason.' Date that today, Juba, and witness Selene's mark."

I listened with a sense of dread. "What have the Isiacs ever done to you that you want to destroy them?"

The emperor snatched the scroll from Juba and laid it before me, pressing a pen into my hand. "They represent everything I fought against. They hold un-Roman ideas that spread like contagion. They condone immoral relations between men and women. They encourage the little people to think that the gods actually have an interest in them. They're a dangerous and influential cult, and I cannot tolerate their opposition. And none of this is even to mention how they conspired with Antony's old partisans when they thought I was dying in Spain! If your mother is alive, I'll not leave them whole to give her succor and assistance. Infiltrators and traitors all, even those in Rome. It's time I'm finally rid of this troublesome sect. Now sign it."

I had cooperated and the Egyptian gladiator lived. It had not been a lesson lost on me, but now I held the scroll away from me as if it were poisoned. "You'll just sign it and say I did either way."

"Don't make this uglier, Selene," the emperor said.

He wanted me to choose. He wanted me to prove my loyalty. I held the pen in my hand, but I couldn't write. "What will happen once I've signed it?"

"I'll have Agrippa leak it to the Senate," he said smugly. "They'll get curious about what I'm hiding. Then I'll make a great show of being forced to bring this complaint into the open. The Senate will be outraged on our behalf and take action. The temples will come down and the Isiacs will be persecuted."

He was bragging. He wanted us to take in the details of his plan and appreciate its horrifying simplicity; he always needed an audience to appreciate his genius. Now the emperor's gold furnishings winked with glittering mockery as I flailed in his trap. There would be no point in refusing him. The only thing my refusal would accomplish would be to spare me of complicity in destroying my goddess and her followers.

Juba watched my struggle and put a hand on my upper arm. "Make your mark, Selene."

Questions ran riot through my mind. How could I fight him? What would my mother do? The most famous story of my mother is how, when she had nothing else to bargain with, she delivered herself to Julius Caesar. But this was a different Caesar.

Could I soften his heart, the way my mother had softened two Romans before him? Could I make Octavian a better, more merciful ruler? "If I sign this, it'll destroy my influence with the Isiacs," I said softly, making my gambit. "Why oppress them when I could influence them?"

"Don't play games, Selene." The emperor had already begun to rise. He'd thought of this, I was sure. Weighed it. Measured it. And decided against it.

I had to change his mind.

"Isis speaks through me, so perhaps I can win her followers to your cause."

"Or conspire with my enemies," the emperor mused.

"Have I been disloyal to you yet, Caesar?" I let him have my dead brother's name. "Let me go to the Temple of Isis and speak with her followers. Send Agrippa with me if you fear it."

The emperor snorted. "I daresay Agrippa would do most anything for me, but there he might draw the line. You know how he feels about that religion."

"Then send Juba with me, but don't destroy the temples in my name! If you do, what use will I be to your empire?"

Octavian looked annoyed. "What use, indeed?"

I said a silent prayer that I understood the emperor's motives. "When you build your port in Mauretania, you'll need someone to sway the natives to your cause. If they believe in me, maybe I can convince them not to fight you."

"Maybe I'll send your twin, and while he's there he can have a tragic boating accident. I don't need you, Selene."

My heart stopped in my chest. Was he just trying to frighten me, or did the emperor hate Helios that much?

"But you *do* need me," I forced myself to say. "I come from a line of rulers who take disparate peoples and bind them together. A line of builders. You need a Ptolemy in Africa and I am that Ptolemy."

I could see that the messages on my hands had put poisonous doubts into the emperor's mind. Where he'd been so smug riding in his chariot today, now he was undone. "Your name may hold power, but you're just a girl. A very unusual girl, I admit, but just a girl."

"I am *not* just a girl. I'm *Cleopatra's daughter.*"

Silence.

The emperor stared at me, trying to penetrate my walls, trying to see into my mind, but I'd somehow found my pharaoh's mask again. I lifted my chin as he stared at me. Let the emperor look at me and think of my mother.

"You *are* Cleopatra's daughter," he finally said. "But will you be mine, Selene? That's the question, isn't it?"

I could see it then, for the first time, as I'd never seen it; he needed a protégé. He wanted me to belong to him, in spite of himself. My mother had also played this game with dangerous Romans. I must learn to play too. "Caesar, I'm yours," I said, hiding the shudder that went through my bones. "Everything I want can come to me through you alone. You're the only father that I have now."

It made me sick to say that. Sick in heart, sick to my stomach, and sick in my limbs. Loyalty to Isis had overcome loyalty to my father and it hurt more than I could have imagined. But I wasn't sorry.

"When you want things, Selene, you want them very much," the emperor said.

"So do you," I shot back.

"What I want is for you to marry Juba."

It stunned me into silence. I glanced at Juba whose cheeks colored, but he didn't look surprised. Clearly, they'd spoken of this before, and that realization made *my* cheeks color. I'd feared that the emperor would match me with some wrinkled ally in the Senate, that I'd be sent away from my brothers, to serve an old man, never to lay eyes on Egypt again. I'd never expected *this*.

Juba was young and handsome, and when he looked at me, sometimes my belly fluttered. Most important, being married to Juba might mean that I could stay near my brothers. Had I charmed him into asking the emperor for my hand?

How foolish I'd been to bind my breasts, to keep him from seeing me as more than a girl. Now, the bindings felt useless and I

wanted to tear them off. I'd never wear them again—for I understood that my strength now lay in being a woman.

"I'll announce the betrothal when it pleases me," the emperor
was saying. "But I'll have your assent and your cooperation now
in exchange for my clemency toward the Isiacs."

He didn't need my assent. He could marry me to whomever
he wanted. He had all the power and I had none—except for this.
He *wanted* my assent. And I would give it to him. I didn't look
at my intended bridegroom as I said, "You have my assent and
cooperation. When will we marry?"

"Soon," the emperor said. "Perhaps you can wed together with
Julia, since whoever she marries will be my heir."

He had it all wrapped neatly as a package. Julia and I were
chattel to bind chosen men to his side. I again nodded my assent
and watched the emperor throw the document accusing the Isiacs
of attacking me into the fire. The bargain had been struck.

Twenty-two

JUBA walked me back to Octavia's house, and as we made our way there, in spite of how much worse things could have turned out, I slipped into a solemn silence.

"You did the right thing," Juba said.

I didn't want to speak, but I found myself asking, "Would my father think so?"

"Your father wouldn't encourage a child's rebellion. You had no other choice than to cooperate . . . but I'd hoped you would like this match between us."

"Maybe I would like it more if you stopped calling me a child."

Juba stopped beneath a columned archway where green vines crept up the stone and clung. "You're a young lady—more mature than most I know. That's why I want to marry you."

Juba's eyes were filled with affection and I realized now how much I'd wanted to hear him say such words to me, and yet how could I believe them? "You flatter me, Juba."

"You doubt my sincerity? I'm fonder of you than it would be appropriate to admit."

"You needn't say such things." I leaned against the wall to still my shaking knees. "I know that ours is a political arrangement."

"Yes, political," Juba said, abashed. "But your mother's marriages were political and that didn't lessen their reported passion."

I knew what kind of things they said in Rome about my mother's reported passion and worried to have that reputation. "If this marriage will help serve Isis, then I'm glad for it."

Juba winced at my neutrality. "You resent how this was presented to you, and I don't blame you. Did I know the emperor might want us to marry one day? I did. But I didn't know how much I'd welcome it. I didn't expect to care for you as I do. I didn't know that we'd have things in common, like literature and—"

"A love of Africa?" I looked at him hopefully.

"That too." He pulled me from the archway into the torch-lit garden. "I'll give you a good life, Selene. An exciting life. We'll travel. We'll write. We'll meet all the most important people in the world. Our pasts are so much the same. Don't you think it's fitting, in a way?" At a loss for words, I studied him as he studied me and Juba brushed a lock of hair out of my eyes. "Selene, won't you like me a little?"

"But I *do* like you," I said. I liked his intelligence, I liked his curiosity, and I liked the sensitivity in his eyes. Still, this was no moment for romance. Today, I'd found Isis again and all that filled my thoughts was that I needed to see Helios. I'd kept so many secrets from my twin, and all that had to change. I needed to tell him everything—about Euphronius and about my bargain with the emperor. He'd see that I'd fight for our family, for our people, and for our faith as hard as he did. He'd see what I was willing to sacrifice for Egypt and he'd forgive me and maybe even help me.

WHEN I came through the door of my room, Bast had been dozing on my bed, and she came awake from her catnap with all her fur on end, as if my blood-covered visage were a terror even to her. I went to the washbasin and sponged my arms, then changed into clean clothes. "Are you better, Selene?" Philadelphus asked from the doorway.

"Yes. So much better . . ." I went to him and hugged him close. "Isis sent a warning for the emperor and he thinks Mother sent it!"

"Did she?" Philadelphus asked.

It was a surprising question. My mother had been called the New Isis, and perhaps she'd carried the words and the will of the goddess when she was alive. Perhaps the part of my mother that had been Isis sent the emperor a warning, but I didn't think so. "No," I finally said. "It's Isis who speaks through me, but I think Octavian *wants* it to be our mother. It unsettles him, it haunts him, and yet he *wants* it to be her." Philadelphus chewed his lip, clearly bewildered. Perhaps my twin would understand. "Where's Helios?"

"He won't come to see you," Philadelphus said. "I told him not to fight, but he's mule-headed."

"Let's see if we can convince him," I said, crouching under the desk to reach for the loose brick. I pulled it toward me, out of the wall, and found that Helios had blocked the hole with his bed on the other side. "Helios?" I sighed miserably when he didn't answer.

Philadelphus crouched beside me. "He'll forgive you."

I stared for a long time. "How do you know?"

Philadelphus peeked up beneath auburn lashes. "I just know."

I remembered all the strange things that my little brother said, and the words that my mother had spoken when she put his amulet around his neck the day she died. "Philadelphus, you knew that I'd save the gladiator at the games today. You knew it before it happened. You read the Rivers of Time, don't you?"

"Yes," Philadelphus admitted. "I see things sometimes, before they happen. Other times, the things I see don't happen, because the river has changed course. It's wide like the Nile, with all possible futures. Sometimes I catch up the water in my hands and see so clearly. Other times I look down again and the river goes a different direction and whatever I saw is gone."

"Can you see mother?"

"Sometimes," he said shyly. "Sometimes I see her victorious, with our father, and the eagle of Egypt flies over the whole world. I see Helios married to Iotape and Caesarion wearing his pharaoh's crown and Antyllus a great lord. But sometimes I see our mother in chains and the temples of Isis crumbled to dust."

I only dared ask the question in a whisper. "Is our mother alive?"

Philadelphus tilted his head. "Somewhere. Somewhere I see her with Julius Caesar and they laugh together and we don't exist at all. But mostly she's in the afterworld . . . Selene, don't be angry at me."

I wrapped my arms around Philadelphus to reassure him. "Why would I be angry?"

"Lady Octavia says people might think I worked magic, and they'd be angry and crucify me. She said not to tell anyone. Not even the emperor. She said she'd keep my secret safe."

I paled at the idea that Octavia knew more of my little brother's gifts than I did. How could I have left it to Octavia to protect Philadelphus? "Do you trust Lady Octavia? Does she treat you well?"

"She's very nice and she says I have our father's hair." Philadelphus took a curl in his fingers. "I used to know just what he looked like, but I can't remember anymore."

I ached at the sadness of his admission. It hurt worse when I tried to remember my father's face myself. The details were fading. How much longer before I forgot what he looked like entirely? Just then, Chryssa knocked at the door. Philadelphus and I crawled out from under the desk and let the slave girl inside immediately because her eyes were red and teary.

"I didn't think he would do it," Chryssa kept saying, sniffling and wiping her eyes. "Oh, my lady, I only showed him the tunnels to explain my comings and goings. I never thought he'd use them."

Tunnels. I remembered Helios talking about the tunnels as a way to escape before. My heart began to race. "What are you talking about?"

Chryssa cried, "Master Helios is gone!"

Twenty-three

HELIOS was *gone*. Of all the words that I could have heard, none would have made me feel so lost, for in my world, when people left they never came back. I stared at Chryssa wordlessly, overtaken by despair. I stood so still that I thought I'd turned into stone.

"Say something," Chryssa pleaded.

In answer, my hand struck like an asp, slapping her full across the face. But hitting her once wasn't enough to diffuse my rage. I struck her again and she went to her knees. Isis forgive me, so soon after finding your mercy, I wanted someone else to feel pain. I screamed at her. "How could you let him go?" Philadelphus stood in wide-eyed shock at my violence. Then I rounded on him too. "Did Helios tell you anything about this?"

He shook his head, his own distress obvious. The slave put her hand to her cheek where the red marks of my fingers lingered and her tears dripped on the floor, but when pity welled within me, I shoved it back down. "Where's Helios? What did you show him?"

"There's a tunnel near the Temple of Apollo," Chryssa said,

voice wavering. "The emperor built it so he can go back and forth without being bothered by clients, but slaves use it too. There are guards at the end of the tunnel. Helios might still be there, waiting for an opportunity to slip past."

"Maybe if we run, we can catch him," I said, making Chryssa get up. I grabbed Philadelphus with one hand, took up my skirt with the other, and led the way, racing down the corridor toward the gardens. I wanted to run as fast as my legs would carry me, but that would arouse suspicion. Instead, we strode with unquestionable purpose, as if summoned by the emperor himself. We wove through the arbors, where the scent of jasmine filled the warm night air, but just as we turned a corner into the privacy of the hedge, Chryssa pulled me back.

The house was quiet, everyone having been quite exhausted by the games, and yet I heard soft laughter. In the torchlight I glimpsed Julia and my Roman half brother in an alcove, locked in a kiss. Iullus had both his hands on her cheeks and kissed Julia as if she were a woman grown. The sound of Philadelphus's gasp caught their attention, and they broke apart. Then Julia sprang to her feet and Iullus sneered in my direction. "Shouldn't you be bleeding half to death somewhere, Selene? What are you doing here?"

What were *we* doing here? What was *he* doing here with the emperor's daughter was the better question, but I didn't have time to scold them now. "Have you seen Helios?"

Iullus smirked. "Do you mean *Marcus Julius Alexander*?"

Even in the dim torchlight, I could see that Julia's cheeks burned. "Selene, we didn't see Helios, but if he saw us, he wouldn't tell father, would he?"

That's when Philadelphus broke in with, "We think he might have run away into the tunnels."

Once again, I despaired of ever having a sibling who knew when to stay quiet, but Julia looked fascinated, as if exhilarated by my brother's nerve. "Ran away?"

Iullus found this terribly funny. He laughed aloud. "Won't the emperor be so pleased with his new favorite when he finds out."

I counted all the people who held power over me and with whom I must curry favor. Livia. Octavia. Agrippa. Octavian. My half brother, Iullus, wasn't on the list, so I said, "Listen to me, you bitter worm. You may hate the family you were born into, but if you don't help me find Helios, I'll make you sorry you were ever born at all!"

Iullus stared at me as if he were doing a calculation of his own. Now that I knew about him kissing the emperor's daughter, I had something to hold over him. I was a girl, but he knew I was clever. In the game of imperial politics, I might win. He shrugged at me in surrender. "He's probably still in the tunnels. They're guarded by the praetorians, you know."

I nodded. "Show us where the tunnels are, Chryssa. We're all going after Helios."

But no sooner had the words left my mouth than we heard a praetorian running up a path toward us. "What are you children doing out of your beds? Don't you know the hour?"

When we didn't answer, he said, "There may be an intruder in the compound. Augustus wants all the grounds checked, and you should be in your room, Lady Julia! Your father will worry."

"I somehow doubt that," Julia said, but guilt flittered across her puckish features as she looked to me for help.

I had none to give her. "What intruder?"

"A guard was found unconscious at his post at the Temple of Apollo. A big, bloody lump on his head. We think someone tried to get past him to come into the compound."

Iullus smirked his infernal smirk. "Or someone tried to leave."

THE emperor was a deep sleeper. He went to bed early and rose just before dawn, so interruptions of his schedule put him in the foulest humor. The day's events had already unnerved him, and being awakened by the guards with news of an intrusion made it worse. He entered the *tabulinum* wearing slippers. His hair was in disarray and his gray eyes were bloodshot. "Where's Agrippa?"

"On his way, Caesar," the guard told him.

The emperor grumbled. "Would that he brought my niece back to live in my house instead of Antony's. I'm surrounded by womenfolk and children, day and night, with their clamor." Then the emperor turned his attention to us. "You say that you realized Helios was gone, you suspected that he went out through the tunnel, so you came running to find him and stop him?"

My palms were sweaty, but I noticed that the emperor no longer seemed to care what Helios's name was. "Yes. That's what happened."

The emperor leaned toward me. "And you have no idea where he's going, Selene?"

But I knew what he really meant. He wanted to know if Helios had gone to find my mother, wherever she was. "No. Of course I don't know where he's gone." It wasn't entirely a lie. I knew that Helios would go searching for Euphronius and that he'd search for Isiacs sympathetic to our cause. But then what? Would Helios try to go to Egypt? And what if he succeeded? Would I be glad for him, or would being left behind be more than I could bear?

The emperor eyed my little brother. "Philadelphus, you share a room with Helios . . ."

Philadelphus shrunk back, wordlessly, and I answered for him. "He doesn't know anything."

Then the emperor's stony glare rested on Julia as if she were a great nuisance. "How did my daughter get involved?"

Iullus's eyes darted around the room as if he could hide his guilt amongst the tapestries and sparking braziers that lit the room. I enjoyed seeing his smugness evaporate and a part of me wanted to expose his secret, but nothing good could come of that. Besides, if I lied for him, maybe Iullus would feel bound to aid me. So I took a deep breath, and said, "I asked Iullus to help me find Helios. He suggested that we check your house and when we got here, I insisted on getting Julia to help, too."

The emperor looked skeptical. "And Julia, being a dutiful daughter, of course, alerted the guards?"

Julia lied as effortlessly as I did. "No. I thought Helios might be in the garden. He likes to draw his ships there sometimes."

I knew what would please the emperor and now I did it reflexively. "Please find him, Caesar. Please don't let anything happen to my twin!"

He'd always liked to see me beg, and this time was no exception. It gave him a chance to fulfill the role of *paterfamilias* that he so cherished and he peered down at me with something akin to benevolence. "Don't fret, Selene. A boy of royal breeding isn't likely to get very far in the city of Rome. I'll be shocked if he even finds his way to the Forum."

Just then Agrippa burst into the room, his armor askew. He'd obviously been roused from sleep. "I've got my best men on it. We'll find him."

"Be discreet," the emperor said. "I don't want all of Rome knowing about this."

Agrippa nodded. "What do you want done with the injured guard? I'd have him beaten unconscious again, but the blow itself nearly killed him."

"But how did the boy do it?" the emperor asked. "Helios hasn't even completed his soldier's training."

Agrippa paused to rub his chin. "He just whacked the guard with a marble bust. We found it broken."

The emperor cringed, the hapless guard forgotten. "Not the new bust of Divine Julius, I hope. That cost a fortune!"

"No, Augustus." Agrippa worked his jaw. "It was the one of you."

Twenty-four

TO find Helios, Agrippa posted guards at every shrine and Temple of Isis in the city. If Helios wasn't hiding with the Isiacs, we assumed he'd make his way to the port in Ostia, then try to sail to Egypt. But days passed without a clue to my brother's whereabouts and Agrippa was singularly frustrated. "When we find that boy, let's enroll him in the legions as a scout; he's sneakier than anyone under my command."

This was as close as Agrippa would come to making excuses. The emperor was counting on him to find Helios, and so was I. The longer Helios was gone, the more difficult it was to keep secret. What's more, if my brother actually made it to Egypt and declared himself king, all would be lost. Childhood rebellion would become war and Rome wouldn't spare us a second time.

Meanwhile, the emperor was seeing my mother everywhere now. When an eagle roosted upon the new Temple of Apollo— the spot that had been designated by lightning—the emperor was outraged, for an eagle upon a lightning bolt was the Ptolemaic symbol. Later that week, an obelisk slipped as workmen installed it and one of the workman's hands was crushed; the workers murmured that it was Cleopatra's Curse, and the emperor was livid. That same day, a Roman courtesan passed the emperor in the street wearing an Egyptian wig, and the emperor had her jailed. He seemed to unravel more each day and decided to make good on his promise by taking out his anger at my brother on his slave girl.

He had Chryssa beaten during our afternoon meal so that we could hear her screams while our food was served. Chryssa's naked body undulated as the whip came down on her skin, leaving hot red welts upon her back, and it seemed to me as if Iullus was watching with more than morbid fascination.

As the slave girl screamed, Julia dropped her spoon twice. Juba kept clearing his throat and Philadelphus whimpered. As for me, my stomach clenched so tightly I thought I might vomit.

"Selene, you've become so thin since Helios ran off," Octavia said. "You have to eat something, dear."

But I couldn't eat, and it wasn't only because Helios was gone. Watching the stripes of pain break across Chryssa's ribs, I remembered that I'd struck Chryssa unfairly. In my wrath, I hadn't recognized myself. It was as if, without Helios, I couldn't serve Isis as I was meant to do, and I was as angry with him as I was fearful. It was hard to believe that Helios had abandoned Chryssa to take his punishment. Harder still to know that he'd abandoned Philadelphus and me too.

It ached as much as any physical injury. Was Helios sorry for leaving us here, or relieved to get away? Had he found Euphronius? Was he hurt? Was he frightened? Was he lying dead somewhere? No. Surely I'd know if he were.

When the flogging stopped and Chryssa's screams at last softened to groans, the emperor looked up from his barley soup and announced, "I'm considering another wedding—a match between Juba and Selene."

Juba and I both greeted the announcement with silence,

but Julia gasped. "Surely not! Selene was once a queen . . ." She glanced at Juba, whose status she was implying was far below mine. He'd only been a prince and his family name far less prestigious; he was no Ptolemy. "I'm sorry, but she *was*."

To my surprise, Julia wasn't the only one offended on my behalf. My half sister Antonia also voiced her strenuous objection. "We love Juba, but if Selene must marry a foreigner, it should at least be a king."

Juba winced and I pitied him for his embarrassment. Meanwhile, the emperor stared, clearly not having expected opposition to his plan. He was unused to criticism, especially from girls. "Nonsense. We're Romans. What use do we have for kings?"

"Juba, forgive me," Marcella added. "But Selene is the daughter of Mark Antony and you're not even *half* Roman."

This seemed to offend Juba most of all, and it made him sit up in his seat. The emperor sputtered at the sudden mutiny. "Not Roman? I *made* him Roman. Isn't he Gaius Julius Juba? Wasn't he raised in my household?"

I couldn't fathom why the girls were arguing with the emperor on my behalf. Did they worry that if he made a poor match for me, he might make an even poorer match for them? But when Julia reached out and squeezed my hand, and the two Antonias looked at me in reassurance, I realized that over the years I'd become more than an exotic pet. They saw me as part of their family.

The emperor finally threw up his hands. "By Apollo, all I did was wonder aloud about a match. It just seems to me that Juba and Selene have a great deal in common. What do you think, Octavia?"

"I've approved of this match from the beginning," his sister replied, shocking me even more. "In fact, I recall it as my own idea."

Livia sniffed at her wine. "Does the emperor have some matches in mind for *my* sons?"

For the first time, Tiberius and Drusus became interested

in the conversation. The emperor scowled and said, "Tiberius is already betrothed to Agrippa's daughter, Vipsania."

Livia gasped. "But that was years ago, before Actium. I thought we had agreed such an arrangement was outdated and that you would consider greater marriages for my sons."

The emperor said, "Well, I haven't considered it yet."

Livia's gaze narrowed, holding special venom just for me. That the emperor was arranging my marital prospects before her sons was a slap in the face and she blamed me for it. Perhaps Julia knew it too, because she drew Livia's attention to herself. "Maybe I should be betrothed to Tiberius this summer . . ."

"Julia, it's improper for a girl to suggest her own match," Octavia scolded.

Livia slammed down her cup. "You only say that because she wants *my* son, not *yours!*"

Whoever married Julia would be the emperor's heir, and both women plainly coveted that honor for their own flesh and blood. "I'm confident in Julia's affections for Marcellus," Octavia countered, and the two towers of matronly virtue glared daggers at one another.

"That's enough," the emperor said. "How you women natter on. Take note, young men. This is what happens when you let a woman have the mistaken notion that she should have a say. Out. I want all things female out of my sight so that I can eat in peace."

THE emperor commanded that the household carry on as usual, as if the gaping hole that Helios's absence left in my life should go unnoticed. And yet, he remained nervous about how my father's old partisans might react. Perhaps, having bribed men like Plancus once before, he feared they could be turned against him again.

With Helios missing, the emperor no longer trusted me to leave the household, so my whole existence was once again confined to the Palatine Hill, and Bast was my most constant companion. On a market day during which I was feeling particularly abandoned, Julia agreed to keep me company at the looms. "You're very worried, aren't you?"

It was more than worry. Without Helios, I felt a rope inside me tightening, unraveling, ready to snap. I couldn't even think clearly. The day Euphronius had asked me to run, he'd sent me back to the villa to fetch my brothers. I would never have left without them, but Helios had left without me. Perhaps he'd found Euphronius. Perhaps he'd learned my secret, and what must he have thought? I couldn't even explain myself to him and it made me want to cry.

Julia bit her lower lip. "Maybe I can distract you. If I tell you something, will you keep it a secret?"

I nodded, slowly, never sure that it was a good idea to promise anything to Julia.

Her eyes shone and her rosebud lips parted with a sigh. "Iullus has written me a poem. A love poem."

"What would your father think of that?" I asked. "He doesn't even know about how you kissed Iullus in the garden . . . the risks you take!"

"I'll never have father's approval anyway. *You're* his little favorite." And when I winced, she added, "He praises you because you're foreign. You're a Ptolemy. You can be smart. But me? I'm to stay silent and convey the status of heir upon the man he chooses. You see how he is with me, Selene. Nothing I ever say or do pleases him, so why should I even try?"

"Did you somehow think it would please him to find out that you're meeting clandestinely with the son of his enemy?"

Julia made a face at me, as if I sounded just like an old Roman matron and I probably did. "You don't understand. I *love* Iullus."

I'd been embroidering and her words surprised me so much that I stabbed myself with the needle. I wasn't yet fifteen years old, but everything I knew of love told me it was deadly. Bringing the scarlet drop of blood to my lips, I said, "You shouldn't say that."

"Why not? It's true. I love Iullus *fervently!*"

"My parents loved fervently and it cost them everything."

That silenced her, at least for a moment. When she spoke again, she was sullen. "They say that, in Egypt, a woman can choose."

I'd boasted about the brave women in my family who had taken power and wielded it. Had Julia felt her face rubbed in it every time I told those stories, knowing her father would always discount her? Still, it galled me to listen to Julia complaining about a lack of choice in her life when I was being forced to marry Juba. Given a free choice, I might have chosen my handsome young tutor for myself, but I chafed knowing that it wasn't a free choice at all.

Julia continued on, oblivious to my concerns. "They say, in Egypt, a woman can even take lovers before she's married."

"Not royal women. Or at least they're not supposed to." Admittedly, I had a rather hazy idea of the chronology of my mother's pregnancies and marriages, and it was hard to sort out the truth from the emperor's propaganda.

"Well, I'm not royal," Julia said.

"You're also not Egyptian," I replied, irritated with my own prudish tone. "Maybe you should ask your father to marry you to Iullus instead of sneaking about in the gardens."

Julia snorted. "Father will never betroth me to Iullus because neither Octavia nor Livia champion him. Livia hasn't been able to give my father a son, so I'm his only path to having an heir. Why do you think Octavia and Livia are at each other's throats over whether I should marry Tiberius or Marcellus?"

"Which of them do you prefer?" I asked.

"Neither of them. It would break my heart to be given to any man but Iullus, but if I have to choose, I'd choose Marcellus. Tiberius is always so gloomy. Besides, any man that came from Livia's womb can be nothing but poison to me."

If I had a mother like Livia, I thought I'd be just as gloomy as Tiberius, so it seemed unfair to blame him for it. "Livia *is* an unpleasant woman."

"I hate her," Julia said with surprising vehemence. "She wants influence and pretends not to. She wants power for herself, while decrying it for anyone else. I think she wishes she were a man! She lectures on propriety and sin, all the while helping my father to—" Julia cut herself off.

"All while helping your father to what?" I prompted.

Julia worked the loom with an angry clatter. "It's enough to say that Livia would have poisoned me a hundred times over if she thought she could get away with it. As long as I live, her position as Mistress of Rome is threatened. She wants to be rid of me. Watch how she undermines me in my father's eyes."

"What were you saying before?" I pressed. "What does she help your father do?"

Julia didn't even pretend to answer my question and there was nothing I could do to make her. Whatever she knew about Livia, she wasn't going to tell me. Inelegantly changing the subject, she announced, "You must be outraged about this proposed match to Juba. Oh, I grant you that he's pretty to look at. I've even heard he's a decent soldier in the field. And I think my father actually means well by this match, in his way. For him, it's the best Roman story—two exiled children of foreign royalty come under the sway of Rome to find romance. He knows it will make the *plebs* sigh and clutch their breasts with tender feelings for his generosity and mercy."

I studied her, realizing for the first time how well she understood her father.

SINCE the emperor wouldn't let me out of the house without an escort, Juba came to take me for a walk through the gardens. He led me through the courtyard where the boys were sparring.

I hoped to see Helios amongst them but I didn't, and again I was left feeling hollow and alone. "Juba, have you heard anything about my brother?"

"You're very worried about him, aren't you?"

"You'd tell me if you heard something, Juba?" I asked, fighting back tears. "You *would* tell me, wouldn't you?"

Juba nodded. "But I haven't. Helios is still missing. This is bad news, as you know."

"I'm beside myself," I admitted.

"I know. You don't eat, you sleep little, and you don't speak in class. You don't even speak to me, though we're to be wed."

I took a deep breath, worried that I had offended. "I'm sorry."

"There's no need to apologize. Your brother is lucky to have your love." Here Juba paused. "I hope to inspire such loyalty from you one day."

"And I want to be a loyal wife." I meant it earnestly. Oh, Isis, how innocent I was. I didn't know anything of marriage, but I wanted to please him, and it made him smile.

Quietly, we strolled through the gardens where Livia's slaves had trimmed box trees in the shape of animals. "It's lovely, isn't it?" Juba asked, draping his arms over a marble railing. "We can build gardens like this in our own home if all goes according to plan."

I wrapped my arms around myself. "I'd rather that whatever we build be more like Alexandria than Rome."

"Do you even remember Alexandria after these years? Are you sure it was really so much preferable?"

Did he even have to ask? "Have you been to Alexandria?"

"I haven't had the pleasure," he said.

I sighed. "Then you couldn't understand."

Juba plucked a blossom from a hedge and handed it to me, a most romantic gesture. "If you explain, I'll try to understand. You can be the teacher today and I the pupil."

He was trying hard to win my affections, as if he didn't realize that he already had them. I wasn't distant from Juba because

I didn't care for him, but because I could think of little else than my missing twin. I took the flower and inhaled its scent while gathering my thoughts. "First, consider Rome," I began. "She crows with worry about the loss of old Roman values, and everywhere you turn, the emperor tries to reverse time. Everything new is suspect. Everything that's practical utility is not immediately evident is worthless. Beauty is frivolity, and books are stowed away in temples reserved for only a few. Rome is always looking over her shoulder and wishing for what once was."

Juba's brows knit in concentration. "Go on."

"But Alexandria isn't just a city," I said. "She's an idea. She isn't about what came before but about what can be. She has the best university, inviting the greatest thinkers of our time to collaborate and discover. The Great Library pools human genius from all over the world, or at least it did before the Romans came. Above all, Alexandria embraces the free mind."

Juba walked with me a few steps and then said, "How free can a mind be under a monarchy? It's not as if you Ptolemies adopted Athenian democracy. But even granting that, some say that a free mind is an undisciplined mind. The Alexandrians are the most rebellious and immoral people in the world."

I took a deep breath. "Sometimes I think *immoral* is just a word Romans use for things they fear. Why must passion be immoral? Why must pleasure be sin? Why should it matter which woman sleeps with which man?"

"Selene!" he said, scandalized. "You know why it matters."

And I did know. Yet, I could see that he was enraptured by what I was saying and I let myself fall under the same sway. For that moment, I imagined myself in his arms. Juba moved closer to me and I wondered if he'd embrace me. I wondered too what it would be like if he kissed me the way Iullus kissed Julia that night in the garden. I could feel his breath on my cheeks. He smelled like cinnamon and sand and incense. Like the upturned petals of a flower, I lifted my face to him in offering.

But Juba only kissed my forehead.

"When you care about something, you care about it fiercely," he said. "If your brother feels as strongly as you do, it's no wonder that he'd try to escape to go back home. But if he's gone much longer—"

"Perhaps he hasn't gone home," I said, a little dizzied by Juba's proximity, and remembering the words Euphronius spoke to me in the grasses outside Livia's villa. "Perhaps Helios has only gone east. Maybe to India."

The spell between us was slowly subsiding, as Juba said, "Even if Helios isn't in Egypt, the Egyptians may take up his banner in the hopes that he'll soon arrive. If they declare him king, then the emperor will send me back to Africa again to help put an end to it."

"Again?" I asked, taken aback. "When were you last in Africa?"

He straightened as if steadying himself for a blow. "During the war."

Something warned me in advance that I shouldn't ask the next question, and yet I couldn't stop myself. "Which war?"

Juba let go of my hand. "Selene, what's past is past."

My blood seemed to turn to water. I needed to hear him say it. "Which war?"

Juba didn't look at me. "The war with your parents."

"You were in Egypt?"

"And surrounds," Juba said. "It was my job to help keep other Africans from rushing to your father's legions. It was my job to help convince those who served your father to abandon him."

"You helped spread the tale that my father fled Actium after my mother like a coward . . ."

"Yes."

Just moments before, I'd wondered what it might be like to have Juba kiss me. I'd let down my walls, let myself feel close to him, and this was my reward. This was the man that I was to marry? This was that man?

"And what was your payment for these services, Juba?" I knew the answer to that too. It was me. "The emperor promised me to you, all that time ago. I'm your wages for your part in Egypt's defeat."

"Please try not to think of it that way," Juba pleaded.

Were it not beneath my dignity, I would have spit at him. "What other way is there to think of it? You always knew the emperor wouldn't harm me, because he'd already promised me as your slave girl prize. Did you think marrying me would help you regain your Numidian throne? Or did the glamour of marrying a Ptolemy entice you, Juba?"

"It doesn't matter why I wanted you," he said. "The point is that if it would help bring peace to the empire, I'd do everything again a thousand times."

I laughed bitterly. "I think you would."

I started to walk away from him, then changed my mind after a few paces. I spun on my heel to say, "If my brother finds his way to Egypt and is declared king, they'll send you to work against him. They'll have you use my name, as my husband, to what? To fight Helios? To kill him?"

"Yes," Juba said.

Of course. Just as Romans had pitted my mother against her siblings, this is what they would try to do to us. This is why the emperor had wanted my assent. He wanted to divide Helios and me through this marriage and weaken our claim to Egypt. But I wasn't some simpering Roman woman who would take her husband's part over all else, and the emperor, of all people, should have known it. I'd never take up against Helios. Not for Juba or anyone else.

My fingers curled into fists at my side, one hand crushing the blossom Juba had given me. How I wanted to hit him. How I wanted to scream. But someone was calling my name.

It was Julia and she was waving both her hands. "Selene! Virgil is here and he's telling everyone that he's seen Helios."

Twenty-five

TURNING away from Juba, I raced up the garden path and burst into the *tabulinum* where the emperor was supervising slaves in arranging chairs and benches for the night's lecture. Virgil stood by, sweating.

"Is it true?" I demanded. "Have you seen Helios?"

The emperor snapped at my intrusion. "Selene!"

"He's my brother. I have to know."

Juba and Julia arrived on my heels and the emperor fanned himself with his hat, waving us all into the room. "Well, Virgil," he said, "it appears I have a new interrogator in my employ and she may be more effective than Agrippa. Go ahead. Answer her."

"I'm afraid it's a very confusing tale," Virgil began, glancing at my arm, perhaps expecting to find my mother's snake bracelet wrapped around it, but it'd been secreted away since the day he gave it to me.

"I'll simplify this confusing tale," the emperor broke in, his expression somewhere between outrage and amusement. "Helios tried to burn down Virgil's house."

I was sure I'd misheard.

Virgil shifted from foot to foot nervously. "I own a country estate near Cumae. It's easier to work there, away from the crowds and the heat of Rome. One evening, I returned to find my slaves shouting and throwing buckets of water into my study, which was on fire."

I was astonished. "Why would you think Helios had anything to do with it?"

"Because my slaves managed to capture the arsonist and they brought him before me. Imagine my surprise to see it was your brother. But punishing the guilty party was hardly my concern. Saving my house was my priority and in the chaos of the moment your brother escaped with an old man in priestly garments that none of my servants could identify."

"An Isiac, no doubt!" The emperor snorted.

He was more right than he knew. It could only be Euphronius with Helios, but the Romans had long forgotten our old tutor, and I wouldn't remind them.

"Selene," the emperor said quietly, swatting at a mosquito that plagued him. "Your brother has done more than run away from me; now he's betrayed me."

"By offending Virgil?" I asked, as if I didn't know what he meant.

"Helios is trying to destroy the epic work I commissioned to glorify Rome."

My future groom was agape. "You think he was trying to destroy Virgil's *Aeneid*?" Juba asked.

I gripped the back of a chair and lied without reservation or hesitation. "My brother pays no attention to Roman poets. He couldn't care less about Virgil's work."

"Really?" the emperor asked. "Of all the country estates on the Italian peninsula, he manages to find Virgil's and set it aflame? It's a symbolic gesture. A way of striking back at me. Unusually subtle for your brother, I must add."

It was entirely *too* subtle for Helios, but it wasn't beyond our old wizard. If Virgil was writing a treatise that would glorify Rome and degrade my mother, they'd want to destroy it. But didn't Euphronius know what danger he was putting my brother in, and didn't he care?

When he'd urged me to escape with my brothers, Euphronius had said nothing about starting fires. He talked only of escaping Rome. So why hadn't they left yet? Were they waiting for Philadelphus and me? Were they coming for us?

"The fire was put out, I trust," Juba wondered.

"Yes," Virgil replied. "Thankfully nothing of import was destroyed. A couch, some draperies, and a scorched door were the worst of it. It all happened rather quickly and I was able to save my writings."

The emperor pinched the bridge of his nose. I could almost hear him counting in his head the thousands of man-hours he'd wasted hunting for my brother at Ostia. But who could've predicted Helios would go to Cumae? "Selene, while I've often decried your mother's morals, I never denied that she was shrewd. And yet they say her brothers were drooling idiots. Is this is a hereditary problem in your family?"

"I don't know . . ."

"It was a rhetorical question!"

I looked at Virgil. "Are you sure it was Helios?"

It was the emperor who answered. "Of course he's sure. Do you think there are many other startlingly blond boys of royal breeding running around trying to ruin my legacy?"

It had been a string of bad days and the emperor's eyes were sunken and his skin more afflicted than usual with splotches. "Leave me. All of you. Julia, go to your room!"

Julia's eyes widened at the injustice of it. What had she done, after all? "But—"

"Julia, go. Juba, send for Agrippa. Selene, serve Virgil some refreshments while we await Agrippa. He might have more questions for him. Now get out. Go!"

I led Virgil to another room where I knew I could find him some honeyed wine. As we walked through silk curtains, I noticed that Virgil was still sweating and fretting.

As soon as he was sure we were alone, he said, "Selene, I didn't tell the emperor quite everything. There's a message."

I remembered the last time Virgil had delivered a message to me, so I was wary. "What message?"

"It's from your brother. He asked me to give it to you before he ran off."

Virgil pressed a small scrap of paper into my hand, and I realized it was Helios's writing.

> *I was afraid the emperor would realize that you're dearer to me than a slave girl, dearer to me than my name, and dearer to me than Egypt. Now that I'm free, I'll learn for the both of us. The sun lets the moon rest, and the moon shines when the sun is tired.*

When I finished reading, my eyes filled with tears. I memorized the words and, with great reluctance, tore up the note into small pieces lest the emperor see it. "Ah, my dear, it seems I always deliver news that upsets you," Virgil said. "I confess that I tried not too hard to capture Helios. But he'll not get so lucky with Agrippa's men."

As if summoned by his name, Agrippa burst into Livia's dining room and nearly tripped over a low table. A fruit platter clattered to the floor. "Virgil!" the admiral bellowed. "How in Jupiter's name could you let the boy get away?"

"His villa was on fire," I interjected.

"Selene, go back to Octavia's house!" Agrippa barked.

"Helios is my brother, I—"

"Now!"

In his own way, Agrippa was less reasonable than the emperor sometimes. This was one of them. I trudged toward my room, my emotions a jumble.

I found Chryssa skulking by my bedroom door. She was hugging her knees, careful not to press against the wall. The lacerations from her recent flogging still wept blood into the bandages beneath her *tunica*, and she winced as she stood to greet me. "Lady, I've come to ask your intercession."

I opened the door to my room and motioned her to follow me inside. "I'm sorry that you're being whipped for my brother's misdeeds, and I'm sorry I struck you. You deserve none of it."

"You have no need to apologize," she said. "I'm just a slave and you are a vessel of Isis."

"But Isis teaches compassion," I said ruefully. "I should follow her example. I'm trying, but it's difficult to be as I'd like to be." And with that, I started to cry. Deeply humiliated that I let a slave see my tears, I tried to wipe them away with the backs of my hands. "I'll try to help you," I sniffled. "But I already walk a very narrow ledge with the emperor."

"It's an intercession of another kind I wish to ask."

Trying to get myself under control, I sat down at my dressing table and began to unwind the plaits in my hair. My lower lip was still trembling, and I bit it to keep it still. "I'll help you if I can."

Chryssa took a deep breath before saying, "I vowed to save my virginity for Isis. My vow has been broken." I was still young enough to be scandalized. I turned to look at her as she stammered, "S-s-someone found out that I was still a virgin. I was br-brought . . ."

"Brought where?" I gently prompted. I was painfully curious.

"To the emperor's chambers," she said, and my eyes must have flown wide in surprise because she added, "It was foolish of me to make a vow over that which I have no control. Now I fear that Isis won't forgive me. If you were to pray for me, surely she'd listen."

I noted Chryssa's bruised lips, her red-rimmed eyes, and the way her hands shook. I tried valiantly not to envision the perverse horror of her beneath the sickly ruler of the world. No. I *couldn't* imagine it—and my pity turned to suspicion. "Did you fight him?"

"I wasn't so foolish, nor so faithful. Will you ask Isis to forgive me?"

She lowered her head, awaiting my absolution, but I'd noticed evasions. *Someone* had discovered she was a virgin? *Someone* led her to the emperor's chambers? Who?

What could she hope to gain by telling these lies? Perhaps she'd resorted to this to win back my favor, but I already felt guilty for the way I'd treated her. "I'm sure Isis will forgive you. If you tell it true, it wasn't your fault. If it happened as you say, the emperor did it out of petty vengeance against Helios, and against Isis to be sure."

"Will you pray for me?" she asked again.

"I will," I said. After all, Isis offered forgiveness and compassion to all. "But when you pray to her yourself, you must tell her only the truth of what happened, and all of it."

I knew Chryssa was one of the few people who would take solace in the news that Helios was alive, so I tried to cheer her. "I have some tidings that might be welcome. They've seen Helios. He's somewhere near Rome."

She gasped. "Have they caught him?"

"Not yet. He's with Euphronius. Doing *what* I'm not sure, but I thought you'd like to know."

"Thank you, my lady," she said, and I could see she was sincere. She didn't even eye my jewelry with her usual covetousness, so I motioned for her to rise and make herself comfortable on my bed. She winced when she took a seat, her flesh still tender from the lashing.

"I hope they don't catch him," she said. "He's too strong and brave."

"How can you praise him after he left you to take his punishments?"

"I don't mind," the slave girl replied. "I told him not to worry about that when he left. It was a sacrifice I was glad to make for him."

Chryssa realized her error just as I did and dropped her eyes. My nostrils flared. I slammed down my comb and turned on her like a lion in the arena. "You said you had no idea he was going to run away. You lied to me!"

"My lady, please forgive me, but we didn't know what you'd do if you thought I had any part in him leaving."

I wanted to slap her again and so much harder than before. But if I did, I thought I might never stop. "Helios told you not to trust me?"

She held up her hands in supplication. "He said that when Juba carried you out of the arena, he worried that you might say the wrong thing to the wrong person."

Oh, how it stung.

"That's not fair," I said, my voice hoarse. "I called for Helios, not Juba. I called for him."

"He said that he couldn't become Marcus Julius Alexander."

"Don't you know how dangerous this is? If he's gone much longer, it's a king's rebellion and he'll end up drowned in the Nile in his golden armor, like my mother's brother! You tell me where he is, or so help me—"

"I only know that he went to find Euphronius," Chryssa insisted.

"It's been three years since the Ptolemies ruled in Egypt. Do they even remember us anymore? What does Euphronius want with my twin?"

"What all the Isiacs want of him. We want him to return the throne to Isis, to safeguard a kingdom where people may worship her freely and her mysteries can be preserved. Since your mother's death, Isis has been without a home. You and your brother must give one back to her again. Then, perhaps, there'll be a Golden Age."

I spoke through clenched teeth. "Everyone babbles about a *Golden Age* but not once has Isis mentioned it, even when she carved messages into my flesh!"

"The rumors are already spreading of Helios's divine strength, my lady, and that he'll free Egypt of Roman tyranny. Soon the uprisings may begin in Rome itself."

My mouth went dry. "If that happens, the emperor will be forced to kill him. Don't you see that?"

"Or maybe Helios will be forced to kill the emperor."

My anger was volcanic. It was as if without my twin, my own rage was unleashed and I could barely restrain it. I didn't feel like serene, loving Isis now. I felt the destructive wrath of my mother inside me. "You tell me where Helios is and you tell me now!"

Chryssa shrank back in fear. "I've told you all I know."

"Chryssa, if you're lying to me, so help me, I'll pour salt and vinegar in your wounds. I'll make you suffer. I'll make you more miserable than the emperor could ever think to."

"I swear by Isis, I don't know where Helios is."

"Do you know anything, you lying, worthless slave? Get out!"

Chryssa rose quickly. I took a nearby oil lamp and launched it after her as she fled. It crashed against the door frame as she escaped; clay shards and oil spattered everywhere.

I couldn't sleep.

A damp chill had settled in my woolen blankets while a rain-storm howled outside. Inside, the anger that Chryssa had unleashed in me still screamed through my veins. Now that I knew she'd lied to me about Helios, I was sure she'd lied about everything else—especially her ridiculous story about the emperor taking her virginity.

But alone with myself, tossing and turning in my bed, I had

to admit that it wasn't the slave who upset me. It was Helios. I was tortured by the knowledge that he hadn't trusted me. And why should he have? I'd been lying to him practically since the day we'd come to Rome. Lies of omission, to be sure, but lies still. Helios thought I'd betray him to the emperor and maybe I would have. Maybe I *still* would if it kept him safe.

When Euphronius had asked me to escape with him, there was at least some reason to think that with Octavian dead we might prevail. But now? Helios had to know how a confrontation with the emperor would end, but perhaps, like my mother, my brother saw virtue in fighting even when he couldn't possibly win. And like my mother, he'd left me.

Meanwhile, I was to marry a man I now loathed. Treacherous Juba. Once, I'd sought out Juba's attention because of my childhood infatuation, but now I knew I was just his laurel leaf crown. From now on, whenever I remembered those shadowy nights when my father brooded in the cabin by the shore, contemplating his suicide, I'd blame Juba.

How would I bear being married to him? *Traitor.*

Did Helios think the same of me?

Between the splashes of rainwater outside, two frogs croaked at one another in Octavia's atrium and one of them sounded as if it were laughing at me.

WHEN I heard the brick in the wall being moved, I threw the blankets off and bolted out of bed. "Helios?"

"No, it's just me," Philadelphus said, looking through the hole in the wall with one wild eye.

I tried not to show how much my heart sank to see him. I loved Philadelphus. I needed him now more than ever, but he wasn't my twin. "What's wrong?"

Philadelphus said, "I think it's my fault Helios is gone."

I couldn't help but sigh with him, sharing that ache, and

wondering if I hadn't failed both of my brothers. "Your fault? No. It was mine."

"He knew that I could see things, Selene, and he wanted me to try, but I was too frightened. Lady Octavia warned me not to."

"Perhaps you were right to listen to her," I said.

"I can't see things just because I want to anyway," Philadelphus said. "But I think it might be different for you."

"What do you mean?" I asked, not sure I wanted to know the answer.

"I saw something in the Rivers of Time. I think I know how Isis comes through you. She's the goddess who sewed together the severed limbs of Osiris. She's moved by the suffering of those she loves. She's called by our blood."

"Blood?" I held my hands up and stared. The first time the hieroglyphics appeared was the day after I was spattered with the blood of the Prince of Emesa on the steps of the Temple of Jupiter. The second and third messages had followed my touching or tending to Helios's wounds. Yet I'd tended my own cuts and scrapes, and touched my own menstrual blood, and nothing had ever happened. "Are you sure?"

Philadelphus nodded. "And I've seen other things too. Now that the Isiacs in Egypt know that Helios is free, they plan to rise up and riot."

"Sweet Isis!" I pressed my hands flat to my face. It was madness. "Is Helios declaring himself King of Egypt?"

"Shhh!" Philadelphus spoke in a voice that wasn't entirely his own. "Helios is trying to save Isis, for if there's no throne for Isis, everything will change. There'll be no more goddesses in the world, only gods. Ages and ages pass and all the goddesses are washed away."

My eyes widened. "That's what you see?"

Philadelphus blinked rapidly. "Without Isis, people forget female divinity. Isis must be saved."

I'd heard this before, but still my question remained. "How does one save a goddess?"

Philadelphus had the same kind of bewilderment upon his face that I always felt when I received messages upon my hands. I'd been a messenger for Isis, but I hadn't always understood the messages. So too it seemed with Philadelphus and I wished I could comfort him.

So many nights I'd reached through this small hole under my desk for my twin's comforting grasp. In fact, Philadelphus and I had both always reached for Helios. Now all we had was each other. But in each other, we also had Isis. Perhaps our goddess couldn't protect us from all harm, and perhaps faith alone couldn't solve all that vexed us, but Isis bound us together as surely as she bound the pieces of Osiris.

I remembered the way the doomed gladiator called her name as he lay splayed in the sand of the arena, his throat exposed to the sword. He'd called for help, and through me, Isis had answered him. I couldn't bear a world in which such simple magic wasn't possible. Whatever else happened, whatever wrongs I'd done, Isis must still live on in me.

I reached beneath my mattress and drew out the frog amulet on its golden chain. The carved jade glowed green in the lamplight, so delicate, so beautiful, so precious. I fastened the chain around my neck and kissed the inscription, the stone cool and soothing to my lips. *I am the Resurrection*, it read, and I whispered the words to myself.

The night I chose not to run with Euphronius, I made the right choice. Perhaps a lucky choice. But I'd been wrong—so wrong—to turn away from Isis. I didn't believe my twin's defiance nor Juba's capitulation was the way to save my faith, but with the love of Isis, I'd find my own way.

Twenty-six

AS the imperial family settled into their usual seats, the emperor's temper was anything *but* usual. His tooth had been bothering him and he puffed his outrage through a swollen cheek. "Three riots outside of Rome in two days!"

I didn't see why this was particularly worrisome. The Romans rioted about everything when the weather got warmer, but the emperor dug his stylus into the wax tablet and said, "Word has spread that Helios has disappeared. Some are even saying that I killed him. This is what mercy gets you."

As my stomach clenched, Juba said, "There's no sense hiding anymore that he's run off. Caesar, the truth might serve us very well in this case."

I dared not look at Juba. His voice had once sounded sweet to my ears, but now everything he did made me angry.

Agrippa broke in. "If they think we've killed the boy, they're not going to believe that he ran off. Maybe it's time the people took less interest in Antony's children. Antony was a traitor to

Rome. We've ruled his birthday an evil day and prohibited his name. They can't seriously be rioting over one of his brats!"

Iullus tensed in his seat. Octavia held Philadelphus closer and the admiral had the grace to look away. I knew it was just his frustration talking, but his words hurt. My father had been vanquished, but Rome still loved and remembered him. Someday, though, the Romans might not remember Antony and when that happened, our fates might change too.

"Well," Juba said softly. "Perhaps we should trot Virgil out to tell the people how Helios tried to burn down his house."

"Who will believe that lunacy even if it's true?" the emperor asked. "Besides, they're not rioting over Helios so much as they're using this as an excuse to protest my policies."

The children of the household were mostly quiet during this exchange and I noticed Chryssa hovering in the doorway with some of the other slaves. Iullus glanced at her and from my vantage point, I could see that his expression was unmistakably lurid.

Suddenly, the emperor slammed his tablet down. "I'm going to close every Isiac temple within the walls of Rome. They're behind this unrest and I won't have it!"

Did he plan to break his bargain with me? I tried to hide the creep of anger that reddened my cheeks—especially since I knew he was right. This time, it probably *was* the Isiacs who were to blame for the riots.

As I tried to disguise these thoughts, I realized the emperor was looking at me, his eyes sharp as flint and heavy with expectation. He wanted something from me. When the emperor played this game with Agrippa he always led the admiral down an obvious path. It had started that way with me too, but the better I became at anticipating what he wanted, the less obvious he made it. I'd have to become better still at this game. Better still at riding this serpent that might turn and strike at any moment if I wasn't careful.

Now that I no longer bound my breasts, the clasps holding my *tunica* seemed to cut into my skin. I fidgeted until it draped properly. The chair I sat on felt too stiff. I didn't know what the emperor was fishing for, but I knew what I must do. "Emperor, if the Isiacs are behind this rioting, let me tell them that Helios ran away and has been seen alive. I'm his sister. They'll believe me. I'll tell them he left because of a scuffle with Iullus. I'll tell them it's boyhood rebellion. I'll say whatever you want me to."

Whether he was pleased or displeased, he didn't show. "I'll think on it. There are certain additional conditions that would have to be met, Selene."

"I'll meet them," I promised.

That I was willing to renegotiate wasn't lost on the emperor. His cool gray eyes met mine in understanding before turning in wrath on Agrippa. "How does this boy evade capture? Are your men incompetents?"

Agrippa squared his shoulders defensively. "The Isiacs are like vermin. They can infest even the best of households. There are more of them in the city now than there were last year, and more last year than the year before. Some of them claim that Helios is—"

"I know who they think he is," the emperor said bitterly. "Some might rally to him because of their Isiac fantasies, others might rally to him because he's Antony's son. Well, all Rome knows Helios is missing now, so you might as well alert the urban cohort."

Livia stirred a tonic for the emperor's tooth and set it beside him. "With the city rioting, perhaps we can distract people with a wedding. Julia expressed an interest in marrying Tiberius . . ."

The emperor didn't look at his wife. He didn't look at Julia. He only looked at his sister when he said, "Julia is going to marry Marcellus."

The room went completely and utterly silent. It was as if the torches were afraid to sputter and no one dared to breathe. Although the tension in the room was palpable, Lady Octavia clasped her hands to her heart and smiled, but she was the only one who did. Marcellus froze in his seat as everyone stared at him. Livia glared like some gorgon, ready to turn everyone to stone. Especially her son Tiberius, who had apparently fallen short of expectations.

For her part, Julia was stricken. She fought back her tears and it must have killed her not to look at Iullus, so I looked at him for her. My half brother had spent the better part of his life learning to school his features to please the emperor, but now even his expression faltered. I had to admit that he actually looked crestfallen when he reached for his goblet and drained it of watered wine.

"But—but what if I don't want to marry Marcellus?" Julia asked.

Sensing her chance, Livia jumped in to say, "The poor girl is in love with Tiberius, can't you see that?"

For just a moment, it seemed as if Julia might be foolish enough to speak the truth about her feelings for Iullus, but I watched her swallow down all her anguish and mask herself, just as I had always done. "It's not true."

"And it wouldn't matter anyway," the emperor said. "Tiberius isn't my son."

"Neither is Marcellus," Livia replied.

"Marcellus has the blood of the *Julii* in him," the emperor replied. "My nephew descends from Venus just as I do. And when Virgil finishes writing the *Aeneid*, it will help shape the mythos around our dynasty. Marcellus will get me a grandson upon Julia. One with my bloodline. That's the end of it."

"But Julia's still so young," Livia dared to say. "Can't it wait a little longer?"

"She can breed, so she's old enough. When she gives me a grandson, she'll have finally done something to make herself useful to me."

At that, Julia started to cry and Lady Octavia started toward her. "Oh, Julia, my dear. Marcellus will be a kind husband to you. I swear it." But Julia pulled away. Big teardrops flowed down her cheeks, and her slender frame was wracked with sudden sobs.

"Selene," the emperor said. "Talk some sense into my daughter."

And now I understood that this was his new condition. I was to make Julia behave. I was to persuade his daughter to be as biddable to his plans as I was.

LATER, I found Julia and Iullus on the marble bench by the hedges, exactly where they had been before. This time, Julia was sitting on Iullus's lap, and he was rubbing her knee with his hand, fingers inching the fabric up, mouth on her neck like a lover. There were still tears on her cheeks but something more too. A breathless desperation as she kissed him. A needy sound in her throat as she let Iullus touch her anywhere he wanted to. I was both fascinated and upset by the sight, my heart thumping in my chest. Was this what love looked like? Might it have been this way between Juba and me if only I'd never asked him about his part in the war?

I stared for a few more moments than I ought to have before making my presence known. It was Iullus who saw me first. "Selene, you're the nosiest person I know. Have you come to make matters worse?"

I blushed. I blushed for what I'd seen, I blushed for blushing, and I blushed with fear for them. "You're going to get caught, don't you realize that? And now that Julia is betrothed to Marcellus, the emperor will think you've betrayed him. How much provocation does the emperor need to eliminate another troublesome son of Antony?"

Iullus bristled. "The emperor doesn't see me as a troublesome son of Antony. He doesn't think of *me* like that. I'm not like Helios. I've been a member of this family since I was a little child. He thinks of me as one of his own. I'm not a foreigner like you or your brothers."

I could see that Agrippa's earlier remarks were still ringing in his mind, though, and so I pressed on. "Neither was Antyllus."

Our dead brother's name must not have twisted with grief in Iullus's heart as it still did in mine, for his face remained stony. He looked me in the eye and said, "Antyllus was an enemy of Rome."

A traitor for loving our father, he meant. A traitor for having come to Egypt, he meant. Antyllus was a traitor for having been my brother in truth, though he was Iullus's brother by blood. "Is it now treason to show filial piety?"

"It is when your father is a traitor," Iullus said, staring off toward the Roman hills, lit purple by the setting sun. "I reject Antony and embrace Caesar. I don't try to have it both ways, like you do. Someday the emperor will see through you."

Suddenly, I understood Iullus—the little boy lost, trying to find a new father. He thought I was trying to do the same, and that fueled his hatred for me. He thought I'd stolen one father from him and was now trying to steal the other. I felt for him a mixture of compassion and contempt and used my words like the surgeon uses a scalpel to cut out disease. "Iullus, the emperor has just shown you what he thinks of you. They say that no one served him more faithfully in Spain than you did. But who did he choose just now, to wed his daughter? He chose Marcellus. At least the Antonias are related to him by blood and my mother was a queen. You're just the son of an uppity Roman woman who dared to make war on him. You're of no value to the emperor and it's time you realized it."

This time, Iullus offered no snide quip. His fists balled and he rose to face me, but I wasn't afraid of him. I stood my ground. Then he turned and stormed off toward Octavia's home, his sandals crunching over bushes and flowers as he went. Julia called after him, but he waved her away. We both watched him go. "You were cruel to him," Julia said, drying her teary eyes with the back of her hands. *"Cruel."*

"I was kind, Julia. Your father has no interest in Iullus beyond using him as an example of how merciful he can be. You say you care for Iullus, but you're risking his ruin. You're betrothed to Marcellus now. You can't ever kiss Iullus again. It's too dangerous."

"It's only dangerous if you tell," Julia said.

I wouldn't tell. Iullus might never think of me as a sister. He might never accept me as anything other than the daughter of an Egyptian whore, but I would protect what remained of my family, whether they wanted my protection or not. "I'm not going to say anything, but—"

"Thank you!" Julia embraced me in a fit of spontaneous exuberance. "I *love* him, Selene."

This time, when she said it, I believed her. I wanted to cut that out of her too. "It doesn't matter if you love him. He doesn't love you. I know you think he does, because he gets Horace to help him write you love poetry. But Iullus only thinks you're important because you're the emperor's daughter. He wants you because he can't have you."

She recoiled from me. "Why are you being so mean?"

"I'm not trying to be mean. I'm trying to tell you that Iullus isn't a nice person. He has a darkness inside that he doesn't even struggle against."

Julia wrapped her arms around herself. "How can you say that?"

"I think he forced himself upon my brother's slave." When Julia's eyes sparked with jealousy I explained, "Chryssa swore her virginity to Isis, but she claims—"

"I've heard of this," Julia interrupted, her voice lowering a notch. "Of women who dedicate their virginity at fertility rituals in the Isiac temples."

I felt my blood run unexpectedly hot. "I don't think it was like that. Followers of Isis often make vows of chastity. They make sacrifices for spiritual enlightenment."

"But some of them also debase themselves in fertility rites, don't they?" Julia asked.

"It's not debasement," I argued before I could stop myself. "It's something very old that is sometimes practiced at her temples. It's a rare thing, but sometimes the temple prostitutes and other worshippers gather and initiate newcomers."

"Initiate?" Julia was always one for the salacious details.

I sat down on the marble bench with her. I was exasperated, but I tried to appear more sophisticated about the subject than I really was. "They mate. It brings about the blessings of Isis to the land so that new children can be born."

Julia's eyes were wide. "Are you saying that Isiacs go to the temples and . . . breed with complete strangers?"

"I think so. I don't know. Sometimes. But that's not—"

Julia howled. "Worshippers of Isis do *that* and you're worried about my kissing Iullus in the garden?"

"What should it matter? It's a holy rite that has been sacred for thousands of years and it is probably gossiped about more than it's ever been practiced. Even if Chryssa were going to do that, she's an unmarried slave. You, however, are the emperor's daughter."

Julia seemed determined to divert me from the intended course of the conversation. "What happens if the women in this ritual were to get pregnant?"

"They're *supposed* to," I said. "Children are good to bring to a marriage. Sometimes married women go to the temple for the rituals if they are having trouble conceiving, with the blessings of their husbands." I was likely confirming everything the emperor said about my mother and my people, but it was Julia, and I wasn't about to feel shame before her. "It isn't as if they're taking lovers in amorous affairs!"

Julia looked at me dubiously. "You're making that up."

"It's true. It's referred to even in the Hebrew holy book. It's the tree and the fruit and the snake, symbols of Isis that their creation story warns against—as they were no friends to the Isiacs even before King Herod came to power."

"How can they know who fathered the child?" Julia objected, mesmerized.

"They can't, and my mother said we ought to curse the day men ever learned that they fathered children, because that's when they started treating them like possessions."

We were both silent for a moment. Julia was looking at me with a mixture of admiration, envy, and fear. "Perhaps Livia should go to one of these rituals—then maybe she could provide my father with the son he needs and then I wouldn't have to marry Marcellus."

"Julia . . ."

"Perhaps *I* should go. Then no matter who my father married me to, I'd still get to choose who fathered my child. Perhaps then I could choose Iullus."

I was frightened by how seriously she said it. "Don't speak it. Don't even *think* it. I should have never mentioned it."

"Then why did you?" Julia leaned back against the vines on the low wall and her little mouth puckered in thought.

"I just want you to think twice. Iullus isn't the boy you think he is and he likely violated Chryssa, though she made up this outrageous story about your father."

"My father?" Julia said, with a tilt of her delicate head.

I'd come this far, there was no point stopping now. "She said someone found out that she was a virgin and brought her to the emperor's bed." I expected Julia to laugh or to be outraged and disgusted, but she showed no signs of surprise whatsoever. When she didn't say anything, I rambled on with, "Clearly that's a lie, but Chryssa was upset. And I've seen the looks Iullus gives her."

Julia folded her arms over herself. "Sometimes you're so clever, Selene, and sometimes you don't know anything."

I bit my lower lip. "I know how your father feels about such things. He's even told me it's not proper or legal for Romans to bed with their slaves."

"First of all," Julia said, "when he lectures about propriety, purity, and chastity, he's talking about women. Second, even if he were talking about men, that doesn't mean it applies to *him*."

"The emperor preaches about homespun and he wears it," I pointed out. "He preaches about simple food and he eats it."

Julia rolled her eyes. She took a stone from near her foot, and threw it into the bushes. "My father also preaches about a moderate homestead and you've seen his office. You've seen the temple he's built for himself while telling Rome it's for Apollo. My father is like one of those actors from the theater. Everything is a show. So why don't you stop blaming Iullus when anyone could tell you that deflowering virgins is my father's favorite pastime."

I sat there, still as a statue. "That's absurd."

"It's true. His friends try to discourage him, but it's of no use. There was even an instance where my father sent for a girl, and when he opened the carriage, a friend leapt out with a knife to show him how vulnerable he was. I think Maecenas hoped that my father would be content to take Terentilla as his mistress, but she apparently isn't young enough, or pure enough."

"You're making that up."

"Like you made up the fertility rites of Isis?"

My expression soured as I struggled to readjust my perceptions. "I just—my point was just that you shouldn't so easily trust Iullus. Even if you're right about your father, Chryssa said someone brought her to the emperor. That was surely Iullus, trying to impress."

Julia stood up and started to walk away. She was like me in so many ways, a reflection and a shadow all at once. And no matter how foolishly placed her loyalty to Iullus was, I couldn't hate her for it. "Fine!" I said. "Maybe it wasn't Iullus that brought Chryssa to the emperor. It could have been anyone. You're right."

"Oh, it wasn't anyone, Selene," Julia said, whirling back to face me. "It was Livia."

I sputtered with sudden, absurd, laughter. "Livia!"

But Julia wasn't laughing. "Why do you think she even thought there was a *chance* that he'd choose Tiberius as his heir? She wins his loyalty by granting his every depraved whim. She practically scours the city to find virgins for him to despoil. Some of the slaves even say she tries to find highborn women to bear him a son that she can take in as her own."

A flash of memory from my first Saturnalia passed through my mind. I remembered the girl outside the emperor's bedroom and the way Livia had been caressing her cheek, then commanding her. Heat crept up my neck at the memory.

"Don't look so shocked, Selene," Julia said. "Livia tends to *all* my father's needs."

ON the other side of the wall, Philadelphus pressed the sharpened needle against the fleshy part of his hand. "I don't know if I can do it, Selene. I've never stabbed myself before."

"Don't do it too hard," I said. "Just a little blood."

We had a theory about the hieroglyphics. Only when I touched other people's blood did the messages arrive. In all three instances, the blood had belonged to someone I cared about. Someone who believed. Now it was time to test the theory. A chair blocked my door to keep out intruders, but I was still nervous that Julia or Octavia might come bursting in, and I was irritated that Bast kept yowling to be let out.

Philadelphus still hesitated. "But every time you get a message, there's trouble, and the emperor is in a foul temper already."

"The emperor doesn't know what causes the messages. Last time I had one, it made him unsteady. With Helios gone, I think I must *keep* him unsteady. It's when he's cool and calm that he's most dangerous."

"But the messages hurt you," Philadelphus said.

"Not that much," I lied, but I was desperate for guidance. I didn't know if the bargain I'd struck with the emperor was right or wrong, and I hoped Isis might tell me.

Philadelphus whimpered, handing me the needle. "I can't."

I thought about how hard it must have been for my father to

drive his own sword into his heart, or for my mother to bare her arm to the bite of the cobra, and I felt shamed for asking this of Philadelphus. "It's all right. I'll think of another way."

Philadelphus pushed his hand through the hole. "This is the way, but you do it for me."

My first attempt was ineffectual, causing pain without breaking the skin and Philadelphus yelped. "Sorry! I'm sorry." Finally, I took a deep breath and plunged the needle into his hand, a trickle of blood welling where I'd made the puncture.

"Ow!" He yanked his hand back and shook it.

I reached for his hand and pulled it back, smearing his red blood on both of mine, and whispering, "Isis, let me be your vessel."

When the crimson drops settled into the lines of my palms, I didn't know what to do next. Was I to leave my brother's blood on my hands? Wash it off? We had chores to do, and if I didn't complete mine, Octavia would be wroth.

"Now what?" Philadelphus asked, putting his lips to the wound.

"I guess we wait."

SUMMER was upon us and the Romans complained about the unbearable heat. Perhaps it was the nervousness that made me feel it too, because as I slipped onto a couch with Julia for our meal, I needed to wipe the perspiration from my brow. I had a hard time looking at her as the slaves served us millet porridge with thick ribbons of honey stirred through it. I couldn't look at Livia either. Not after what Julia had said about her. Livia liked to say that she never feared the emperor would divorce her because she'd always done whatever he asked of her, willingly and without complaint. But what would the people think of Livia, the perfect matron, pimping the virgins of Rome to her husband? Rome would forgive the emperor this vice—perhaps even admire him—but Livia? *Never.*

Given that the emperor had just announced the betrothal of Julia to Marcellus, Livia's position was more precarious than ever, and I knew it was a secret she'd kill to protect. I feared she could read the knowledge on my skin. In fact, I almost jumped when the emperor ambled into the room with some scrolls tucked under his arm.

"We're going to have *two* weddings this summer," he announced, and a spoonful of half-swallowed porridge caught in my throat. "Julia will marry Marcellus and Juba is going to take Selene as a wife."

My intended groom smiled broadly, but Livia's eyes flashed only briefly with resentment before drifting half-closed. It was her reptilian instinct to reserve energy. I knew she'd strike only when she felt strongest. My eyes lifted to the emperor who stood over me smugly, awaiting my reaction. I surveyed the room. Livia glared, but the tension and upset that had accompanied Julia's wedding announcement was absent here. Everyone else smiled at me or gasped their surprise. Even Agrippa seemed strangely happy for me and raised his wineglass to us. I could scarcely believe it.

Even if someone had been ready to protest, the emperor held up his hand. "You said that only a king would do for Selene? Only a king would do for a Ptolemy? Now you'll have one. I'm giving Juba back his ancestral lands. Congratulate King Juba."

"King Juba?" My eyebrows shot upward. "You've given him back Numidia?"

How was this possible? Was Numidia really to be deprovincialized and given back to its native prince, or was this a title in name only? Either way, Juba looked as if he might burst with pride. But I couldn't be happy for him. In the first place, I mistrusted this declaration. Surely there should be some manner of document to prove that the Romans would withdraw from Numidia in favor of Juba's rule. In the second place, I thought of my father kneeling over his sword when his troops abandoned him, the job well done on Juba's part for which he was now being rewarded.

"What have you to say, Selene?" the emperor asked me.

I'd already agreed to marry Juba so I'd gain nothing by refusing now, even if it meant I'd be dragged to Numidia—a world away. I loved Helios, I loved Philadelphus, I loved the Isiacs, and I loved Egypt. It wasn't a difficult choice, though I choked on the words like a bitter draft. "I'm honored."

The emperor was clearly enjoying the drama he was creating. He played the part of the benevolent dictator and he expected everyone to appreciate his largesse. "Haven't you a question about your dowry?"

My cheeks burned at the question. I had no dowry. He'd taken from us everything we'd ever owned. As if some man needed to be paid to marry me anyhow! The indignity of it stung. "A dowry, Augustus?"

He threw a scroll down on the table. I was afraid to read it, and when I did I was filled with dread. Juba was the rightful heir to Numidia—perhaps giving him back his kingdom was the natural thing to do—but as dowry for a Ptolemaic princess, the emperor was gifting Juba with a kingdom that didn't even belong to him: Mauretania. I'd asked the emperor to send us to Mauretania, to allow us to persuade the people there to build a port. I had *not* asked that he subjugate them under pseudo-Roman rule. "So, Juba will rule both Numidia and Mauretania?"

"How else will you build my trade port?" the emperor asked, entirely pleased with himself. "If I require a Ptolemy in Africa, I'll have one as the king's consort, although I don't envy Juba's task of keeping you in your place."

"What about Egypt?" I dared to whisper. My true inheritance was Egypt and we both knew it. Was the emperor going to make Juba pharaoh too?

The emperor actually laughed. "A moment ago you had little more to your name than a cat and a harp. Now I've furnished you with a royal marriage, yet always your mind is on Egypt!"

"Egypt starves without a pharaoh," I said quietly, cursing

myself for the dangerous line I walked. If I continued, I'd remind him that my twin was in open rebellion.

"Egypt is a chained crocodile," the emperor declared, swishing his purple bordered toga. "She's no threat to anyone and no longer gives us enough grain. Africa is the future. If you and Juba do your part there, then we'll see about ceding you back parts of the old Ptolemaic Empire. After that, perhaps we'll speak of Egypt." It was too rich a plum to dangle before me. He knew it. "Now, after the betrothal announcement, you'll go to the Temple of Isis and look for your brother."

My heart soared at the prospect of visiting the Temple of Isis, but my joy was tempered by the sinister purpose for which I was being sent. I knew I must get used to this. In becoming Juba's queen, I'd have to rationalize and realize the emperor's vision. I'd have to leave Rome and perhaps leave my brothers too, but it would save their lives and, perhaps, our faith. "Selene?" The emperor tired of waiting for my gratitude. I peeked at Juba and his eyes pleaded with me to use this as an excuse to finally invest myself fully, heart and soul, into Octavian's dreams. My bargain with the emperor had been struck before Helios ran, so I donned my own mask of the gracious and grateful ward. "Caesar, you're so very generous that I'm moved beyond words."

Marriage, thrones, and the love of family now formed golden chains around me tighter than the ones I wore when they dragged me through the streets of Rome.

Twenty-seven

FOR our betrothal announcement, I was obliged to dress for the occasion in an embroidered white gown fastened with pearl brooches at each shoulder. Silvered ribbons ornamented the dark waves of my hair, and I wore my mother's pearl necklace. Julia, Marcellus, Juba, and I stood together in the heart of the city where our betrothals had been published in the *Acta Diurna* for passersby to read. Then the herald made the announcement and the crowds swarmed around us in congratulations.

I was always frightened amidst Roman crowds—the memory of Octavian's Triumph never far from my mind—but on this day the faces were curious and friendly. As Juba displayed me on his arm like a prized falcon, children threw flower petals, and there was a general atmosphere of merriment. The people were so enchanted with the idea of Julia and Marcellus that they had no apparent concern that the ruler of Rome saw fit to name kings and queens of faraway places, for now Rome owned the entire world.

For my part, I pretended that I didn't loathe the man I was to marry. I smiled at senators. I waved to children and merchants. All the while, my eyes searched the crowd for Helios. Would I glimpse his golden curls beneath a farmer's hat? Would I see Euphronius first, sun gleaming off his bald head? I looked past braying mules with packs on their backs and searched the faces of young men gathered by the cisterns. I squinted in the sunlight, past the glitter of coins being exchanged, but I didn't see Helios.

We left Julia and Marcellus to their admirers, for the new King of Mauretania and I still had work to do. "Selene, can't you enjoy this day with me?" Juba asked as we passed the rostra which the emperor had adorned with the battle rams of my mother's defeated ships. "We're friends at least, aren't we?"

"We *were* friends," I said, a wisp of my hair escaping and lifting on the breeze. "That was before I learned that you're a traitor, and a liar."

"I never lied to you—"

"Yes, you did. You told me that you watched your own father die, but you can't have remembered that. I've studied my history. You were too young. If I weren't such a fool, I'd have realized it sooner."

Juba looked pained. "Selene, I only wanted to win your trust. To make you feel less alone. Besides, I have heard the story of my father's death told so many times I feel as if I *do* remember it. I've always been your friend. What can I do to prove that to you?"

I thought about this earnestly, and then lifted my eyes to answer. "You can swear by Isis you'll never help the emperor to hurt Helios or my family or Egypt."

Juba stared into the blue sky but didn't swear. "Can't we get past this?"

A tavern keeper toasted us in the street outside his shop, and I forced a tight smile. When I spoke to Juba, my teeth remained clenched. "Can we get past the fact that my parents and two of my brothers are dead because of you? I don't think so."

"Not because of me," Juba protested. "It was the emperor's

war, Agrippa's war, your parents' war—not mine. How can you hold me responsible?"

"Because the emperor, for all his vileness, is convinced he fought for family and country. What's more, it may be said for Agrippa that he at least met my father in open battle. But you're no Roman and you did your part in the shadows, with bribes and lies."

Juba's public face was slipping. "If I'm a traitor because I sided with the Romans, what does that make your mother when she fought beside Julius Caesar?"

"Are you comparing yourself to my mother?" I laughed. "Did you roll yourself out at his feet before *your* Caesar took you to bed?"

Juba blanched. I knew he would. His Roman dignity couldn't withstand the taunt. His footsteps stopped, there beneath the shadow of some unsightly brick building, in the middle of the street. He trembled with anger. "Selene, you go too far—"

"Oh, Juba, you mustn't scowl," I singsonged, holding fast to his arm. "Aren't we to be seen as the happy couple? If I must endure it, so must you."

Juba worked his jaw. "I suppose I shall just have to be grateful that the people aren't rioting."

Our wedding announcement had taken attention off my missing brother and helped give the impression that the emperor meant my mother's children no harm—in fact, it gave the impression that he meant to glorify us. It also meant that the emperor was playing one Ptolemy sibling off the other, just as the Romans had done in my mother's time. In the end, my mother's brother ended up drowned by Roman soldiers, and she in Caesar's bed.

That wasn't a fate I relished for Helios or for myself.

MY heart soared as the temple came into sight on the Campus Martius. Bright red, blue, and yellow pillars were a welcoming balm to my weary spirit—a speck of color in a more drab Roman world. Though the Senate had desecrated, destroyed, and banned Isiac temples before, my father promised to bring Isis back to Rome because the people demanded it. Now here she was, waiting for me.

Roman temples opened to the street, but the Temple of Isis was a quiet sanctuary for the faithful. A walled-in garden surrounded the temple, and from it I could smell magic. I could feel the *heka*, as if it hummed from every fuchsia acanthus flower I passed. So bright and silvery were the multitudes of lamps and candles that warmed the sanctum, the temple interior shone like the full moon at midnight. A reflecting pool glistened green as only the water of the Nile could—or was it a trick of the mosaic stones beneath?

Here the public gathered to view the statue of the goddess, rising in stone before us. I went soft to see her, my heart squeezing with unexpected joy.

Oh, Isis!

For so long I'd been away from her, from her mercy, and here she was seated, her carved gown tied in the mystical *tiet* knot between her breasts. Horus, the divine child, was suckling. For a moment, I forgot Juba and I forgot Rome, transfixed by the serenity of Isis's face. The features weren't my mother's, yet I could feel my mother's presence here, as if she'd just walked past me and the air was still tinged with her perfume.

In a chamber to the right of her statue, sacred crocodiles lay side by side at the end of their chains and the public steered clear of their dangerous jaws. I looked into their cold reptilian eyes and still found warmth. They, like me, were so far away from home.

"Selene, remember why we're here," Juba told me, guiding me by the arm. The emperor had made clear what was expected of me. I was to undo the damage Helios had inflicted by raising the hopes of the rebellious against the emperor's reign.

Turning to the crowd, Juba announced, "I present to you Cleopatra Selene of House Ptolemy."

Priests and priestesses dropped to their knees before me and some of the commoner citizens too. "Sacred twin," they whispered, but I stood before them a living being, of flesh, close enough to touch and without my other half.

"Daughter of Isis," one priestess said reverently. "We've been waiting for you."

These were the Isiacs that the emperor so loathed and feared— these holy people? With Juba watching, I knew I must be careful with my every gesture. "Please, rise. I'm honored the emperor has seen fit to allow me to come. He's a great man of much wisdom and he wished for me to spend time with the worshippers of Isis and share the news of my good fortune."

"You consider your fate good fortune, my lady?"

Everyone strained to listen for my answer; they seemed hungry for everything I had to say. It felt wrong to tell them half truths, but what choice did I have? "It's good fortune for me and good fortune for those who love Isis that I'm to be wed to Gaius Julius Juba, soon to be King of Numidia and Mauretania."

I forced a smile and the artifice ached inside me.

"You'll be King and Queen Consort of Mauretania but not of Egypt?" the priest asked.

The Isiacs understood the twining of religion and politics. My throne was deeply relevant to them and even everyday worshippers gathered around me to listen. "No, not Egypt." In a sudden flash of inspiration I added, "But in Mauretania, we'll build the greatest Iseum the world has ever known! A new harbor, a new world to let Isis be a throne once more, to give her a home where her worshippers may find safe harbor."

This was only a dream or a lie—which, I couldn't tell. Given the way Juba stared at me, a hint of warning behind his eyes, I knew he'd never let me do such a thing, but he dared not interrupt me now. Not when they were listening with rapt attention. Not when I'd captured their imaginations. This was the moment. "But to do all this, to honor Isis, I'll need my twin brother, Helios, by my side."

"So it says in the prophecies," someone whispered.

I spoke quickly. "By now, you must have heard that Helios ran away from the emperor's home. I worry for him and want him back home with his family, under the emperor's protection. If you've seen my brother—any of you—I beg that you ask him to return. I can't bear to be apart from him. I need him."

My throat tightened with emotion because that last part of my statement was true. Without Helios, I was desperately adrift and I let them see it in my eyes. If any of them had seen Helios, though, they didn't reveal it.

I adjusted the brooch at my shoulder and smoothed down my gown while they absorbed what I'd said. More crowded into the temple to see me with questions on their faces: Could it be true that Octavian, who had denounced Cleopatra, denounced Egypt, denounced Isis—could he possibly allow Cleopatra Selene to renew the faith? I had to convince them. "The emperor has given me leave to join your worship today."

"Come, then, for the Lamentations," the priestess said. "Wash your hands with the tears of Isis, which I bear in this consecrated bowl. As the tears of Isis are sacred to us, know that your tears are also sacred to her. It is Isis who wails for us and we are washed by her tears."

The familiar words of ritual came back to me from my childhood as Juba washed his hands in the sacred water. As soon as I dipped my fingertips into the bowl, my amulet warmed at my throat. I saw the Nile as I saw it the day my mother died, green as my twin brother's eyes. Teeming with life that danced at my fingertips. Something was happening to me and the world seemed like only one stream that fed an ocean in which all things were possible. In which Egypt was ascendant and in ruins. In which Rome was conqueror and conquered. In which Golden Ages died and dawned. It was the hum of *heka!*

As I struggled to come back to myself, my fingers dripping with the sacred water, I realized that the priestess was telling the story of Isis. "Once Isis ruled in partnership with her husband and their reign was glorious. But the dark god became jealous of their love. He murdered Osiris, dismembered his body, and scattered the pieces. Isis wandered the world in great sorrow and collected her husband's remains. Crying each night, searching each day, she walked the world leaving a trail of tears. Let us now walk the Path of Tears."

I'd missed the beauty of this ceremony and it made me miss Helios even more.

"As Isis unbound her hair in her mourning, so we unbind our hair," the priestess said.

I unfastened the ribbons that held my hair, and let it spill over my shoulders, braving Juba's admonishing glance. Then the priest walked past me carrying an urn and he smudged my face with ashes, chanting, "As Isis streaked her face with ashes in her pain and in her weeping, so do we streak our faces and weep with her."

I felt raw, naked, exposed. I felt the weight of my heart in my chest and tears sprang to my eyes.

Juba pulled me toward him. "This emotion is unseemly."

I ignored him.

A priestess took up a chant. "We weep for the poisoned earth that warfare makes unclean."

The people repeated the phrase, and like any good Roman, Juba tensed at the mention that war was not glorious. But there was more yet to come that made me understand why Rome, and particularly the emperor, wished to silence the Isiacs.

I'd been a little girl when last I shared the rites. Now, with new eyes, I realized that our ceremonies weren't merely spiritual but also profoundly concerned with the political. And profoundly un-Roman.

"We weep for those who deny that there's an afterworld in which we'll all be judged," the priestess said. "We weep for the greed that breeds humiliation, and poverty, and slavery."

This startled even me. The temple was challenging temporal

authority based on moral precepts. The temple was calling for a new order between man and the divine, between man and each other.

"Brother, what do you weep for?" the priestess asked a peasant.

This too departed sharply from any Roman religion. To have the common masses participate in ritual—so personally—was unheard of. "I weep for my father, lost in a battle in Spain," was the peasant's answer.

"Sister, what do you weep for?" the priestess asked the woman closest to me.

Her hair was red as copper and her back bore the mark of lashes; she was assuredly a slave, and she said, "I weep for a barren womb."

One after another, people confessed their fears, their hurts, their sorrows and regrets. They opened themselves to the judgments of complete strangers, and it humbled me.

"Sister, what do you weep for?" Now it was my turn. I was sharply aware that every person in the room had offered his or her pain to Isis. They took strength from her. They'd come here with honesty whereas my heart was heavy with guilt. I wanted to weep for so many things, but my weeping would have to wait. *Isis, forgive me.* I couldn't even look at the priests when I spoke. "I weep that Helios has fled an honorable and loving home and that people should think the emperor has done him harm."

This time, I could see that my words touched the Isiacs and was grateful when the priests handed out blindfolds, so that I could hide. With the linen wrapped around my eyes, I reached out into the darkness, where the faithful Isis gathered the pieces of Osiris's body and used her *heka* to restore him, giving him new life. I too embraced the night. My frog amulet wasn't merely warm at my throat but hot. With one hand I touched it, and thought my silent prayer. *Isis, please bring Helios back to me. Without him, I'm so alone.*

I heard a voice in my mind, familiar and terrifying. *You are not alone. You are never alone. You are the daughter of Isis.*

Am I a traitor? I wondered.

You know what you are, the voice said.

I did know. The words came out of me, clear and bold. *"I am the Resurrection."*

Isis was with me. She was in me. She was everywhere!

I shouted it. *"I AM THE RESURRECTION!"*

Power surged through me. Life force. *Heka*. It filled me and overflowed. I was like a jug in a waterfall. I'd always thought the frog amulet gave me power, but I knew now that it only amplified what was inside me. It was more like a lever, something to center my magic and intensify its force. Only at the Temple of Isis did I finally understand. Here, where thousands, maybe millions, of worshippers had come to leave their tears as a well of magic for me to draw upon. This is what had been missing since leaving Alexandria. And now that it had returned, I opened myself to carry a message for Isis.

I felt the stinging fire in my hands, words carving themselves into my flesh. I ripped off the blindfold and held up my fingers. Blood already dripped from them. But I wasn't surprised this time. Nor would I hide it. My shouts had caused a commotion and people began removing their blindfolds, crying out as hieroglyphics scrolled down my arms.

Juba grabbed at me, trying to cover my wounds but my blood dripped to the marble floor between us and flowers sprung whole, blossoming like a fortress of petals around me. Someone gasped. The barren slave with the red hair screamed. I turned to her in my fit of ecstasy and put my bleeding hands on her belly. "I am the Resurrection! I put my hands in the Nile and fish dance to life. The dried brown plants become green. The dead snake shimmers to life for me. So too will your womb become fertile!"

"Savior," she called me, and wept.

"Selene," Juba hissed, daring to pull me from the woman.

"Let go of me." I threw off his hand as if it were something putrid with rot.

Then, before he could reach for me again, I broke away, fleeing toward the shelter of the divine statue. I wasn't mindful of where I was running, and people screamed, warning of crocodiles.

In that moment, it seemed better to be eaten by sacred beasts than defiled by Juba. Before she died, my mother warned me that one day crocodiles would be my judge. If my acts were wicked, let them eat my heart. If my heart was light, let it be saved. The largest crocodile rushed toward me, legs splayed widely as it slid its belly along the floor, powerful tail whipping water into the air. I feared it would catch me up in its jaws and tear me to pieces, but when we collided, I fell and the creature dropped before me, resting his head in my lap like the most docile dog.

"No, Selene!" Juba cried.

I paid him no heed. The hide of a Nile crocodile is rough and scaled, and the animal in my lap was of a dark olive hue with brown cross bands. I embraced the head of the great beast and leaned over to kiss him, my blood dripping upon his majestic snout. He was a dangerous creature to whom I'd run for safety, and he, in turn, put his trust in me. He sighed, his reptilian eyes closing in bliss while temple-goers stared.

We were one another's refuge. Here, we felt safe—the crocodile and I—refugees from Egypt.

Juba lunged to grab me and the other crocodile rushed him. A snort reverberated through the temple. Flashing teeth snapped and narrowly missed taking off Juba's arm at the elbow. My betrothed leapt back as the crocodile thrashed at the end of its chain and Juba's voice rose in pitch. "Selene, come here this instant."

"You do not command me," I said.

I knew Isis more completely now and I was forever changed.

"Drag her away from those beasts," Juba said to the priests and worshippers.

But none of them obeyed.

I held my hands aloft to read the twisting hieroglyphics while the barren woman knelt on the marble, weeping. The crowd gathered with eyes glistening and dreamy. Some trembled. Others murmured prayers and clutched hands. As I looked upon their faces, I knew that I'd unleashed something more powerful than myself.

I was the Resurrection.

Like Isis, I would gather every piece of my parents' legacy. I would collect their family, their beliefs and ambitions, their faith, and foster them in the swamp of my heart.

"Selene, if you don't come, I'll call for the praetorians," Juba threatened.

Yes, he *would* do such a horrible thing. He would bring soldiers into this holy sanctuary, and being Romans, they would kill the crocodiles. For once, I didn't fear the Roman soldiers, but neither would I allow them to desecrate this place, so I rose and walked toward Juba, eyes afire.

The crowd parted as I stepped over the crimson flowers born of my blood, and Juba took a step back. The magic in me was powerful; even he could sense it. Pain burned through my arms and blood dripped off my fingertips as I stood before him like a gladiatrix. I wasn't helpless, not this time. I had only a few words for him, and they were: "I have a message for the emperor."

Twenty-eight

AS I walked up the road in my bloodstained white gown, passing citizens stared. Still, I was unafraid. For so long in Rome, I'd lived like a timid mouse, feeling myself unworthy of the power of my legacy. Now, with this *heka* from the temple coursing through me, I felt like a lioness. Hundreds of people had seen the divine power of Isis working through me—they would tell their friends. Soon thousands would know. There was no hiding these mystical powers now.

"Just a little farther," Juba said, but I didn't need his reassurance. Isis was still with me.

As we entered the house, Livia gasped at my bloodstained appearance and her slave nearly dropped the amphora she was carrying. "What have you done, you wicked girl?"

I was a child of Isis. Livia was nothing to me. When I looked at her, zeal must have shone in my eyes, because she said nothing more and simply let me pass. The last time I'd served as a vessel for the goddess, I'd been a frightened child, and Juba had to carry me up the stairs. This time, gathering the white folds of my betrothal gown into my bleeding hands, I walked by myself.

I didn't knock but swung the doors of the emperor's study wide, standing in the threshold where he could see me. He was already standing, in armor and cloak. Whether a runner had warned him, or he'd seen me from the windows, I couldn't say, but now we stared at one another like two towering colossi on either side of a road.

If I was some part Isis, then he was some part of the dark god Set. "Is the message for me?" the emperor finally asked with cold fury.

I held my chin high. "Yes."

As the emperor circled me, I held up both bleeding hands to let him see the thousands of little cuts upon my skin. I didn't wither under his scrutiny. "Translate," he said.

I was eager to.

"As you refuse Isis her throne, be assured your descendants will never inherit yours. Deny me, and your ignoble name will fade to dust."

Before I could translate more, the emperor seized me roughly by both shoulders. "And where shall I have my retort, Cleopatra? Shall I point out that *you* descend from an inbred line of fat kin murderers, most of whom squandered Alexander's legacy until Egypt was an indebted skeleton for you to inherit at Caesar's sufferance?"

He shook me until my teeth rattled. Still, I knew it wasn't me he was screaming at. No, he was speaking to my mother. Perhaps he didn't want to think that he defied a goddess, or perhaps some part of him needed to grapple with my mother still.

We stared at one another, both of us aware of every sound in the room, of every breath. I'd brought this on myself to strike at him, and I felt both satisfied and unsettled by the effects. Though he'd held my life in his hands since before I'd even met him, he'd never laid hands on me like this. He was a cool-tempered man who rarely spoke an unintended word, but now his fingers dug into my shoulders like talons.

"You're hurting me," I whispered.

He looked right through me, trembling with rage. And his eyes—oh, his eyes. "*Who* are you?"

"Selene," I murmured.

"No. You think like *her*. You talk like *her*," he accused. Then his hand went to the nape of my neck, where he bunched my hair in his fist. My arms went limp at my sides, and droplets of blood splashed the woven carpet beneath us.

I was perfectly still. I heard my own heartbeat in my ears; it beat only a pace slower than his. We were locked together now, almost like an embrace. "I'm Selene . . ."

At last, he released me, returning to his chair with a great show of propriety, as if he hadn't touched me at all. My blood was now smeared on his breastplate. He didn't seem to notice. It took me a moment to find my voice. "There's more."

"I've heard enough." His voice was like a sword being slowly slid back into its scabbard for use another day. He stared out the window and my pain began to overshadow the euphoria.

"The symbols aren't healing as they usually do," I told him. "Isis is still in me and my hands won't stop bleeding until you've heard it all."

"Don't say it as if it were my fault. *She* does this to you, not me."

Did he want me to feel angry with my goddess? With my mother? The days of that were long past. I'd shared the tears of Isis, praised her name, and she'd infused me with power that I hadn't known I could draw upon. I stood there. Waiting. It felt as if hours passed before the emperor finally made a motion with his hand.

"Read the rest."

"The spirit of Isis survives. I will lurk in depictions of mother and child. I will live in the shadows waiting for the Golden Age. Justum bellum, Octavian."

Each wound closed up as I finished translating, leaving my hands bloody but healed. Now my strength was failing me. I couldn't stand any longer and took a seat unbidden.

Octavian was quiet, letting his head tilt upward, to stare at the ceiling. "You sound very much like her."

Like a trainer with a dangerous asp, I knew not to make any sudden moves that might provoke him to strike again. "I'm sorry."

"I remember how your mother spoke about justice for Caesar's murderers. We were allies then, your parents and I. Did you know that?"

I *did* know it. "It's sad that Julius Caesar's legacy was fought over by those who loved him best."

"*Did* she love him?" the emperor asked. "I've always wondered. Oh, I know she bewitched and ruined him by parading their affair before all of Rome. She even let him put her statue in the Temple of Venus Genetrix. What humiliation for my family! But did she love him?"

I could see that he genuinely wanted to know. Beneath his blood-smeared breastplate, his chest rose and fell with the effort to restrain his emotions, as if he still grieved for his uncle. His shoulders were knotted and tense. I could almost feel compassion for him until I remembered that he'd killed Julius Caesar's only son—my brother Caesarion. And in truth, if he *was* Julius Caesar's son, then Caesarion was the emperor's brother too. And he'd killed him anyway. With that thought, what compassion I had for him drifted away. "Yes, she loved him. My mother loved Julius Caesar and she fought for him until her death."

"No, I think she still lives somehow," he said, almost entirely to himself. His tone was flat, detached, as if he'd gone somewhere to erect his defenses. "And yet I'm strangely gratified."

He was as rattled as I'd ever seen him. By now, he would have normally ordered me away so that he might have time to think. But instead, he had me linger, that strange intensity still in his eyes.

"Gratified?" I asked.

"Did your mother tell you that I would have killed her? If she did, she was wrong. I know what they say—that I wanted her dead. That it was convenient for me. And it was. But in spite of the politics of the matter, I wanted her *alive*."

I balanced on the edge of my seat. "To torture her?"

"To make her appreciate it!" he snapped.

His calm was only armor of another kind and I'd dented it, badly. "Don't you see, Selene? Your mother would have understood what I've accomplished. Even in defeat, she would have appreciated it as no one else can. Cleopatra dismissed me as a boy, but I wasn't so different from her. She was a teenaged queen and I was the youngest consul in history. I was outmaneuvering Antony before I was twenty years of age!"

He ran his fingers over the golden dolphins by his desk. My mother's. The rug was hers too. The furnishings and even the agate cup he drank from once belonged to my mother. He'd surrounded himself with her things and her children.

"Look now," he continued. "I find myself alone in a world filled with such *little* people. The great ones are all dead. Marius. Sulla. Pompey. Cato. Cicero. Caesar. Brutus. Cassius. Antony. All gone now, but me. Yes, *Octavian* triumphed where they failed."

He'd used his real name; he might be telling the truth, but I was wary. Always at war in him were his cautious instincts and his desire for an audience. He needed not just those watchers who fell under the spell of his performance but also the critics who grasped the cleverness of his play. "I'm sure my mother understood the enormity of what you've done."

"It's dangerous to humor me right now," the emperor said. "I know you. I know how you think. You may look like an innocent lily floating on the Nile, but you are like the blue ones that submerge at night. You show the world one face during the day, but like your namesake, the moon, you are changeable. Beneath the surface of you lurks a creature of ravenous appetite. I know you as I know your mother. Cleopatra and I understand one another. We know what we're fighting for."

The emperor looked down at his breastplate, where my blood dried between the grooves of the carving that depicted his victory at Actium. Madness shone in his eyes. "We fight for the world. A war to determine all—which ideologies dominate and which gods survive."

"And you've won, Caesar," I said, wading into the depths of the swamp, leaving only my eyes visible through the reeds of my intention. Like Isis, I must hide until I was stronger.

His eyes, however, betrayed him. They were the eyes of the hunted and haunted. "In declaring war upon Egypt, I said we must allow no woman to make herself equal to a man. The Egyptian queen, Cleopatra of House Ptolemy, the Egyptian whore who worships reptiles and beasts, must be vanquished. We declare a just and righteous war. *Justum bellum.*"

Remembering it seemed to bring back fire from a lost time, and his fist tensed. He was slowly coming into possession of himself again. "I wished for peace, yet it seems Cleopatra is still alive and wishes to keep fighting. Where, I wonder, will she find another Roman warrior to champion her cause?"

"I don't know." I wrapped my arms around myself. I didn't like to see how his memories renewed his strength. I didn't like to see how his obsession with my mother blinded him.

"Not your brother," he mused. "He's just a boy. Not Agrippa; he's too loyal. No doubt Plancus and Sosius and all your father's old partisans who now pretend to be mine would entertain her cause, but none are great enough to face me now. As I said, the world is filled with *little* people."

"I am just the messenger," I whispered.

I wasn't just the messenger. I was the Resurrection, and he seemed to know it. He stood, placing both palms on the desk and leaning toward me in a stance of threat. "You're more than that. Perhaps your mother plans to find her new warrior amongst the Isiacs you inflamed with your demonstration today?"

My heart beat erratically. He'd taken a gamble in sending me to the temple; it wasn't too late for him to bury his mistakes. "Caesar, I won't go to the temple again. What happened there today can be denied."

"Oh no, Selene. The stage has been set and we're now both trapped upon it. Your fortune and mine are entwined. So you may go to the temple. Bleed. Cavort with crocodiles. Weave your Ptolemy spell over the masses. Play at divinity. And be in love with Juba, the blush of it on your cheeks. The more potent symbol you are, the more powerful tool you make for me. Make them bow, make them weep. Let them think you're their savior, for I am yours. Your mother may be emboldened by your brother's escape—Helios may be with her, wherever she is, even now. But she forgets one crucial thing. You belong to me."

Twenty-nine

OUTSIDE the emperor's study, my insides quaked and my knees shook beneath my gown, but I forced myself to stand tall. The magic had taken a deep toll on me. I ached deep in my bones. My stomach felt cramped and sick. The black pillars holding up the roof seemed to weave before my eyes.

"Let me walk you back to Octavia's house so you can be cleaned up," Juba said, tentatively extending a hand to me.

"Just leave me alone, Gaius Julius Juba."

"Selene, be reasonable. You can barely stand, much less walk back on your own."

He wasn't wrong. When I looked down at the ground, it seemed to fall away from me. The breeze in the trees sounded rhythmic and harsh, impossibly loud. My arms were stiff with drying blood, uncomfortable, and tight. I must have fallen because Juba steadied me and I was startled by his touch. I hadn't realized he was so close to me, because I seemed so far from myself. Even though he had likely rescued me from cracking my head open on the stairs, I glared at him. But I was too weak to pull away from his grasp.

Juba shook his head. "Today . . . Selene, how did you know the crocodiles wouldn't harm you?"

"I didn't."

This answer plunged Juba into a temporary but welcome silence. When he spoke again, he was hoarse. "Did you make that woman fertile? The woman in the temple whom you laid hands upon. Do you have that power?"

I looked him in the eye. "What do you believe?"

He studied me. "Are you trying to frighten me?"

"I'm trying to save my brother's life. I'm trying to spare Egypt. I'm trying to spread my faith and honor my goddess. If that frightens you, I don't care."

Juba sighed. "I'm to be your husband . . ."

"But you're not my husband yet, are you?" I asked, pulling away and walking on my own.

He fell into stride beside me. "In a few weeks, I *will* be your husband. Everyone is anticipating it."

I was so weary, I couldn't even be bothered to brush away the flies. "Don't fret, Juba. I'm willing to make the sacrifice of marrying you, but until that day, don't touch me."

"Sacrifice?" he asked stooping down to one knee so that he could look at my face. "Will marriage to me be so terrible? We belong together. Imagine what we'll do. You can't tell me that you aren't eager to return to Africa."

A part of me was eager. I couldn't have Egypt without Africa, and I couldn't have Africa without Juba. But the fact that he could kneel before me and try to speak of our life together while my blood dried on my arms made me laugh.

There was nothing else to do.

CHRYSSA undressed me with great care. Then she helped me step into the bath because I was too weak to do it on my own. I lolled there, in the water, half-asleep. Meanwhile, Bast circled the room, puffed up and tail twitching as if she sensed the *heka* that'd worked itself through me this day. Her fur formed a ridge along the top of her back, and she wouldn't be settled.

"Is it true?" Chryssa asked. "What they say about the temple today . . . my sister Phoebe heard that you experienced the ecstasy of Isis, then confronted the emperor."

I'd resented her for such a long time, but now I understood that we were bound, she and I. I didn't know that I could ever forgive Chryssa for helping Helios escape or for lying to me, but Julia had confirmed Chryssa's story about the emperor having taken her virginity and I felt sorry for her. I couldn't stay angry. "It's true. I felt the power of Isis and even the crocodiles could see it upon me."

"I can feel the magic around you even now," Chryssa explained, then quietly sponged me with perfumed oil—the kind that Octavia disapproved as a foreign extravagance, but which Julia and I both preferred to olive oil and a scraper. "The temple replenishes your power. Euphronius told me it's stored in you and will dwindle slowly with every spell you cast."

"I don't know how to cast spells," I said, mindful of the doorway. Speaking of magic in Octavia's household was never to be taken lightly. "Chryssa, I know you've lied to me before, and I know I've been unfair to you, but this is the most vital time for you to be truthful because Isis spoke through me today. You must tell me if you know where Helios is."

Chryssa lifted wet hands from the water. "I swear to you that I don't know."

This time, I believed her.

"Are you still in pain?" Chryssa asked as she returned to scrubbing the blood off my skin.

"Yes." I'd successfully fought the battle to remain conscious, but my body was limp, my head ached, and I fought nausea. "But I think I came to understand something in the temple today about suffering and the sharing in it. It is an important step to . . . to something else."

"To rebirth," Chryssa said.

I nodded my head slowly, closing my eyes.

I can't have been asleep for very long when I was rudely awakened by the emperor's wife. Wet tendrils of my hair were cool against my forehead and I tried to focus my eyes. "You stupid girl!" Livia screamed.

Bast hissed, Chryssa skittered to a corner, and I blinked several times in confusion. This was Octavia's villa, and Livia seldom ventured here uninvited. But here she was, her face twisted with anger. "Selene, this household has been turned upside down to marry you and Julia off properly. I even purchased your wedding attire myself! I spent all day making arrangements, only for you to embarrass our family, whipping up the masses against us with your blood and ravings."

Normally I'd have been frightened of Livia, but something had changed inside me at the Temple of Isis. I didn't even sink down into the pool to hide my nakedness. "You've been misinformed. I said nothing against you or this family."

"You didn't have to. You just had to put on your Ptolemaic charm and the slaves bowed down before you like slobbering idiots." Livia looked at Chryssa pointedly before her gaze returned to me. "Did you use chicken blood or some tawdry little tricks to put on that show?"

"Isis came to me," I said. "Perhaps you should visit her temple for guidance."

Livia reeled. "You're an impudent wretch. Won't this episode just wipe that self-contented look right off Octavia's face? Maybe the shame of having a witch in her household will make her think twice about taking up for the likes of you."

I lifted my chin, pride overcoming wisdom. "Why should there be shame in my following the emperor's dictates? I went to the temple today and did exactly as instructed. I just came from his study and he gave his approval, so perhaps you aren't as privy to his wishes as you think you are."

Livia's eyes narrowed and her fists clenched. I'd known exactly where to strike her vanity. While all of Rome might think of her as eternal serenity, this was the side of Livia that I knew best. Petty and mean, red-faced and furious. "Who are you to question my marriage?" she asked.

I stood up, climbed the stairs out of the bath and snatched a robe from where Chryssa cowered. Today I'd been the vessel of Isis. I'd seen life beyond life. I didn't shrink from Livia this time. "If the emperor finds no fault with me, why should you?"

Livia sputtered, "I find fault with you because he doesn't. You're a dangerous little viper! You're a distraction to good Romans, just like your mother was. You cloud his senses. He thinks he's using you, but you're using *him*. Why am I the only one to see it? His good judgment fades the longer you're in this house, but I won't allow my husband to become another Roman seduced and brought low by an Egyptian whore."

I squinted. "The emperor is a *father* to me."

"Liar!" Livia shrieked. "I know what women like you are, what you really want and I swear that I'll ship you off with Juba as soon as possible now that all Rome knows you dabble in bestiality with crocodiles."

"*Bestiality?*" It was even more absurd than it was insulting.

"Your mother was no stranger to perversion," Livia hissed. "So why should anyone expect better of you?"

How could I endure this from the woman who scoured the city for unwilling virgins to bring to her husband's bed? After all that had happened this day, it was too much to bear. "Livia, of all people, *you* have no standing to attack me on the subject of perversion."

Involuntarily, my eyes darted to Chryssa and Livia took my meaning at once. Then the emperor's wife turned scarlet and I knew I'd made a terrible mistake. Livia gave Chryssa a murder-ous glance before taking the measure of me. "I don't know what you mean."

I struggled with the certain knowledge of my error, hoping to quickly cover it up lest Chryssa pay the price. "I spoke nonsense. You upset me, and I've had a long day. I'd like to retire to bed."

Livia stared at me for moments that seemed to stretch on interminably. "I don't think so. You plan your words carefully, Selene. You always do. So, I dare you to make yourself plain."

I could almost feel Chryssa's fear. I kept my eyes on Livia and now I knew, for certain, that Julia was right. "I just mean—"

"Livia?" Octavia was in the doorway, rescuing me from another fabrication. "What are you doing here?"

Livia turned toward her sister-in-law and her voice dripped with poisoned honey. "I came to tell Selene that wedding gifts have already started to arrive."

"You might have sent the message with a slave," Octavia said. "You needn't have troubled yourself."

"I wanted to trouble myself," Livia said. It was plain she didn't appreciate Octavia's intrusion, but neither did she want the emperor's sister to know her secret. "I came to speak to Selene, if you don't mind."

"Well, I do mind," Octavia said, standing her ground.

This time, it was Livia who blinked first and took her leave.

AFTERWARD, Octavia ushered me into bed and snuffed out most of the oil lamps. It seemed that I fell asleep as soon as I closed my eyes. I slept a dreamless sleep, the kind where there's only peaceful blackness, oblivion to pain, as if Isis took me back into her womb. So when I woke, I was surprised to find Octavia still there.

"Is the light disturbing you?" she asked, coming to the side of my bed to put her hands upon my forehead.

"No," I whispered. My tongue was thick in my mouth and my head was pounding. "But I'm thirsty."

"I have some cool broth for you. It'll help," she said.

Her simple kindness moved me. I wished to ease her mind, I wished I could tell her that I hadn't worked magic, but this time it would be a lie. Philadelphus and I had made this happen, and I wasn't sorry.

Octavia sat beside me on the bed. "It takes a heavier toll each time. You worship a cruel goddess."

"She's the kindest one, if only you could understand," I said. "Thank you for before. With Livia."

"I'm capable of taking care of the children in my home without Livia's help."

It occurred to me then that it needn't have been Octavia that took us in. If the emperor had wanted to keep us as wards, we could've lived with Livia instead. "Why *did* you take us?"

Octavia's fleshy hands drifted down to tuck the linens in around my shoulders. Her eyes were guarded. "It was something that I could do for your father."

I loved my father, but he'd never been a constant presence, even before his death. It was hard, even for me, to understand how and why my father had so many children and former wives. "Everyone knows how poorly he treated you. Why do you feel you owe him anything?"

She sighed, as if in pain. "I owe your father, because had I not loved him, he might still be alive."

I was silent, prompting her to say more.

"It's true that Mark Antony was my rightful husband," Octavia said. "It's also true that your mother took him from me and from Rome. But there's another truth, which is my sin: I took him away from your mother first."

I swallowed, and some inexplicable impulse made me touch her hand, as if to give her permission to stop, but now that she'd started her story, it all came out. She took a deep breath and said, "When things went sour with Fulvia, your father could have divorced her and taken a new Roman wife, but he stayed in Egypt. Your father was happy with your mother, especially after she bore him twins."

I tried to keep the judgment from my eyes, but her cheeks crimsoned. "You must understand that I'd loved Mark Antony since I was young. I met him at my uncle's home—at Julius Caesar's table—and he was like no man I'd ever met before. With a booming laugh, a lion's skin over one shoulder like Hercules, and a leer in his eye . . . there was no one like him."

"It's not wrong to be drawn to a strong persona," I reassured her, though it made me feel disloyal to do so.

The truth was, my mother had hated Octavia, but I no longer did. And now her eyes met mine as if for absolution. "I couldn't accept that he loved a foreign woman. I couldn't believe that he meant to make a life with Cleopatra. It wasn't right. It wasn't legal. So when my brother sought a way to make peace with your father, I offered myself. Leave Cleopatra and her twins and marry me. It was the most immodest proposal I've ever made, and many people died because of it."

"Because he couldn't give us up," I whispered.

Octavia stared at her hands. "He tried to love me, I think. But once he saw her again, he was bewitched. He divorced me to marry Cleopatra and appeared to the entire world as having divorced Rome for Egypt. My fault. It was all my fault . . ."

"No." Didn't she realize that her love for my father had only been convenient to the emperor's purposes? "The war would have come anyway."

"The war might have come anyway," she agreed. "But it wouldn't have been for my honor. Every effort I made to be a good wife to your father was turned into propaganda against him, for Romans saw his rejection of me as a rejection of them."

She laid one of my hands over the other and clasped them

softly in her own. "Your father lives now only in his children. So I pay my debt to them. I don't understand what happened today in the Temple of Isis with the crocodiles, and I don't condone it. But before you marry Juba and go to Africa where I may not see you again—well, I'd wish for you to remember me kindly."

Lady Octavia was her brother's creature; it was true. She would always choose the emperor over everything, even over her own heart. But I had a brother too—one that I loved just as much. It was hard for me not to feel sympathy. "Octavia, in my faith, the most sacred thing a person can do is to honor the lives of those they love by gathering the torn pieces and putting them together again. You did that with my father's children, so I hope you'll remember me kindly too."

Octavia had allowed herself to be more sentimental than she perhaps intended. Smiling softly, she blew out the lamp beside my bed, shrouding the room in darkness. But before she left, she stooped over my bed, and pressed her lips to my cheek.

As tender a kiss as a mother might give a child.

And I thought to myself as I drifted to sleep, *Isis dwells in her too.*

Thirty

IN the morning, I dressed and wandered the curiously empty house. It was a market day, so I hoped everyone was just visiting the Forum and not avoiding me. The family had seen me bleed before, at the Trojan Games, but how would the girls treat me when they heard that crocodiles had submitted themselves to me and flowers had sprung from my blood?

In the kitchen, I found only slaves who were cleaning up the mangled remains of a rat that Bast had helpfully dropped at the threshold for them. The slaves stopped talking when I entered, and they curtsied. It was rather awkward, so I took some sun-dried dates and went to find Philadelphus. He was in his bedroom, in the middle of the day, sitting cross-legged on his bed. He rolled some bone *tali* dice, playing a game the emperor had taught him. He looked pale, and he was still in his bedclothes.

"What's wrong?" I asked, putting the bowl of dates near his bed.

"I have a cough," Philadelphus said, and then proceeded to hack phlegm as if in demonstration.

As we talked about what had happened in the temple, I sat upon Helios's abandoned bed and ran my fingers over the fabric, searching for a trace of him. I imagined that I could smell him, like faint echoes of sea breeze and sun-bleached sand. It brought out a pain in my heart at once sweet and sorrowful. "It seems odd that in a temple where Isis teaches that war pollutes the world, I should get a message declaring a just war against the emperor."

"Not all wars are about killing. Maybe some wars are about ideas." Philadelphus took some dates and began to eat them. "I don't really understand everything I see. But I think someday you'll be a great queen."

"You do?" I played with a stray hair on Helios's pillow. It was curled and blond.

"I've seen it. In so many of the rivers, I see that you restore a throne to Isis. You'll bring her back home. You'll preserve her worship right in the center of the Roman world . . ."

I stared at him, hungry to believe. If what he said was true, then maybe I was *meant* to marry Juba. What if Rome and the emperor were stepping-stones to my destiny?

TEMPERS in the imperial compound were blistering. Agrippa's soldiers terrorized Isiacs, slaves, and freedmen searching for Helios. That Augustus had "misplaced" Cleopatra's son lowered his esteem in the eyes of the people, and it made Agrippa—who had won so many battles and built so many public works for the Romans—look like an incompetent. All the while, my star rose. Word of my miracles spread throughout the city, and the glamour of my impending wedding added to the allure, so the emperor kept me by his side.

Some days he asked me to translate; others he simply wanted me to play the *kithara* for him. I knew that he kept me close out of fear that like my twin, I might run, but there was something else too. He watched me, always looking for my mother in my eyes. For my part, I gave him no cause for alarm. I'd shaken him enough with the last bloody message; now I did everything he asked, without complaint. Like Isis, I plotted in the reeds. I didn't show how desperately I missed Helios and I busied myself with the emperor's concerns. I willed myself to care about the things he cared about. I forced myself to appreciate his good qualities—for the best lies require you to believe them, in part.

One day, when we two were alone in his office, he looked up from his correspondence and asked, "What are you reading?"

I shifted upon the plush carpet at the foot of his desk, rolling to one side. "I'm learning Punic," I explained. "I want to be able to speak to Juba's people in their native tongue."

I wondered how the Africans would see us, as we entered with legionnaires and Roman settlers. Would they view us as Romans come to conquer, or would they celebrate Juba at the helm? It had been no exaggeration when I told the emperor that he needed a Ptolemy in Africa. It would be my task to make Roman settlers remember that my father was Antony and to remind the natives that my mother was Cleopatra.

I'd have to do it all for my husband's glorious reign. I knew that *my* crown was to be only symbolic and that Mauretania did not belong to me, but I'd been raised to rule and wanted to learn everything I could about the kingdoms my intended bridegroom had been given. Of Juba's two kingdoms, Mauretania would be the richer by far. The fish swam so plentifully, it was said you could cast a net into the water and draw it out moments later with your dinner.

Juba and the emperor hired architects. They recruited settlers. They chose officials and administrators, and I watched as the machinery of nation building began to turn, as I served only as a figurehead. I was my mother's daughter and a Ptolemy and I wanted more.

PHILADELPHUS was ill.

"He has a fever!" Octavia cried, guiding me into Philadelphus's room. "He collapsed while playing ball in the courtyard today. I thought it was just the heat at first, but now Chryssa says he won't eat anything."

Philadelphus was on his back, the bed linens twisted around his legs and his tunic plastered to his chest with sweat. His hair clung to his face in wet ringlets, and though his skin was red and hot to the touch, he shivered. "Selene!" he shouted when he saw me, his eyes wide and feral as they'd been when last he looked through the Rivers of Time. I could see that he was lost in visions now, looking at me and *through* me at once. He whimpered, fingers curling around mine. "Don't feel sorry, Selene. You have to go."

"He keeps saying things like that," Octavia said, taking a wet cloth from his forehead and rinsing it in a basin before gently laying it upon his brow once again.

I put both of my hands over my throat, trying to calm myself. "I don't want Livia to see him like this," I finally said. Truthfully, I didn't want anyone seeing Philadelphus like this. "Please, let me tend to him. Leave us."

But Octavia stood firm. "Selene, Philadelphus needs a healer. I know a physician who specializes in fevers. His name is Musa. I'll send for him."

"Is this physician at least Greek or Egyptian? Is he competent?"

"He's helped the emperor before."

If the often sickly constitution of the emperor was Musa's best recommendation, I had much to fear from this physician. I'd heard of the fevers that ravaged Rome in the summer. Julius Caesar himself had once drained the marshes to prevent the spread of the illness, but children still died of it each year. Philadelphus was the last of my family with me and I knew I couldn't bear to lose him.

"His name is *Antonius* Musa. He was your father's freedman and though I have never demanded that he confirm it, I believe he worships your goddess. We can trust him and you must trust me, my dear." Octavia glanced down at my little brother, where he writhed with discomfort. "If I'd given Antony a son, I think he'd have been just like Philadelphus . . . I won't let anything happen to him."

How Roman Octavia looked in her dowdy garments and with her hair so severely pulled back. How my mother and father had detested her. How loyal she was to her brother—at least as loyal as I was to mine. But I remembered her motherly kiss in the dark. "Do you promise? Do you promise me?"

Octavia nodded solemnly. "I promise. Make Philadelphus understand that he must be quiet when the healer is here." Then Octavia's eyes fell upon the Collar of Gold that hung from Philadelphus's neck. "I only let you children keep those amulets because I thought them similar to the *bullas* that Roman children wear, but now I think he shouldn't be wearing things that invite evil and illness."

I self-consciously wrapped my free hand around the frog amulet I had once removed but would not now part with for my life. "It's the last thing my mother ever gave him. She'd never give him something that would make him sick."

Octavia pursed her lips again in matronly disapproval, but when Philadelphus clutched at his amulet, the issue seemed to decide itself. "Selene! I see Helios and he wants to stop you from marrying Juba."

I forgot how to breathe. I looked at Octavia desperately. "Whatever he says about Helios, you can't tell the emperor!" I was asking her to commit a grave act of disloyalty and we both knew it.

Octavia's pinched expression became more pronounced, then she shook her head, retreating behind denial. "There's nothing to tell. It's fevered ranting. I'm going to fetch the healer." With that, Octavia strode from the room and left us alone.

"Philadelphus, they're going to bring a healer to you, and you mustn't say anything about the Rivers of Time or tell them anything you see about Helios. Do you understand?"

Philadelphus's eyes were wild. He was somewhere else, in

another place. "Helios doesn't want you to marry Juba, but you almost always marry Juba. Euphronius knows that too."

I put my hands on my face. If the healer came and heard Euphronius's name, it would be that much worse. Up until now, I'd kept to myself the identity of the priest with Helios. If the emperor found out, he'd smell conspiracy. "Don't look into the Rivers of Time anymore today. You're too sick," I said as I brought the water basin to his side.

I had to calm him before the physician came. I made Philadelphus sit up and remove his tunic, discarding the sweaty garment as he reached with both hands into the water basin, splashing water onto himself. At first I thought he did it to cool off, but then he cupped water into his hands and stared. "You marry Juba." Then he dropped that handful of water and took up a new one. "You marry him again."

Fevered as he was, I didn't know whether Philadelphus was having true visions, but he'd been right the last time he saw things. He'd been right about the blood causing my stigmata too. "You can see that in the water? I always marry Juba?"

"Sometimes Helios raises an army," Philadelphus said.

My heart leapt to my throat. "What about this time? What about in *this* River of Time? Is Helios trying to raise an army?"

Philadelphus fell back onto the bed and let the water slosh onto the floor. I took the basin from him and used the washrag to wipe down his body. "Have the visions passed?"

He nodded weakly.

"When the healer comes, you must be quiet, even if the visions come back. Can you be quiet?"

Philadelphus pulled the bed linens up around him, but nodded. Still, his eyes were faraway. "The river bent and the silt churned, and now I can't see what happens as clearly."

Thirty-one

❦

THE physician believed that the way to cure my little brother's fever was to plunge him first in a hot bath, then in a cold one. So poor Philadelphus spent the mornings in the *caldarium* breathing in steam, and the afternoons in the *frigidarium*, soaking in cold water until his lips turned blue and his teeth chattered. But still, Philadelphus's fever burned.

For that matter, so did Rome.

First, the armories were set ablaze. Siege engines and barracks went up in smoke on the Campus Martius before the fire brigade could battle the flames under control. Next came the warehouses, some of which still housed portions of my mother's seized treasure.

Finally, the villas burned. Most wealthy homes on the Palatine were abandoned in summer while nobles vacationed in their villas by the ocean. Thus did several homes perish in flame without anyone being home to stop it. No one wondered that they were the homes of the emperor's most loyal senators. But they should have.

When Agrippa's own house burned down, there was no question in my mind that it was arson. That house had belonged to my father, and I didn't even have to remember the way Helios set his toy ship aflame in Alexandria to know this was his doing. I remembered the birthmark on his arm. The *uraeus*, the spitter of fire.

Yet the emperor never publicly accused Helios. In fact, deceptive official explanations for the fires were put out. An overturned lamp for the villas. A lightning strike at the docks. A careless soldier at the barracks.

Even so, now that Marcella and Agrippa had been forced to live in the imperial compound with the rest of us, I waited for the day of reckoning. Since my visit to the Temple of Isis, I was no longer afraid for myself. But the emperor still held power over the people I loved, and for them, I was afraid.

One day, when I was staring out the gate, no longer sure whether I should hope for Helios to return, the emperor emerged beneath an archway, scrolls tucked beneath one arm. I felt his eyes on me in a way that made my senses prickle with alarm. He said, "I could have soldiers go house to house, rooting out every Isiac in the city. I could have them rounded up and thrown into the arena with lions."

"But Caesar is more merciful than that," I said, suddenly conscious of the thin garment I wore on this hot day, and the less-than-fatherly way he stared at me.

"Yes, I'm merciful. Which is why I'm only sending Agrippa to close temples and prohibiting the worship of Isis within the inner sanctum of the city."

I started to object. I started to remind him that this was in violation of the bargain we'd struck, but he held up his hand. "It's as much for their protection as for mine. The Senate blames the Isiacs for the fires."

"But closing the temples makes it look as if *you* blame them too," I said, rising to my feet. "You'll make them look guilty."

He brought his face near to mine. "Would you prefer that I told the people the truth?"

No. Beneath us, the city of Rome fanned out and I knew that somewhere in that maze of dark passages and brick hovels, Helios hid, waiting to strike fear into the most powerful nation in the world. If the emperor told the Romans that it was Helios setting their city on fire, the mob would do worse than kill my twin. We both knew it, and all the fight went out of me. "What would you have me do?"

"Write a letter asking the Isiacs to peaceably give up their temples and altars in the city. They all remember your dalliance with the crocodile. They'll listen to you."

I reached up to pluck a branch of laurel knowing I'd always associate the scent of sweet bay with Rome—with the Palatine Hill and with the wreath Octavian wore when he, like some dark god, dragged me through the city streets in chains.

Surely Isis wouldn't want her followers to abandon her temples, but when Isis faced her own dark god, she fled to the marshes. So too would her followers have to flee now. "I'll write your letter," I said, knowing it might be the bitterest thing I'd ever done.

THAT afternoon, Juba came to see me on the terrace where I was reading medical texts in the hopes that I might find some cure for Philadelphus. "How do you fare?" Juba asked me.

"Not well," I admitted. I was still angry with him, but I had no ire to spare. The weddings drew nearer and Philadelphus had told me that I almost always married Juba in the Rivers of Time, so I forced myself to be civil. "What if they catch Helios and blame him for the fires? What will happen to me and Philadelphus?"

Juba sat beside me. "If that happens, the emperor will need you even more than he does now. Denounce Helios as a traitor and the emperor will be even happier to elevate you. Your mother declared *her* brother a traitor when he fought against Julius Caesar, after all."

Comparing Helios to my wicked uncle was an outrage. "I'll never denounce Helios."

Juba sighed. "I wouldn't be so sure, Selene. You and I must accept the fact that we'll be forced to stand against your brother if he continues this course."

"I fear that as I fear little else in life, but I don't accept it."

Juba took the scrolls from my hand and set them aside. "Let me distract you with talk of our future. We don't have much time to gather everything that we'll need for the voyage. Our kingdom is still wild—"

"Is it?" I asked, for this wasn't what I'd read. Mauretania might be unsettled, but as a Roman province, at least Numidia had cities.

"Well, it's wild in some parts, so we'll have to bring everything."

I squinted at him. "Not *everything*, certainly." There wasn't any reason we couldn't live in one of his ancestral palaces . . . unless the Romans didn't intend to leave and Numidia was to be granted to him in name only.

"I've already started to ready ships and sailors for the journey," Juba continued. "Securing a stable food supply is our first priority. We'll have to do all we can to send grain back to Rome."

Grain for Rome. Another price to be paid. Like my mother before me, my destiny would be to feed the ungrateful Roman masses. "Juba, have you only thought of the soldiers and the ships and the maps? We must also have musicians, poets, and people to travel with us and make our royal court their new home. We'll need our own royal guard."

He tilted his head. "Royal guard?"

"Will a Roman guard taste your food for poison?" I asked, taking perverse joy in deflating him. "King or no, the Romans look upon you as an equal at best, a barbarian at worst, certainly not someone to die for. Will you entrust your life to them?"

Juba didn't like hearing this, if the way he knit his brows was any indication. "A royal guard, then. Anything else that *Your Royal Highness* would like?"

"Yes, as a matter of fact. We'll need gifts for the important personages we'll encounter. Perfumes, paintings, silk, incense, furniture, gold plate . . ."

"How about statuary?" Juba asked, finally warming to the subject. "And tradesmen. If we build a new city, we can't wait for native talent to present itself."

A new city. The idea called to my blood. A summer bee circled lazily in front of us, stopping on a nearby acanthus flower, and I was wary of its stinger. My Ptolemaic ambition was my strength and my weakness. Juba knew he could exploit it to draw me nearer to him because the founding of a city was a magnificent thing—even my mother hadn't accomplished it in her lifetime. If I could do that, wouldn't I prove myself worthy of the Ptolemy line? Would she be proud of me from beyond?

"In whatever city we construct, there must be a Great Library," I whispered before I could stop myself.

Was it possible to rebuild everything that had been destroyed? Was it possible to steal back all that had been stolen from my family? I served Isis one way, and perhaps Helios served her another way. Which one of us was right, I couldn't say.

OCTAVIA sat dutifully beside my brother's sickbed, smoothing back his hair while the physician attended him. Philadelphus's chest rose and fell as he wheezed under the watchful gaze of Bast, who dozed on a ledge, her whiskers twitching every time my little brother coughed.

It hurt to see that my little brother's skin was pallid and untouched by the sun yet kissed with the dew of fever. He seemed smaller somehow, limp with exhaustion.

In Egypt we'd have brought him to the shore to be cooled by

the breeze and with ostrich-feather fans. Musicians would have played to soothe him, and the best physicians in the world would have attended him. But here in Rome, they kept him in this fetid room.

Octavia looked relieved to see me. "Ah, Selene. Good. I can stretch my legs a little bit."

The owlish physician squinted at me, then put his things away in a satchel. I noticed he was short, squat, and had difficulty meeting my eyes, and I feared what Philadelphus may have revealed in his feverish rantings. "You must be Musa," I said with an imperious air. "I'm Cleopatra Selene and I'd like to hear your report on my brother's health."

"It's malaria," the physician said. "I've seen this fever many times. Bad air rises from the swamps and sickens people. We should expect nausea and vomiting. There may be a yellowing of the skin and eyes if it progresses."

He related these things to me in a very factual way, as if he were insensible to the distress it would cause. I had trouble keeping my composure. "Th-then what?"

"Then we must continue his hot and cold baths and hope it runs its course," Musa replied. He made ready to leave with Octavia but then stopped in the doorway. "He says things that make me wonder—"

I stopped him before he said another word. "Certainly a physician of your reputation has seen delirium before."

"Certainly," he said. "I just want you to know that your father was a very good master. He granted me my freedom and I feel as if I owe a debt to his children. If there is anything you should ever need of me, you need not hesitate to ask."

Then he let Octavia lead him away.

I took her place beside Philadelphus's bed and whispered, "You have to get better. Please, you have to get better." I didn't know if he heard me, but that's when I felt a shadow behind me, in the doorway.

I was surprised to see that it belonged to Agrippa. He seldom ventured into the privacy of Octavia's villa, but with his own house—my father's house—burned down, he was restless. I watched him shift awkwardly from foot to foot.

"Lady Octavia just left," I told him. "You can find her in the gardens."

Agrippa cleared his throat, as if embarrassed at my suggestion. "I came to see the boy. Is there any change?"

I shook my head and Agrippa wiped sweat off his brow with the back of one forearm, then unclasped the right side of his breastplate. "Selene, I know of a folk remedy. It might break the boy's fever."

I quickly fastened onto any scrap of hope. "What is it?"

Agrippa rubbed the back of his neck and rolled one massive shoulder. "A weed of some sort. Sweet wormwood, they call it. I don't know if it works or if the physician will let him have it, but I'll have it sent for anyway . . . if you think I should."

It was strange to have him defer to me in this way. "Is there anyone to vouch for this remedy?"

Agrippa grimaced, leaning against the door. "Your father did. A long time ago."

I failed to smother my surprise. "My father?"

"You know we served together before he . . . went Egyptian. There were swamps at Philippi. Men fell sick. This plant, well, Antony gave it to some of the men. It helped."

"Then please, yes, send for some." Agrippa nodded, but just stood there in silence. I knew it made him uncomfortable to discuss my family, but he'd brought it up in the first place, so I pressed the matter. "Did you *always* hate my father?"

"No." Agrippa let his eyes trail over Philadelphus. "Antony was once a soldier's soldier."

Coming from Agrippa, that was the highest compliment, and yet the defeats that he'd perpetrated upon my father were the kind that denied him any honor. It hadn't been enough, after all, to crush the Egyptian fleet at Actium; it'd also been necessary to slur my father's manhood with the lie that he'd run away to chase after his Egyptian whore. "My parents broke your blockade to save their ships to fight another day. My father didn't run away from you like a coward, but you had Juba say that he did. You must have hated him."

"Aye, by that time, I did."

"Why? What made you hate him so much?"

Agrippa hadn't shaved yet that day. He looked as if he hadn't slept much either. Now he looked over his shoulder as if for an avenue of escape, then back at me. At length, he said two words: "Lady Octavia." Then a lifetime of jealousy bubbled up from within him and spilled over for me to see. "I wanted her, but she wanted Antony."

I stared, wondering how I'd ever been so stupid. The emperor had ensured with a single divorce that my father would not only enrage Rome but set Agrippa against him too. It was brilliant and diabolical. My mother had used her personal relationships to shape the world. Now I realized that the emperor used people's relationships to each other to do the same.

"You still love her," I said. "Even though you're married to her daughter."

Agrippa stiffened, his arms crossing over his chest. "We all have our duties, Selene. We make sacrifices for honor, and we take our happiness where we may."

"I stay in Rome," Philadelphus murmured feverishly.

"I'd better go before I wake him," Agrippa said, turning on his heel. I watched him retreat, wondering what it would take to win the loyalty of men like Agrippa.

Thirty-two

❦

THE most famous story about Rome's founding is about Romulus and Remus, the wolf-nursed brothers who fought for supremacy. But there was another story about the early men of Rome. They had no wives of their own, so they invited a neighboring tribe, the Sabines, to a feast. Once the Sabines were drunk with wine and filled with food, the Romans kidnapped the women and chased off their men.

When the Sabine warriors returned with allies to liberate their wives and sisters, the women had already been raped by the Romans and borne Roman sons; by now, the Sabine women had lived amongst the Romans and shared their triumphs and their pains. New loyalties had been forged. And so, as the two armies were about to come to blows, the Sabine women rushed onto the battlefield to intervene. The women forgave the Roman men and convinced their fathers and their brothers to lay down their arms and let the tribes join as one.

Thus was Rome born.

It was a story that resonated with me in every way. Day by

day, it became more difficult for me to tell my enemies from my allies. I'd lived for years now as the emperor's hostage, his ward, and his favorite. I'd seen the Romans in all their shades of gray. Somewhere out there in the world, my twin was setting Rome ablaze, but it was Romans who tried to heal Philadelphus. And I couldn't forget that.

Agrippa sent his fastest messengers to fetch the folk remedy, and no one could fault Octavia's devotion. She sat hour after hour, tending to my youngest brother. The emperor too, for all in him that I loathed, was ensuring a prosperous marriage for me. He insisted that my wedding was an important event to the world, for the territory that Juba would rule was the largest of any client kingdom in the empire, and the only one in the West. We represented the emperor's new dynastic order, and everything had to be just right.

The wedding day drew closer and client kings began to arrive, bearing gifts. The emperor gave generously too. Pearls, gold, jewelry boxes, and silk. Like Octavia, perhaps he felt he owed my parents some debt or form of penance. And now I felt myself confused.

Had my mother wrestled with her loyalties the way I wrestled with mine? As much as I loved Helios, as much as I loved Egypt, I now had loved ones in Rome as well. So it was that when Octavia told me that Julia was also ill with fever, I ran to her as if she were my own blood sister.

I found Julia in bed, on her side, her back to the door, with the linens tangled about her knees. She turned over to look at me, then reached out a trembling hand for the cup of water by her bed. I gave it to her and she drank greedily, her fingers shaking as she did so. It frightened me to see her like this.

"Close the door," she whispered.

"Julia, you'll get a breeze if you leave it open."

"Close it." She lay back as if drinking had taken all her strength. I closed the door, half-terrified she'd slip away from life while my back was turned. But no sooner was the door closed than Julia sat upright. "Thank the gods! I was getting so bored. I thought you'd never come."

I stared, dumbfounded. "I came as soon as they'd let me."

Julia threw the covers off to reveal some poetry she'd hidden. "I'm reading Catullus and it's perfectly filthy. You *must* read it. He's so passionate. Catullus loves her. He hates her. He calls her a prostitute. He's tormented, all because of a woman!"

I took the seat with the tasseled cushion beside her bed. "Julia, aren't you ill?"

"Of course I am," she replied, sobering. "I'm sick to death of weddings. Aren't you?"

Anger washed over me. "Julia, the whole household is terrified for you. Your father is beside himself with worry."

Her countenance turned soft and wistful—an expression she rarely employed and probably wasn't conscious of. "He *did* seem worried when he came to see me. Of course, he wouldn't step all the way into the room. My father's health is delicate, you know. He can't risk it. Besides, he's been having nightmares."

My own nightmares usually came in the form of a basket of figs. But what disturbed the emperor's sleep? This I had to know. "Does he say anything to you about what upsets him?"

Julia shrugged. "He cries out in his sleep about Cleopatra."

My mouth fell slightly open. "Does he?"

"Oh yes, he's so dramatic . . . is it any wonder that I had to fake a fever to get his attention?"

"Julia, you have everyone afraid that you'll die."

"Oh, I bet they are, because if I died, who would marry Marcellus and give my father the grandson he wants?"

"Well, you worried *me!* How are you doing it? You tricked the physician."

Julia looked bored. "It's easy. If I want them to catch me with a fever, I jump up and down until I'm red and sweaty from this heat, then collapse in the bed. Mostly I moan and clutch at my stomach. I have Musa so worried that he said I don't have to do any chores until the weather turns colder."

"But *why* are you doing this?"

"So they'll call off my wedding, of course!" Julia grasped my hands. "All we need is a little time. Time for Iullus to become a *quaestor* and prove himself as an elected official. He's not as good at numbers as I am, but I can help him with his work at the treasury, keeping track of all my father's gold."

I put my face in my hands. "Julia, didn't you hear anything your father said? He wants you to marry one of the *Julii* and there's only one left you can marry. *Marcellus.* I know he isn't the man you want to be with, but—"

"Are you blind, Selene? Marcellus doesn't even like girls. He's a catamite!"

That silenced me. Completely. Utterly. I'd noticed how Virgil doted on Marcellus, of course. Everyone had. But that didn't mean anything. Now that I thought more carefully, though, I couldn't ever remember hearing rumors about Marcellus and the slave girls. Or any girls. But a *catamite*? It was one thing for a Roman man to enjoy the favors of a boy, but quite another to *be* that boy. "Does your father know?"

"Of course not," Julia said. "Even I'm not selfish enough to tell him. My father is a hypocritical monster. He'd punish Marcellus for it and it would break Octavia's heart. What's more, Livia would use it to her advantage. I don't want to marry Marcellus, but I don't want him ruined either. He has a good nature."

"Then you just have to marry him," I said glumly. "And ignore the rest. It's what we told Marcella when she married Agrippa."

"But I'm not like Marcella. All *she* really wanted in life was a household of her own, and once she went to live with Agrippa we hardly ever saw her until the house burned down. But you and I are different. I write Greek and I've read my father's speeches.

I could improve upon his rhetoric. I could be twice the Roman magistrate that any of the boys are, but he'll never call upon me for anything but to marry the man of his choice." I couldn't argue. It wasn't arrogance or self-aggrandizement. Everything Julia had said was true. "Neither of us should have to marry anyone we don't wish to," she continued. "Unless you *want* to marry Juba."

"I don't," I insisted.

Julia's big brown eyes fastened on me like an interrogator. "Don't lie. You've always fancied him."

Yes, I had fancied Juba. But those feelings had been dashed the day he told me about his part in Egypt's defeat. "Maybe once, but no more."

Julia didn't seem to believe me. "Every girl that looks at Juba must imagine kissing such handsome lips, but even if he were an ugly old scab, you'd still want to marry him now that he's a king. Have you seen the wedding gifts arriving for you? Jewelry and gowns, braziers and incense . . . I'm Caesar's daughter, but all the best gifts are for you. My father has purchased no fewer than twenty slaves to attend you, and that doesn't even count the ones he's giving Juba. Some foreign king even sent you a gilded carriage with two snow white stallions to pull it!"

I bit my lower lip not to seem too eager to embrace my new fortune. But Julia's jealousy was short-lived. "He's also going to give Chryssa to you. He says that your brother has forfeited his property, but I suppose my father doesn't know what else to do with her now that she's a virgin no more."

I winced to hear of Chryssa so casually disposed of; like a used-up castoff, she would now become mine.

Julia crossed her arms over herself and said, "Selene, the worst part is that I'm going to lose you too. It's not bad enough that I can't be with Iullus, but now you're going to leave for Africa and never come back."

"I'll come back," I promised. "After all, I have family here."

"Philadelphus isn't going with you?"

I shook my head. "Eventually. Not now. He's too sick."

She had the grace to look guilty for only pretending to be ill with fever while my little brother truly suffered. "Can't you heal him, with your powers? I heard what happened at the Temple of Isis the day our betrothals were announced. Everyone is talking about it. You bled, but crocodiles defended you, and you made a barren woman fertile by placing your hands on her."

"Is that what they're saying?" I asked, closing my eyes as if I could recapture the feeling of Isis flowing through me. "I felt I could make her fertile, but I don't know if I did. I can't explain it, but I don't know how to heal anyone."

Julia sighed. "I want to believe in your Isis the way you do, but what use is magic if you can't fix anyone?"

What use indeed?

LEAVING Julia's room, I was distracted. I almost walked right into the salon but stopped when I heard Livia's voice. "Please adopt my sons," she was saying. "Adopt Marcellus too, if you must. Don't rely upon these marriages. Will you let everything depend on the fate of one frail girl?"

I hovered outside the doorway where I couldn't be seen, but I heard the emperor's reply. "Julia will be fine. How many times did they say that I'd die of my frail constitution, and yet I've outlived all of my family but my sister."

"Perhaps Julia will recover, but if she doesn't, then where will we be?"

I wished I could have seen the emperor's expression when he snapped, "It is not my fault that you're barren!" I held my breath. When Livia didn't reply, the emperor moderated his tone. "I decided to marry you when you were still Nero's wife, heavily pregnant with his child. I thought it was sure proof of your fertility, but, oh, how the gods laugh. I suppose it isn't your fault. You've provided for me in all ways but giving me an heir. It's just the way of it."

"It doesn't change the situation," Livia said quietly. "Wouldn't the Republic feel more secure knowing that you had heirs before the worst should befall you? You have no idea what it was like when we thought you were dying in Spain. The chaos, the fear, the insecurity."

"Let Rome be insecure," the emperor spat out. "Let the people worry about what will happen without me. Antony's partisans are still scurrying about the city. Even the senators dare to criticize me. Let them see how indispensable I am. Perhaps, someday, I'll just walk away and watch them all come crawling back."

I listened to hear Livia's reply, but instead I heard the distinct scrape of *caligae* boots in the hall. Soldiers were coming. I withdrew from the doorway and started to retreat. Then I saw that it was Agrippa and an escort of guards. He was grim-faced. "I have news for the emperor!" he bellowed. "You'll want to hear this too."

He caught my arm in his viselike grip and yanked me with him into the salon. Livia rose to her feet, and Agrippa made a smart salute. "Hail, Caesar!"

"What is it?" the emperor asked irritably.

"I've received word from Cornelius Gallus." I knew this man was the Prefect of Egypt; the news couldn't be good. "Alexandria is holding, but Thebes is in open revolt," Agrippa continued. "The Thebans have declared Alexander Helios king and pharaoh."

The room spun before my eyes. Not even Livia's potent glare could break through the dizziness and I was suddenly grateful for the balance Agrippa's hold on me afforded. It was the worst imaginable news. Helios. Helios. What had he done?

Thirty-three

ONE of my brothers lay dying of fever and the other would soon be crushed by all the might of Rome's legions. The weight of that reality might have sent me to my knees if Agrippa hadn't been holding me by the arm. Nonetheless, I wrenched away from him. "Let me go, you ineffectual baboon! How all Rome must be laughing; the Hero of Actium brought low by a boy."

"She's right," the emperor said with an impatience rarely directed at his lieutenant. "The fires convinced you the boy was in Rome. Now you say he's in Egypt starting rebellion? Which is it? Does Gallus say?"

Failure made Agrippa's shoulders sag. "No one knows. Perhaps not even the Egyptians themselves. According to the messages, he hasn't declared himself king. Rather, the mob has declared him so."

"They wouldn't dare without assurances that he was en route to Egypt," the emperor said, eyes accusatory. "Think, will you? The boy has gone to Egypt to take his throne. Antony's partisans and the Isiacs are burning the city and maybe our fleets to prevent our following him. Send word to Gallus to march on Thebes. Round up the Isiacs in Rome. Crucify them all and put an end to this cult."

It was all slipping out of my hands, beyond my control. As emotion swelled in my breast, the amulet around my neck grew warm. Even my arms started to tingle. Then the air seemed tinged with a dark perfume, metallic, like the scent of a sword being pounded in a forge. The taste of it was in my throat as I confronted the emperor. "You promised you wouldn't hurt the Isiacs, you *liar*."

Livia, who had thus far stood mutely, slapped me across the face. One of my hands came up to my cheek where she'd struck me and the other rose up like a shield. The sting of the blow spread across my skin. Anger blinded me. Rage had been building in me for so long; I suddenly felt my shadow-self unleashed.

As Livia raised her hand for a second strike, I said, "Don't you ever touch me again!"

Heka flowed from the inside of my elbow where it swirled around my birthmark like the pen of a scribe, tracing the pattern of a sail. Then it flowed out of my fingertips in a torrent. I felt undone by it, overwhelmed by the potency of magic that flowed through me.

Wind blew from my hand.

I didn't know how I did it or how to control it. It was unlike any natural wind. It was a gale force. A chair blew across the room and tilted against the far wall, balancing on two legs before crashing to the floor. Then a crushing wall of air burst out of my body and slammed into Livia, knocking her to the ground.

For a moment, the world stood still. I heard my breath, staccato gasps. The shuttered door slammed open and shut, reminding me of that long-ago day when they told me Caesarion was dead.

I felt the emperor's gray eyes on me as tendrils of my hair whipped up around my face. Agrippa stared agape while Livia panted where she lay splayed on the floor, her nostrils flaring, her expression twisted with fear. Her lips were a thin, mean gash. "You *are* a witch."

The great weariness I usually felt after my hands bled was coming to me now, the expenditure of *heka* costing me dear. Nausea rose in me and my knees threatened to buckle, but though my limbs were leaden, I turned and simply walked out.

When guards tried to stop me, I lifted hands and blew them away.

I'D never sought sanctuary in a foreign temple, but I was inescapably drawn to the Temple of Venus Genetrix. It was the temple of the *Julii*, where it had all started. Trembling with *heka* sickness, I passed through the pillars and walked up the staircase into the shadowed antechamber. Someone should have stopped me, but perhaps no one dared. In the face of the winds still harkening to my fingertips, the attending priests fled.

And then I was alone.

I ignored the lavish artwork. I barely noticed the engraved gemstones and pearl encrusted breastplate brought all the way from Britannia. My eyes were only for Venus, who was beautifully indecent, carved so that one rounded breast was bared, its nipple puckered taut. The rest of her was covered in a transparent fabric that made obvious even the erotic folds between her legs. She was scandalous and lovely; she was everything about a woman the Romans wished to cover up.

In one hand, Venus held an apple. It was, perhaps, the apple of the *Iliad*, the apple Paris had awarded her when he chose the fairest goddess, but it looked to me more like the beckoning fruit of knowledge that Isis offered to all. I still remembered the words Isis carved on my arms all those years ago: *The Athenians call me Athena. The Cyprians and Romans know me as Venus . . . I am one goddess. I am all goddesses.*

Looking at Venus now, I decided it was true.

My eyes danced to the alcove below where two smaller statues stood. One portrayed Julius Caesar and—more important to me—the other was a gilded statue of my mother. She wasn't here portrayed as the Whore of the Nile, naked and clutching snakes to her breast like her wax effigy in Octavian's Triumph. No, here my mother was as she was in life and my throat tightened at the memory of her.

I'd never seen my mother's face as young as it was on this statue and I realized she'd been not much older than me when she faced civil war and the annexation of Egypt. She'd not been much older than me when she played this same, very dangerous game with the Romans.

I marveled at the knot of Isis between her breasts, the serpent bracelet carved upon her arm and the slight swell of her stomach. And there, atop her shoulder, was a little boy. *Caesarion*. He was posed like Cupid clinging to Venus, the clearest statement Julius Caesar could've made that my mother was the mother of his son.

By putting this statue of my mother here, Caesar had proclaimed us family—Ptolemies and Julians, Romans and Egyptians, men and women. I knelt before my mother's statue and pressed my cheek to her knees as I had when I was a girl. I regretted that I'd once judged her. I hadn't wanted to look like her, hadn't wanted to carry her burdens, and hadn't wanted to feel her spirit inside me. But that had all changed and come full circle now, and I was grateful for these quiet moments with her.

When I heard the slow footsteps behind me, I wasn't surprised; I'd known the emperor would come for me. I turned to see that he was dressed for battle and his *lictors* flanked him, as if they thought I posed a grave danger. They'd seen me lift my hands and call forth the wind. They'd seen me make toy soldiers of the guards who tried to restrain me. They'd seen that I was capable of more than just bleeding. The emperor had seen it too and I wondered, *Was he afraid of me now?*

From where I knelt, I let a small smile play at my lips. As if he knew I was mocking him for a coward, he dismissed his guards. Then we were alone.

"My family temple?" His voice filled the quiet chamber. "A strange choice."

"It's my family too," I said.

"Get up, Selene," the emperor commanded.

"Why? What more could you want from me?"

His footsteps echoed as he crossed the temple. Then I saw him screw up his courage as he took me by the arms and pulled me to my feet. He forced me to look at him, and there I saw a strange triumph and thrill. "I want a great deal more from you."

I remembered the way he'd grabbed me in his study, trying to reach through to my mother, but this was different. This time he was actually seeing *me* and his eyes were filled with avarice. His hold on me was almost a caress. "You have powers you never told me about. Powers that are mine to harness. That's what I want from you, amongst other things."

"What other things?"

"You'll marry Juba."

"I've already said I would."

"You'll also denounce your brother as a traitor."

I stiffened defiantly. "That I won't do."

He smiled a malicious smile. "We had a bargain, Selene."

"Which you've broken numerous times," I reminded him.

He shrugged. "What Caesar gives, Caesar can take away."

"Why do you need me to denounce Helios? Why isn't King Juba's word enough? Why should the Senate need to hear from me?"

I could see from the amusement in his eyes that my taunting didn't anger him. He was in the game, encouraging my next move. "Because I want them to hear it from you."

No. It was because he wanted me to be like the treacherous Danaids that he'd put around his Temple of Apollo. When we saw those statues, Helios had said that all Rome wondered which of us held the dagger. The emperor thought it was me. But he couldn't make me plunge it into Helios's heart.

"What if I refuse? What if I refuse this marriage? What if I say that I hope Helios raises an army to smash Rome, for it will be no less than you deserve? Will you capture me? Will you march me behind your chariot again? I'd be your easiest conquest. A battle won in a temple. You wouldn't even need Agrippa. It'd be the first battle you won for yourself."

The emperor slowly released me and took a step back. He adjusted the belt of his uniform. Every gesture he made was a dare. "Or I could set you free, Selene. I could send you to Egypt to come to your brother's aid."

I wasn't so foolish as to mistake this as a genuine offer. It would give me only the freedom to bring ruination to Africa. More loot for Roman Triumphs. More victories for Octavian. More misery and bloodshed. "Have you no message for the Senate?" he asked.

I stared at him. He stared back, but I didn't shrink from it. Did he take me still for that scared little girl who cowered before him and begged for her life? "Oh, Great Caesar," I said, my voice dripping with sarcasm. "If I'm to be your puppet, why not simply tell me what to say?"

"Not my puppet," the emperor said very slowly. "My *Cleopatra*."

My mouth was too dry to spit at him. "I hate you."

"You wish you hated me. But you're just like me, Selene. You quest for power. It's in your Ptolemy blood. You gave me your allegiance and your loyalty. You said you were Cleopatra's daughter and mine. Now we'll see."

He was mad. Obsessed. It was the only advantage I held.

"I can't help you kill Helios," I said. "I won't."

The emperor pursed his lips at my defiance. "There may be clemency for him if you cooperate with my plans. After all, Agrippa says that Helios hasn't declared himself king. That counts for much."

He was lying. Having spared my brother once, he wouldn't

spare him again. Still, how could I not cling to the possibility that Helios might yet be saved? "You'd pardon my twin?"

"There'd be consequences. Exile, at a minimum. He'd have to live in obscurity with you in Mauretania and give up his name. But Helios hasn't taken the *toga virilis* of manhood yet, so he might be pardoned. You must trust in Caesar and do everything I tell you."

Trust in Caesar. Had he said these words to my mother and then gone on to murder her son? The thought hardened me. Always the emperor demanded promises of me while he broke his own, but he'd underestimated how much I'd learned from him. In fact, I was his star pupil. Whatever I must become to fight him, I'd become.

Again, the emperor and I stood facing one another like colossi on each side of a road. If I was some part Isis, he was some part Set. I felt Isis and Egypt in me. As we stood in that shadowy temple, I found my inner iron. "I have conditions."

He shook his head. "You've nothing to bargain with."

"Don't I?" I asked, remembering the way wind had come from my fingertips. What magic could one day be at my disposal? I didn't know, but neither did he. "While you've held us hostage, the East has submitted to you. Now Helios slips away for only a few months, and Thebes has already risen up. Alexandria will be next, then the Kushites, the Numidians, the Mauretanians, all of Africa and Spain. You need me to bring about your Golden Age—not the real one but the pretty vision that Virgil propagandizes in his *Aeneid*. You need me."

"I can always send Juba to Africa without you," the emperor said, averting his gaze from Venus. This place made him uncomfortable, and I was glad.

I felt the weight of my frog amulet at my throat. "Who will accept a Romanized king named Gaius Julius Juba without even a royal wife at his side? But they've all heard the name Ptolemy. They all know the name Cleopatra."

"If they reject Juba as their king, we'll fight them."

"Then they'll ally with the Spanish tribes," I said, showing that I'd learned my lesson well. "On how many fronts can you afford to fight?"

His face reddened. "As many as it takes. Roman soldiers are the envy of the world."

"Perhaps you're right," I told him sweetly. "But how many able generals do you have left? Agrippa can only be in one place at a time. Aren't you always telling us how we must grow up quickly because there are no leaders left in Rome?"

He didn't answer me.

"Perhaps the prophecies are wrong," I continued, my voice melodious. "Perhaps you really *have* eliminated every rival. Perhaps you're luckier than Julius Caesar, but can you be sure?"

I watched as the emperor's eyes fell upon the statue of his uncle. A leader just like him, who had eventually been stabbed to death in the Senate by the very men he thought were his friends. The emperor's jaw tightened.

"Why risk it when I'm offering reasonable conditions?" I asked. "Don't you like to say, 'Better a safe commander than a bold'?"

The emperor lifted his chin. "What are these reasonable conditions of yours?"

"You won't persecute the followers of Isis. No crucifixions of Isiacs. None."

The emperor waved this away. "I suppose that's in as much my interest as yours. If the Isiacs are divided between you and your brother, it makes little sense to focus their hatred on me."

"I'll denounce the rebellion in Thebes," I offered. "But I'll never denounce Helios or call him a traitor."

He adjusted his armor impatiently, but didn't refuse me. "Any more conditions?"

I breathed deeply and said, "Make me Queen of Egypt."

At this, his face jerked up, his eyes rounded, and something pulsed at the base of his throat. "No. Rome has made that mistake before."

I could see his mind was set, but so was mine. I had plotted and planned. "Then give me Mauretania."

"You're already going to be—"

"Juba's wife. Queen consort. That's not the same. If you're going to take Mauretania, don't make it a dowry for Juba. Give it to me."

"I've already promised Mauretania to Juba!"

"What Caesar gives, Caesar can take away," I said slowly.

The way his lips parted, I couldn't tell if he were staring at me in outrage or admiration. "Selene, I can make you a co-ruler in the Hellenistic tradition, but Romans will only acknowledge you as queen because you're Juba's wife."

"Then acknowledge me as a queen in my own right. Confirm my right to Cyrenaica. My father gave it to me; now you can give it back."

I thought he might choke. With Egypt, Cyrenaica, Numidia, and now Mauretania, I could lay claim to rule all of northern Africa. More than any Ptolemy before me. The audacity of it seemed to stun him. "You know that I could do such a thing only as a symbolic gesture."

"It will be enough." To start with.

"Selene, understand that in all the empire, I have only client kings, not client queens."

"Now you'll have one. You'll have *me*," I said.

All those years he'd made me play the *kithara* harp for him, but now it was his strings that I plucked. In the shadow of the statues, I could see that his reason was at war with something deeper inside him, something darker and more dangerous by far. The emperor was Roman, but he too had a *khaibit* in which his secrets lurked. This specter was a part of himself he didn't see or understand, and it was wholly mine to exploit.

"Very well," he finally said.

As simply as that. Had Julius Caesar said it so simply to my mother when he made her the most powerful woman in the world? Everything, *everything* had changed in an instant and I tried to show neither surprise nor doubt. "Philadelphus must come with me to Mauretania."

"Your brother isn't well enough to travel."

"The remedy Agrippa sought for him is helping. He's getting well."

The emperor abandoned all pretense. "Philadelphus will stay in Rome to ensure your loyalty. As long as you do my bidding, Philadelphus will be treated kindly. Now I tire of this. You'll marry Juba, you'll help me end rebellion in Egypt, and I'll confirm your right to rule as co-ruler with Juba."

"How do I know you'll keep your word?" I asked.

"You don't," he snapped.

"I'd be a poor sort of queen to accept that answer."

"You'll have it written and sealed at your wedding."

"That isn't good enough," I said, scenting the moss that had grown at the corners of the masonry, and beneath those earthy notes, I sensed something deeper still. Could there be magic even in a Roman temple? It wasn't enough to fill me with power, but the ache of *heka* sickness that had been in my limbs began to ebb, and I stood straighter. "Why don't you worship here? Julius Caesar built this temple, after all."

"And it was the death of him," the emperor replied.

"You do seem genuinely grieved," I admitted, glancing over my shoulder at the Divine Julius. "You asked me once if my mother loved Julius Caesar. Did *you*?"

"He was my father."

"He was your *uncle*," I said, shaking my head.

"No," the emperor said, crossing his arms over his chest. "I don't remember the man who put me in my mother's womb. He died when I was only four years old and I don't remember a single thing about him. But I remember Julius Caesar, who was my father in every way that matters."

"Then *be* like him," I said. "You ask me to be your Cleopatra, so be my Caesar."

His eyes snapped to me and when he tried to speak he struggled. It was now his mouth that had run dry. I was Egyptian; I'd learned about all the parts of the soul—I knew that a man was not only himself but also who he wished to be. The emperor didn't want to be only humble Octavian, even if he'd conquered the world. He wasn't enough at peace with all the things he'd done to be easy with the man he was.

He'd always held all the power; nothing had ever forced him to bargain with me, not truly. When I said that he needed me, I'd been telling only a partial truth. He *wanted* to need me because it made of him another man. That's why I knew I would triumph this day. "Be my Caesar," I said again.

"How?" he rasped.

"May I have your blade?"

He eyed me suspiciously, but slowly withdrew the *gladius* at his hip and handed it to me. He was too curious, I think, to deny me. The weapon was more of a dagger than the typical legionnaire's *gladius*, and I gripped it by the carved hilt which fit perfectly in my palm. I was pleased it was made of ivory, fashioned from the tusk of a great African elephant whose spirit might be watching me now as I lifted the hem of my gown and pierced the fabric with the sword.

"What are you doing?" the emperor asked.

A distinct tearing noise answered him as I ripped the cloth. "I'm making a diadem," I said. "Alexander the Great wore only a ribbon upon his head as a symbol of his divine royalty; it will be sufficient for me."

The emperor arched a brow. "I imagine *his* was made of some fine shimmering fabric and not torn from a homespun gown like a raggedy bandage."

Indeed, the strip of cloth in my fingers with its jagged edges *did* look like a bandage, and seeing that made something tighten in my chest. In Egypt we wrapped our dead in bandages to preserve their souls. Just so, Isis bound together with bandages the pieces of her dead husband and brought him to life. A bandage was a sacred thing.

"I can't crown you within the walls of Rome," the emperor said. "It's against the law."

He didn't care about the law, as we both well knew. He only cared that he not be caught breaking it. "We're in a sacred space here," I said. "Beyond the laws, and what we do isn't to be witnessed by outsiders."

"What's the point of a coronation without witnesses?"

"Oh, there will be witnesses," I said, gesturing toward the statues that hovered over us. "Can you not feel their *kas*? They're watching: Julius Caesar, Cleopatra, and Venus too."

He looked at the statues and the strain in the emperor's shoulders drained away. He took the knife back from me and slowly slid it back into its scabbard as if in a dream, and then his jaw went lax. Perhaps he felt the faint traces of *heka* in this place too and fell under its spell.

"Make your pledge to me," I said. "Your oath in our family temple as witnessed by *my* mother and *your* father. What you promise in front of them, I'll take on faith."

"Faith," he said slowly.

"Faith," I repeated. Then he held out his hand to me. Reverently, I kissed the ribbon before placing it in the emperor's outstretched hand.

Though it was torn from my dress, a strip of cloth he'd mocked just moments before, I saw something in him change as he touched it. His fingers caressed it as if it were made of the finest silk, and then his gray eyes fastened upon me with deadly earnest. "To rule is a responsibility."

When I was a girl, I hadn't known what it meant to be queen.

I hadn't understood when my mother asked her people not to fight anymore—when she put her hand into that basket for their sake and mine. But I understood now that being queen wasn't about sparkling crowns or scepters. It wasn't about the beautiful palaces, the silvered sandals, and elegant gowns. Not about the adoring crowds and the thrones made of gold.

It was about the people whose lives you held in your hands. I'd never lived in Cyrenaica nor Mauretania, but I knew without reservation that I'd rule more justly than any Roman governor and more gloriously than Juba ever could. "It's a responsibility I accept; I claim the crown."

The emperor's eyes burned like some dark metal in a forge and he brushed my shoulder as he passed behind me. We were both facing the statues now.

Had I been crowned Pharaoh of Egypt, it would've been done in Memphis and I'd have worn the two crowns and held the crook and the flail. But I was in Rome and the land I'd rule held no such traditions. There could only be this—but under the eyes of my mother, it was still sacred. A flicker of torchlight lit up my mother's face and it seemed as if she smiled.

The emperor was very close behind me now, his breath on the back of my neck. I should've feared that he might take that cloth, wrap it around my throat, and strangle me. After all, he'd murdered Antyllus in a temple too. But I didn't fear. With faint traces of *heka* thrumming warm through my body, I was, in this moment, certain no mortal hand could destroy me.

The emperor reached around me and I felt his breastplate against my back as he wrapped the cloth around my forehead; the diadem kissed my brow like the lips of a lover. I closed my eyes as the emperor fastened it at the nape of my neck. Then I whispered in Egyptian, words that came from some past that wasn't my own:

"Hear me, Queen of Heaven,
Let there be terror of me like the terror of thee,

Let there be fear of me like the fear of thee,
Let there be awe of me like the awe of thee,
Let there be love of me like the love of thee,
Let me rule, a leader of the living,
Let me be powerful, a leader of spirits,
Oh, Mother, thou hast come forth from me,
And I have come forth from thee."

I flushed at the power of it. The warmth flowed from my heart, to my lips, and all my most secret places. After all I'd endured and all that'd been endured for me, there was this sweetness. Tears welled in my eyes as I reflected that this diadem was a bandage to bind back together all the broken pieces of my family and my faith. I'd make it so. I had come to Rome in chains, but I would leave Rome a queen.

I turned, shoulders high as if I were floating toward the sky. He paused for a moment, as if he didn't recognize me. "You're a sovereign now. So what say you then on Egypt's rebellion against Rome? What stance shall you take in a war, if it comes? Choose."

This would be the first—and most important—decision I'd ever make for my people. It was a summer evening, and outside frogs called to one another. The warm night air was tinged with possibility. But there was only one choice. Holding my amulet at my throat with one hand, I lifted my chin and pronounced, "We remain a Friend and Ally of the Roman People."

"A good choice, Queen Selene."

Queen Selene.

He smiled and I smiled in return. It was my Isis smile, my eyes still secreted in the reeds. He thought I would build my kingdom on the blood and bones of my brothers, but he'd soon learn he was wrong. The emperor had bemoaned living in a world of little people. He wished for an equal. Well, I would make myself his. He wanted in me, his own Cleopatra. Well, he would get one.

Win or Die.

Cleopatra's daughter was born at the cusp of a religious awakening and came of age in a dangerous political world. Like her more famous mother, this young girl also forged important alliances with the Romans and charmed her way into power. It may even be argued that she did so more successfully, and with less bloodshed. But Selene's importance may have to do more with her religious influence than with her statecraft.

Today, we take for granted the concept of personal spirituality or a relationship with God. In much of the ancient world, however, religion was a covenant between the state and the divine realm. Insofar as personal or household gods existed for the Romans, worship was more *orthopraxy* than *orthodoxy*. That is to say, the emphasis was on correct ritual rather than on faith or intimate prayer. For the early Romans especially, religion was more a matter for men than women.

All of this started to change with the rise of henotheistic mystery cults, and as a forerunner of Christianity, the Isiac religion was one of the few in the ancient world to concern itself with social justice. In challenging temporal authority, the spread of Isiac worship nurtured a nascent concept of personal spirituality without which our world might be very different today. And were it not for the influence of Cleopatra Selene as the foremost proponent of Isis during the Augustan Age, such a transition may never have taken hold.

In spite of her role in fostering a religion that paved the way for modern-day spirituality, the historical record of Cleopatra Selene's remarkable life is scant. Plutarch, Suetonius, and Dio Cassius give us only brief but tantalizing clues. It was for this reason that I imagined the truth of Selene's story in terms of magic.

The idea that Octavian may have been obsessed with Cleopatra is not my original innovation. After her death, Octavian not only allowed Cleopatra's legend to grow, but he actively cultivated it. This was, no doubt, because it glorified *him* to have defeated an extraordinary woman, but historians like Diana E. E. Kleiner in *Cleopatra and Rome* have described a fascination that may have gone beyond the political, and it is hard not to imagine the influence that Selene may have had in sustaining her mother's image in the mind of her conqueror.

I departed from the historical record concerning the campaign in Spain insofar as Augustus wasn't able to return to Rome before Julia's wedding to Marcellus in 25 B.C. Juba was made King of Mauretania that same year, probably while serving with Octavian in Tarraco. It's possible that Juba went directly to Africa to claim his throne with Selene, without returning to Rome. The dedication of the Temple of Apollo occurred earlier than my novel would indicate, as did the rebellion in Thebes. For the sake of brevity, I also omitted the mention of Hyginos as one of the orphans in the imperial compound and made no mention of Octavia's eldest daughter, also named Marcella.

No ancient sources mention Iullus in Spain, but given the fact that Octavian took all the other young men of his household of fighting age, including Juba, it's the most likely time that Iullus would have obtained military experience to qualify him for the political offices he would later hold. As for Selene's other brothers, Alexander Helios and Ptolemy Philadelphus, the historical record is ambiguous. For example, while the twins are specifically referenced as having been marched in Octavian's Triumph, Philadelphus is not mentioned. This may be because he perished before he could march, was spared on account of his age, or simply lived a relatively obscure life and wasn't acknowledged again by historical sources except by those who claimed that both boys went to live with Selene in Mauretania. Modern scholars have theorized that the boys must have died young, but for purposes of the novel's narrative arc, I've embraced the uncertainty surrounding their fate.

Lastly, while references to Christianity might seem anachronistic in a book set thirty years before Christ's birth, it's important to remember that Christianity didn't arise in a vacuum. If we accept Matthew's Massacre of the Innocents as valid gospel, we must acknowledge that Selene's life intersected with important people like King Herod who played a role in the Christian faith. What's more, Christianity was not only influenced by Isis worshippers but also shared many symbols and ideals with the Isiacs.

I hope you've enjoyed *Lily of the Nile* and that you'll look for its sequel, which will explore Selene's journey to Africa and how this fascinating but as yet uncelebrated young queen went on to influence the Roman world, their faith, and our own.

For a more detailed bibliography and a list of Frequently Asked Questions, please visit my website at www.stephaniedray.com.

READERS GUIDE

LILY OF THE NILE

DISCUSSION QUESTIONS

On the Story

DISCUSS THE CHARACTERS, THE MAGIC, AND THE MEANING

1. How do Selene's feelings about her mother's death change over the course of the novel?

2. In antiquity, girls were considered to be marriageable at the age of twelve, but what experiences in Selene's life made her older and wiser than her years?

3. How do the powers Cleopatra gives to her children suit each of them, and do you think their characters would have changed had they been matched with another power?

4. What role does Selene's twin brother play in her life? How does her relationship with him differ from her relationship with her other siblings?

5. Selene learns to lie at a very young age and we watch her evolve into a schemer. Can these traits be forgiven as the tools of survival or do they represent a fundamental weakness in her character?

6. Octavian's desire to rebuild the Roman Republic and end the civil wars is juxtaposed against the unhappiness of the many children that he's decided to adopt as his own. Does Selene give him enough credit for sparing her life and for trying to be a just ruler?

7. In what way does Selene become more like the emperor than she is like her mother or father?

8. There is an emphasis placed on magic throughout the novel. Discuss what magic is to the Romans and the attitude that they hold for it, as well as what magic means to Cleopatra's children and the followers of Isis. Are their attitudes at all similar and how do they change throughout the course of the plot?

9. When Selene refuses to run away with their old wizard, it puts a barrier between her and her brothers. Is this a breach that can be healed?

10. In the middle of the book, Selene abandons her faith and removes her frog medallion. Why do you think she turns her back on Isis when she seems to need her most? How does this decision impact the story?

11. Helios was furious with Selene for helping the emperor deprive him of his name during the Trojan Games. Did you agree with her choice or with Helios?

12. How is Selene a different person once Helios goes missing?

13. Julia faces a harsh reality when she realizes that she has no choice when it comes to her future. Every decision is made for her and serves a specific purpose for Caesar. What do you wish for Julia, and what kind of woman do you think she will become?

14. Is Selene disloyal to her family for coming to love some of the Romans?

15. Should Selene forgive Juba for his part in her parents' defeat?

16. What do you think the emperor means when he says that he wants Selene to be his Cleopatra?

On the History

DISCUSS ROME, EGYPT, AND THE AUGUSTAN AGE

1. While much is known about the allegedly scandalous Cleopatra, her more cautious daughter is virtually unknown. Why do you think that is?

2. Cleopatra's death has caused speculation and sensationalism for centuries. Given accounts that Octavian called for snake-poison healers to try to revive her, and her subsequent portrayals in his Triumph, it has long been believed that she died by the poisonous bite of an Egyptian cobra. More recent theories include the idea that she was poisoned or was forced to kill herself because she was an inconvenience to Rome. How do you think she died?

3. After Cleopatra's death, Rome went through a period of Egypto-mania, fueled in part by Octavian himself. Why do you think he remained so fascinated with the country and the woman he had conquered?

4. It is said that Caesarion was killed because "two Caesars is one too many." But Antony's son Antyllus was also killed. What does this tell us about Rome's intentions toward Egypt?

5. One of the most noticeable features of Rome today are the many obelisks that were transferred from Egypt and placed around the city. In the book, Selene takes notice of Octavian's obsessive behavior toward her mother. How did it benefit him to keep the legend of Cleopatra alive?

6. The society of Egypt and that of Rome are often compared throughout the novel. One serves as a symbol of success through a fostered liberty under a monarch, and the other serves as a symbol of success through organized power under the guise of a republic. How do both of these symbols interact throughout the novel and why do you think it is important to see them functioning side by side?

7. There are often references to a Golden Age. Augustus's reign lead to two centuries of peace known as the *Pax Romana*. How was he able to bring this about?

8. Whereas Julius Caesar was assassinated by those he had counted as friends, Augustus's reign featured many loyal allies including Agrippa, Maecenas, Juba, Livia, Octavia, and others. How was he able to secure such loyalty?

9. While Augustus's family grew to an enormous size, including many grandchildren, nieces, and nephews, the Julio-Claudian dynasty was ultimately dominated by Livia's side of the family. Why do you think this is?

10. The month of August is named after Octavian. What other traces of his rule can be found in the world today?

On the Cultural Implications of the Novel

DISCUSS RELIGION, FEMINISM, AND PROPAGANDA

1. Rome was generally very tolerant of religious diversity in the peoples that they conquered, but during the Age of Augustus, the Isiac faith was actively persecuted. Why?

2. How did the Isiac religion clash with the more traditional Roman view of the relationship between man and the gods? Why should it matter that slaves and women were allowed to worship in the temple and participate in rites as equals to their male counterparts?

3. Selene was born approximately forty years before the birth of Christ, and was heralded upon her birth as a savior. The entire ancient world was awaiting a Golden Age. What light does this shed upon Christianity? And how might Jesus have fared differently if he had been born into a world ruled by Cleopatra and Antony's heirs, rather than Augustus's successors?

4. Isiacism was one of the first religions of the ancient world to concern itself with social justice. Slavery, warfare, and care for the less

fortunate were themes these religions addressed, to the consternation of the ruling elite. How have these traditions come down to us today?

5. Virgil's *Aeneid* was, as they say, an instant classic. Commissioned by Augustus, and passed down as the quintessential creation myth of the Roman state, it tells Rome's story as the Romans themselves would have wanted us to see it. Was Augustus wise to hire a cadre of esteemed artists such as Virgil to create his propaganda?

6. *Lily of the Nile* examines the hardships of even a highborn Roman woman's life and the lengths that society went to preserve a woman's sanctity and meekness. Selene's antithesis, Octavian, shadows his household's every decision. How do his presence and his beliefs shape the plot of the novel? How would the plot change had he not been adherent to his strict policies and viewpoints on the role of a Roman woman?

7. Could Selene's story be used to empower young women in society today? Why or why not? Are there any parallels between the decisions that she has had to make for her family and the decisions some young women make for their families today?

8. How did Augustus's morality and attitudes toward women shape Rome and influence our society even today?

9. Selene had a variety of female role models to choose from. Her mother, Livia, Octavia, and even Marcella. How do each of these women embody a different approach to the patriarchal world into which they'd been born?

10. Discuss the personalities of the male characters and their contributions to the story line. What were the expectations for a Roman man, and how does this impact Juba, Helios, and even the sickly emperor himself?